Secrets in the Mist...

~ SHATTERED DREAMS ~

C. L. STEVENS

COVER ART: ERIN K. KATICH

PAGE PUBLISHING
Conneaut Lake, PA

First originally published by Page Publishing 2023

ISBN 979-8-88960-092-3 (pbk)
ISBN 979-8-88960-099-2 (hc)
ISBN 979-8-88960-096-1 (digital)

Printed in the United States of America

A dedication page is truly a special page indeed. It is a page to say "thank you." It is a page to say "I couldn't have written this book without the following people…"

So with those thoughts in mind, I'd like to dedicate my first book to the following people and inspirations:

To my family, for those who have encouraged me to keep writing, to be positive and to keep persevering and continue to move forward. With all my heart, I thank Keith, Erin and Nick, Clark/"EC" and Steph, Marie and family members, and my high school study hall students and other students and staff at Bay High School for always encouraging me and giving me praise for my accomplishment!

To Mr. Joe King, my guide, my inspiration, my mentor. Joe, you put a fire under me to get this book to print. I thank you for always encouraging me and being there for me. Not only are you a wonderful children's author and musician/composer, but an amazing and talented artist as well, You write and paint with all your heart and soul, and you have that way of bringing a magical life to the written page.

You will always hold such a special place in my heart. I thank you for your endless guidance, your generosity, and your kindness. I am eternally grateful...

To all my inspirations in my life, for the life experiences, lessons learned, and the many people who have crossed my pathway and gave me the inspiration to breathe life into these pages...

To the paper and the number 2 pencils and my ability to dream...for without these items, my book and story would never have come to be.

And finally, to all my readers out there in the universe. Please don't be afraid to dream, to write, to keep a diary—even if it's just notebook paper in a three-ring binder! Write your thoughts down. Keep a memory book on your nightstand next to your bed for you never know where your thoughts may take and lead you. You are truly the master of your own universe. Explore, discover, and reach for the stars! Believe me, you can achieve your dream. And you never know...you, too, may be that next inspiration for someone else's dreams yet to be discovered!

Happy reading, everyone.

—C. L. Stevens

PART 1
Genesis

CHAPTER 1

The eve of the wedding

In the distance, a ten-piece orchestra played a lively, jazzy tune. The music drifted on the warm, light breeze outside the Dennyson Mansion's ballroom. It was the eve of Melanie Dennyson's marriage to David Williams.

Dusk had fallen. Melanie, who resided on the premises of the estate, lived in a quaint, cozy cottage that her father had renovated for her. Melanie was preparing for the celebration. Her wedding dress was ready for the next day—her nuptials to her beloved David. It was beautifully displayed on the wicker dress mannequin before her. Melanie stepped back to admire the beautiful dream bridal gown she had created and designed herself. She clapped her hands and squealed in delight. It was, indeed, one of her proudest and happiest moments. Her dream wedding dress was displayed before her—the flow of the organza material in a beautiful soft ivory tone and all the fresh-water pearl beads that adorned the dress were exquisite. The back of Melanie's creation had appliques of pearl beads in a patterned design. They were flowing and cascading down the long train. The tiny patterned buttons on the back started at the midback of the gown and would hug Melanie's beautiful petite body. Her silhouette would be breathtaking for anyone to behold. Melanie had been dreaming of this day for a very long time. She literally had dreamt of this beautiful wedding dress. One morning, she abruptly awoke and quickly sketched the drawing of her dream wedding gown. She often kept a sketch pad and drawing pencil next to her bed—just in case ideas would come to her while she was sleeping or awake just resting in bed. And on this particular morning, after Melanie awakened, her ideal wedding dress came to be.

Melanie stepped back a little more to further admire her work, as she envisioned herself in her beautiful design. Tomorrow was the big day—the day she had been waiting for forever. Her dreams were finally coming true. She closed her eyes, and her thoughts took her back to her college days at Whitmore College, where she'd first met David. She smiled and thought to herself just how perfect her world was right now—and just how perfect her life with David was going to be from this day forward… forever.

Melanie majored in fashion design and minored in business to please her father. Her four years at Whitmore College taught her organization, discipline, and determination. She studied and worked very hard. She wanted to prove that although she was born into a wealthy family, she was *not* a spoiled, brainless, self-centered woman. Melanie wanted to prove that she was more than that. She had goals for her life and was driven to accomplish just that. Yes, she had an easy lifestyle with no financial worries, but her father worked very hard to get where he got. He became a successful, savvy businessman who made wise, sound business decisions. The result? A very successful company—Dennyson Toys—and the maker of the Kelli Doll, the most successful doll of the toy industry to date!

Melanie and her father had a very close and loving relationship. Her mother, Anne, had tragically died in a fatal car accident. She was killed by a drunk driver. Melanie had been very young. Her father never remarried. He never really dated either or was ever in search of a mother replacement for his only child, Melanie. Arthur never felt that any woman, in comparison, could—or would—ever come close to his beloved wife, Anne. They had a perfect marriage—as some would often say. They complemented each other in every way. Anne would always be at Arthur's side, and she would be the best hostess and planner of the many galas Arthur would often host. She had her faith and was Arthur's rock in every way. Death had taken Anne way too soon. Soon after the funeral, the very next day, Arthur delved deeply back into his work—Dennyson Toys. He never found any time for any possible relationships to develop. His life was Dennyson Toys and his beautiful little girl, Melanie.

With the help of a handful of dedicated and loving staff (mostly Melanie's nanny, Irene), Melanie grew up as normal as possible. She developed into a well-adjusted, beautiful, and thoughtful young lady. Her close companion and nanny, Irene, was at Melanie's side each and every day. If Melanie could choose a perfect mother—as she often thought—she would envision someone just like Irene. Irene was loving and caring without being smothering and hovering. She was a mentor and a teacher—patient and kind. And even on the busiest of days (which one would never know), she would stop whatever she was doing and welcome Melanie with open arms.

Irene would often say, "What can I help my darling girl with today? Just name it!" And she would follow with, "I will always be here for you, Melanie. I love you with all my heart."

Irene had actually been one of Anne's dearest friends. Irene had lost her husband, Gordon, very early and didn't know where to turn after his funeral. She had been devastated—lost. Melanie's mother, Anne, soon said after the funeral (as Irene had told Melanie several times) to Irene, "Irene, you come stay here with Arthur and I—live with us. This house is so big. You can have your own wing if you'd like! And *no* for an answer will *not* be acceptable!" Anne was like that. She would make anyone who walked through her doorway feel special in every way. She would give them her undivided attention—as if she had nothing any more important to take care of or do.

According to Irene, Anne was God's earth angel.

When her best friend, Anne, had died, Irene never thought of being anywhere else. She'd stayed on, as she felt Anne would want, to take care of Melanie. Anne and Arthur had done so much for her. They always made her feel like a part of the family. Arthur was like the brother she had always hoped to have—loving and supportive—especially when going through the most troubled times when her husband, Gordon, passed away. Arthur was so indebted to Irene for staying on to watch over and take care of Melanie. He'd said so many times, "Irene, I don't know what I would have done if it wasn't for you! My Anne—and your Anne—would be so happy, as I am sure she is now, that you stayed on to help me with raising our Melanie."

"Oh my goodness, Arthur. I couldn't think of any other place in this world I'd rather be than here!" Irene said fondly.

Irene helped Melanie with everyday living. Irene loved and guided her young charge through any problems a young lady might have. She nurtured Melanie with all the love she had. Irene didn't have any children of her own. She and her husband, Gordon, tried having children, but it just wasn't meant to be. In a way, ironically, Melanie, filled the void of not having a child of her own. Irene was happy and content and felt like her life had purpose.

Melanie grew up and went to college after high school. She graduated from Whitmore College with a degree in fashion design and a minor in business. She now headed up the Design Division of Dennyson

Toys—specifically the Kelli Doll. She worked alongside her father. She worked diligently just like her father, mirroring his integrity and business savvy and knowledge. Arthur was so proud of the young woman Melanie had become. He knew Anne would be very proud of her little girl.

While at Whitmore, Melanie met David Williams. David was a business major working on his MBA. He was Melanie's grad assistant, and he fell deeply in love with her—at first sight. Her bubbly, witty personality, her contagious laugh, and her beautiful long blonde hair was enough for any young man to become captured and fall under her spell. She was truly a dream come true! Melanie was a smart, beautiful girl who David fell madly in love with. And lucky for him, Melanie fell deeply in love with him. It was a match made in heaven. They, of course, waited to start dating until after Melanie completed the course David was teaching. Naturally, it wasn't school policy to allow dating a student. So they waited. But after the semester ended and Melanie completed the business course, Melanie and David soon became a couple. They started going out together and were never apart from that official first date—ever.

It was a fairy-tale romance, and it was going to be a fairy-tale wedding—with all the glitter and glam. It was going to be a beautiful wedding and celebration. It would be a wedding given in love by a father who couldn't love his daughter more. It was a dream come true…or so it seemed.

CHAPTER 2

Several days before, David was sitting in Arthur's office, waiting for Arthur to get off the phone with a client.

Wow, Arthur Dennyson, my future father-in-law! Who would have guessed that! David thought to himself.

David looked around the room. *Am I dreaming? Is this real?*

David always took pride in his work. He studied hard—he got excellent grades. He received his bachelor's degree and continued to work on his master's. He became a grad assistant and ultimately, graduated, earning his MBA from Whitmore College. He never thought it could get any better than that! Then he met and fell in love with Melanie Dennyson—and she fell in love with him!

David reminisced about the first day of class as a grad assistant. He'd been so nervous. He'd tried not to get too overwhelmed about his teaching students, grading, his other classes, studying, etc. And then Melanie had walked into the room.

Man, how does she do that, David often thought. It was so stupid to say, but when Melanie walked in, she made everything better. David had shaken his head. *I'm a goner!*

He'd thought Melanie was too good to be true. He'd thought about the typical things a guy would think about—a beautiful girl they just saw, probably has a boyfriend. *She's beautiful, but is that all she is? Is she smart, funny, kind, witty, or just pretty to look at?*

David had thought to himself, *I'm not looking to find my future wife—not now! I'm not ready to meet my soulmate. I'm not ready for that!*

But there she was. Melanie was everything David had ever hoped for in a soulmate—a life partner, a wife, and in the future, a mother for their children. She was a dream come true. She was his dream come true.

"David," Arthur said firmly.

"Oh, sorry, Mr. Dennyson," David replied apologetically. "I was just daydreaming…reminiscing. Sorry."

"That's okay, son. No apologies necessary. I remember those days all too well. I trust everything is okay?" Arthur asked with a smile.

"Yes, sir, everything is very okay!" David smiled back.

"Well, it is my turn for an apology. I'm sorry, too! I was on the phone with Mr. Anderson. We're trying to figure out this new acquisition. Maybe you can weigh in with us, David, and give us your opinion?" Arthur asked.

"I'd be glad to," David replied.

"Great! Let's do a conference call this next week and get this deal rolling."

Arthur was so glad to have David on board with the company. He had his board of directors, his sales staff, his support staff, but Arthur always wished to have a son to work alongside with him to help run his toy business. Of course, Arthur didn't mean to be a sexist. It certainly didn't mean that Melanie wouldn't inherit the business, but a man sometimes missed having a son. Anne and he had hoped for a son, but Anne had the miscarriage—before Melanie— and tragically lost the fetus. It would have been their son. It wasn't meant to be. They didn't have a funeral for Daniel. The miscarriage came at the end of Anne's third trimester. Both Anne and Arthur were so devastated. And then with the "doors and windows" philosophy, Anne became pregnant once again. And nine months later, a beautiful baby girl came into their world, making it complete. Anne and Arthur had thought how nice it would have been for Melanie to have an older brother to look out for her—a big brother. Anne had even taken it harder, thinking it was something she had done wrong. But Dr. Simpson said it wasn't anything she did wrong. Sometimes, these things just happen—fate. They had thought that even after Melanie, they would try again to maybe give Melanie a brother or a sister, but then the tragic car accident happened. Anne had died. There would be no hope for another Daniel or any other child or children ever again.

Just then, a knock at the door brought both Arthur and David back to reality.

"Come in," Arthur said.

"Hey, Dad! Hi, David! I'm sorry to interrupt... am I interrupting?" Melanie asked with enthusiasm.

"No, honey. David and I are just discussing some business. What do you have on your mind?" Arthur asked kindly.

"I just wanted to get your opinion—and David's, of course—about some new ideas I had to help expand the Kelli Doll line. Is that okay?" Melanie asked.

"Sure, honey. David, okay with you?"

"Absolutely!" David replied enthusiastically.

Melanie kissed David on the cheek, closed the door slightly, leaving it ajar just a crack. She probably should have closed it entirely so their conversation would be private. And as she walked over to her father and rested her hand on his shoulder, a few extra ears were, unknowingly to them, listening in on their conversation. Those two sets of ears were always looking for any opportunity to eavesdrop on any and every conversation.

CHAPTER 3

Nancy and Gina were college classmates of Melanie's at Whitmore College. They both felt Melanie was a spoiled, rotten, rich bitch who got everything she ever wanted. As a college major and class assignments go, Melanie, Gina, and Nancy were usually in the same classes together. As Nancy would always put it, "Melanie was *always* the star! She *always* had the best designs, *always* the best A+ presentations, and, of course, *always* the best grades!" Nancy and Gina hated her—with a passion!

Nancy was the brains of the diabolical duo. There always seems to be a leader, one who devises the plans, the driving force, the pulse of any and every operation.

Nancy and Gina grew up together as well. They had known each other practically their whole lives. Gina and her family moved when Gina was very young—when she was in the first grade. It was hard enough moving when you were young, and moving to another state was even worse! Gina was always pretty quiet. She didn't make friends easily. Then as a mentoring program, Gina was "coupled" with Nancy—an outgoing, friendly student of Mrs.

Stewart's first grade class. She thought Nancy mentoring Gina would be a good fit. She always wanted each of her students to feel comfortable and welcome in her classroom. And when having the initial meeting with Gina and her mother, Gwen Brown, she immediately thought that her student Nancy Smith would be the perfect matchup for Gina. Nancy was a natural-born leader—even in the first grade. Mrs. Stewart could tell already that Nancy Smith, one day, would have the potential to be a good leader, someone who had the determination and drive to become whatever—and whoever—she wanted to become.

Gina, on the other hand, was very quiet and shy. In talking with Gina's mother, Gwen Brown, this was a hard move for her family. It was just Gwen and her two children—Gina and her brother, Greg. Gwen was divorced and had a difficult time making everything work after the divorce. And staying in the same city, the same location as her ex, was not helpful either. It was hard enough trying to scramble to find yourself, decide on a career, find a job, and be the sole one responsible for two small children—without a husband to rely on and an income for support. Yes, Mr. Brown, the asshole, made a good appearance in court every time. And he talked a good line about making child support and alimony payments. But as we all know, that doesn't always pan out. He started out well, then the payments stopped coming. Gwen tried to collect, going through all the proper channels, but the court system was slow. They never saw the urgency in dealing with the problem. Her husband—now ex-husband, Sonny Brown—worked in the Service Department for the city they lived in. Gwen knew there was favoritism there, and Sonny was very well liked. Gwen knew things were covered up—excuses were made, and payments to her were somehow lost. It was the typical "good ol' boy" network in this city, and there wasn't a damn thing she could do about it! Gwen was really just fighting city hall and losing the battle. Sonny had a lot of friends in high and low places. When she thought back, hell, everyone covered up the affair Sonny was having with his secretary—for three years! Gwen hadn't had a clue. Well, there were several times when she thought that Sonny might be having an affair, but then she soon dismissed it. She thought back and said to herself, "I was such a damn fool! I had all the red flags and just chose to ignore each and every one of them!" She often heard of others telling stories of their husbands having affairs or flings, but Gwen thought, *No, not my Sonny! We were childhood sweethearts all through school. Sonny would never do that to me! We have a family. We were happy and content—a good, wholesome, all-American family of four! Well, I certainly was the poorest excuse for judgment on that one!* It hit Gwen straight between the eyes.

One day, Sonny came home from work, exhausted as usual (from work…or so she thought), and he told his wife of ten years, he wanted a divorce as soon as possible. He stumbled through his words as he explained to Gwen that he fell in love with his secretary, Marilyn. Of course, it wasn't intentional (it never is). He never meant for it to happen. He tried to justify it by telling Gwen how wonderful Marilyn was, how she was always there for him, so efficient, even consoling—as he reminded Gwen of the occasional times they had problems in their marriage.

Gwen just sat there, in the kitchen chair, numb all over. She was half listening to Sonny go on and on and on about Marilyn. She just couldn't take it anymore. She was going to be sick! She was thinking back throughout their marriage, *How did I miss this? What did I do wrong? Did I miss the red flags—the signals?*

Then all of a sudden, Gwen was jolted back to reality and heard the word *pregnant.*

Sonny raised his voice, "Gwen, you listening to me? Are you hearing anything I've been saying? Answer me! Say something, goddammit!" Sonny screamed out loud. "And that's why it *never* worked for us!" he finished.

Gwen suddenly looked up—blank stare and all. She didn't know what to say. She was dumbfounded. She was so glad a neighbor had kept the kids over. Thank God for neighbors—your true friends! She just had to run to the store for a few quick moments to pick up some spaghetti sauce for dinner. Sometimes, bringing Gina and Greg with her was such a hassle—car seats, etc. It was just easier to leave them with a neighbor. She was very grateful she had Mrs. Swenson next door. She was thinking that Mrs. Swenson—Margaret—must be worrying since she probably knew that Gwen was home and not coming over to pick up her children, although Margaret also knew the family history. There must be something going on, again, with Sonny. She knew keeping the children with her for a little while longer wasn't going to be that big of a deal. She felt sorry for Gwen—lovely, a hardworking woman, a dedicated mother. Margaret knew the family didn't have a lot of money, so she never accepted any money from Gwen when she watched her children, Gina and Greg. They were lovely children—never a problem. They were a delight to have around. It was actually nice to have children around again. Margaret had no grandchildren or great-grandchildren living near her—they were all living out of state now.

Gwen thought moving away would be good for her and her two children. A cousin of hers, Brian, found her a job up north. She would be eternally grateful to him. It would be a fresh start. She probably wouldn't be getting any more financial support—not that she had gotten that much from the beginning. It was time to move on, to leave this bad memory behind them. Sonny ended up marrying Marilyn soon after their divorce was final. And now, he was starting a family with someone else. All Gwen could say about that scenario was, "Good luck— you'll need it!"

CHAPTER 4

Nancy and Gina soon became fast friends and best buddies throughout all of school—grade school, junior high, and high school. They even decided to go to the same college—Whitmore College. It was a good college—not big. Gina liked that. She thought she worked hard, although schooling and learning didn't come easy to her—not like it seemed to for Nancy. Nancy's tactics and philosophies for learning weren't the same as Gina's. Nancy always had this way of achieving without ever really doing the work. She would pair herself up with the right students who worked hard and were smart. Nancy just had this way of finding out who would be in her classes, strategically lining up and being placed with the smart students. She would act like she was doing her fair share of the work (and didn't), and yet somehow got the grades. She would even get the answers to tests. Although not the most athletic, Nancy even managed to get on the sports teams she wanted. And when it was time for working out and conditioning, Nancy would conveniently disappear and find secret spots to hide out so she wouldn't have to run or exercise.

How did she do that? Gina wondered. Nancy would joke about that all the time. She would gloat how she could pull off her wins. Gina would always wonder, in the back of her mind, if she was the only one that Nancy ever confided in and told her secrets to. Gina always felt burdened about knowing all the bad things that Nancy did. *Did anyone else ever know? Did she confide to anybody else? Probably not.* Nancy was good about that—never having anything to "clean up." If anything, Nancy was neat and tidy and thorough!

Whitmore College had a nice campus. Nancy and Gina roomed together throughout their four years there. Gina followed in Nancy's footsteps as far as deciding on a major—fashion design. Nancy said it would be a piece of cake and a lot of fun. Gina was definitely a follower and thought that one day, it might get her into a lot of trouble. But for now, the adventure with Nancy was anything but boring!

Nancy and Gina met Melanie Dennyson in their first fashion design class together. Gina thought Melanie was nice enough—very pretty and full of life. Of course, Nancy hated her—maybe it was jealousy. Nancy always used the word *hated* when she was describing girls that seemed to have it "all." She would be obsessed with "destroying" them, as she would put it. And she had this way of always manipulating Gina into doing whatever she wanted her to do—to get the job done. At times, Gina would be frightened. She sometimes thought if there were any limits to what Nancy would do…

As Nancy scathingly said many times to Gina, "That bitch! She may be all that, but when it comes to common sense, dumb as they come." Then Nancy would laugh.

Melanie Dennyson was kind and somewhat innocent—to a fault. She always looked—and found—the good in everyone—always! She felt that if she looked deep enough, there was good in everyone. And sometimes when she would come across someone that wasn't that way—good—she was, unbelievably, dumbfounded.

She liked Gina and Nancy enough. She felt they both could have worked harder. Melanie felt that everyone would, naturally, work hard in their field of study. Why wouldn't they? They chose that field to make their career in. Melanie didn't dwell too much on other students in her classes. She just concentrated on herself and her goals and what she needed to do to complete them. She had plenty to do and plenty to accomplish. There wasn't any time to waste on other people's issues, etc. She did have the opportunity, on several occasions, to work on a tag team with Nancy and Gina. She did find that she did most of the work, but both Nancy and Gina seemed to struggle a bit, and Melanie didn't mind helping them along if needed. It was a group effort, and if she could help for the common good/cause, she would. It was all good. She didn't mind—she always wanted to be helpful.

Nancy and Gina weren't the brightest of students. Neither one ever put their best effort into their classes. They were lazy—to a fault. Well... at least Nancy was. They always took the easy way out—even cheating if need be. If they could cut corners, they would—and did. They did whatever they had to do...whatever it took. No one ever knew that, however. No one caught on. They were crafty and shrewd, sneaky and conniving. On the surface, they were dedicated, diligent, and hardworking, but underneath and in reality, just the exact opposite of their classmate, Melanie Dennyson.

Nancy's hatred and pent-up anger would come full circle for her. Gina's fears and premonitions would also come to fruition. The bottled-up feelings that Nancy had possessing her would surface. Her anger, her loathing, and her abhorrence would overpower her and take control. The results would be overwhelming. The results would be horrifying, the results would be fatal...for some.

There would be no turning back.

CHAPTER 5

The orchestra was playing beautifully. Arthur, Irene, and David looked around the glass-enclosed ballroom. There were so many people there to celebrate the upcoming marriage of Arthur's daughter, Melanie, to David Williams, soon-to-be son-in-law of Arthur Dennyson.

Arthur was very well respected and liked. He had many business associates and friends—friendships to last a lifetime. He looked around the room. These people were his rock. Most were there for him when Anne had passed away. Most of them sent congratulations and gifts on the announcement of the birth of their daughter, Melanie.

There was dancing and laughter and lots of lively conversation. People were all enjoying the luscious food that Arthur's staff had provided. Arthur was grateful for his dedicated house staff. They were a part of the well-oiled working machine that Arthur created. He liked that! Everything was moving along quite nicely.

"Irene, where is Melanie?" Arthur asked. "It isn't like her to be late, and it is not like her to miss an extravagant party—especially in her honor!"

"I don't know Arthur," Irene replied, a little puzzled. "I talked and checked on her earlier. Everything was fine."

David jumped into the conversation. "I'll go see where my beautiful bride-to-be is!"

David felt bad. He expected to have a little more time after working with Arthur on that acquisition with Mr. Anderson. They had the conference call, and everything went smoothly. Afterward, he and Melanie and her father talked a little while about Melanie's ideas for the Kelli Doll. Melanie felt things were getting stale. She wanted to boost things up a bit with new ideas to help promote the stagnant sales. She thought some new clothing/wardrobe styles, accessories, new houses, etc. would help increase sales in the upcoming holiday season. Melanie even thought of several new ideas—movies, TV programs, games—all surrounding the Kelli Doll. She felt something new would keep the continued target audience excited and also bring in new customers. It was a sound advertising and marketing strategy, and both Arthur and David were eager and enthusiastic to get started on her plan. They all got caught up in the brainstorming. Melanie's excitement was contagious. Arthur was more enthusiastic than ever.

David really liked Arthur. He was grateful and thankful that Arthur was welcoming him into the multimillion dollar business. They got along very well, and that pleased Melanie so very much.

The other night when they were alone, Melanie, cradled in David's arms, said, "I love you, David, with all my heart. You have made me the happiest girl in the entire world." She smiled. "How did I ever get so lucky?" Melanie sheepishly asked her beloved.

David replied, "No, I'm the lucky one! I fell in love with you the very first day I saw you."

David laughed. "Look at us, we sound like a couple of sappy idiots! Anyone who would listen and hear us would laugh and roll their eyes!"

"Ya, I guess they would," Melanie replied. "But I don't care! I'm blissfully happy, and no one is going to ever spoil that or take that away from me!"

A little stifled giggle was heard outside. Nancy and Gina both cupped their mouths as they let out a laugh. Nancy had made a little hole in the back of Melanie's cottage so she could peak in whenever she wanted. She knew Melanie would never find the hole. "She's not that bright," Nancy would often say. After a while, Nancy put in a few more holes around the cottage—for convenience.

Gina was horrified. How could Nancy do such a thing? Gina always thought there would never be limits to what Nancy would do, but this?

"Geez, Nancy! What the hell!" Gina exclaimed in disgust.

"Oh please, Gina. Like you never take a peek while the bitch is in there! I've caught you several times! I swear you like her—I mean, *really* like her!" Nancy said wickedly.

"Stop it, Nancy!" Gina yelled angrily. "I don't like her like *that*! I'm just curious, that's all!"

"You tryin' to convince me or yourself, G?" Nancy replied.

Nancy often called Gina "G." Gina actually liked that. It was kind of tough—just like Gina had always hoped she would be.

Nancy and Gina slipped back to their hiding place—the shed that was tucked away on the other side, next to the wooded area. The shed held all the gardening tools that the gardener, Richard, used to keep the beautiful gardens on the estate looking exquisite. It overlooked the backyard gardens and was right next to the wooded area that surrounded the mansion.

Melanie loved her little cottage. When she was young, she would pretend she was off in the wilderness on an exciting adventure. When she was little, Irene would always let her play in the cottage. It was Melanie's playhouse. Irene always kept a watchful eye on her dear, but she also wanted Melanie to feel some sense of independence too. Irene didn't want to become overprotective and smothering. Arthur respected Irene and marveled at how well she took care of Melanie. He felt if his Anne were alive, she would have raised Melanie very much the same way, using the same philosophies and love—always love.

CHAPTER 6

The night before the wedding, Arthur insisted on throwing a celebration for Melanie and David. Oh, of course, there would be a magnificent wedding and reception at Covington Country Club. It was going to be spectacular! Arthur would make sure of that! But tonight he wanted this special celebration here at his home—at Dennyson Mansion. He loved this big, grand, beautiful estate. It was like no other home in the area. He made some changes in the architecture—updating the kitchen, powder rooms, and bathrooms, and of course, adding the huge glass windows in the back of the ballroom. Other than that, he thought the estate was magnificent. It was a home—his home. It was a home that he was very proud of, a home fit for a queen, his queen—his Anne. Arthur felt if he worked hard and he made the money, why not enjoy it. He employed enough people to take care of his home. Arthur's last hire was Richard, his gardener and caretaker of all the beautiful gardens. Richard was a good man—a hard-working man. Richard and his small crew designed and cared for the beautiful gardens on the estate. He also made a vegetable and herb garden near the back of the kitchen area so that the chef and kitchen staff would have fresh herbs and vegetables for the table.

It was Richard's idea for the vegetable and herb garden. He wanted, of course, to approach Mr. Dennyson before he started.

Richard saw Mr. Dennyson sitting on the patio one early morning with a cup of black coffee in hand. Arthur enjoyed getting up very early—even on the weekends. He was glancing at the newspaper. Richard was tending to one of the many rose gardens in the back. He, too, liked to get up early and get his start on his duties.

"Good morning, Mr. Dennyson," Richard said joyfully.

"Good morning, Richard. How are you this fine morning?" Arthur replied.

"Fine, sir, thank you," Richard responded. "Sir, do you have a moment? I'd like to ask your permission about putting in an additional garden—a vegetable and herb garden—near the back of the kitchen area. Would you approve of that, sir?"

"Richard, that's a splendid idea! I would love it. There's nothing more I wouldn't love than a fresh vegetable and herb garden. Go to it, man!" Arthur responded enthusiastically.

"Great, sir! I was hoping you'd be pleased. You know, sir, Ms. Anne always wanted an herb and vegetable garden, and I just thought—"

Arthur interrupted Richard by holding up his hand, "I know, Richard. Say no more. Ms. Anne would have definitely loved an herb and vegetable garden. Please go ahead. I look forward to all the fruits of your labor!" Arthur smiled.

Anne's passing affected everyone who worked for Arthur—especially the staff at Dennyson Mansion. Everyone adored Ms. Anne, as they would call her. Anne loved the staff as well. She would always remember each and every one on special occasions—birthdays, holidays, special moments in each of their lives. Richard always worked hard to please Anne. He loved showing her all the gardens—especially the rose beds. Anne always loved her roses—her favorite flower. She loved watching Richard work her rose and shaded beds. Anne always was so pleased with Richard's green thumb and his knack for growing things—the natural beauty he always created. On some afternoons, when Anne would be sitting outside on the kitchen patio, she would ask Richard to join her for a glass of iced tea or lemonade and conversation. She was a gracious lady and a sincere, kind human being.

CHAPTER 7

David listened to the melodic, lively piece the orchestra was playing as he looked outside the glass windows of the huge ballroom. The entire back of the ballroom were floor-to-ceiling windows. Melanie had told him that her father replaced the shorter windows with entire glass. He said he had a beautiful backyard filled with exquisite colorful gardens and a lovely wooded area filled with beautiful pine trees and nature. He and Anne and Melanie wanted to enjoy the view—*not* cover it up!

A bloodcurdling scream was heard outside. It came from the back of the estate. It was, unfortunately, muffled by the clear sweet sounds of the orchestra playing.

David stepped outside into the gardens.

Gina was screaming as she was holding and cradling her head in her hands. She was freaking out.

"Oh my god, oh my god, oh my god! Nancy, what did you do!" Gina screamed uncontrollably as she rocked back and forth on the floor.

Gina was just about hyperventilating as she saw Melanie's crumpled body in a pool of thick bright red blood on the floor. There was so much blood, so much blood everywhere.

Melanie was lying on the floor of her beautiful, quaint little cottage in her wedding dress and veil. Her wicker mannequin was bare now. It used to hold Melanie's beautiful wedding dress—her beautiful design. It was now ripped and torn. The beautiful lace that she added as a final touch was soaked with bright red blood. It was soaked in some spots, and flecks of blood were splattered elsewhere.

Melanie knew she was running a bit late, but she just wanted to try on her wedding dress just one more time before tomorrow. She brought, ever so gently, the veil out of her closet. It was her mother's veil—the veil she had worn at her own marriage ceremony. Anne had it put away for her daughter—to be kept and hopefully worn again one day. Anne and Arthur had a simple wedding ceremony before a justice of the peace. It was nothing special. They couldn't afford more than that. Anne wore a lovely white shantung chambray suit. She did have a beautiful veil that was given to her by her mother. It was so delicate now. She envisioned her daughter, if she had one, wearing it someday.

Nancy had a heavy wrench in her back pocket. She hoped it would be enough to do the job.

One whack and electricity was out! She laughed.

Nancy sent Gina back to the shed for the pitchfork. She knew she was going to be needing it very soon. It gave Nancy a few minutes to go to the outside of the cottage to kill the electricity. Nancy thought to herself, *Good thing I have great night vision. It's going to come in very handy very soon.* Nancy grinned.

Nancy had been waiting for this moment for months—years even. She thought back to several weeks ago when she and Gina were working on a project for Melanie—something for the Kelli Doll. Nancy hated that doll, but it paid the bills. Her and Gina worked for hours on this particular project— actually worked on it—using their own ideas, etc. They were both really proud that they actually did something on their own. They were proud of their own work. They then presented it to Melanie. She hated it and squashed the whole idea! All their time and work went for nothing! Nancy was furious. Gina was truly disappointed.

"No, that's not really what I wanted. I guess I'll just do it myself," Melanie responded disappointedly. She responded in a huff.

Nancy and Gina just stared at Melanie in total disbelief. They were sitting in Melanie's office, slumped down in the two chairs that faced Melanie's large expensive mahogany desk.

"No, no, no, this won't do. This won't work!" Melanie replied in frustration. "This isn't what I was looking for. Okay, well, I'll just do it myself. No worries, girls." Melanie looked at both Nancy and Gina with a forced smile.

Nancy hated that look—that fake smile that Melanie would occasionally show to her and Gina, especially these past few months. Melanie was never satisfied with any of their work, it seemed. The anger in Nancy was growing.

Nancy thought back to when her and Gina were sitting in their small, furnished apartment one day after working with Melanie. It was a very modest apartment. It was all they could afford. Nancy was always angry these days. She was especially angry at the modest pay that she and Gina were receiving for all the hard work they were doing for Melanie. While the rich people lived in their highfalutin' mansion, they were sitting here in this dump of an apartment! But Nancy thought everything out very carefully—cold and calculating. It wouldn't be long till she got her final revenge. This would all pay off. Just a little longer...

Nancy and Gina were sitting in their tiny apartment. They were sitting at the small kitchen table. Nancy was fuming. Gina could always tell when Nancy was angry, and she was extremely angry that day. She was drowning her anger in her fifth cold beer when Gina finally opened her mouth to speak.

"Nancy, don't you think you had enough?" Gina said timidly.

"Stop, Gina, just stop! I know when I've had enough!" Nancy replied in disgust. "I *know* I've had enough of that bitch!"

Gina was actually scared at that very moment. She always thought that Nancy was a little nuts—especially with that thing that happened at college. A girl they knew—although reluctantly—gave Nancy answers to an exam that she had taken earlier in the day. Nancy had intentions of paying her right away, but explained the money would be a little late coming. Nancy hadn't gotten paid yet. Nancy and Gina had jobs on campus in one of the cafeterias, but because of the holiday, the checks were going to be delayed a couple of days. The girl was getting very impatient.

"Nancy, I want my money. I gave you the answers. Now give me my cash!" Miranda exclaimed.

"I'll get you your money—on Monday. My boss didn't give out the paychecks yet. I'll get my check on Monday. You can wait till Monday!" Nancy yelled back.

"You bitch!" Miranda shouted. "You lied to me!"

"What did you call me?" Nancy screamed in a very threatening voice.

Gina just stood back behind them and hoped no one else heard them arguing. It was a dark, deserted area right off campus. Nancy wanted to make sure there wouldn't be anyone around—as always. She made sure the process, the transaction, would go unnoticed—with the exception of Gina being present, of course. Nancy trusted Gina. Gina had often thought just how long that would go on—Nancy trusting her. Gina would sometimes think that there may come a time when Nancy would turn on her. Gina shuddered to think about that terrible thought. She always had that fear.

The local police department found the girl's body several days later—in a ditch. Her head was bashed in. She was dead.

Nancy panicked. Gina panicked.

"Oh my god! What did I do?" Gina shouted in panic. "Oh my god!"

"Gina, it's okay. I'll help you," Nancy said all too calmly.

"Oh my god! I didn't mean to kill her!" Gina was freaking out.

Gina threw the heavy rock down on the ground, although it was more like a small boulder. Gina had come at Miranda with the large rock she had found on the ground nearby. Miranda had started lunging at Nancy, strangling and choking her. Gina had to defend her friend—and she did. She came from behind and approached Miranda. With all the physical strength she could muster, she struck Miranda on the back of the head. Miranda fell to the ground immediately.

"Thanks, G," Nancy said gratefully as she was holding her hands and massaging her throat. "Way to go! You clocked her!" Nancy was actually quite proud of her best friend—and surprised.

"She's not moving!" Gina exclaimed hysterically.

"Gina, don't worry. I'll help you get rid of the body. It's going to be okay. You were just trying to save me." Nancy was trying to reason and reassure Gina.

"We're gonna die!" Gina said frightfully.

"No," Nancy said calmly. "You're going to prison. I didn't kill her...you did!"

Gina started to cry. Nancy smiled and tried to comfort Gina—kind of.

"Gina, we'll get rid of the body," Nancy said in a peaceful tone. "No one will ever know that we—or rather you—had anything to do with it. No one will be able to link us to this. Trust me."

And so it began...

CHAPTER 8

Melanie wanted to see herself in her beautiful wedding dress and veil in the long oval mirror just one more time. She thought to herself, *Brides really never get to see themselves... They're so busy. I just want to make sure I'm perfect.*

Just then, the lights went out in the cottage—total darkness. Melanie spun around. She thought she saw something—someone peering in at her. She never really felt creeped out living here alone at her little cottage. She felt confused. And now it was definitely a different feeling. She felt a premonition of sheer panic and fear.

Melanie reluctantly opened the back door a crack and spoke out, "David...Daddy? Hello, anybody there? Who is it? I'm in no mood for games, not tonight, not on the eve of my wedding!"

"That rips it!" Nancy exclaimed in anger. "I've had enough!"

Things happened so fast. Nancy came out of nowhere, Gina trailing behind. Nancy had a heavy wooden pitchfork squarely secured in her hands as she rammed Melanie right in the stomach—fork end first.

"Nancy, no!" Gina screamed.

Melanie fought with everything she had in her, but she stumbled back. She looked down. She held her stomach where the pitchfork entered her. Her blood was oozing out of her belly now—everywhere. She knew she was going to die that night. Melanie thought, *No, not tonight...not on the eve of my wedding...I'll never get the chance to have my perfect wedding...I'll never marry my David. Oh...David...I'm so sorry...so very sorry...*

Nancy had pulled out the pitchfork and wacked Melanie across her head and face. "I am going to destroy you, bitch, finally—once and for all!"

Melanie collapsed and crumbled to the floor. Her spirit was slowly drifting up...she was dying.

"There, how do you like the color red for your be-au-tiful wedding dress!" Nancy cackled out loud.

Gina was rocking back and forth on the floor in the corner. She was catatonic. She was screaming and holding her head.

"No...no...no...no!" Gina said on and on, over and over. She kept repeating it as she rocked back and forth. She was so in shock at the horror she had just witnessed.

"Gina, come on...get up! We gotta get out of here. They're gonna come lookin' for us...or for someone who did this! Gina, come on!" Nancy screamed in panic. "Oh, Jesus Christ! Gina, don't go catatonic on me now. Get up! We gotta go!" Nancy pleaded with Gina, thinking she could be reasoned with. Now. Nancy was getting scared.

Nancy grabbed the pitchfork. "I can't leave the murder weapon here."

Nancy knocked Gina out and picked her up. She threw Gina over her shoulder. Nancy thought to herself, *Thank God she's light!* She quickly took a fast glance at the floor of the cottage—nothing to tie her to the crime. They were outta there.

Nancy took Gina back to the shed. She, as quietly as possible, while balancing Gina on her shoulder, opened the shed door as she propped up the murder weapon against the shed. She laid Gina gently down on the floor. She knew she couldn't leave the pitchfork anywhere in the area—too obvious. She hoped Gina wouldn't be too mad at her. She'd had to knock her out—she wouldn't budge, and she wouldn't move. Gina left her no alternative—she'd had to club her.

Nancy thought she would just take the pitchfork with her and Gina. They had to go back to the apartment quickly get some things and get out of Dodge. She had wiped off the wrench and buried it behind the shed. It would be fine. No one would ever find it. Now to find a place for the pitchfork.

Nancy opened the shed door. She heard moaning coming from inside. Gina was waking up.

"Gina, you okay?" Nancy innocently asked.

"My head…it's splitting. It hurts so bad…what happened to me?" Gina asked groggily.

"You don't know?" Nancy asked her.

"No, did I fall…stumble? My head's killing me!" Gina was puzzled and confused.

Gina took her hand and with the palm of her hand pressed gently against her forehead.

"Ouch!" Gina cried.

Blood was trickling down her forehead.

"Seriously, you don't know what happened?" Nancy asked again.

"No, dammit! What happened to me?" Gina yelled.

"You really don't remember? Well…you fell and hit your head against the shed outside," Nancy said calmly.

Nancy thought to herself, *Wow, Gina doesn't remember a damn thing! This is perfect! I couldn't have planned this any better! Gina doesn't remember a damn thing!*

The shock of everything happening put Gina in a temporary amnesia.

I am saved, Nancy thought to herself. *Neat and tidy!*

Nancy grabbed in her pocket for her keys.

"Dammit, where's my keys?" Nancy panicked. "Dammit, where are they? We gotta get out of here!"

Gina just lay there on the floor of the shed as she looked at Nancy, confused.

Still holding on to her head, Gina said, "Just chill, Nancy. You probably dropped them somewhere when you picked me up from falling."

"Oh ya, no worries," Nancy replied. "That's probably it."

That's it, Nancy thought to herself. She'd heard something fall back in the cottage—on the floor.

She'd heard a clunk. She'd been so busy killing that bitch that she didn't stop to look at what might have dropped. It was her keys that fell out of her pocket of her overalls.

"Goddammit," Nancy said under her breath in a low tone. "I have to go back."

"Nancy, go back where?" Gina asked.

Man, she really doesn't remember a goddamn thing, Nancy thought. *This is beautiful. Now I won't have to clean up another mess by killing Gina. Perfect!*

"Gina, you stay here and rest. You have a nasty bump on your head. I'm just going to close the door so you have some peace and quiet. I'm going to go and look for my keys. Now don't try to move. Don't get up. I'll be right back, okay?"

Gina nodded.

Great, Nancy thought to herself. *And if Gina falls asleep, maybe she'll fall into a coma—better yet. Death might be good for her.* Nancy had hoped that she wouldn't have to kill Gina later if she started remembering. She wouldn't look forward to that, but if she had to, then she had to. It may not be a bad thing...

Neat and tidy was always a must!

CHAPTER 9

David took one of the stone pathways that led back to Melanie's cottage. The air was crisp and cool and uncannily quiet. The night sky was dark but lit up with all the beautiful stars. It was a gorgeous night for a stroll.

There were no lights on at the cottage.

That's funny, David thought to himself. *Melanie always leaves the lights on at the cottage—even when she's not there and especially at night. She's obsessed with leaving lights on—at least several night-lights on at night. And even if she's still there, she still leaves plenty of lights on. The cottage should be a blooming beacon!*

"Something's wrong," David said to himself. "Something's very wrong…it's not right."

David wished he had a flashlight on him, although he did have fairly good night vision. He just needed a few moments to adjust his eyes to the darkness of the cottage. He knocked. Nothing…silence. He did think he heard a rustling of some sort though.

"Melanie, honey, you okay? It's David."

He slowly opened the front door. It creaked. He took a mental note—fix that.

"Shit," Nancy whispered to herself.

41

Nancy was crouched down behind the couch, fumbling and feeling around for her keys when she heard someone coming up the pathway and then opening the front door.

"Dammit, I gotta kill another!" Nancy said to herself in disgust. "Another mess, another cleanup I gotta do!"

David opened the door. He couldn't see clearly yet. Damn! His eyes weren't adjusting to the darkness as quickly as he wanted. He knew the layout of the cottage. His thigh bumped into an end table. He raised his arms and used his hands to feel ahead of him.

"Melanie?" David said out loud. He was panicking now. "Where the hell was Melanie?"

Nancy silently kept to the floor and was able to crawl to the back corner. She knew David didn't see her. He didn't even know anyone else was there in the cottage with him. Nancy was always good with that—being able to move around undetected and invisible.

She felt around for something—anything. She felt behind her. Oh good, the kitchen.

David fell. He stumbled onto something. He fell onto Melanie. He felt something wet and sticky on his hands. He felt her ice cold body, her face—she was covered in blood. He felt the moisture and lace. *Oh my god…no!*

"Melanie!" David screamed a blood-chilling scream. "Oh my god! No…no…no…Melanie!"

He cradled her in his arms, rocking her back and forth, crying habitually. "No...no...not my Melanie!"

All of a sudden, a blow came to the back of his head and then a stab in his back, his side, the back of his neck, his upper back again. He was going to die too, just like his Melanie, alongside his Melanie. He fell on top of her in a thump. He felt the life and spirit slowly leaving his body. He was gone just like Melanie. No wedding, no future, no nothing...

Nancy slipped out the back door undetected. David tried to move, to call out. No one would ever hear him. The orchestra was playing. The music was so loud and blaring. They were so very far away. He couldn't move. He wanted to. He wanted to know who would do such a horrific thing. Melanie was nearing death, and he probably was too...soon. He wanted to pick her up. He heard a door close, a click, maybe the back door. He saw shoes...boots...but that was all.

David tried with every existing muscle in his body to turn over. He had to try to pick up Melanie. Maybe he could carry her. There was still hope.

With everything he had, he pulled himself up to his knees, stumbling. He had no energy. He knew he had lost some blood. He struggled but picked up Melanie—carried her like a baby. How would he get the door open? He didn't want to drop her. She was relatively light to carry, his betrothed. He maneuvered himself, cradled Melanie, and went for the front door handle. He tried to turn the handle and push with all his might.

Wow, that was easy, David thought as he stumbled through the front door.

David pushed right through...right through the door. He was a bit disoriented. He hoped to find someone...anyone...who could help him with his beloved Melanie. He looked down at her...so peaceful, like she was sleeping. She had blood on her. Her wedding dress...it was torn but still beautiful, just like his Melanie. She really wasn't heavy at all. He wandered through the woods...searching... searching...

David didn't hear the music any longer. The estate...where was it? He might have been turned around a bit, that's all. He was just a little confused because of the bump, scratches. Was he stabbed? He'd felt, at one time, a type of stabbing feeling, but all those feelings were gone. He must have healed. He was a quick healer. His mother always told him that.

Pushing through the darkness...stumbling and wandering in the woods...the forest...

"Can anyone help me? Can anyone hear me?"

I need to get my Melanie to a doctor...a hospital...

PART 2
The Coming

CHAPTER 10

"These dreams go on when I close my eyes every second of the night. I live another life...these dreams..."

Reagan was humming and singing along with her favorite vocal group Heart. "These Dreams" was one of her favorite songs.

Reagan was tired, exhausted. She hasn't slept well these past couple of weeks—months. These last couple of months have been insane. If someone would have predicted that she would be contacted by an attorney, been told that you have become the sole heir to a house—a mansion—she would have said you were crazy, absolutely crazy!

But that was exactly what happened.

Reagan came home from pulling a double shift at the hospital. She was a pediatric nurse at Lincoln Memorial Hospital. She had worked an eleven-to-seven shift for a fellow nurse and then worked a seven-to-three shift when another nurse came down with the flu. She was beat. All Reagan wanted to do was sleep. She checked her mail and pressed to listen to her messages on her answering machine—she had five messages.

"Hi, Reagan, it's Maggie. Just checking with you about Friday." She clicked to the next.

"Hey, Reagan, it's Mark…just checking to see what you might be doing tonight…dinner?"

"Sleeping!" Reagan responded out loud.

"Reagan, hi. It's Marcy. Just wanted to say thanks again for covering my shift for me. I owe you one! I'm feeling much better." She clicked to the next one.

"Hello, this is just a reminder that your car is due for an oil change soon, so please call us at…"

And then message number 5.

"Hello, Ms. Dennyson. You do not know me. My name is Carl Hogan. I'm an attorney with Remington, Remington, and Holden. Please call me back at your earliest convenience. It is urgent. This is not a hoax. Please call me at 1-800-555-2095. Please…as soon as possible. Thank you."

Reagan listened to the last message again. *Hmmm…what was his name? Carl Hogan? I'd better write this down*, Reagan thought to herself. *Although it is not a message one could easily forget. The message said urgent. What the hell? What could this possibly be all about?*

Reagan looked at her watch…too late to call now. *I'll call in the morning. I'm off tomorrow—a gift for pulling a double shift at the hospital. Yay!*

Hopefully, Reagan would get some sleep tonight. Melatonin, Reagan thought, may be her choice again tonight. It had been the sleep aid of choice for Reagan these past couple of weeks—months. Reagan had never been a great, sound sleeper. It all started back about sixteen years ago…

CHAPTER 11

"Reagan, come on! Hurry up!" Rachel yelled impatiently. "I want to go to the lake! You are so slow!"

"I'm coming! Hold your horses!" Reagan yelled back.

Rachel was Reagan's twin sister. They were identical twins. Reagan and Rachel did everything together—had the same set of friends, liked playing the same games, enjoyed the same programs on TV. Of course, they did have their differences too. Rachel loved peanut butter—absolutely loved it! Reagan, on the other hand, could take it or leave it. Reagan loved mostly all foods, including fruits and vegetables. Rachel was more finicky—a picky eater.

Reagan was born a minute and a half earlier than Rachel—not that it necessarily meant anything. Some may say the twin that is born first may be a little bigger in size, a little smarter, a little stronger, maybe more outgoing. But Rachel wasn't anything less than Reagan. Rachel was actually the more outgoing and headstrong of the two. They were both very healthy girls—and very normal in all instances.

Vincent and Carole Dennyson were Reagan and Rachel's parents. A very normal family—as normal goes. When the girls were born and Carole would take them out for a walk in the twin stroller, people would stop and take a peek. Carole was always pleased to show off her girls. They really were beautiful—light brown hair, blue eyes. Their features were fine. Their skin was pink, plump, and beautiful. Everyone always remarked how angelic and beautiful her babies were. Carole just smiled, graciously agreed, and thanked them. Carole loved taking her morning walk with the girls. The morning hours were her favorite time of day. When her and Vincent found out that they were pregnant and then, having twins, they decided that Carole would stop working. Being pregnant, of course, didn't always mean one had to stop working, but having twins was another story. Carole was always pretty healthy. She had no complications during her pregnancy—aside from swollen ankles toward the end and being tired, of course. She was diligent about taking her prenatal vitamins, eating healthy, and no alcohol or caffeine. All in all, Carole felt pretty good all through her nine months. Vincent was always very supportive—a good husband. He went with Carole to her doctor appointments when he could get away from work. Vincent worked for the big neighborhood car dealership. He worked very hard. He was knowledgeable about his product. He was honest and had integrity. He was very well liked. He knew his stuff as his fellow workers and customers would often say. He was friendly and really loved what he did—selling cars. He actually met Carole at the dealership.

Carole worked in the office. She was very knowledgeable and skilled. She worked a variety of tasks—customer service, accounts payable (if needed if Penny was away), accounts receivable. Whatever needed to be done, Carole could do it. Vincent loved that about Carole. She was always kind, a winning smile—never moody. Carole, too, had a great work ethic and was always honest. Customers liked her. Vincent liked her. It was the largest car dealership in the area and always winning quotas and awards for customer satisfaction and selling the most vehicles.

Don McCormick owned the dealership and several others in the nearby cities. He was successful and had high expectations from his employees—all of them—including the service department and support staff. He believed everyone needed to pull their own weight and work together as a team—and they did. Don also believed in rewarding for a job well done. At the end of a promotion, end of the year, and holidays, he rewarded his employees with bonuses, parties, and incentives. He felt if you treat your employees well, then they would work that much harder. Don wanted happy, contented employees who had integrity and knowledge. Sometimes, Don would take on new recruits, as he would call them—high school grads or college students who would like to learn the car business—on kind of an internship program. He would pair them up with a couple of his best car salesmen to learn the business. If they worked out well, he would offer them a position with one of his dealerships. This program worked out very well, Don thought. It was a win-win situation in his eyes. He was teaching good, sound business principles and philosophies, a business trade, and in turn, may get decent employees that he had already created some history with. That's how he got Vincent Dennyson. Vincent didn't attend college, but he always wanted to sell cars and work for Mr. McCormick. He liked Mr. McCormick—always smiling and laughing. Mr. McCormick was successful and a nice, genuine man—a good role model and a hard worker.

When Carole and Vincent found out that Carole was having twins, and they told Don McCormick, a wonderful baby shower was thrown for them. Everyone at the dealership was invited. Carole and Vincent were truly touched. It was a surprise baby shower put on by Mr. McCormick and his wife, Penny. Penny took care of accounts payable. They spared no expense, and the baby shower was held at the neighborhood restaurant and pub— Browning's Restaurant and Pub. Browning's wasn't ostentatious—it was warm and inviting. The interior was all wood paneled, with enough lighting for a warm, glowing effect. It had a large enough capacity—but not like a cafeteria. There were individual rooms off to each side for people to have individual, private parties if they chose. The tables were set up and arranged nicely and perfect for socializing. The bar area was a fun area for people to gather. The bar was U shaped with plenty of comfortable stools. The backdrop of the bar was long mirrors and glass shelves, which housed all the extensive selections of booze and alcohol. Whatever one wanted, Mr. Browning was sure to have it—or he would get it for you! And, of course, the food was delicious. The Brownings—Alice and Tom—came over from Ireland and settled here in the United States. Tom's family owned a pub over in Ireland, and when his family—parents passed away—and his siblings didn't want to carry on the tradition of keeping the pub open, Tom thought "what the heck, I'll just bring the pub to America!" He became acquainted and became good friends with Marcus, an American who was temporarily working where Tom had his pub.

When Tom's parents passed away, Marcus said to Tom, "Tom, you love this place, but you know you can't run it by yourself. Pack the pub up, come to America, and I'll help you run it! Hell, I'm ready for a change, a new beginning, a new pathway to follow. I'd love to work alongside my new best friend! What do you say?" Marcus asked enthusiastically.

Tom replied, looking upward and pondering for a moment or two, "Damn, I like that idea. I'll do it!"

Tom and Marcus shook hands to seal the deal, and they'd been business partners—and best friends—ever since!

The shipping of the bar itself—the most important focal point of the pub—would be tricky. Of course, the barstools would accompany the bar as well. Everything else could easily be duplicated, but the bar and stools had to be shipped over. It wasn't easy, but it was done. And Browning's Restaurant and Pub came to be. It's a fun place to go—good ale, good liquor, and good Irish food—and Tom throws in, of course, American fare as well.

The baby shower was wonderful, and as it got too difficult for Carole to work any longer, she took a leave of absence—that turned into a permanent leave. It was just too hard and quite inconceivable for Carole to think she could return to work—not with taking care of and raising the twins, Rachel and Reagan. Mr. McCormick understood completely. He also wanted Carole to know that if, at any time, she wished to come back to work—even part time—he (along with his wife, Penny) would welcome her with open arms. Carole—along with Vincent—were like his children. He, along with Penny, loved them both as if they were their own.

Carole got settled into an organized routine with Reagan and Rachel. By 7:00 p.m., it was baths, bottles, rocking, and bed. As she would lay them in their cribs—all cozy and comfortable—soft music would always be playing, and the soft glow of a night-light would be seen. The babies were all settled in and good for the night.

The girls grew and were delightful. They played together nicely in their playpens with always watchful eyes—Carole's. She was a good mother—loving, protective, and nurturing. She treated each with equal amounts of love and attention, but it was exhausting. With twins, come twin everything—twin feedings, twin laundry, twin baths, etc. Vincent was always as helpful as he could be—when he could. Even though he would be exhausted, too, from working a full day, he still came home with a smile knowing in his heart that Carole probably just had an equally hard, tiring day as well. They would both take care of Rachel and Reagan, put them to bed, and have a relaxing rest of the evening of good food, maybe a glass of wine and conversation about the day's activities. Life was good.

But life can change in the blink of an eye, in a moment's notice, and sometimes tragically too...

CHAPTER 12

It was a normal Saturday in June, as normal Saturdays go. Vincent was at the car dealership, putting in a few hours. He would finish up by noon or one and come home to spend the rest of the Saturday and weekend with his family.

The girls were eight years old now, and each had their own individual personalities. Carole and Vincent often talked about how Rachel and Reagan had maybe looked almost exactly alike, but when it came to personality traits, each was their own person. Carole and Vincent encouraged each girl to just be themselves. Even though they were only eight years old, their personalities were forming into their own individual molds.

Carole was busy working on some bills. The girls were good company for each other, and Carole always knew, well hopefully, what the girls were up to and where they were.

"Mommy," Reagan asked, "can Rachel and I go to the lake just for a little while? We'll be good, and we'll be safe—promise!" Reagan pleaded.

Rachel chided in, "Please, Mommy, please?"

"Girls, you know the rules—only with adult supervision, meaning Daddy or I. You know that," Carole reminded them in a raised voice.

"Mommy, we promise we won't go into the water. We'll just look at it." Rachel put her hands together in a praying format. "Please," she continued pleading and smiled.

Carole was being worn down. She just needed to get the bills done. She wanted to, at least, complete one task today!

"Girls, Daddy should be home in a little while. Just wait until then please!"

Rachel and Reagan stormed off in a huff. They didn't throw temper tantrums, as Carole's sister's kids usually did. She was very grateful for that. Although she, along with her husband, Vincent, believed temper tantrums were cultivated. Their girls were usually very good. It's how a child or children are raised, Carole would often say. A child's behavior is not just the luck of the draw. It's the skill in how that child is raised—what's allowed and what's not, what rules and parameters are formed. Carole and Vincent knew their girls were not perfect—not by a long shot. But all in all, they were good girls.

Rachel and Reagan were sitting in their bedroom. Reagan could tell that Rachel was unusually quiet, and that usually meant that Rachel was scheming up a thought—an idea. Rachel really wanted to go to the lake. She was a determined child. Reagan knew her twin sister well.

"Reagan, let's sneak out. Mom will never know. We'll be back in plenty of time for when Daddy gets home. C'mon…please?" Rachel whined.

"Rachel, no! You heard what Mom said. We need to wait till Daddy gets home," Reagan retorted. She knew Rachel's routine all too well.

"Well, you can stay here, but I'm going!" Rachel said in a stubborn, almost spoiled tone. "I'm going to the lake. If you want to stop me, you'll just have to come too!"

"Ughhh, why are you so stubborn, Rachel! What's waiting a little while longer gonna hurt? We need to wait for Daddy!" Reagan insisted.

Rachel wasn't even listening to her twin sister any longer. She quietly slipped out of the bedroom and left the door open. She usually could get Reagan to go along with whatever she wanted. Rachel liked adventure. Reagan, on the other hand, was more compliant and dutiful.

But, and Rachel knew this, Reagan was always very protective of her sister as well. And as predicted, Reagan would follow Rachel. Rachel was so manipulative, which can be a very dangerous quality to possess. Reagan heard Rachel tell Mom that she was just going out into the backyard to play.

"Where's your sister?" Carole asked Rachel.

"She's reading," Rachel replied in the most innocent voice she had.

"Oh, okay," Carole answered.

At first, Carole thought that was odd. The two girls always did things together. They usually didn't do anything apart from one another. The brief notion was quickly dismissed as Carole turned her concentration back to finish up paying the bills—just two more to go…

And that unfortunately, little did Carole know, would be the last time, the very last and final time, that she would ever see and talk to her daughter, Rachel.

It was all such a blur from that point on…

Reagan heard the back door slam. She knew Rachel had lied to Mom. She also knew if she hurried up and followed her, then at least Rachel wouldn't be alone at the lake. Temptation was always an evil factor for Rachel.

Reagan came into the kitchen, where her Mom was working at the kitchen table.

"Mom, I'm going out to play with Rachel. Is that okay?" Reagan asked.

"I thought you were reading, honey? No, that's okay. Please stay in the backyard and keep your sister with you please. I just have a little more to finish up, then I'll come out too, okay?" Carole looked up from her checkbook and smiled.

"Okay, Mommy," Reagan replied dutifully.

Carole knew that Reagan would watch over Rachel. She was the more mature—grounded—of the two. She felt better about the previous thought about her two girls not being together. She laughed a little and shrugged off her nagging negative thoughts—premonition. They'd be fine. She was not a "hovering helicopter" mom, just a loving, protective one. They'd be fine.

"Come on, Reagan, hurry up!" Rachel yelled. "You take forever!"

"I'm coming! Hold your horses!" Reagan yelled back.

They both looked back at the back door, making sure their mother wasn't there or didn't hear them talking of their escape. Carole was still sitting at the kitchen table, finishing up writing checks for the bills.

The girls giggled and skipped lively as they headed down to the lake—Lake Bremen. It was a warm summer day. The sun was shining brightly. The lake was shimmering—it was beautiful. But as beautiful as Lake Bremen was, it was also a deep lake and a dangerous one. People in the area knew just how Lake Bremen could be. It was shallow at first, then it dropped off dramatically. There were jagged rocks everywhere. Whenever Carole and Vincent took the girls to the lake, water shoes were always worn and hand-holding a must.

There was an area that was a favorite of the girls. It was a woodsy area—trees, then some rocks—always an area that was fun to explore. It was so much fun to find that special stone. Rachel and Reagan collected stones from the lake. They had a huge collection in a box in their bedroom. They could spend hours and afternoons going through their collection of favorite rocks. They wanted to eventually paint on them—

painting faces of animals, flowers, designs. They loved doing that and creating their own artwork!

"Hey, Reagan, let's go look for more stones to add to our collection!" Rachel yelled back to her.

The rainstorm yesterday had left that woody area damp and slightly muddy.

Rachel scurried off to her favorite place.

"Rachel, wait!" Reagan screamed at her sister.

Rachel was off and running. Reagan stumbled, stopped, and bent down to tie one of her shoes. She didn't think it was very long. And then she heard a bloodcurdling scream. It was a voice that she knew well—Rachel's.

"Rachel!" Reagan yelled.

Reagan panicked. She ran to where Rachel went. She stumbled and fell. It was muddy. She got up and ran to where she heard Rachel scream.

She saw her in the water near the woodsy area. Rachel had just bent down to pick up a beautiful, glistening stone when she stumbled and fell into the water. She'd tried to grab and hold on to a branch of a tree to keep herself from falling into one of the deepest parts of the lake. It was muddy, and the rocks were jagged and sharp. She tumbled down and hit her head. Rachel fell into the water. The water was moving and still was very cold in temperature.

Reagan found Rachel. Her head was bleeding, and she was swallowing a lot of water. Neither were great swimmers. Reagan held on to the tree with her arm.

"Rachel, grab my hand!" Reagan screamed in panic.

Rachel tried reaching out to Reagan, but it was too hard. Rachel was weak. The sharp bump on her head made her dizzy. She felt she was going under the water. She kept trying to reach Reagan, but it was futile. Reagan finally had Rachel's hand—for a moment—and then Rachel slipped away down under the water.

Reagan was crying habitually. She was in a state of panic. She didn't want to leave her sister, but she needed to go for help. She wasn't a good swimmer. She was afraid she would end up helpless like Rachel.

She kept calling out to her sister, "Rachel, Rachel!"

Reagan grabbed anything she could find that maybe Rachel could grab on to, but she couldn't see her. She must have gone under. She kept calling out to her. She thought, for a moment, she saw Rachel's head bobbing, then nothing. She wasn't there…as if she was never there.

She ran as fast as she could to get back to the house. Vincent was just getting home from the car dealership when Reagan ran up to him in a panic, screaming uncontrollably. Vincent had just stepped out of the car.

"Daddy, Daddy, come quick!" Reagan was crying and pleading with Vincent as she pulled on his jacket.

"Calm down, Reagan. What is it?"

"It's Rachel! She fell into the lake! I can't find her, Daddy! Daddy, come quick!"

Vincent yelled out for Carole. Carole came out quickly.

"What's the matter? Hi, honey. Reagan, where's your sister? Where's Rachel?" Carole was panicking now and screaming.

"Come on, hurry!" Reagan waved at her parents with both arms. "We have to go! We have to save Rachel!"

They ran to Lake Bremen as fast as they could. It wasn't that far away, but when there's an emergency, it always feels like forever in getting to where one needs to be.

Reagan pointed to where Rachel fell into the water. Vincent immediately jumped in, clothes and all. As he kept diving under the cold, icy water, he could hear his wife, Carole, yelling at Reagan.

"Reagan, what were you two thinking! I told you to wait. All you had to do was wait!"

She and Reagan were crying hysterically now. They both kept their eyes frozen on the spot where Vincent went under to look for his other daughter.

There were other homes nearby. People soon ran out of their houses. They heard the commotion, and some who'd lived in the area for a while knew all too well the familiar sounds of panic and fear. It was coming from the lake—Lake Bremen. It was never good…never a good sign…never, never good…

Someone called the police and emergency squad. Squad cars and emergency vehicles came quickly—along with the EMTs. The blaring sound of the sirens piercing through the air were frightening as they raced down Cumberland Road. They were hurrying once again to Lake Bremen. Lights were flashing everywhere.

Soon, a large group of people were gathering on the beach. Some were lined up on the side of Cumberland Road with outstretched necks, watching in morbid curiosity. Some people were praying, some were watching in silence, some were talking quietly. But everyone was hoping the little girl would be found…and hopefully alive and safe.

It was just like ten years ago when Billy Sawyer drowned at Lake Bremen. Another normal, sunny, summer day, another tragedy, another life taken by Lake Bremen. It had taken another victim.

CHAPTER 13

Dickinson's Funeral Home was not at peace or at rest today—not when a child inhabited the funeral home. Today was the wake of Rachel Marie Dennyson—daughter to Vincent and Carole Dennyson, twin sister to Reagan Katherine Dennyson. It was a jam-packed room filled with family and so many friends and neighbors to Carole and Vincent. Soft music was playing. It was coming out from the sound system and speakers overhead the visitation room where Rachel was laid out. Of course, no one could hear the solemn music playing. The crying and talking drowned out any possibility of the music ever bringing any kind of comfort to the room or the people that had gathered there that day and evening. Pink and white flowers were every-where. There wasn't an inch of space available for any other floral or plant arrangements. Carole and Vincent had a hard time deciding whether to leave the coffin lid closed or open for the wake. Rachel was dressed in a beautiful light ballet pink dress. It was laced with fluffy ruffles, as Rachel would often call them. It was her very favorite dress-up dress. Reagan had picked it out. Rachel looked like a little angel—

and probably was now. They placed her favorite soft, fluffy white-and-pink stuffed bunny in her arms. She never could—or would—go to sleep without Bunny at her side and in her warm little hands. And now her hands, although embracing Bunny, were ice cold… and forever would be. Her Bunny would now be with Rachel for always.

It was a very, very long and exhausting day and evening. Vincent, Carole, and Reagan were at Dickinson's at 9:00 a.m. They were all dressed in their Sunday best. All three looked the part—a family that had been, and would continue to be, grieving. They may have looked the part, but on the inside, they were all suffering so very much. Carole and Vincent were going through the motions of "thank you for coming" and "we're doing the best we can." They were just words one usually says when close ones died. The words were vacant and empty and unfeeling. Although Vincent and Carole, and maybe Reagan, were grateful for all who attended and paid tribute to their beautiful little girl, the words, although dutiful, felt meaningless.

That day that took Rachel away from her family was like a dream—a very bad, horrid dream, a nightmare. It didn't feel real—like it really happened. Was it just a terrible dream? Would Carole, Vincent, and Reagan wake up—and hopefully Rachel too? Would they just sit at the breakfast table and maybe laugh like it was the silliest, most awful nightmare anyone could have had? No, unfortunately, it was not the case. It was real. It was the most awful nightmare that any family could ever have. There would be a space left vacant at the table. A space that always seated an energetic, bubbly, happy-go-lucky little girl. A little girl who would go crazy if she couldn't find Bunny. A little girl who didn't even have the opportunity to fully enjoy a life—a life that may have been filled with a future filled with wonder and excitement and adventure. No, this was the reality for the Dennyson family. A moment in time would change this family's thinking and feelings forever.

Reagan made sure that day and evening at Dickinson's Funeral Home to stay away and keep her distance from Rachel and her coffin and all the flowers that surrounded her now. Reagan couldn't even look at Rachel. She was scared to death that if she did take a look, a glance, that Rachel would lift and turn her head toward Reagan and stare at her with her lifeless eyes. Reagan was scared that Rachel would come after her and yell at her for not saving her in that God-awful, freezing, deep Lake Bremen. Reagan thought it was her fault that Rachel died, and she was convinced that Rachel must have thought that too. Reagan didn't move fast enough. She didn't hold on tight enough. She didn't convince her sister enough. Reagan didn't keep Rachel from going to the lake and ultimately found her doom. From then on, Reagan would have trouble sleeping. She wouldn't experience a comforting full night's sleep for a very long time.

Reagan just sat in a corner of Dickinson's Funeral Home in a comfortable overstuffed chair. Her mother and father were quietly talking to Mr. Brown, the funeral director. Reagan was tired of crying. Her mother, Carole, motioned to her, calling out to her to let her know that she and her father would be right back. They had to sign another piece of paper that finalized Rachel's funeral. Her twin sister, her best friend in the whole world, who had just died, would never bother her again. Rachel would never coax or coerce her sister to come with her, get another cookie from Mom, never collect beautiful stones and rocks to paint. Reagan would never have her sister around her ever again to laugh with, to dance with, to play games with, to walk with her to school with. It was just Reagan now.

Reagan was just gazing off into space, trying not to think about anything. Her mother came into the room and talked to her.

"Reagan, honey, you okay?" Carole spoke softly in a concerned tone of voice. "Daddy and I just need to step out for a moment and go to Mr. Brown's office to…" Carole started crying.

Carole composed herself and tried speaking again. "We need to finish the paperwork. We'll be right back. Do you want to come with us, or are you okay with just sitting here for a few more moments?" Carole asked.

Carole and Vincent knew this had to be so hard on Reagan. It was certainly the most difficult thing that her and Vincent had ever experienced in their combined lives. She knew they had each other, and they both had to be strong for each other and for Reagan. Carole thought to herself that this had to be a really bad nightmare, and she would soon wake up and realize it was just a stupid dream.

Reagan just shook her head. "No, I'm okay, Mommy. I'll wait for you and Daddy here."

This was so unbelievably difficult for Reagan. Reagan knew she shouldn't have let Rachel go to the lake by herself. She should have told her mother right away. As we all know, hindsight is twenty-twenty. Reagan had such a hard time sleeping at all. She slept just for short periods of time.

She would break her sleep by waking up abruptly and screaming, always screaming. The nightmares were frequent and the same over and over again… Reagan grabbing and trying to hold on to Rachel's hand, it slipping away into the deep, icy, dark pool of water. There were bubbles in the water. The water was circling and circling like a tornado. Then Rachel came out of the water, rising up slowly. She was soaked and bruised and covered in mud and looking so gray in color. She was scary looking, black holes where her beautiful blue eyes should have been. Her once beautiful hair was now dirty, stringy, and dripping in blood. Her face was pasty white and gray and bloody. She was floating closer and closer to where Reagan was, sitting on the ledge of the wooded area. Rachel's little arms, so bruised and gray and gangly, were outstretched and reaching for her sister, Reagan. She kept coming closer and closer, floating to where Reagan was. Reagan kept leaning back, unable to move or get up. She was paralyzed—frozen.

"Reagan," Rachel was speaking slowly and softly. "You left me to drown...you let me die...you left me...you left me...Come play with me, Reagan... come play with me in the lake. I don't want to be alone...I don't want to be lonely. You said we would always be together...forever...for always..."

Then Rachel grabbed on to Reagan's arms and pulled her into the lake with her. The screaming started. Reagan was going down under the water, going deeper and deeper. It became darker and darker...

It would always be the same routine every night. It would be silent. Carole and Vincent and Reagan slept in the same bedroom every night. It started the first night when Rachel's body was found—when everyone knew for sure that Rachel had died. There were no more questions—no more doubts, no more maybes that Rachel would be found alive. It didn't take long before the search and rescue team found Rachel's tiny, little body downstream. Her body had floated to where it became caught on the ledge and side of a large tree on the edge of the wooded area. The large tree roots were exposed and jutting out into the lake. They'd found Rachel there caught on the tree's roots.

They buried Rachel the next morning in the town's cemetery—Lincoln Park Cemetery. Rows and rows of so many people were buried there. And now a new plot was dug. The dirt was freshly turned and waiting for their next inhabitant, their new resident. This time, it was a small child—an innocent, full-of-life, beautiful little girl, a little girl that would never grow up, never live and love life ever again.

CHAPTER 14

Reagan sat silently in Dickinson's Funeral Home. She cautiously and timidly looked around the room, searching and watching to make sure she was alone. That day would be Reagan's very first experience with the paranormal. She had felt very uneasy being around Rachel and the casket. Reagan was confused, but she knew she was frightened. Was it the guilt she was feeling? She wondered why, at that moment, the atmosphere changed in the room. She wanted out of there. She had an incessant urge to get up from the chair and run. But she didn't.

Reagan gazed and looked upon the light silver gray coffin that housed her sister, Rachel. The flowers all surrounded Rachel's coffin like they were protecting and shielding her from any harm. The flowers were defending her and making the space a safe haven for her. Reagan thought she saw something...maybe something move? Did one of the plants or flowers move? She was definitely frightened. Since that day at the lake, being scared was a feeling she always felt day and night. It was the last day she had spent with her sister, Rachel.

Reagan looked across the room. There was a white mist that started to form near the coffin. Reagan thought she was dreaming, imagining it. The air was cool and getting colder. The mist formed quickly, swirling. Were the drapes moving? Maybe a little. Then the lid of Rachel's coffin rose to open very slowly. It was opening up by itself.

Reagan quietly spoke out loud, calling out to Carole, "Mommy…"

"Shhhh…Reagan, don't be afraid. It's just me… it's Rachel. I won't hurt you. I just want to see you…" It was Rachel's spirit communicating to Reagan.

Rachel's spirit started floating out and above her coffin. She floated across the room toward Reagan. Reagan could see right through her. Rachel was kind of transparent. The room turned ice cold. It was so cold that Reagan could see her breath. She was shivering as she folded and rubbed her arms. Rachel was a soft white mist. Reagan got this waft of a clean, soapy, bubble bath smell that started to surround her. Reagan was just sitting there, frozen. She couldn't move a muscle.

"Reagan, please don't be scared. It's just me, Rachel…I'm lonely. I miss you, Reagan."

Reagan squeezed her eyes tight. She didn't want to open them, fearing what she would see. It took all the bravery Reagan had to open her eyes and say the next few words.

"Rachel, is that you?"

"Yes, it's me, Reagan."

"But how...how can you do that? How can I see you?" Reagan was so confused—and frightened.

"How can you see me, Reagan? I don't know... but you can," Rachel softly replied.

And so it began...

CHAPTER 15

Reagan woke up quite early Wednesday morning. She showered and got dressed into some dress slacks and a comfortable sweater. She made her coffee strong that morning. She knew she was going to need it. Maybe a premonition, she thought.

She had called back Carl Hogan. He was an attorney with Remington, Remington, and Holden. Reagan was nervous—and curious. She dialed. She thought she would have at least a couple of moments to gather her thoughts together, but he answered the call.

"Mr. Hogan, this is Reagan Dennyson. I received your voice message yesterday, and I'm just returning your call. And, needless to say, extremely confused…and curious," Reagan said.

"Ms. Dennyson, I'm so glad you called me back. I was afraid I was going to have to make a second phone call to you. I thought you might think I was a prank or someone running a scam," Carl Hogan replied, laughing a little.

"Are you, Mr. Hogan? Are you running a scam or something?" Reagan asked.

"Oh my goodness, no, Ms. Dennyson. I assure you...and please believe me when I say that this phone call and conversation we are about to have is very legit and true!"

"Okay," Reagan answered nervously.

"Ms. Dennyson, I'd really like for you to come to my office to discuss this matter...not over the phone but in person. It is urgent and imperative that we meet in person as soon as possible please," Mr. Hogan stated matter-of-factly.

Carl Hogan wanted to settle and close this matter as soon as possible. He had a vacation pending, and he wanted to wrap up this matter as soon as he could.

"Am I in some kind of trouble, Mr. Hogan?" Reagan asked—hoping for a negative response, of course!

"No, no, of course not, Ms. Dennyson. I'm sorry. I certainly don't mean to be vague. Okay, let me tell you one thing, and then please promise that we'll set up a time this afternoon—tomorrow morning to come in. Deal, Ms. Dennyson?" Carl Hogan curtly asked.

"Deal, Mr. Hogan."

"Okay, well, to put it bluntly, Ms. Dennyson, you've inherited a mansion."

"What did you just say? Did you say I just inherited a mansion, Mr. Hogan?"

Reagan thought she was going to keel over in shock, pure shock. A mansion? Reagan inherited a mansion? And it came with a heavy amount of baggage, to say the least.

The next morning, Reagan went to Carl Hogan's office.

"Ms. Dennyson." Carl Hogan extended his hand. "I'm very pleased to meet you. I'm Carl Hogan. Please come in and have a seat. Can my secretary get you something to drink? Water? Some coffee perhaps?"

Carl wanted to make Reagan as comfortable as possible. He needed to set the atmosphere to a conducive environment, the most comfortable environment—one where one can tell a young person, someone who has just started their adult life, that they are the heir to a mansion. And not just any mansion but *the* Dennyson Mansion—a widely, publicly, well-known mansion that just happens to have the reputation of being haunted! The story broke out in the news media at eleven:

DAUGHTER AND SOON-TO-BE SON-IN-LAW OF WELL-KNOWN MILLIONAIRE AND SUCCESSFUL BUSINESSMAN, ARTHUR DENNYSON, FOUND BRUTALLY MURDERED

It was all over the papers, newscasts, radio, the Internet. What a story, a story that doesn't go away, nor would it ever.

But if solved…

Reagan couldn't believe what she was hearing. Mr. Hogan spoke of the facts surrounding her inher-

itance—and not just a measly dollar-amount inheritance. She'd inherited a house and not just a house
but a mansion, and not just any mansion but *the*
Dennyson Mansion, and not just that, it was well
known throughout and was said to be haunted. No
would ever touch that place!

And so it continues...

CHAPTER 16

The music from the ballroom was still playing. The guests were all wondering if something was going on. They were all wondering where Melanie and David were.

"Ladies and gentlemen, friends," Arthur announced. "Please excuse this interruption. I seemed to have misplaced my beautiful daughter, Melanie, and her husband-to-be. Please continue to enjoy the food, drinks, and fine music, and hopefully, we'll continue with the celebration when the loving couple are present," Arthur concluded.

Arthur tried to make the situation as light as possible. He didn't want to display any kind of emotion that centered around concern for his daughter and future son-in-law's welfare.

"Irene, I am going to Melanie's cottage. I know David left a while ago, and now neither have returned!"

"Arthur, I'll go with you. Maybe Melanie needs some help with final touches on her dress, and maybe David can't help her. I'm sure there's a simple, logical explanation as to why they are not here yet," Irene replied sensibly.

Irene hoped by saying that explanation, it would take the edge off anything other than simplicity and logic. But unfortunately, she, along with Arthur, would soon find out that their lives would yet again change again dramatically—and for the worse.

Arthur and Irene walked down the pathway, just as David did a little while ago, to Melanie's cottage. It was indeed the walk of doom. The night sky was a beautiful indigo ink color. It was filled with thousands of blinking stars. The moon—a full moon—was huge that night. It was enhanced with the most entrancing glow that lit up the entire sky. It was bewitchingly beautiful.

Arthur and Irene saw that Melanie's front door was opened a crack, but no light illuminated from inside. It was eerie and silent within.

"That's funny," Arthur said in a questioning tone.

It was very dark inside, and a putrid, awful smell was emanating from Melanie's living room. It was a gagging, sour smell. Irene reached into the pocket of her dress. She took out her keys with a small flashlight attached. She pressed it on. She always carried it with her. She always wanted to be prepared—if she ever needed it. Now would be a time for it. She would remember this night for the rest of her life for what she and Arthur would soon view would be the most horrific, terrifying sight each would ever know.

"Arthur, what's that God-awful smell?" Irene yelled.

"I don't know, Irene. I'm not feeling good about this," Arthur replied.

Arthur was frightened, and so was Irene.

Arthur felt, with his fingers, the small lamp that was just inside the entrance located on the small desk near the doorway. He pressed the light switch to on. It didn't turn on. *Okay, the electricity is out—that's a problem*, he thought.

Arthur was very glad, and so was Irene, that Irene had a flashlight, even though it was very small. Any light would be better than none. They both stepped inside the cottage, and Irene started flashing the light around the living area to get a feel of what may be going on.

"Arthur!" Irene gasped, holding her hand over her mouth. "Oh my god in heaven!" Irene screamed in horror.

There, on the floor, behind the couch, lay Melanie and David…lifeless, crumpled. Pools of blood were everywhere. Melanie was in her wedding dress and the veil that belonged to her mother, Anne. Everything was soaked in blood. Melanie's matted hair was crusted over with her blood. It had started to dry. Pools of blood surrounded Melanie and David, as if protecting them.

Arthur dropped to the floor, grabbing his chest and head. He couldn't believe the horror he was seeing.

The scene he saw before him was just too much to bear. He collapsed to the floor. The bloodbath and two crumpled, mutilated bodies that once belonged to his beloved Melanie and her fiancé, David, was just too much to see. The horror of that night, that display, was too horrific for anyone to see. Irene just stood in total disbelief. She screamed a bloodcurdling scream. It broke through the ever beautiful silence and stillness of the night. The shriek pierced through the cold, chilling night air.

It would be the demise and finish of Arthur Dennyson. He just couldn't take any more heartache in his life. That was the last straw. His mind, his body, his soul would soon give out...and give up. He, too, would lose the battle of life.

Irene ran out of the cottage. She ran back to the mansion, the ballroom. She yelled for anyone to call 911 reporting two murders and Arthur's collapse.

Friends and guests were in uproar. Panic erupted throughout the ballroom. The servants came together for Irene to take control. One went straight to Irene to help her. A couple of Arthur's associates took control of the guests. As Irene pointed toward the cottage, the colleagues ran to the cottage to find Arthur. Irene was led to a nearby sitting area in the living room. She collapsed onto one of the sofas.

"Run and get a cool cloth and some water. Hurry!" Marie screamed.

Marie and Irene had become fast friends. Marie came to the Dennyson Mansion soon after Anne had passed away. Arthur felt more help would be needed, and he actually had Irene do the interviewing. Arthur trusted Irene implicitly. As Irene was interviewing Marie, her heart went out to her. As she listened to

Marie's story as to why she was seeking employment, Irene knew firsthand just how Marie felt. Her husband, too, had passed away suddenly, and she needed to find a job. Finding employment would certainly help Marie with her grieving process as well, but most importantly, she had to get a job—to work, to make a living. Irene explained to Marie how exactly she understood her plight. Irene had experienced the same situation many years ago as well. What Anne did for Irene, Irene would do for Marie. Irene told Arthur, and he agreed immediately.

"Hire Marie," he said firmly.

After accepting the job offer, Marie moved into the mansion—just like Irene did—those many years back. There were living quarters where the help could live comfortably. It worked out perfectly for Marie. Irene and Marie became good friends. And tonight, especially tonight, Irene needed a good friend.

Tragedy had been a major part of the Dennyson family. People said there was a huge black cloud over the family. There were so many tragedies, so much suffering. How could that possibly exist in just one family? It seemed to be one tragedy after another.

The murders of Melanie Dennyson and David Williams were never solved. Arthur Dennyson died of a fatal heart attack soon after. The Dennyson Mansion was willed to Arthur's brother, Vincent, and Irene equally. After Anne had died so tragically, Arthur had to change his will.

Ultimately, he left everything to his daughter, Melanie, and left plenty to Irene. It was so that Irene would never ever have to worry financially again. And with Melanie's death being so untimely and unexpected, Arthur had to yet again change his will. He left the mansion to his brother, Vincent, and Irene.

After that night, Arthur felt ill and never really recovered. He never got any better. He had no will to live—his life was slowly being sucked out of him. He stockholders, his board of directors, his close associates were all so very concerned, gravely concerned for Arthur. He next in command and vice president, Douglas Montgomery, met with him a few months after the joint funerals of Melanie and David.

"Arthur, we need to discuss some things," Douglas said to Arthur solemnly.

Arthur was getting weaker by the day. He certainly wasn't the man he was a year ago, and rightfully and understandably so. Irene felt she needed to stay with Arthur. It wasn't an obligation. Irene wanted to stay. For everything that Arthur and Anne had done for her when they didn't have to, Irene never wanted to be anywhere else. Anne and Arthur were her family. Arthur was the brother she always wished she had. Her heart was breaking once again.

"Irene, you don't have to leave," Arthur said quietly one morning.

Irene often had gone to Arthur's room each morning. Arthur couldn't leave his room, and meals, although very small in size, were being brought to him. His personal butler, James, was always very close by nowadays. He never left his side.

One morning, Irene had pulled up a chair and sat next to Arthur at his bedside. She held a cup of warm tea that he was slowly sipping. It was difficult getting Arthur to eat or drink anything any longer. James was tidying up in the room and listening to Irene's and Arthur's conversation.

James came over to Arthur. "Sir, do you want me to step out for a moment while you talk with Ms. Irene?" James asked dutifully.

Arthur just shook his head—along with Irene. "No, James, of course not. You're fine to stay—always." Irene nodded in agreement.

Arthur wanted Irene to think of Dennyson Mansion as her home—her permanent home.

"Arthur, I will do whatever you want and whatever I can to help you. I don't know what to do. I feel so useless and so helpless now. And I feel lost yet again." Irene had tears welling up in her tired eyes.

Arthur just weakly nodded his head in agreement. He was barely able to get out the words. "I know...me too." Irene saw that Arthur was struggling with wanting to say more. He wanted to tell Irene something more.

With James's assistance, Arthur repositioned himself in bed so that he was sitting up more. Irene could tell it took so much out of Arthur just to sit up in bed. Thank God for James. He was dutiful, but he was also loyal, patient, and kind.

Arthur had changed his will again. He'd left the mansion to Irene and to his brother, Vincent.

"Arthur, my god, you do not have to do this. You are under no obligation to take care of me. I don't know what to say." Irene was dumbfounded.

It was hard for Arthur to get any of the words out. He struggled but was able to say a few words.

"Irene, please, you have been Anne's and my lifesaver for many years. I don't have to tell you again just how valuable you have been to me in raising Melanie all those years."

It was so hard for Arthur to even say his deceased daughter's name. Tears started rolling down his tired, thin, drawn cheeks.

He continued, "Irene, you are the sister I never had…and the sister Anne never had…and then… the mother you came to be for our Melanie. I feel this is a way I can convey my feelings and deepest gratitude…for everything you have done to make our lives better. Please accept this gesture that I have willed to you."

"But, Arthur, what about Vincent?" Irene asked. "He may resent my getting half of the mansion. Vincent should have all of it," Irene pleaded.

"I've talked to Vincent, and he agrees. That is it…all is fine," Arthur assured Irene.

A couple of months passed. Arthur was hanging on—barely. He was getting weaker. He had a small stroke that left his right side paralyzed. The rehab was not helping very much. Arthur was getting weaker. His health worsened.

A month later, Arthur Dennyson collapsed, having a massive heart attack. He passed away, leaving the mansion in Vincent's and Irene's hands.

Vincent had come to visit Irene at the mansion after the funeral. He wanted to talk with Irene. Vincent, too, wasn't doing too well healthwise. The tragic death of his daughter, Rachel, and dealing with the health of his wife, Carole, and Reagan's issues took a toll too. How ironic that he and his brother had similar tragedies—both their daughters dying unexpectedly and horrifically.

CHAPTER 17

Fate was not finished with the Dennyson family. After Reagan graduated from nursing school, her mother, Carole, contracted breast cancer. Carole passed away at the end of that year. Vincent and Reagan were devastated. The cancer took Carole so fast. It spread so fast.

Reagan found a job very quickly with Lincoln Memorial Hospital. She wanted to stay and live at home with her father, but Vincent was insistent that she move out and find an apartment nearer to the hospital. He told her she wouldn't be that far away, and she needed to start a life of her own. She had a close relationship and special bond with her father, Vincent.

After Rachel passed away, Reagan always felt that her mother, Carole, blamed her for Rachel's death. Carole was never the same spirited self after Rachel's death. As Reagan grew up, she felt there was no pleasing her mother. Reagan was certainly troubled all through her growing-up years. Her mother and her dad and she went to grief counseling for the next year and a half after Rachel died. It was helpful for them, but the nightmares that Reagan was experiencing wouldn't go away. The family was tired beyond sanity. The counselor suggested taking Reagan to a child psychologist, thinking that may be helpful.

Carole explained one day, confidentially, that she thought Reagan was having additional difficulties with Rachel's death. Carole would sometimes hear Reagan talking to someone—maybe herself. No one was ever in her bedroom but her, and still Carole could hear Reagan talking. When Carole knocked on her bedroom door and then opened it, she asked, "Reagan, who are you talking to?"

Reagan would reply, "No one, Mom, it's just the radio."

"Honey, is everything okay? Is there anything you want to talk about? Do you want to do something together today?"

"No, Mom, I'm fine," Reagan would always respond.

Reagan was fine. She finally got used to the fact that Rachel was always with her. They would have conversations all the time. It was as if Rachel never left, never died. Obviously, Reagan couldn't hug her, feel her. It was always very cold around Rachel. Reagan soon accepted her "gift" of being able to see Rachel. She never told her parents, Carole and Vincent, that she could see Rachel and have conversations with her. It was her and Rachel's little secret. Reagan didn't know if she should tell her parents about seeing Rachel. What would they think? Would they believe her? Think she was crazy? Send her to another child psychologist? She had enough of those! Reagan just let things be. She actually found it kind of comforting having Rachel around—after she got used to it. Rachel said she would always protect her and always be with her until they would be together again. But Rachel assured her sister it wouldn't be for a very long time. Reagan would have a wonderful and full life.

"Does it hurt, Rachel? Did it hurt to die?" Reagan asked one morning in their bedroom. They were talking in conversation like they always did all the time now.

"No, not really," Rachel responded. "I mean, it did at first—when I was dying. I mean, when I thought I was dying. My head and tummy hurt going under the water. It was so cold, and it got colder. Then I died. After that, I didn't feel a thing."

Reagan started to cry at that moment. "Rachel, I am so sorry. I didn't mean to let go and let you die. I should have come in after you, and I didn't."

"Reagan, it's all right," Rachel tried to reassure and comfort her.

Rachel came over to where Reagan was. Reagan was sitting on Rachel's bed. Reagan liked to sit on her sister's bed—it was somehow comforting for her.

Rachel made the motion of putting her arms around her sister, funny as it seemed—a ghost trying to comfort the living.

Not even death would keep Reagan and Rachel apart. Rachel would always be with her twin sister. If ever she needed her, Rachel was just a beckon away. All Reagan had to do was call out her name, and Rachel would always appear to her…always.

CHAPTER 18

Vincent Dennyson laid in the hospital bed weak and solemn. Reagan was at her father's side.

She never left him these past few days—months.

"Reagan, you should go home and get some needed rest. I'm not going anywhere," Vincent said quietly.

Vincent had no more strength. His muscles and physical strength were gone. His frail body was weak. As the Dennyson tragedy saga continued, another tragedy struck—Vincent. He, too, developed cancer, and there was just a short time left until Vincent's body would just give out. The doctors said it wouldn't be long now.

Reagan sat quietly next to her father. His face was drawn and thin. His body was just skin over bone. He was barely recognizable as the handsome, healthy man he once was. Reagan was thinking to herself how some people who are diagnosed with cancer have the luck to conquer and overcome, and yet others struggle and succumb and fail. She had so wished her parents were the ones to conquer and overcome, but as it goes, everything happens for a reason. One's life happens as it should. Plans are made...life happens. Reagan remembers so many personal philosophies that her mother would have. A special one comes to her mind now:

"Life is like a huge puzzle. There are puzzle pieces you want to fit in a particular spot, but they just won't fit in—no matter how hard you try to make it so. The puzzle piece is just not meant to be there. And then, on the other hand, there are puzzle pieces that fit just perfectly—like they were meant to be there. They slip right into the space. So no matter how much you try to make plans, a job, a person fit into your life, and whether it's the timing, etc. that doesn't make it happen—it's just not meant to be. And yet there are opportunities, etc. and people that fit into our lives perfectly. It is part of the grand design."

It was an early evening. Reagan was sitting at Vincent's bedside. She was doing a little reading. She listened at the weak, labored breaths that Vincent was taking. He was sleeping and resting most of the time now. She looked up occasionally from the book that she was reading, glancing at her father. He happened to open up his eyes. She smiled endearingly at him.

"Daddy, I love you," Reagan quietly said.

He mouthed with much effort, "I love you, too, punkin."

He would always call his girls his "little punkins." It was one of those endearing names that parents give their children.

Reagan's eyes started welling up with tears. Reagan knew it wasn't going to be much longer before

Vincent would be taken from her. First, Rachel, then Mom, and now, Dad. It was inevitable—Reagan would soon be alone.

Reagan wanted to tell her father something—something was nagging at her. This last year when Vincent was diagnosed with cancer, he wanted to have a long heart-to-heart conversation with his Reagan. He didn't want to leave anything out. He knew it would be his last chance to tell her things that maybe he, conveniently, left out of everyday conversations with her. He wanted her to know first and foremost that he loved her. He wanted her to know that her mother loved her very much, and that absolutely neither he, nor her mother, ever blamed her for her sister's death.

The years following Rachel's death were very difficult on Reagan's family. Laughter and joy weren't heard throughout the household like before when Rachel and Reagan were younger. The death of Rachel took a toll on everyone. Vincent delved right back into work. He tried to convince Carole to go back to work, even on a part-time basis. Even when Reagan got older and could easily be on her own for a while, Carole refused to go back to work. Vincent thought it would be good for Carole to get out of the house and put her mind on something else during the day. Mr. McCormick would have been happy to have Carole return. He, too, tried to convince her. "It would be good for you, honey. Penny would love the companionship. She misses you, dear. Please consider coming back—even just a couple days a week. Just think about it, okay?"

Carole was so overprotective of Reagan now—more than ever. She would still go to the therapist. She needed that continued outside support system. Carole did feel it helped her. It is never easy—of course not—when losing a child. Usually through the grieving process, guilt feelings step in and become a lasting factor. The should haves, would haves, and could haves set in and eventually tear you apart—and tear the family apart—if one lets it!

The Vincent Dennyson family, although smaller in size now, was mighty. They held together like glue. They fought hard and became stronger. They held on tight to one another. Others saw just how strong they had become. Carole and Vincent were an inspiration to all around them. People marveled at their diligent strength and the love they had for each other. Vincent and Carole tried to never place any guilt onto their daughter, Reagan. Although a hard pill to swallow, they worked through their grief and bitter feelings and dealt with their sadness each and every day. Their normal, everyday habits changed, however, since that day at Lake Bremen. Neither Vincent, nor Carole, nor Reagan ever went to that lake again. Carole and Vincent thought a fresh start would help too. They found a lovely house located near the car dealership. It was on a lovely cul-de-sac. A girl in Reagan's class actually lived on Spencer Court. She was a real nice girl named Gracie. She had a nice family, and Reagan and Gracie became very good and close friends. The move was easy. The house was cheery—three bed-rooms, two and a half baths. It was a split-level home. It had a lower-level family room and basement/rec-reation room area. It didn't have an attic, but it had plenty of storage areas. It was a fresh start for the family. But it was very confusing for Rachel.

Reagan was unpacking her boxes in her new bedroom. It had soft blue wallpaper with tiny rows of white flowers. There were white Priscilla curtains framing her windows. Reagan just loved her new bedroom. It was her own room.

She was making her bed with the new bedspread her and her mother picked out one day. Reagan had just finished folding a soft, fluffy matching comforter at the end of the bed. Reagan plopped down onto her just made bed. She rested her head on the over-sized fluffy pillows and stretched out her arms and placed them behind her head. She just lay there in peace, staring at the ceiling, daydreaming. She was beginning to feel better, which was a miracle, con-sidering how this year had been going. Reagan was just about to nod off for a nap. She was tired but felt so good. She needed some restful sleep—not a sleep filled with terrible nightmares.

Reagan woke up abruptly. Something had star-tled her. The bed shook slightly. A dent was seen next to her on the side of the bed. It was cold again in the room. The temperature had taken a drastic dive. It was Rachel.

"Reagan, wake up," Rachel said to her.

Reagan could feel the coldness now that was in the room. She smelled Rachel's scent, and she saw her form as she woke up and focused. Rachel was looking at her in a confused way. Reagan knew that look all too well.

"Reagan, why did you and Mom and Dad move?" Rachel asked.

Reagan looked up at Rachel's ghostly form. She was used to getting startled by Rachel now. At first, she would feel very uneasy. But now, it was "normal" to see Rachel popping in from time to time.

Reagan had thought, many times, why Rachel never crossed over into the light and went up to heaven. She had asked her one day, but Rachel just stared at her with that confused look on her face. At times, Rachel would just say, "I just want to stay here with you, Reagan. I don't want to leave you. I never want to leave you, Reagan...ever."

The room was dark, but there was a small glow from a lamp that Reagan brought into his room.

Vincent hated the hospital room lighting. It hurt his eyes. They were so bright.

Vincent was looking with glazed eyes at his daughter, Reagan, with so much love in his heart. He knew this was going to be so difficult for her. There was nothing he could do. Fate was going to take him away from her. She would be alone. He tried to fight the battle, but he was going to lose—very soon.

"Honey, I'm so sorry," Vincent whispered. He was getting weaker by the moment. He had no strength left. It was all he could do to mouth the words and get them out.

"Daddy, don't talk. It's all right. I know." Reagan was wiping the tears as they were rolling down her face. "Daddy, I want you to know something. You don't have to say anything. Just listen, okay?"

Vincent gave a weak smile.

"Daddy, I can see and talk to Rachel. I've been able to for a long time—actually since Rachel died. I wanted you to know that, and I wanted to apologize to you for never telling you—or Mom—ever." Reagan was crying uncontrollably now.

Vincent smiled at his beloved daughter. He wasn't surprised. He slowly lifted up his hand now to his daughter. Reagan grabbed his hand and held it like she would never let it go.

Vincent said very weakly, "I know, honey, I know."

"You know? But how?" Reagan replied in a puzzled voice.

"I would see her sometimes…out of the corner of my eye…sometimes," Vincent said.

"But, Dad," Reagan said, "I can't see Mom. It's weird. Why can't I see or talk to Mom?" Reagan was confused and still crying. "If you see one ghostly spirit, why can't you see more? Or all? Or other family members?" Reagan asked.

"Honey, Mom's here. I feel her—I see her in the distance. She's waiting for me. It's time…it's time for me to go…to join your mother…and your sister. I love you, my little punkin'…always."

And with that last thought, Vincent was gone. He took his last breath. As his spirit floated above his tired, frail body below, he watched as his daughter, Reagan, uncontrollably cry. She was hugging his fragile body.

"It'll take time, but Reagan will be all right."

Vincent extended his hand out to Carole, and they left together toward the warm, glowing, bright light.

He was finally free from pain and at peace.

"It'll be all right, honey. We will always be with you…always."

CHAPTER 19

Driving down the road, I get a
feeling that I should have been
home yesterday…yesterday.

—J. Denver

John Denver. Reagan loved John Denver too. He died so tragically, too.

Music helped to comfort Reagan so much. She always felt that music being in her and her sister's life since they were born, was a constant. Her mother, Carole, always had music playing during the day, and in their room at night. It brought a soothing feeling to their room while they were sleeping or napping. It was always a radio station that played music that had a gentle, calming effect. It was comforting.

Reagan looked at the address again—33445 Covington Lane.

When Mr. Hogan contacted her from Remington, Remington, and Holden and told her about her inheritance, she remembered how she hung up the phone and flopped down into a side chair next to her desk in the living room of her apartment. She spoke out loud, "Oh my god!"

Reagan tried to remember her uncle Arthur. They really didn't see or visit Uncle Arthur and Aunt Anne very often. Reagan and Rachel were pretty small.

As Reagan grew, she would sometimes ask her dad about his brother and her uncle. She would ask her dad why they didn't see or visit him very often. The replies were always the same—Uncle Arthur and Aunt Anne were very busy people. Vincent would continue explaining that being very successful had its drawbacks—not much time to fit in for family visits or get-togethers. On holidays, Reagan and Rachel would always get these lavish, beautiful gifts from Uncle Arthur and Aunt Anne. That would be the only time the girls would hear from them. Even that last year before Rachel died, they received these beautiful Kelli Dolls with all sorts of accessories, clothes, dollhouses. The girls would remember their Christmas mornings when her and Rachel would sneak down to take a peek at their presents under the beautiful Christmas tree their mother would always decorate and create. It was such a magical time—their favorite holiday! Carole was so particular on how important decorating the Christmas tree was. It was an art, as Carole would always say. Her Christmas tree was always breathtakingly beautiful—every year! Every ornament, every colored ornament, every personal ornament from her two girls, every white dove and red cardinal was perfectly spaced and placed on the tree. The beautiful angel tree topper was magnificently placed on the top of the perfectly shaped blue spruce Christmas tree. The angel looked like she was the protector of the Christmas tree and a guardian over the home. Both girls would squeal with delight as they would come downstairs on Christmas morning (the second time) and attack their presents with delight! Carole and Vincent would sit back with their cups of coffee and smile as their girls opened each and every gift. Warm hugs and kisses were given out, and "thank you, Mommy and Daddy" was heard all through the morning. The special gifts from Santa were also wonderfully displayed on the couch—never wrapped, of course. Santa didn't have time to wrap all his gifts to the children, but they were always beautifully displayed every Christmas morning with notes back to each girl. The delicious homemade cookies were placed just so, and chilled milk was left in a thermos for Santa. Of course, food for the reindeer—whole carrots—was a must too!

Reagan smiled. It was a good memory to have. She thanked God each and every day for her wonderful childhood memories.

Reagan was jolted back to reality as she finally saw the address at the end of the long—very long white pebbled driveway. It led to a beautiful two-toned stone mansion. There were chimneys jutting out of the tops of the dark gray roof. Black shutters framed each and every paned window. Reagan thought the home to be of Georgian architecture. The estate, the mansion—Dennyson Mansion—sat far back. It was overwhelmingly beautiful. There was a circular driveway in front of the stately manor. The home was surrounded by low manicured shrubbery—no flowers, just greenery. There was a huge tree in the foreground, located at the beginning of the driveway, welcoming everyone to its home. The setting was stunning and elegant. Reagan couldn't believe just how grand Dennyson Mansion was. She had occasionally overheard her parents talk about Uncle Arthur and Aunt Anne's beautiful home. But seeing it now, this breathtaking estate would easily take anyone's breath away.

And so the story goes. It was an elegant, stately mansion that claimed to be haunted. Unfortunately, because of the media, everyone heard of the two brutal murders. Melanie Dennyson and her fiancé, David Williams, were murdered on the eve of their wedding, and the murderer—or murderers—were never found. After the murders, Arthur Dennyson fell apart. He eventually passed away as well and joined his wife, Anne, his stillborn son, Daniel, and his daughter, Melanie, her fiancé, David, in the afterlife. Vincent passed away and joined his wife, Carole, and daughter, Rachel. Reagan was the only living relative of the Dennyson clan left alive. Reagan will share ownership of the mansion with Irene. And even if Reagan could convince Irene to sell this beautiful grand estate, no one would buy it.

Reagan, of course, was no stranger to spirits. She was very curious and somewhat skeptical as to the mansion being haunted. She knows just how the media blew everything out of proportion, thus distorting the truth. But Reagan always had an open mind on the subject matter and was ready to embrace anything ahead of her. It would definitely be an adventure.

Reagan took vacation time from Lincoln Memorial Hospital. And she tacked on extra time so she could sort all this out. Someone named Irene was going to meet her at Dennyson Mansion. She wasn't exactly clear who this Irene was. She thought Mr. Hogan said Irene was living at the mansion—maybe a very close friend of her aunt's or friend of the family? Reagan wasn't exactly sure.

Reagan pulled her car up and around the circular driveway. She pulled up to the grand entrance. The entranceway was white, which offset the rest of the tanned stone structure. It had four large pillars in front. She wasn't quite sure if she should have parked right in front, but of course, cars and parking and traffic wouldn't be an issue.

The home was stately and beautiful up close and personal—not like anything Reagan has seen. She left her suitcases in the car. She got out, stretched, smoothed out her outfit. She wanted to make sure everything was in place and that she looked presentable for the introduction to Irene. She slowly walked up to the front door and rang the doorbell. It had a bellowing, grand sound—very stately.

"Of course," Reagan smiled and said to herself.

As Reagan looked up to the incredible "tallness" of the manor, she thought to herself, *Funny, it doesn't look haunted, but then what is a haunted home supposed to look like?*

She heard a voice inside, "I'll get it, James."

One of the huge wooden double doors slowly opened, and a short very pleasant-looking older woman stood before her.

"Hello, Reagan?" Irene asked with a smile.

"Yes, ma'am, I'm Reagan Dennyson." Reagan extended her hand out to shake the sweet woman's hand.

"I'm Irene, dear. Please, won't you come in? Welcome to Dennyson Mansion," Irene said pleasantly and effortlessly.

Irene motioned Reagan into a sitting room and library located on the side to the grand hallway.

"This is a very beautiful estate, Mrs....," Reagan stumbled, thinking she had maybe forgotten Irene's last name.

"Irene, dear. Please just call me Irene."

"Irene," Reagan said, smiling.

The entrance hallway was large and beautifully decorated with very pricey artwork and period furniture. Everything was painted in beige soft tones, but accent colors of gold and mossy green were throughout. The large archways were outlined in wooded overlays. The woodworking was exquisite. Reagan just looked around in awe.

Irene asked, "Do you have any luggage, dear? Should I assume that you're staying, yes? Or...maybe knowing the details about the mansion, you're staying at a hotel in town or nearby?" Irene was hoping that Reagan would stay here with her. Irene was eager to get to know Arthur's niece. She seemed very nice.

"No, not a hotel, Irene. I would love to stay here—if that's all right with you? My luggage is still in my trunk of the car," Reagan replied.

It was overwhelming for Reagan, listening, as Irene did most of the talking. Irene explained the history of the stories of the mansion. Reagan just sat wide-eyed, soaking up all the details of everything that had happened.

"Wow, Irene, I am so very sorry. I really don't know quite what to say. I never knew everything that had happened. Of course, I was very young," Reagan said apologetically.

"It's okay, dear. Frankly, I went over and over in my mind—so many times—exactly how to approach and to explain everything to you. All the history and the stories I needed to tell you about—there's so much to grasp and take in and digest. It was hard to know where to begin," Irene explained.

"And they never solved the two murders, Irene?" Reagan asked.

"No...no they didn't." Irene, frowned and shook her head. "Don't get me wrong...they tried. There were maybe a couple of leads, but neither led to any arrests. The brutal crimes of our Melanie and her fiancé, David, were left unsolved. Tears were coming as Irene wiped them away. Every anniversary of their deaths, the media comes out in full force. For about a week, you can see it on TV or hear it on the radio or on the Internet. The cases are still left open until they're solved. Every anniversary, messages are conveyed to anyone that may have any information—leads to contact our local police force here in town. The police department and detectives have been beating themselves up over these two deaths. They so want to solve them. A new detective on the force, I think, has reopened it back up hoping to crack the case and solve it."

Reagan sat for a moment taking in all the information. Reagan could tell that Irene was obviously very close to this story—this family, to Melanie Dennyson and to her uncle and aunt. It was also obvious to Reagan to see that reliving this horror story was extremely difficult and may be upsetting her. Reagan wanted to change the subject quickly.

"Irene, I'm a little confused," Reagan spoke up. "Isn't the mansion now yours? You said that Uncle Arthur willed it to you—and, of course, my father. And with my father passing, it would go solely to you. Isn't that right?"

"Well, yes, dear, that is true," Irene continued to explain. "I'm old, dear. There is no way I can take care of this huge place. Your uncle left me in good financial hands—so to speak. There was an addendum in the will where I could leave this mansion to whomever I thought fit. And when I called and spoke to Mr. Hogan, he said there was one living relative left in the Dennyson family—and that would be you dear, Reagan," Irene replied so matter-of-factly.

"I just don't know what to say, Irene. What am I going to do with a mansion? I'm single and have a job as a pediatric nurse. I just don't know. And selling it, although would be a logical option, doesn't seem to be an option right now, because of its horrendous past history. Who would want it?" Reagan exclaimed.

"Well, dear, I do have some thoughts. Maybe we could work something out together. Are you willing?" Irene asked, hoping.

"Okay...I guess," Reagan replied. "What did you have in mind?"

After a bite of lunch and some hot tea, Irene proceeded to take Reagan on a tour of the mansion. Irene had a cleaning company come in to keep up with monthly cleaning, and she had a landscape company come to maintain the grounds and gardens. Richard had since left to join his family down south. There was so much to maintain—a landscaping company was the only way to keep the grounds and gardens looking beautiful. Irene knew it was a sound, logical decision to bring Reagan into the picture. Irene just couldn't do it—even with the small staff of James and a few others. She was getting older and in her twilight years. Although Irene was feeling pretty good and healthy, it was a time for her to slow up and take it easy and relax—maybe travel a little. The staff, inevitably, was getting older as well. Some of the staff had retired and moved down South to a warmer climate and peaceful living. Irene kept a small staff on, but just enough to keep the mansion in good shape.

Reagan and Irene went outside to the rear of the mansion. They were looking over the gardens and beautiful landscape of the woods in the back. Reagan pointed over to where Melanie's cottage once stood.

"Is that where Melanie's cottage was, Irene?" Reagan asked reluctantly.

"Yes," Irene responded solemnly and sadly.

"I'm sorry, Irene. I don't mean to remind you of that terrible night. I can't imagine how terrified you must have felt," Reagan said apologetically.

"It was an absolutely awful night. I never want to go through anything like that ever again. Melanie was such a beautiful young lady. She had such a promising life ahead of her, and David, what a wonderful, handsome young man. He, too, had a wonderful future ahead of him. It was so tragic and senseless. Who would ever want to harm those two?" Irene was talking and reminiscing about that horrible, horrible night. "Anyway," Irene continued, "yes, that is where Melanie's cottage once was. Soon after the police and detectives finished with investigating the cottage and the surrounding area, your uncle Arthur insisted the cottage be torn down. He couldn't look at the cottage another minute. The sight of that cottage—Melanie's cottage—tore your uncle's heart right out. It made him sick when he would see that cottage and relive that horror of a night. He wanted it gone forever!" Irene explained.

It was hard to believe that one whole month had passed since the day of the murders of Melanie and David. Arthur was so insistent with the police department and the detectives assigned to the case to hurry up with investigating the cottage and area around it. They did feel hurried at the time.

"Mr. Dennyson, we certainly sympathize and understand your feelings, but we want to do a thorough investigation of the cottage and this area. This is where your daughter and soon to be son-in-law had their lives taken. We want to make a thorough investigation, and we certainly don't want to overlook any possible clues that could lead us to the murderer or murderers. Please just be patient. Just a little longer, please," Detective Armbruster pleaded.

"But you went over everything, you said," Arthur Dennyson replied in a frustrated tone. "I want this cottage down!" Arthur exclaimed in a very demanding way.

"I know, sir, I know. Please, not much longer. You do want us to find who killed your daughter and fiancé, right?" The detective was working on much lack of sleep. He knew as soon as he said that, he was going to get flack. He was tired too.

The police department brought in the FBI as well. They did a thorough search of Melanie's cottage. They took blood samples from the floor, dusted everywhere for fingerprints. They found a kitchen knife on the floor of the living room. The knife came from the kitchen. There was an empty slot visible in the wooden block where Melanie would keep her kitchen carving knives. They turned up nothing. The blood samples were Melanie's and David's. There were fingerprints on the knife—David's—but it was deduced that David was probably struggling with the murderer. They could tell by the direction of the stab wounds in David. They were even throwing the idea around that maybe David had an argument with his fiancée, Melanie, and then stabbed her—and then had remorse and killed himself. But that notion was soon thrown out. The way the stab wounds entered his body couldn't possibly have been made by him. Then a thought of an argument still being a possibility and maybe Melanie stabbing her betrothed. But the coroner's office said Melanie died before David. That couldn't have taken place either. Another strong factor was that there was another set of muddied footprints that came and led back to the back entranceway to the cottage. They weren't David's nor Melanie's. These footprints were made from boots—hiking boots, work boots. The FBI searched outside the back entranceway. They followed to where they led to a work shed located on the property. The footprints stopped near one of the entrance areas to the woods. And then…nothing. Leads that went nowhere. They found a stab wound located on Melanie's stomach area. The wound was in a line—most likely made by a pitchfork. It was assumed that it would have been a tool kept in the shed on the property, but they never found it. Dead ends everywhere…

The FBI questioned everyone at the party that night and, of course, the staff—at the estate and at Dennyson Toys. Arthur's business associates and anyone else that even remotely had any connections with the Dennyson family was interrogated. They searched for anyone who might have it in for either Arthur or his daughter, Melanie, or even someone who might be after David. But nothing turned up—no leads. However, one curious thing, two of Arthur's employees who had worked closely with Melanie turned up missing also that night of the murders. They vanished with no trace. They were never found either—Nancy Smith and Gina Brown. It was as if they never existed. No one saw them leave; no one heard from them. They had no friends—probably just each other. The college they both attended together and with Melanie was contacted. Hometowns and any possible relatives were contacted—nothing. Of course, speculations were made, employees were questioned again. The same conclusions and questions were being brought up: "Where did they go? Why did they leave? Is it possible that either, or both, had something to do with the murders of Melanie Dennyson and David Williams?"

CHAPTER 20

Irene and Reagan were standing in the center of the ballroom. A chill suddenly filled the air.

"Irene?" Reagan spoke up.

"Yes," Irene responded.

"Do you feel a draft in here? There's a chill all of a sudden." Reagan was rubbing her arms.

Irene chuckled. "No, dear, that's probably your uncle…and maybe your aunt just letting us know that he is here with us," Irene answered.

Irene was quite used to Arthur and Anne popping in from time to time to check up on things—and her. They were still very protective of their Irene.

Reagan looked around the huge open ballroom. It was beautiful with all the magnificent, massive crystal chandeliers hanging from the tall ceiling. Ornate crystal-draped sconces were adorning three of the long walls. Reagan could smell something—a particular aroma, maybe cherry pipe tobacco. She couldn't see any spirits, but she felt something.

After Anne had passed, Arthur would sometimes say to Irene that he would occasionally see his Anne—usually early in the morning, just before daybreak, and sometimes late at night while he was reading by the fireplace in the master bedroom. He would feel the damp and coolness of the air. A mist would begin to form and then Anne's most familiar fragrance—her favorite scent. She didn't speak, but she would be there watching her Arthur. It was comforting for Arthur just knowing that his Anne was always around him. And when he got a whiff of her fragrance, he knew she was nearby.

There were other spirits in the mansion. Unlike Anne, these other spirits weren't so welcoming and comforting. Irene would be very afraid of them. There were rooms in the east wing that she would never go to—including the attic and the basement and wine cellars and storage rooms. There was a room in particular on the second floor corridor—in the east wing. Irene kept the door closed—always. It was a room kind of tucked away in a corner. It was an eerie, forbidding feeling inside that room.

The cleaning crew that came in once a month were always very anxious and nervous to go to the Dennyson Mansion. The Madison Cleaning Group was very reputable, reliable, and thorough. Their customer satisfaction was always good, and Louise always took great pride in her staff and their work ethic.

One day, Louise received a phone call from an Irene Boxler. Irene requested a meeting with Louise in regard to a cleaning job at Dennyson Mansion.

Louise thought to herself, *Oh boy, this is going to be a big job.*

Louise had plenty of crew. Her business was established, and there usually wasn't a job her crew couldn't tackle and complete. But this one, this one was going to be different.

"I'll need a large cleaning crew, but only once a month, I think," Irene explained to Louise. "The estate really doesn't get dirty too much. I have myself and a very small staff nowadays. And I certainly want to keep up with taking care that every room and space is dusted and vacuumed where needed."

"Of course, Mrs. Boxler, we understand," Louise replied assuredly.

"Irene, please. Just Irene." Irene laughed a little. "Also, there are a few other things I feel I need to mention about Dennyson Mansion, Louise."

Louise put her pen down as she was taking notes. She usually took notes with the first visits with clients. The notes would go into a folder to keep and file away. There was no room for error. That way, if there was any additional information or details to add, additional time spent at the business or home, etc., it could be added to the file. The initial file also acted as a reference guide—very necessary.

"Well, Irene, you certainly have my undivided attention." Louise smiled.

"I need to tell you that Dennyson Mansion is haunted, Louise."

"Ummm, okay," Louise remarked with surprise and smirking just a little. "We can work through that! So they're true? I have, of course, heard stories." Louise was thinking again. *Maybe the smirk was inappropriate.*

"Yes, they are true." Irene nodded her head. "They are true. I'm hoping your crew—or the ones you select—will not be skittish and afraid. There have been moments where I and the staff have felt chills, seen things. Shadows, mists, odors are smelled. Maybe we should just leave that section of the mansion alone. It is not an area that is to be gone down."

"It is none of my business, Irene, but have you ever had that section investigated? Where are the blueprints of the mansion?" Louise asked.

"Well, funny you should ask about the blueprints, Louise. Mr. Dennyson had gone to city hall and talked with someone who had found the blueprints. The staff member put the blueprints on his desk while he and Mr. Dennyson had stepped for a moment. When they returned, the blueprints were gone. They never found them again," Irene answered.

"Well, don't worry, Irene, we'll take care of everything. The mansion will be sparkling—from head to toe! Well…almost!" Louise laughed.

CHAPTER 21

Irene led Reagan up the grand staircase. At the top of the stairs, one could go either right or left. The estate was built in the early 1900s, Irene told Reagan. When Arthur Dennyson bought the mansion, he changed the name. Arthur felt that since he spent so much money for it, he could name the estate whatever he wished, so Covington Manor became Dennyson Mansion.

There were bedrooms, sitting rooms, and bathrooms. Irene kept doors closed to each bedroom. The details in the crown moldings, the green velvet period furniture, the heavy jacquard draperies, and the landscape paintings were exquisite and tastefully displayed. It was so quiet on the second floor. The color scheme continued throughout the mansion. The richness and warmth of the gold hues and the accents of the rich forest greens complemented the warmth of the dark brown mahogany furniture pieces. The side tables, accent chairs, lamps adorning and lining the long hallways added to the beauty and stately demeanor of the estate.

Walking down the west corridor, Irene opened each bedroom door to show Reagan each room. Each bedroom had a different pastel color scheme, with the exception of the master bedroom—Arthur's and Anne's bedroom. That bedroom was mostly a beautiful light, creamy ivory beige. As Irene opened up the double doors to the master bedroom, they both stepped inside. The master bedroom had a beautiful mahogany fireplace. It was the only bedroom that had a fireplace. It had an exquisite private master bathroom and large, roomy dressing room—for Anne. There was a huge walk-in closet for Arthur equipped with shelves and hanging rods throughout. In the very back of Arthur's walk-in closet, there was a hidden safe. That was where Arthur kept all his important and valuable documents, paperwork, and jewelry.

Reagan couldn't get over how anyone could live in such lavishness. Oh, of course, Reagan knew of people, millionaires and successful tycoons and entrepreneurs, who lived like that, but she never knew anyone personally—except her Uncle Arthur and Aunt Anne—that lived like that. And she never would have predicted that she could—or ever would—be a part of that world someday. It was all so surreal.

As they walked down the other end of the hallway, the east corridor, the mood quickly changed. Irene seemed very nervous and anxious. There was a sense of reluctance Reagan felt.

"Irene, is something wrong? You okay?" Reagan asked. She was concerned. "We can stop the tour. I'm okay with that." Reagan patted Irene on the shoulder as Irene looked at her.

Irene really hesitated going down that hallway, but why, Reagan wondered. *I wonder what's down there?* Reagan thought. They turned to go back to the center of the second floor and staircase.

"I have an idea," Reagan said excitedly. "Let me treat you to an early dinner. How about it, Irene? Let's get a change of scenery. We'll freshen up, and I'll take us into town. I bet there's a wonderful, little restaurant we can find for dinner!" Reagan said enthusiastically. "We both need to get out of here for a while."

She felt the tension and how tired Irene might be feeling. It could be time for some fun—time to be away from the mansion. A change of scenery was definitely in order.

Irene laughed and replied, "Actually, that sounds like a splendid idea, dear!"

Irene gave Reagan a warm and unexpected embrace. "Thanks, honey. I think I will really love having you around. I think you are just what I need!" Irene said gratefully. "You are a breath of fresh air!"

"Aw, Irene, I'm glad to be here, and I'm glad we're going to be in each other's lives now," Reagan replied warmly. She gave Irene another warm hug.

"You're a good hugger, Reagan! You remind me of my Melanie a little. She was a good hugger too. I guess it runs in the family!" Irene smiled.

Reagan chose the room with the soft peach color scheme. She was never quite the pink, mauvy type. This room seemed to suit her well—very comforting. She got a warm feeling in this room—no negative vibrations were felt. That was good. Reagan was relieved.

Reagan freshened up in her own bathroom—each room had their own individual bathroom, of course! She splashed some cool water on her face. Reagan was never much into the whole makeup thing—just some mascara and a little blush and lipstick suited her just fine. Reagan was a natural beauty. She liked and kept her auburn brown hair long with a simple straight style. Reagan hated to fuss. Her fine features, blue eyes, and naturally shaped brows accented her beautiful curves of her face. Reagan, as well as Rachel, were the spitting image of their mother, Carole, people would often say. Reagan was healthy and looked it. She ate sensibly and wasn't a real drinker. An occasional glass of wine or ice cold beer/ale on a hot day was good enough for Reagan. She was shapely, without looking too athletic.

Reagan freshened up with a new pair of casual slacks, a sweater set, and comfortable flats. She went down the hall to Irene's bedroom and knocked.

"Irene, ready?" Reagan called out.

Reagan thought she heard Irene talking to someone right before she knocked. It was muffled—through the door—of course. Reagan laughed it off, quickly dismissing it. Reflecting back on her conversations with Irene previously, Reagan remembered Irene telling her of seeing her Uncle Arthur and Aunt Anne. Maybe Irene was having a conversation with either—or both—of them. Reagan smiled and totally understood that! Reagan wondered if there was more than Irene was telling her about this mansion. Maybe there were more stories to tell. They had plenty of time to discuss them. There were certain areas in the mansion that Reagan didn't always feel quite right—a little uneasy, kind of "looking over the shoulder" uneasy perhaps. She took another mental note about taking a trip into town one morning and doing some research at the local library about the Dennyson Mansion. She thought the library or city hall would have history of the estate there. And Reagan faintly remembered that the mansion was called something else, another name. She remembered Irene mentioning that the mansion was called Covington Manor. *Hmm...more history maybe.*

"Coming, dear," Irene responded. "I'm just putting on a spot of lipstick. I'll be right down," Irene said through the door.

"Okay, I'll meet you downstairs, Irene," Reagan politely responded.

Out in the hallway, Reagan stood at the top of the staircase. Out of the corner of her eye, she thought she saw a shadow or something at the end of that hallway—the hallway Irene seemed to feel uneasy about. Reagan wanted desperately to go down that hallway to investigate. Reagan wasn't really frightened very easily. Of course, she was introduced and felt comfortable with Rachel's spirit. Sometimes, Reagan would see things—spirits. She wasn't quite sure why. Was she supposed to help them in some way? Why did she have this gift? Was there a purpose? She shrugged it off and felt that the reasoning would somehow show itself one day. The answer will come when it's supposed to. There were so many unanswered questions. She did she a shadow down that hallway. Later, maybe she would go down and look. She felt she had to. It was like beckoning her to come. There were, Reagan was sure, many other parts of the mansion she hadn't seen yet. She was sure Irene would continue their tour—maybe tomorrow. There had to be much more history in this estate— between these walls. There was much more than just the Dennyson family. Reagan was curious to find answers. She was sure there were more stories to tell, mysteries to unfold.

CHAPTER 22

Reagan drove, and she and Irene found a delightful restaurant in town near Covington Square.

"Ooohh, look Irene, let's go there," Reagan exclaimed. "It looks like a wonderful, quaint restaurant!"

Reagan wanted to be enthusiastic and excited. She felt Irene hadn't had much of that for a while. Irene looked tired and a bit on edge. Reagan understood how Dennyson Mansion must have become such a burden to her. For someone living in a place like that, it had to have an effect on them. Irene has been through so much over the years living at Dennyson Mansion. There was so much drama— deadly drama. There was so much tragedy. It had to have an incredible draining, negative effect on Irene. Reagan was amazed that Irene hadn't gone insane and lost her mind! Irene was mostly alone now—aside from James and a few of the staff that was left to take care of her and the mansion and grounds.

Reagan opened the door, and she and Irene stepped inside to the Rosewood Grille and Cafe. Irene said she had heard about a restaurant opening up around here, but she never seemed to have the time to go and visit. It was charming.

"Well, hello there, welcome to the Rosewood! I'm Jayne. Just the two of you today?" Jayne asked.

"Yep," Reagan replied. "Just the two of us!"

"Right this way." Jayne motioned Reagan and Irene to follow her.

The restaurant had a few customers. It was early for a dinner crowd, and maybe a little later for a lunch crowd. It was a cozy, charming little restaurant. It wasn't a stuffy, white-linen-tablecloths type of restaurant—Reagan hated that! Little lamps were on each table, and small woven red checkered tablecloths were on each table—very cozy and inviting. Fresh red rosebuds, with a little baby's breath, in small vases, adorned each table as well. It was a very nice touch.

"Mmmm…something smells delicious!" Reagan smiled and said with excitement.

"Well, that's a good sign!" Jayne laughed. "You must be hungry! Here are your menus, and I'll be right back with your waters."

Irene and Reagan sat at a nice table right by a window.

Looking at the menus, Irene said, "Boy, I'm hungry! This was a great idea, Reagan, Thank you!" Irene was already so grateful to have Reagan in her life. It was just what she needed.

"It was a great idea, wasn't it!" Reagan agreed.

Reagan and Irene got the same selection for their meal—the special of the day: meatloaf, whipped potatoes, fresh asparagus, a tossed salad, and fresh homemade rolls with butter.

They each had water and coffee. They both polished their plates clean. They looked at each other as they finished their last bites, and they laughed at each other.

"We were *very* hungry!" Reagan said.

Irene said to Jayne. "This was delicious! We'll have to come in more often. Thank you!" Irene said complimenting Jayne. Reagan nodded in agreement.

"Well, you're both welcome! Please come back soon—and often! You both from around here? Jayne asked.

Reagan answered first. "Yes, Irene lives at Dennyson Mansion, and I'm the new tenant!" Reagan said laughing out loud.

"Dennyson Mansion…*the* Dennyson Mansion?" Jayne replied, startled at their response. She wasn't expecting that answer—at all!

"Umm…yes," Reagan replied, and Irene nodded. "I didn't know that it was *the* Dennyson Mansion. Irene, when did that change?" Reagan smiled and asked sarcastically.

Jayne immediately responded, "I'm sorry, I didn't mean to infer anything, but it is very historic you both know."

Irene chided, "Yes, it certainly has history—and plenty of it, but I, and possibly Reagan too, call it home."

"It is a beautiful estate, and I apologize, really, for inferring any…" Jayne tried to find the right words to convey her apology.

Irene patted Jayne's arm. "It's okay, dear. I'm sure you weren't expecting that answer, were you?" Irene laughed.

"No, no, I wasn't," Jayne replied, laughing too. It made the moment a little less awkward.

Reagan asked Jayne, "I know you recently opened the Rosewood. Have you lived in Covington long?"

"Actually, yes," Jayne replied. "I've lived here all my life."

Reagan nodded. *Good to know*, she thought to herself.

Well, as it happened, Reagan and Irene frequented the Rosewood Grille and Cafe quite often after that day. Jayne had a daughter, Chelsea, who helped out at the restaurant quite often, along with several other waiters and waitresses. She and Reagan became fast, and soon after, close friends. The food was always good. It was opened at lunch and dinner. Jayne had thought about maybe opening up the cafe part of Rosewood Grille for a light breakfast fare also. It would be good for business. Everyone always looked for a cozy place for coffee, tea, and pastry, etc.

Irene was sitting with Jayne one morning at the cafe. Reagan was off running errands. She dropped Irene off at the restaurant. Jayne was often there and always welcomed the company of Irene.

One morning, during one of Irene and Jayne's visits, Jayne asked Irene a question.

"When are you going to tell Reagan about that one room down in the east corridor, Irene?" Jayne asked.

"I know," Irene replied as she looked off into the distance. "There's so much more history, dark history in that mansion. I'm sure more than I will ever come across."

Irene closed her eyes for a moment and thought back to a particular late afternoon she spent with Anne.

Anne and Irene had been going through some books in the library one day. They were gathering books that would be donated to a local charity event that was being held soon in town. Anne was always very charitable, and she volunteered wherever she could. Her and Arthur were very philanthropic and never ever turned down a charity event where they could be present for and/or donate. Arthur and Anne were well loved and very well respected. Everyone knew that Arthur Dennyson was very rich. Every day, he had many letters coming across his desk. There were many nonprofit organizations, etc. that requested donations. Arthur created the Dennyson Foundation. It was an organization that he founded just for that reason. His secretary, Teri, used to get a little overwhelmed with all the literature that came into the office requesting donations. Upon a meeting one morning with his accountant and financial advisors, Arthur created the Dennyson Foundation.

That way, everything was kept in one account just for that purpose. Of course, Arthur could write off his donations as tax deductions. But it was organized and all in one location. Arthur liked to keep everything organized!

Anne thought she and Irene needed a little break from boxing up some of the books that were to be donated. She was glancing over some of the books she was donating. Erma Bombeck had been a favorite author of Anne's, as well as Agatha Christie. She had some duplicates that were given to her as gifts, and she thought they would be a nice addition to the charity sale. She kept the ones that were gifted to her and donated the ones she had purchased. She was kind of funny that way. She never would give away any of her gifts. She thought gifts were always such thoughtful gestures, and it would be very wrong to give away something that someone gave you. Obviously, someone put time and thought into the gift, so it would be very wrong and inconsiderate to give that gift away.

Iren was over near one of the many bookshelves. She saw a book and tried to pull it down, but it was somehow stuck and wedged in a corner of the bookshelf. She gave it a yank and heard a faint click. The whole bookshelf started to move. It was an eerie, squeaky, cracking sound. It sounded like it had never been opened before. A very musty smell protruded from the dark space. It was dusty—old dust.

"Ummm…Anne…could you come here?" Irene said in an uneasy voice.

Anne was on the other side of the room looking over some other novels and reference books deciding on which to donate and which to hold on to. There were so many books and so many bookshelves in that library. Arthur had his section of the many books that he enjoyed reading. He also had many books dealing with the business, accounting, finance, management, marketing, and research reference books. Arthur had quite an extensive library. He always enjoyed reading in his spare time—when he wasn't out on the golf course or playing tennis.

Anne looked up from one of the books that she was glancing at. She noticed Irene was staring straight at the cracked-open bookshelf—the one that just opened up to display a crack and a wedge of darkness. A putrid, stale odor emerged from that dark crack, and a powder of dust came through as well. Obviously, it was a secret passage to somewhere, and it was also obvious that it hadn't been opened for a very, very long time…or maybe never.

Anne dropped the book. It landed with a loud thump onto the floor. She just stared at Irene and her new discovery.

"What the…Irene, what did you do?" Anne exclaimed.

"Nothing, really. I was just trying to pull down this book, and it must have been caught on this tiny lever of some sort, then this happened." Irene explained, throwing up her hands.

"Should I try to open it further or just close it back up, Anne?" Irene asked, hoping for the latter answer from Anne.

Anne walked over to Irene. "No, Irene, let's see where this leads to."

Irene was wishing that Anne would have just told her to close it back up shut. But it was stupid to think Anne—or maybe anyone else—would do that. The curiosity was at a high right now.

"On second thought," Anne continued, "let's just see if we can close it back up. I'll talk to Arthur later and tell him what we've—or rather, you've—found. I know he'll want to be a part of this investigation—with help, of course!"

As time went on, the secret passageway in the library was never opened again. Soon after that day, Anne was in that fatal car accident that took her life, and Irene never mentioned the secret passageway to Arthur.

For years, Arthur had tried to locate the blueprints for the mansion. He had checked with city hall, and for some reason, the clerk couldn't find them. They had somehow been lost. They disappeared.

"It's the strangest thing, Mr. Dennyson." Jacob scratched his head. "We keep all of our information, documents, etc. archived it one location. We take a lot of pride, and we boast that we have the most organized department. But I'll tell you, sir, this is baffling me today!"

Poor Jacob, Arthur had thought to himself. *This is going to prey on his mind all week!*

"That's okay, Jacob," Arthur replied. "It'll turn up. Maybe the original owner kept the blueprints at the mansion—or, er…what was Dennyson Mansion called before I changed the name?" Arthur tried to remember.

Jacob replied, "Covington Manor, sir. It was called Covington Manor."

"Oh, yes, that's it!" Arthur chuckled. "Well, Jacob, maybe I'll find them tucked away in some secret cubbyhole or compartment somewhere in the mansion. You never know…you just never know."

Arthur never gave it a second thought. He knew Jacob had turned the area upside down looking for those blueprints. And Arthur felt Jacob would continue to look for them thinking they were misplaced somewhere in the archives.

As Arthur turned to leave Jacob's office, he said, "If you happen to come across them, Jacob, please just let me know."

"Will do, sir, I promise," Jacob replied. "Will do."

As Arthur Dennyson left Jacob's office, Jacob thought to himself and said out loud, "I know I put those blueprints on the corner of my desk earlier when I got that phone call from Mr. Dennyson. Where did those blueprints go?"

CHAPTER 23

Reagan was sitting comfortably in the library sipping her first cup of coffee. She was an early riser—usually. The sun shone in on the beautiful stained glass windows which faced the front of the mansion. As beautiful a backdrop the back of the mansion had, the front still had its stately, pleasing view as well.

Reagan was sitting in a comfortable overstuffed dark brown leather Queen Anne style chair. She was enjoying the quiet of the morning hour. Irene didn't wake up and rise quite as early as Reagan. And since the mansion was so large, she probably wouldn't have heard her anyway. Reagan glanced around the library, taking in all the details. It truly was her very favorite room. She felt at home in this room. It had a welcoming feeling—unlike other parts of the mansion that sometimes had a foreboding, uneasy feeling to them.

The quiet stillness of the morning was soon interrupted by James, one of the few staff members left. James chose to stay on with Irene—to finish out his years of service.

Reagan looked up from a book she was reading. "Morning, James," Reagan said cheerily as James came into the library.

"Morning, Ms. Reagan," James replied. "May I warm you up with another spot of coffee? When Ms. Irene awakens and comes down, I'll serve breakfast. I know you rise early, Ms. Reagan. Can I bring you some toast or some fresh baked scones that Cook just pulled out of the oven this morning? It would hold you over until I serve breakfast."

Oh no, that's quite all right, James," Reagan replied. "Although a warm-up on my coffee would be great. Thank you!"

Reagan really liked James. He was quiet and very somber. There were a few times that Reagan caught James off guard. He would be conversing and joking with Irene at times. James has been with the Dennyson family for many, many years—since they arrived here at the mansion. He has been a very loyal and trusting servant to Arthur. He was devastated when Arthur passed away. In conversation one day, Irene mentioned to Reagan how surprised she was that James didn't choose to move on after Arthur passed away. As Reagan was listening to Irene, she thought if Irene even had a clue that James may have stayed on because of her. Reagan felt that there may have been something there between them—a certain fondness that may have developed over the years. Obviously, the loyalty and devotion that each had for Arthur was very apparent. And the last year that Arthur was more bedridden, both were, more than likely, at his side—days and evenings. Some nights, Irene would peek in and see James sitting at Arthur's side, propped in a chair, not looking too comfortable. She would quietly step into the master bedroom and place a light blanket over James. She carefully placed the blanket onto his lap and hoped she wouldn't startle and wake him. Although his eyes didn't open, Irene felt that he knew she had been there to aid in his comfort. Several times, Irene could have sworn she saw a slight smile on James face as she placed the blanket ever so gently on his lap—a smile that said "Thank you for thinking of me." Reagan was sure that a bond, an admiration may have developed between the two of them over the years. She felt that it happened without Irene ever realizing it.

James came back into the library bringing this beautiful silver coffee carafe—a carafe that looked like it had been a family heirloom and in the Dennyson family for years.

"Thank you, James," Reagan said. "That is a beautiful coffee carafe, James. Does it—or did it—belong to my uncle and aunt?"

"Oh no, Ms. Reagan," James replied. "I guess one would say that it came with the home." When Mr. and Mrs. Dennyson moved to Covington Manor, there were many heirlooms left here."

"Oh, really?" Reagan said in a very surprised fashion. "So you are familiar with the mansion when it was Covington Manor, James."

"Yes, miss," James replied very matter-of-factly. "Why, I grew up here. I've been here since I was a small lad."

"Really, James. Wow, I never knew," Regan replied.

"Most people don't know that, miss. Let's say, I'm not usually one who tells people of my life—my history. You might say that I'm sort of a private person, miss," James solemnly replied.

"I'm sorry, James. I didn't mean to pry—really. I'm sorry," Reagan apologized.

"No worries, miss. It's not that I intend to hide anything. I just feel that my life here at Covington Manor—or rather, Dennyson Mansion—is not that fascinating a topic for everyday discussion."

"I understand, James. And thank you for the warm-up!" Reagan said.

"You're welcome, Ms. Reagan."

"James," Reagan spoke up as James turned to leave the room.

"Yes, miss?" James replied.

"Would you mind if sometime in the future, we could sit down together and chat about you growing up here when it was Covington Manor?" Reagan asked with hope.

"I suppose, miss—if you'd be interested in knowing," James responded back.

"I would be interested, James. I really would," Reagan said with a smile.

Just then, Irene came into the library. "Good morning, you two!" Irene looked rested.

"Good morning, Ms. Irene. I'll just go and see if breakfast is ready for you both—now that Ms. Irene was woken." James swiftly left the library.

"Good morning, Irene! I hope you slept well. I've been up for a while. James has been furnishing me with warm cups of coffee! Irene, did you know that James grew up here at the mansion—even back when it was called Covington Manor?" Reagan asked.

"Oh my? Really?" Irene acted surprised. "No, I don't think I ever knew that about James."

Reagan really wanted to talk to James further—if he would talk with her. Reagan was fascinated with the history of this mansion and, of course, the history of Covington Manor. She wasn't sure exactly how old James may be—maybe in his eighties. It would be so interesting to hear about his life here at the mansion and the life and people surrounded Covington Manor. She, of course, didn't want James to get upset, and hopefully, he would be interested and forthcoming about talking about his life as a boy growing up in Covington Manor. It would be very interesting to find out. Reagan would be very excited to hear about it. Soon, she hoped.

Reagan and Irene sat at the beautiful huge Louis XIV dining room table. It seemed so silly that it was just the two of them sitting at a corner of this gorgeous incredibly long piece of furniture. It was graciously surrounded by eighteen beautifully ornate matching high-back chairs. The seat covers were heavy brocade and antique satin materials in a rich burgundy hue. The off-white Louis XIV dining table and chairs were equally matched, with a beautiful sideboard that sat against the side wall. And hung overtop was an exquisite painting of Louis XIV figures conversing and sitting at a small table. The painting was beautifully framed by the same wood and style of the Louis XIV dining room furniture. The frame was gold in color and perfectly enhanced the decor of the dining room. The sideboard was very long and certainly looked like it could handle and amount of banquet it needed. Reagan never saw a more extravagant dining room—maybe in pictures, period movies, or in books. And if someone would have told her that she would be sitting in one of those rooms, she would have called them crazy! The chandelier over the dining table was extraordinary—very old, very ornate, with many antique baroque crystals sparkling and hanging off the massive gold wrought iron chandelier. Reagan could just imagine how the cleaning of the magnificent, multitiered chandelier had to be. It had to take several people to lower, dismantle, and clean—ever so carefully—each and every crystal. As with the entire mansion, it would go without saying, the dining room didn't take a back seat to the beauty and loveliness of the estate. It was definitely a showpiece to be admired and envied by many. The wainscoting, the gilded wallpaper—original, Reagan felt—the sconces adorning the walls, the period pieces of furniture, the exquisite paintings, urns, and other artwork all enhance the rooms beautifully. Ostentatious maybe but elegant and extravagant and breathtakingly lovely.

Reagan was taking her last bite of toast and jam while James was pouring another cup of coffee for Irene.

"Irene," Reagan broke the silence.

"Yes, dear," Irene responded with a smile.

"You may not want to answer this, but may I ask you why you are so uncomfortable with going down the east corridor of the second floor?" Reagan asked.

Irene quickly shot a glance at James, trying not to make it too obvious. James quickly looked away as to not be noticed by Reagan. Although with that question, Irene almost choked on her sip of coffee and James almost dropped the silver coffee carafe. No, not too noticeable…

"Oh dear, I knew that you might be bringing that up soon one day," Irene replied reluctantly.

Irene started explaining, knowing this could be a lengthy topic of discussion.

"This home—this estate—has so much history, dear. It dates back to the early 1900s, when it was built. Mr. Dennyson, your Uncle Arthur, tried—and unsuccessfully, I might add—tried to locate the original blueprints. A while back, he went into town and consulted with a man named Jacob, who worked at city hall in the Records Department. Within that department is also the department that held all the original documents and original blueprints of significant original buildings of Covington. Anyway, Jacob could never locate those original blueprints for Dennyson Mansion—then Covington Manor.

Your uncle, at that time, felt so bad for Jacob. He thought Jacob was going to lose his mind. Jacob said he set them aside and placed them on his desk when your uncle had called him, and they just disappeared. Jacob soon became obsessed in trying to find them—but he never did. It was very strange. Your uncle, feeling so bad for Jacob, never asked again. He knew just how Jacob had become."

"But why wouldn't the blueprints have been kept here at the mansion—or the manor, rather? Reagan asked.

"I don't know, dear. Your Uncle Arthur had always wondered that as well. But after that fiasco, he gave up trying to locate them," Irene responded dryly.

"As to the east corridor, there is always a foreboding, eerie feeling down there. The cleaning company—the staff—refuse to go down there. There was an incident that happened last year while the cleaning company was here. Something startled them—frightened them. They said there are very bad spirits in one of the rooms. The two women were so frightened that they left all their cleaning supplies and ran out of the room as fast as they could. They left everything there. It was such a commotion. They said they would never return and go down that wing. Nor would they return to the mansion."

Irene suddenly had a very puzzled look on her face. Reagan could tell how upset and troubled she was.

"This home is very unsettled," Irene continued. "There were always the rumors of terrible things that may have happened—occurred way back when it was Covington Manor. And, of course, it didn't help that there were the two murders of our dear sweet Melanie and her fiancé, David."

Irene's mind took her back to the time when the murders took place. Oh, how she wished with all her heart that those two murders of Melanie and David had never taken place. And since that wish couldn't be granted, Irene wished that, at least, those murders could be solved. It would give closure and maybe some peace to their troubled spirits, their unrested spirits.

That night, Irene couldn't sleep. She felt so restless and unsettled, too, like the mansion.

CHAPTER 24

It was nearing another anniversary of the brutal killings of Melanie Dennyson and David Williams. Throughout the years, and particularly near the anniversary, Dennyson Mansion seemed to wake up. Noises around the property escalated tremendously. Unexplained sightings, lights, and orchestra music were being seen and heard. The police department was so tired of calls coming in to report everything from hearing orchestra music playing to seeing ghostly apparitions and eerie lights coming from the back of the mansion. Although the cottage where the murders took place is now long gone—torn down by Arthur—screams and crying was still being heard. "Ghost lights" were being seen. The ghostly apparitions of David carrying Melanie's limp, frail body had been seen by many. It's the same vision over and over again—David cradling his beloved betrothed, Melanie, in her torn, bloody wedding dress. He carries her from where the cottage once stood. When you first see David carrying Melanie, the cottage, like a mirage, comes into view. David carries Melanie through the front door and carries her through the wooded area. Every anniversary of their deaths, at the very time they had died, one can usually see the glowing, see-through apparition of David carrying his lifeless bride-to-be adorned in her wedding gown—the once-beautiful laced dress now bloodied and torn. The dress is dragging on the ground. They soon disappear as they meld into the woods.

Every anniversary, local television stations and investigative reporters come around hoping to get yet another interview with Irene about the awful killings. Irene wished it would stop. She doesn't want to relive that terrible, horrific night. God knows the memory of what she saw that night with Arthur would be burned into her mind forever.

Irene sat in her chair by her bedroom window looking out the back of the estate onto the beautiful gardens. Her eyes followed the stone pathway to where Melanie's cottage once stood—the beautiful little cottage that once brought her sweet little Melanie so much enjoyment and comfort. How terrified Melanie must have felt that night. Irene shivered for a moment. Tears welled up in her eyes. She could hardly bear to think how that poor sweet Melanie suffered. The moment she knew that her excitement over her dream-come-true wedding would never take place, would never come to be. Her beautiful wedding dress would never be seen, and the marriage to her dream man would never be. How tragic that these two beautiful, wonderful human beings died so dreadfully and the horror in David's eyes when he first stumbled upon his beautiful, lifeless bride-to-be. Who in their right mind could ever do such a thing—and why? Melanie and David were so loved and liked by many.

The leads in the murder investigation went dry. The Covington Police Department, at that time, was swarmed with phone calls—people giving opinions, sightings, even psychics calling in to give their opinions. The detectives did everything they could—Irene remembered. The murder weapons were never found. The footprints the found on the cottage floor was never matched. Scenario after scenario was discussed, patterns were mapped out, trails were followed that led to nowhere and nothing. The only two suspects that the police department ever came up with were the two employees of Dennyson Toys. And for some reason, they disappeared that night. It was an obvious deduction of the Covington Police Department—particularly the Detective Division—that somehow and for some reason (there was always a reason), these two employees murdered Melanie Dennyson and David Williams. All they needed were the two suspects to be brought in and questioned. But they were never found. Leads ended up nowhere. The detectives were beyond frustration. Lack of sleep and endless hours of overtime turned up nothing! It was as if these two employees never existed after that night. They just fell off the face of the Earth forever.

Irene shook her head and wiped the tears rolling down her cheeks. It was going to be a long night, she felt. She suddenly felt another chill go right through her body. She stood up, a little wobbly, and shuffled back to her warm bed. She would try to forget the faint orchestra music she thought she heard in the distance. It was probably coming from the ballroom again. Irene was used to hearing that same music over and over again. Why couldn't they just play something over that lively jazz piece! Irene left her comfy chair by the window, not wanting to see the ghostly apparitions that would soon be roaming in the far back beyond the beautifully landscaped gardens. Roses still bloomed, but the vegetable garden was just a distant memory. When Richard retired, he joined his daughter and her family down south. Unfortunately, the vegetable garden became in disrepair. Richard was never the same either after Arthur passed on. Irene remembered that conversation she had the last day that Richard was employed. She gave him a warm hug goodbye and said how she understood how he wanted—needed—to move on. He was tired too. Through many conversations, he explained to Irene how his daughter, Jessie, and son-in-law wanted him to join them and live with them in a warmer climate. His son-in-law got transferred, and they were moving. They wanted Richard to come live with them, and they wanted him to enjoy being with his three grandchildren as well. They loved their "Poppa," and they were all excited to think they could have his undivided attention each and every day! They had a suite all ready for Richard—all Richard had to do was say yes. It was time. Richard said yes.

Reagan couldn't sleep either. She didn't know that Irene was having the same problem as she was.

She was sleeping peacefully (a rarity) and then she'd wake up abruptly (not that *that* ever happened before!). She thought she saw something—someone—at the end of her bed. Maybe it was Rachel?

Reagan immediately thought about one of the last times she had spent with Rachel, although Reagan rarely saw or conversed with Rachel anymore. When Reagan and her mother and father moved and Reagan became best friends with Gracie, Reagan didn't spend very much time in her bedroom anymore. Rachel and Reagan would often have their talks and visits in their old bedroom—the one that Rachel was so familiar with. But after the move, Rachel didn't like that Reagan had a bedroom all of her own. It changed—the curtains, the bedding. And it was just one bed. Rachel hated that. She hated light blue! She didn't like the color Reagan picked out, and she didn't like the comforter and curtains at all! Rachel wanted to know where all her things went—her clothes, her books, Bunny. She was confused and upset.

"Rachel, stop! Stop moving all my stuff around! And stop hiding my things!" Reagan yelled angrily.

A faint giggle was heard in the room. Rachel liked to move Reagan's things around—sometimes hiding them. She didn't mean any harm. She loved Reagan, but she was bored. She just liked playing games. Sometimes she just wanted something to do? What else was there?

"Reagan, you're no fun anymore!" Rachel said one day. "Ever since you became friends with Gracie,

143

you're never in your room anymore. I hate that!" Rachel said.

"Well, I'm sorry!" Reagan replied sarcastically. "You're gone now! I can't stay and play and hang around with a ghost for the rest of my life!" Reagan exclaimed.

Rachel's ghostly expression changed—from giddiness to incredible sadness and then a scowl and anger.

Oh great! Reagan thought. *Here comes the anger and then throwing things.*

The last time Rachel got angry at Reagan, she threw one of the rocks that they had collected down at Lake Bremen. It would have hit Reagan square in the head if she hadn't thought quickly and ducked.

"Rachel!" Reagan yelled. "You could have hit me! You could have hurt me! I hate you!"

"I'm sorry," Rachel answered. "I didn't mean to. I just get so mad and angry sometimes. I'm sorry, Reagan. I would never hurt you…never! I love you so much. I just love you. You are my very best friend in the whole wide world. But…we are not in the same world anymore…"

And with those last words, Rachel was gone.

Reagan might not have heard those last words that Rachel spoke. Reagan left her room, slamming the door loudly. It was so final.

Reagan sat up and rubbed her eyes. It was probably nothing. Reagan did have the "gift" to see spirits when they wanted to appear to her. She could also sense if something wasn't right. She thought that maybe she was a sensitive or intuitive. She laughed to herself. *Who knows?* she thought. She did remember on a couple of occasions, reaching out to a psychic—a medium. They always had a hard time reading her. Reagan would usually get disappointed and frustrated. Other people, friends she knew could be read, and wonderful things were said to them, but no, not Reagan. She was more complicated, more complex. Reagan thought maybe Rachel had something to do with it. Reagan would just shake her head and not dwell on it. It was needless. She would say to herself when she would leave the reading, "Well, there's another twenty dollars down the drain!" Sometimes, some of her friends would say, "This one comes highly recommended. She's good—he's good." And then Reagan would usually have the same concluding thoughts—"Ya, right!" She would just shake her head and laugh.

Maybe a walk in the gardens and some fresh air will help me, Reagan thought. She just couldn't sleep. She got us and put on some comfy fleece pants and a sweatshirt. She quietly closed her bedroom door and slipped quietly down the grand staircase.

The moon was glowing—not quite a full moon, but it still flooded the dark night sky with enough light to illuminate the back of the mansion. There was ground solar lighting that illuminated the walkways. Coming down the stairs, Reagan held on to the beautiful long mahogany handrail. During the day, Reagan never had problems walking down the long stairway, but at night, that was another story. There were night-lights glowing throughout the mansion. It was never pitch dark. And with the soft glowing effect, sometimes shadows could be or might be seen. They would appear maybe going from room to room, wing to wing, going through walls, bookcases.

Reagan stopped at the bottom step. She heard music—orchestra music. It was coming from the ballroom.

"Oh, geez," Reagan said quietly out loud. "I knew I should have just stayed in bed—in my room."

Reagan was never a scaredy-cat. She wasn't afraid. With being able to see spirits sometimes—especially Rachel—and feel things, she would meet whatever was coming head-on!

She walked quietly, of course, toward the ballroom doors. It took her a little while to get there. The ballroom was located on the other side of the library. The double doors, of course, were closed. She slowly opened the doors as she still heard the music playing—a jazzy, lively tune, she thought. The ballroom was dark, and the music abruptly stopped. It was silent—dead silent. The glowing light from the moon outside eerily illuminated the whole ballroom. The back of the ballroom was all glass—from floor to ceiling. Reagan remembered the estate tour with Irene and how Irene explained how her uncle and aunt put in new windows. They wanted to enjoy viewing their backyard gardens and wooded area with the beautiful trees. They didn't want it covered up with short windows and no view.

Reagan walked to the center of the ballroom. It was truly magnificent. What a beautiful space—a space that was now never used. No one ever heard music in here anymore. Well, maybe just on special occasions.

Reagan turned around as she looked all around. As soon as she opened the double doors, the music had stopped playing. It was eerily quiet again. She couldn't see anything out of the ordinary—no movements, shadows, orbs. Her eyes took her to the back of the ballroom. She looked outside to the soft glow of the garden lights that lit the pathways. All of a sudden, Reagan saw lights, shadows, something in the back beyond the gardens. She thought to herself, *Isn't that where the cottage once was?*

There were double doors that led out to the patio, backyard gardens, and pathways. Reagan went to the doors and opened them. She left the ballroom, closed the doors quietly, and walked outside. Outside, the air was cool, and there was just a slight breeze. It felt good. She could still see something, shadows moving. She took the pathway that would have led to Melanie's cottage. Ironically, this was the exact pathway that David took, then Arthur and Irene. Reagan remembered Irene telling her that David went to Melanie's cottage to find her, but he didn't ever expect to find her in the condition he did.

"I'm not afraid," Reagan said out loud. "Maybe someone is trying to tell me something. Maybe I'm supposed to be guided somewhere."

147

Reagan didn't know it was near the anniversary of Melanie's and David's deaths. But she did feel something was going on.

"Is anyone here?" Reagan asked out loud. "What do you want? What do you need? I want to help you. Hello?" Reagan kept repeating.

All of a sudden, several feet away, she saw the glimpse of a cottage coming into view.

"What the hell?" Reagan gasped and exclaimed.

It was almost like a mirage. It was there but in a transparent way. And then she saw David. She could see right through him. He was cradling—carrying, she obviously thought—Melanie. He was moving slowly, walking slowly, almost shuffling. He was dragging his own feet, but he was careful as to not to drop his Melanie. Reagan saw him come right through the front door. He was mouthing "Help me!" He looked confused—scared and distraught. He walked toward the wooded area. He didn't seem to see Reagan.

Reagan yelled out, "David!" He didn't hear her. He just kept walking with Melanie's lifeless body cradled in his arms. Reagan picked up her step and followed him. Maybe she could communicate with him—somehow make contact with him. She was getting closer, and then he and Melanie just vanished into thin air just like that! They were gone.

Reagan just stood there—not believing what she had just seen. Did she really just see David and Melanie? Did she really just see a glimpse of the cottage that was? Did she really hear music coming from the ballroom?

All of a sudden, she was startled back to reality. She heard someone behind her. It was Irene and James. Reagan quickly turned around and let out a small gasp of air. She couldn't take on any more ghostly surprises tonight!

Irene spoke, "Reagan, dear, are you all right? James saw you and was worried and alerted me. We came right down. Are you okay, dear?" Irene asked again.

Reagan stumbled to find the words. She was still processing the night's activities.

"I'm okay, I guess. I couldn't sleep, and I thought I might get some fresh air out here and..." Reagan stopped talking.

Irene and James looked at each other and then at Reagan.

"Maybe it's time," Irene said quietly. "I think we should talk over a cup of tea. James, would you mind? And please join us."

"Yes, ma'am," James responded. "I imagine it is time for conversation...and tea."

"Ya," Reagan said. "I think so too."

CHAPTER 25

Sitting in the breakfast nook, James poured two cups of steamy, hot tea—a cup for Reagan and a cup for Irene.

"Thank you, James," Irene spoke thankfully.

"You're welcome," James responded dutifully.

"James, you don't have to stay up—unless you'd like to have a seat with Reagan and myself and join us for a cup of tea," Irene suggested.

"Thank you, madam," James started to reply.

Reagan said, "James, please stay. You're part of this family too." She turned to Irene and said, "I hope I'm not speaking out of turn, Irene, but James, right?"

"Oh my goodness—yes, of course!" Irene patted the chair beside her. "James, please sit and have a cup of tea with us," Irene pleaded.

"Well," James replied, "only if I can add a little something extra to my tea—and I will gladly add to anyone else's if they'd like," James added with a smirk. "I think tonight—on this very strange night—calls for it!"

And so all three nodded in agreement. The choices of spiced rum, whiskey, and Bailey's, and a bourbon all seemed like splendid selections for additions to a hot cup of English tea.

James poured some whiskey into his Earl Grey while Irene and Reagan opted for Irish cream in theirs.

"Well, now that we are feeling nourished," James started the conversation off, "what would you ladies like to discuss?"

"Well," Reagan began," how about the two ghostly, glowing apparitions and the mirage-like vision of a cottage, okay? And the music heard from the ballroom? How about that!" Reagan exclaimed.

Irene chuckled a little after she finished a gulp of tea. She knew there would be no more sleeping that night. All three, unless James left the conversation table, would be greeting the morning light sitting at the breakfast table and not from their cozy, warm beds.

So much to discuss, so much to ponder, so much to uncover and all three wishing the mysteries to be solved.

PART 3

The Ressurection

CHAPTER 26

Hollingsworth Psychiatric Hospital

Gina sat every day in her favorite comfortable chair in the corner next to the southwest window of the solarium. This was where the sun shone brightest. The warmth of the sun made her smile. Gina had to have her favorite crocheted blanket laid precisely across her lap. It had to be perfect. A worn stuffed light brown teddy bear named Teddy was lying just so across her lap as well.

No one ever visited Gina. Her history, according to the facility and the doctors in charge, was sketchy, to say the least.

Years ago, Gina was found, literally, on the doorstep of Hollingsworth Psychiatric Hospital one dark, rainy early morning. She was catatonic and rocking back and forth. She was sitting upright, but her arms were tightly wrapped around her knees, and her head was bent down.

Mrs. Danforth had arrived very early for her shift, as well as several other nurses. Hollingsworth Psychiatric Hospital was not the most desired employer for many. It took a very special kind of nurse that would have any desire at all to work at this type of facility. Brenda Danforth was one of those types of nurses. Brenda had a sister who was mentally challenged. She was a child who always needed special treatment and patience and care. Brenda always knew that when she grew up and had to decide on a career, that psychiatric nursing would be her calling. She has been a nurse for twenty years and wouldn't change a thing about her decision in choosing to become a nurse. She enjoyed working at Hollingsworth. She liked the staff—fellow nurses, doctors, all of them. They worked as a team—together—for the good of the patient. It was a good facility. It had been recognized as a great hospital for the caring and preserving of the mentally challenged. Dr. Raymond Desmond was the head of the facility. He was a caring facilitator and had a reputation of being one of the finest doctors in the care of the mentally ill.

There could be very long days at Hollingsworth. Brenda knew that all too well. The staff cared for 225 patients each and every day. This facility was almost at its maximum capacity. And in the early morning hours on a Monday, Gina Brown became patient number 226.

Brenda was startled to find someone at the entranceway to the hospital. As she pulled into the parking lot and got out of her car, she saw someone on the steps—in a dark corner. At first, she thought it might be a large dog. As she walked carefully up to the entrance, she then knew it wasn't.

"Oh my god! My dear child!" Brenda exclaimed.

As other staff members were pulling into the parking lot, getting out of their cars, one could hear the excitement.

Brenda gently approached Gina. Assessing the situation quickly, it was obvious that this girl—an adult—had been exposed to some very serious traumatic experience.

Adam was following Brenda in the parking lot.

"Adam," Brenda said in a commanding voice, "go see what doctor is available. Dr. Stanbery or Dr. Goodwin may be on this morning. Hurry please!"

"I'll hurry!" Adam replied dutifully.

It was not your typical Monday morning, Brenda was thinking to herself, not by any stretch!

Brenda knew not to startle or charge up to the impending patient. That could very easily put the patient in a far worse mental condition, and it could easily develop into a worse communicative situation. At this time, Brenda could not even assess the communicative abilities of this young woman.

While waiting for a doctor, which seemed to take forever, Brenda noticed a piece of paper that was safety-pinned to the girl's worn sweatshirt jacket. There was nothing on the sweatshirt to denote the whereabouts of this girl. Brenda didn't know if she should even try to collect the piece of paper that was attached to the girl. She didn't want to startle her or make the situation even worse.

"Honey," Brenda said in a soft and kind voice, "you have a piece of paper on your shirt. Do you mind if I take that?"

Brenda gently patted her arm. Gina jerked and pulled away.

"Honey, it's going to be okay. You're safe now. We will take good care of you," Brenda said firmly and, hopefully, convincingly.

Gina just kept rocking back and forth, groaning now—a little.

Brenda still tried to get Gina to look up at her, to make eye contact—anything to maybe distract her, to somehow change the mood.

Brenda saw that Gina had a stuffed teddy bear and a crocheted blanket next to her on the ground. Maybe this would get Gina's attention.

"Honey, is this your bear?" Brenda asked gingerly. "Can I look at him? I promise to give him right back to you. Is that okay?"

That brought Gina around a little. She looked up at Brenda and then back down at her Teddy. She looked back up at Brenda again. She stopped rocking and smiled—just a little.

"Mommy?" Gina very quietly said.

Brenda thought she must have resembled the girl's mother, but that's not always the situation. Any human being could be associated with a patient's familiarity. It's not always a certain or particular resemblance that might trigger a response like that.

"No, honey, my name is Brenda. I'm here to help you." Brenda pointed to herself.

By then, Dr. Will Goodwin came outside. Dr. Goodwin had a very calming voice. That would be good, Brenda thought to herself as soon as she saw Dr. Goodwin.

"Well, good morning," Dr. Goodwin said. "Who do we have here?"

Brenda quickly gave Dr. Goodwin an assessment of the situation. Unfortunately, she hardly had any information to provide to him.

"Okay," Dr. Goodwin said. "Let's get you inside so we can get you warmed up."

Two orderlies came out with Will. With Brenda's help, they were able to get Gina to stand up and walk her into the hospital. That in itself was a miracle. Gina would only go with Brenda at her side. Brenda took her hand, and Gina held on for dear life—almost crushing Brenda's slender fingers.

"It's okay, honey. It's going to be okay," Brenda kept trying to calm, reassure, and comfort Gina.

They finally got Gina to calm down, and they were able to unfasten the note that was attached to her sweatshirt jacket. Brenda was thinking to herself as she sat in a chair next to Gina's bed, *Wow, this is not what I expected my Monday morning would be like!*

Gina was resting peacefully, but only with Brenda there in the room with her. As soon as Brenda would try to leave, Gina would start to get very upset again. As Brenda was watching Gina sleep, she thought how tired she looked and what possibly could have happened to her to bring her to that state of mind.

"That's okay, Dr. Goodwin," Brenda said. "I can stay with her. I must remind her of her mother.

She obviously finds comfort in, at least that," Brenda said calmly.

"Thank you, Brenda," Dr. Goodwin said. "Until we can somehow figure this puzzle out, I want to thank you for accommodating our newest patient. I will clear your schedule for the time being. I will talk to Nurse Conway about this. Don't worry. I'll take care of it. You just stay here with our patient."

"Okay, no problem," Brenda replied and smiled.

The file was started on the newest member at Hollingsworth. But the only piece of information for now was the single sheet of notebook paper that was attached to patient number 226.

Dr. Goodwin was sitting in his office, at his desk, staring at the sheet of notebook paper. It was the only piece of information he had on his newest patient.

Hello, my name is Bea. The person who took care of me can't do this anymore. The best place for me is here. Can you take care of me? I do not talk. I had an accident. I fell and hit my head. I have no memory. Please just take care of me and keep me safe and warm. Teddy and my blanket has to be with me all the time. I like pudding and Jell-O.

Thank you,
Bea

Will chuckled to himself. He spoke out loud and to himself, "Well...that's plenty of information. Our puzzle is complete—not!" Will scowled.

He was interrupted by a knock at his door.

"Come in," Will answered solemnly.

Dr. George Stanbery opened the door.

"Good morning, Will. I hear we have a new patient," Dr. Stanbery said in a matter-of-fact way.

"Oh ya, we do, but there is very little information on her. This may be a tough one. Definitely, a very traumatic experience occurred. We'll need to get a workup on her. The only thing I have is this note." Will pushed the note across his desk to George. "And another thing, this girl will not let Nurse Brenda out of her sight. Brenda can't leave her side," Will explained in a very frustrating voice.

"Well then, Brenda, for the time being, will be glued to the girl's side," Dr. Stanbery replied.

"Okay!" Dr. Goodwin agreed. "Let's get this assessment started!"

Time to assess.

CHAPTER 27

Nancy Smith was sitting in her small one-bedroom studio apartment, thinking, always thinking. She was making sure all loose ends were tied up ever so tightly. Nothing needed to be fixed. All the bases were covered.

Nancy was smoking her third cigarette. She spoke to herself out loud, "I gotta stop these. They'll kill me!" as she squashed the butt end of the cigarette into the ashtray on the kitchen table. She was thinking back on her life so far. She never really planned on her life being like this. She knew she had a temper. People just pissed her off. People made her do the things that she'd done. It wasn't always her fault. She'd had to plug a couple of people, but that was okay. Of course, there was "Hon Bun." That was a different story altogether. She really enjoyed stabbin' the hell out of that bitch and her goody-two-shoes boyfriend. She chuckled out loud.

"Mr. Perfect! Mr. Wonderful! That suckin'-up bastard!" Nancy said, disgusted. "They deserved to die! Makes me sick! They deserved whatever they got comin' to 'em! I fixed 'em both up real fine! They looked much better when I got done with 'em!"

Nancy laughed out devilishly. "I coulda worked for Estee Lauder!" She laughed again.

Nancy's thoughts quickly turned to Gina. Nancy talked to herself a lot these days. She was, of course, a loner. She took up with no one. She held odd jobs here and there. It was a whole lot easier to dump Gina at that asylum! It was a perfect place for her. Nancy tried talking to Gina after that night. She had to drag Gina outta there quick. Nancy was afraid she would be found out—that someone would find them and would know what happened. But they were lucky—so lucky. It was easy. They skipped out of town. No one even knew yet what happened. Nancy heard the music blaring from that mansion. She left Gina locked up in the shed to go back to the cottage to find her keys. She was so hoping to see that bitch again lying in all that blood, just lying there. And then *he* came in and ruined the last best memory she could have had that night. But no worries, *he* then became the last best memory of the night! Double the pleasure, double the fun!

Nancy practically carried Gina back to their apartment. She had to shower, and she had to hose off Gina some too. Carrying her made Gina have some blood on her clothes as well. Nancy took all the clothes and burned them in the back of the building. She buried her boots. Damn, she loved those boots! And she buried the pitchfork along with them. She had to! They were evidence, but evidence no one would ever find! She then garbage bagged everything out of the furnished apartment. Gina just sat limply on the couch. Then after some physical transformation, they left town.

Nancy knew that she had to change her and Gina's looks. That very night, she cut both of their hair. She died her hair dark and cut it very short—in a man's style. She had a very hard time with Gina. Gina was squirming and wouldn't sit still. It was impossible! She did the best she could with Gina's hair. She figured out different names they could choose. Nancey became "Butch."

Nancy was quite proud of herself as she stared at herself in the mirror. "Wow! I make a damn good-lookin' dude! This is going to be easy—a new look, a new gender! I can dig that!" Nancy—or Butch, rather—tried to do as much alteration to Gina as possible. She needed to sit still long enough to get the temporary hair dye in.

"It'll work," Nancy/Butch said. "Now a name for you…" Gina always liked Nancy to call her G, but that would be too easy to track.

"Well, how about B? That'll work! *B* or *Bea* it is."

Nancy drove far enough away. But taking care of Gina or Bea—it was just too much. She had to find a job, and there would be no one to take care of Gina/Bea. And for once in her life, Nancy just couldn't kill, not Gina. She was the only person she just couldn't do in. She did try on two separate occasions, but Nancy just couldn't do it. She knew Gina would never come out of her state of mind—so Nancy was safe there. Gina wouldn't tell anybody anything—she couldn't. She would stay like that for the rest of her sorry life. Nancy's secrets would stay and die with Gina. Nancy was safe yet again. As Nancy would often say, "Somebody *down there* loves me! Always lookin' out for number 1!"

Nancy wrote the note and told Gina that they were going for a ride. She pinned the note to Gina's sweatshirt and took her to Hollingsworth Psychiatric Hospital. It was dark out, but Gina didn't care. Gina didn't care about much of anything these days. Nancy was exhausted taking care of her all the time. The money Nancy stashed away was going to be running out soon. A change had to be made. Gina did whatever Nancy told her to do. She never talked. She just stared off into the distance. At times, Nancy tried to talk to Gina. She'd yell at her, "Look at me, Gina!" Gina would just start rocking again and groan. Nancy would try to refresh Gina's memory about that night. She wanted to make sure she was safe and that Gina wouldn't remember. Gina would begin screaming again and rock back and forth continuously and moan. Nancy soon gave up and knew her secrets were safe. No one would ever figure out what she did that night—ever! Nancy would often turn on the TV after that night. She wanted to keep updated on any new developments in the murder cases. She'd say to herself, "Dumbasses! They got nothin'!" Nancy would exclaim out loud, laughing, "I got you, you bastards!" She'd yell at the television, "You'll *never* figure it out…*never*!"

Nancy was quite proud of herself. She fooled everybody! One night, however, she panicked. There was an interview on a TV station. They were interviewing one of the detectives. He said they might have narrowed it down. They found a footprint of a boot in the cottage that night, and they were trying to match it. They also said that they were looking for two possible suspects. They showed her and Gina's photos and gave their names. They were the photos that were taken when they were first employed at Dennyson Toys. The detective said he just wanted to bring them in for questioning. And that's all.

"Right," Nancy said, disgusted, under her breath. "I'm not falling for that shit! They want to fry our asses! That's what they want to do! No damn way!" Nancy yelled at the TV. Nancy's yelling caught Gina's attention. She started rocking again back and forth...back and forth.

That dark, rainy morning, Nancy took Gina to Hollingsworth Psychiatric Hospital. She pulled up to the entranceway after she scoped out the surrounding area. It didn't appear that anyone was around. It was dark—that helped. She left her old, beat-up Chevy running, as she got out and went around to open the door to get Gina out. Gina had just sat in the car, staring straight ahead. She didn't even flinch a muscle while Nancy pinned the note to her sweatshirt. Gina had her crocheted blanket that her mom made her. It was her "prized" possession. It was the only thing she had left from her mother before she died. She also had her teddy bear that she had as a little girl. There was no one left in Gina's family. Her brother, Greg, had died from an overdose, and her mom drank herself to death after that. It was no life for Gina, but she had Nancy.

Nancy got Gina out of the car and brought her to the top step and alcove. It would be somewhat dry and would keep Gina dry and out of the rain.

"You just sit here. Someone will come for you. Understand? Do you understand, Gina?" Nancy was looking for an acknowledgment of any kind from Gina. Gina looked up, and somehow Nancy felt she knew.

It was time for Nancy to go. It was time for her to start her new life as Butch. She was sad—a little— to leave Gina. But Nancy took comfort in knowing that Hollingsworth would be a good place, a place that had people to take care of her. She would live the rest of her life out there. At least that was something.

CHAPTER 28

After teatime, the sun was coming up. Reagan and Irene were still sitting at the breakfast table. James had retired to his room to catch a few winks of sleep. Reagan was thinking.

"Irene, we have to bring Melanie and David to rest. They are wandering because there was *no* rest for them. Someone has to solve this horrible mystery once and for all! And I guess that someone has to be me!" Reagan came to the conclusion.

"Reagan, dear, the police department and several detectives tried, but they constantly came up empty handed," Irene said firmly.

"The case is still open, isn't it?" Reagan asked.

"Yes, it is…until it is solved," Irene replied. "Until it is solved…"

"Well then, it is time for a trip to the Covington Police Department. Is there anyone specific I should ask for?" Reagan asked Irene.

"No, not that I can remember." Irene shook her head. "I wish you luck, dear. I wish you luck."

CHAPTER 29

Josh Winters sat at his desk in the back of the Covington Police Station. Covington wasn't a huge community, so a huge police department was entirely out of the question. It was a little cramped with just two detectives in one room. Josh shared the office with Harry Trimble, a seasoned officer and detective. Harry had been with the police department coming up on thirty years—twenty-five with the department and five with the detective division. Josh had great respect for Harry and always looked forward to working with him on whatever case came up. Josh was very bright and caught on quickly. He was finishing up his first year as a detective. Josh graduated at the top of his class at the academy. He took the police exam and interviewed with the chief of police in Covington. It went very smoothly. Josh had always wanted to be a policeman like his father and grandfather before him.

Harry had just returned with his fifth cup of coffee in hand. Harry loved his coffee.

"Harry, number 5 really? You really need to cut down on that stuff. It'll kill ya!" Josh scolded Harry.

"Thanks, Mom!" Harry replied sarcastically. "I know, I know! But I just *love* my coffee!" Harry smiled as he held up his coffee like he was toasting Josh.

"Then drink decaf—or half and half, man!" Josh continued lecturing Harry.

"They're not the same, my boy! They're just not the same!" Harry retorted back to Josh.

Josh Winters was in great shape, and he was very conscientious and healthy when it came to his diet. He was working on Harry. He hoped at least some of his healthy dietary habits would rub off on him. He really liked Harry—almost like a father figure. He wanted to be able to stay around for a while. Josh would keep on trying to get through to Harry. He was stubborn too.

Harry walked over to Josh's desk as he was sipping his fresh-brewed coffee. It was midmorning. The two would usually go over any cases they were working on. Josh was moving around a couple of files on his desk when he uncovered a file labeled "Dennyson, Melanie." And then the next one was "Williams, David." They were both exposed on the corner of Josh's desk.

Harry pointed to the exposed files and said, "You know, son [sometimes Harry would call Josh that in a loving way], you're never gonna solve those cases. You do know that, right?" Harry told Josh, "We got nothin'!"

"You don't know that for sure, Harry. Something could turn up," Josh replied. He was optimistic—as always. "The anniversary is coming up again. I'm just refreshing my memory. We're going to get interviewed again. You know that, right?" Josh mimicked Harry with a grin.

The anniversary was soon approaching again. Every year like clockwork, the television stations set up camp at two places—outside the Dennyson Mansion and the Covington Police Department Pretty soon, it was time for more interviews.

Just then, Josh and Harry's conversation was interrupted by a knock on their office door. It was Jennifer.

"Come in." Harry said.

"Excuse me, boys, you have a visitor requesting a meeting with one or both of you," Jennifer said as she opened the door a crack.

Harry replied, "Who and what?" Harry's favorite two words to say.

"It's a Ms. Reagan Dennyson," Jennifer replied.

Josh and Harry just shot a glance at each other.

Josh replied, "Reagan Dennyson—from *the* Dennysons?" Josh asked. "Well, isn't that a surprise!" He looked at Harry. With that answer from Jennifer, Josh's expression looked as if he had just won the lottery!

"On that note," Harry entered the conversation. "I'm leaving. You handle it, flyboy! Do the preliminaries—you know the run. And I'll catch up with you later, okay? It's all yours, son!" Harry waved at him. "I'll just work on that Remington case we were talking about the other day. I'll be down the hall in one of the conference rooms. We'll catch up later. Sound good?" Harry asked Josh.

"Sounds great!" Josh replied to Harry.

Josh looked over at Jennifer. She was waiting patiently by the door for a response from either of the detectives.

"Jennifer, send Ms. Dennyson back—or escort her back, please," Josh said. "Did Ms. Dennyson say why she was here? Did she mention what this visit is in regard to?" Josh asked Jennifer.

Jennifer replied to Josh, "She said she wanted to talk to a detective about the Dennyson murders. I think she said—and I quote—'It's time these crimes were solved!'"

"Well, alrighty then!" Josh answered sarcastically. "Well then, I'm glad Ms. Dennyson's here. We'll be able to wrap these cases up! Goody!" Josh chuckled.

Harry was gathering some paperwork and files off his desk. "God, I'm glad I'm leaving. But it would be fun to be a fly on the wall!" Harry laughed. "Have fun, my boy!"

Joking aside, both detectives would have been very happy—as well as the chief—if these crimes were solved. The whole Covington Police Department would not have to carry that burden and have hanging over their heads one of the most well-known and publicized murders to date.

Harry left the back office and walked down the hall to one of the conference rooms. Jennifer was bringing back Reagan to the detectives' office.

The door to the detectives' office was open. Josh was at his desk waiting for this Ms. Dennyson to arrive. He looked up and saw Jennifer and Reagan walking to the office doorway.

Josh rose from his desk. "Thank you, Jennifer," Josh said. He extended his hand to Reagan to welcome her. And Reagan did the same.

"Ms. Dennyson, please come and have a seat," Josh said with a smile.

"Thank you, Detective…" Reagan felt awkward trying to remember the detective's last name.

Josh jumped right in, "Josh Winters, Ms. Dennyson."

"Oh, thank you." Reagan laughed. "I'm sorry. That was a bit awkward. I'm usually good with remembering names."

"That's quite all right," Josh tried to put Reagan at ease. "What can I do for you, Ms. Dennyson?"

"Reagan please," Reagan replied back.

Josh again motioned Reagan to have a seat as he went around to his chair at his desk.

Reagan sat down with leather binder and pen in hand.

Josh noticed. "I see you've come prepared to take notes, Ms. Dennyson—Reagan."

"Yes, I always bring a notebook with me— only if I expect to take notes, of course!" Reagan responded with a smile. Reagan was always proud of herself for staying organized. And she didn't want to miss any details that she wanted to add to what Irene had already told her.

"So," as Josh started again, "Reagan, what can I do for you? I understand you are interested in the murders of Melanie Dennyson and her fiancé, David Williams. Am I right? And I see you have the same name. May I ask how you are related?" Josh asked curiously.

"My father was Vincent Dennyson—Arthur Dennyson's brother. Arthur Dennyson was my uncle. Recently, I was notified that I inherited—or partially inherited, rather—Dennyson Mansion. I share that inheritance with the woman who has lived in the mansion for many years—Irene Boxler. She was a dear, close friend of my Uncle Arthur and Aunt Anne. She continued to live in the mansion after the death of my uncle. It is in his will, Detective, so please understand that I am not, in any way, challenging that. I do know that the anniversary of the two murders is approaching. I don't know what Irene and I want to do with the mansion as far as keeping it or selling it, but I do know that due to the circumstances, selling wouldn't even be an option right now. I want to—if possible—research these murders and hopefully solve them once and for all.

"As do we, Reagan," Josh answered. "As do we. The two murders are, of course, still open cases until they are solved. And actually, I have those files on my desk now." Josh pointed to the two manila file folders on his desk.

"Is this possible, Detective? Is this possible that I can be included in helping to solve these crimes? I, of course, don't know policies and police procedures.

And please understand, I do want to help. I actually have seen things on the property, just the other night actually…" Reagan's voice trailed as she remembered her experience seeing Melanie and David's spirits in the back of the mansion.

"Ms. Dennyson—Reagan, please be assured that we are trying our best to solve these horrendous crimes. We would like to close these two cases just as much as you and this Irene. I can see you have a vested interest in this with being a part of the Dennyson family. If you would like to take part, I can keep you informed of any new information we may receive. Of course, being an ongoing criminal investigation, this office and police department will have limits as to what we can divulge to you or Irene. But we will do the best we can to keep you informed."

Reagan just looked at Josh. She didn't think she would get anywhere with this interview. She was sure she was displaying a disappointed reaction. She didn't mean to.

"I know this is probably not what you wanted to hear, Reagan. I wish I had more for you. If you or Irene are contacted in any way by someone who has new information, please contact us here at the station." Josh reached down to grab his contact card from his desk. "Do you have any new information that would help to bring us closer to solving these murders, Reagan?"

"No, I don't," Reagan replied. "But I do want to help. I mean, I don't mean to be pretentious and all," Reagan said apologetically.

Josh was remembering when Reagan was explaining how she was related to the Dennysons. "You said your father was Arthur Dennyson's brother. But you said *was*. Your father, I'm gathering, is also deceased?" Josh asked with hesitation.

"Yes, he is," Reagan replied sadly.

"I'm sorry," Josh responded. "I didn't mean to remind you of this. I just wanted to remember how you were related. I'm sorry."

"That's okay, Josh," Reagan said. "My father was Vincent Dennyson. He passed away last year. My heart breaks with all the heartache this family has had. I have had my share—just within my own family. The Dennyson families have suffered greatly over the years. And I am the last member of the Dennyson clan. My mother and my father have both passed. It started with my sister, Rachel—" Reagan stopped talking and suddenly looked very sorrowful.

Josh stood up from his chair and came around to the front of his desk. He sat on the edge facing Reagan.

"You, okay?" Josh asked in a concerned voice.

Josh patted Reagan's arm. Reagan was staring off into the distance, thinking about how long it had been since she saw Rachel. It had been a while. Reagan blinked and refocused and realized that Josh was sitting on the edge of his desk directly in front of her. It startled her a bit.

"What? Oh, okay, I'm fine. It's just that...," Reagan started, stumbling for a response.

Josh interrupted, "Ms. Dennyson—Reagan, I'm really very sorry for all the tragedy your family has had to bear all this time. I really wish and hope someday that we can finally find some closure for the Dennyson family…and for the Covington Police Department and this department as well," Josh said candidly.

Reagan spent more time than she had planned at the Covington Police Department and in the office of Detective Josh Winters. Josh didn't really have anything of dire importance to complete that day. Harry worked on a few cases while Josh was mostly with Reagan. He confided to Reagan that the murders were something he vowed to solve when he became a detective. He wanted more than ever to solve these crimes of passion.

After their conversation, Josh had asked Reagan if she might be hungry and would want to join him for a bite of lunch. He felt that maybe a change of scenery and some food might make Reagan feel a little better. He suggested that they go to Rosewood Grille and Cafe—his treat!

After that afternoon, Josh and Reagan planned to meet to work on and go over every bit of information, news articles, interviews—everything and anything they could find on these murders. They would put their minds together and work together, and maybe who knows. It was worth the effort.

Along with that, Reagan and Josh became fast friends…and maybe more than that.

CHAPTER 30

Reagan was sitting on the floor of Josh's apartment, nibbling on the sausage-and-onion pizza Josh had picked up after work. Along with the two tall glasses of iced tea and a tossed chef's salad, they continued on their nightly routine. There were light tan computer paper boxes sitting on the floor. They housed all the information that was compiled about the two murders. Reagan and Josh started at the very beginning, going through evidence, interviews, and reports. Reagan was certain there was something that might have been missed—overlooked.

Josh brought over a second glass of iced tea to Reagan. He kissed the top of her head as he handed the glass to her.

"Well…anything?" Josh asked.

Reagan looked up and smiled at Josh and thanked him for the tea. He caught her and captured a light kiss. She giggled.

It was inevitable that Josh and Reagan might fall in love and become a couple. Neither one was looking for someone or for a relationship. It just happened—as sometimes it does. It was so easy for the both of them. They fit together like a hand in glove. Reagan had ultimately decided to terminate her nursing job at Lincoln Memorial and move permanently into Dennyson Mansion. Irene was thrilled when Reagan had discussed her decision with her.

"Oh, Reagan, I am so pleased!" Irene said with the widest smile on her face. She clapped her hands together.

Irene was so hoping—and praying—that Reagan would want to come and live permanently at Dennyson Mansion. This huge estate, Irene said so often, was so lonely without people in it. And Irene had grown quite fond of Reagan. She was like a daughter to her...maybe a granddaughter. Irene never wanted to hear about the day that Reagan might decide to leave—to go back to her home. Dennyson Mansion was her home now too.

"Oh, Irene," as Reagan gave her a big, warm hug, "I could never leave you ever...not now!" Reagan exclaimed.

"You know," Irene added, "you give the warmest hugs!"

They laughed out loud. The bond between Reagan and Irene was solid. They each filled an emptiness—a void in each other's lives. Both had experienced such despair and emptiness in their lives. Reagan would often say "doors and windows." People come into your life when you need them the most. Some stay for a short time, and some stay for the duration. Maybe Arthur and Anne and her father and mother were all watching over both of them.

They knew that each needed each other to comfort and to bring strength and companionship.

Now if only they could help guide us to solving these murders! Reagan often thought.

Josh came over and sat beside her on the couch.

"I don't know, Josh," Reagan said in a frustrated voice. "I think we just have to find those two employees of Dennyson Toys. I'm sure they had something to do with the murders. There just isn't anyone else to point a finger to."

"I agree," Josh said. "But both seemed to have just vanished—disappeared after that night. But someone had to have seen them somewhere. The apartment complex they lived in—the owner, the custodian, manager knew nothing. The rent was paid on time and in full—and in cash. There were never any unusual noises. Both tenants were pretty quiet. They were never any trouble."

Both Josh and Reagan wanted to revisit the apartment building and maybe talk to the owner or manager or custodian of the building. The owner had passed on, and the ownership had gone to his only son. The apartment single building had fallen into disrepair and was soon going to be torn down. The son was planning to sell it to a developer. The son lived out of state and had no intentions of keeping it, repairing it, etc. More dead ends.

Reagan fell asleep on the couch—as she often would. Josh bent down to waken Reagan and maybe have her stay the night—as sometimes, she would. Josh covered Reagan with a blanket and went back to the kitchen table to work on some paperwork. He'd let Reagan sleep a little longer and then try waking her again.

Josh looked at his watch. He thought it was time to try and wake Reagan up again.

"Honey, Reagan, you need to get some decent sleep—and not here on my couch." Josh gently nudged her. "You want to stay here tonight?"

Reagan fluttered her eyes open to see Josh leaning over her. "Oh, I'm sorry, Josh. I guess I didn't realize how tired I was. No, I better go back to the mansion. Do you mind driving me home?" Reagan asked.

Those soulful eyes and Reagan's beauty melted Josh's heart. If only Reagan knew just how much he was in love with her. Since the day she walked into his office, he had been a goner. He would do anything for Reagan—anything. All she had to do was ask. And maybe Josh did—or didn't know—the feeling was mutual. Reagan loved Josh too. She never imagined she would fall so hard, so fast for anyone. She'd walked into the office that morning, and she just knew that her and Josh would be together. It was weird how she just knew it. It was a romance that was meant to be.

"Come on, honey. I'll take you home," Josh replied dutifully. "That way you can get a good night's sleep hopefully and feel rested in the morning."

"I hate to leave Irene alone," Reagan said sleepily.

"I know you do. It's no problem—I understand," Josh said.

"You know, Irene has grown quite fond of you, Josh." Reagan wanted Josh to know that Irene approved of them dating and being in a relationship.

"Ya, she's a sweet lady. I hate that she rambles around that big old mansion."

"You know, Josh," Reagan interrupted, "you should just move in with the both of us. There's plenty of room at the mansion. Why, you could have your own wing!" Reagan answered like she was having an epiphany. "But not that one wing…it's pretty creepy down there!" Reagan shivered to think about that one corridor. There was something down there.

Irene looked at her clock on her nightstand next to her bed. Reagan wasn't home yet. Irene usually heard her coming up the staircase. Irene hadn't been sleeping very soundly lately. She had turned into a light sleeper. Irene was usually found in the library, sitting in one of her favorite leather chairs with a blanket across her lap. She would have a cup of tea and a good book to read. Irene loved sitting in the library. There were a number—a very large number—of great novels to read. And a cup of hot tea and a good book to read in her favorite room was all Irene needed. Even though the ceiling was very high, the library still managed to contain the coziness and comforting feeling. It was Arthur's favorite room as well.

Irene was reading one evening. James came in to ask if she wanted another cup of tea or anything else before he retired for the evening.

"No, I'm fine, James. Thank you," Irene replied.

James turned and left the library, moving a little slower these days. He seemed more tired than usual, Irene thought to herself.

All of a sudden, that familiar smell of cherry tobacco filled the area that Irene was sitting in. It was Arthur's signature smell that would usually signal that Arthur was nearby. Irene looked away from her novel she was reading.

"Good evening, Arthur," Irene said out loud. She smiled.

It got incredibly cold in the library. A cloudy mist started to form over by the large stone fireplace—Arthur's favorite spot in the library.

"Is Anne with you? I miss you both so very much, you know." Irene was hoping they could hear and understand her. Just then, as Irene asked about Anne, her signature fragrance wafted through the room. Irene smiled. "Hi, my love—my friend. God, how I miss you both."

Irene looked over toward the fireplace and soon started to see the forms of her two best friends. Arthur had his arm propped up against the mantel of the fireplace. He had on his favorite smoking jacket. Anne stood next to him and just smiled that warm, lovely smile—the smile that made everyone around her feel special. They both looked good, Irene thought. Happy and content.

Irene turned and brought up her hand to her lips and blew them both a kiss. "I love you both, you know. I miss you both terribly. Did I say thank you for bringing Reagan to me? I love her you know—like she was my very own. You two are the best, and I thank you from the bottom of my beating heart that you always look out for me." As Irene was softly speaking to her two best friends, each smiled back. They both were still somewhat transparent but were both undeniably there in the room with her. They were indeed watching over their best friend. And did they have something to do with bringing Reagan to Irene? Well, maybe…

Just then, as quickly as they appeared, they were gone. Irene had heard a car pull up to the entranceway. You could hear the rubber tires of a car make that crinkly sound. It must be Reagan. Josh must have brought her home. Irene felt so protective of Reagan. When Reagan brought Josh home to introduce him to her, she knew Reagan would be nervous. Irene could tell that Reagan wanted her to like Josh—and Irene did. Josh was very friendly. He was a likeable fellow. He wasn't boastful or pretentious. He was kind. Irene could tell that Josh and Reagan were in love—just like her and her Gordon. She was very happy for Reagan. Yes, Irene liked Josh right away. He had no hidden agendas. He was very natural—very nice. Reagan probably knew that Irene may be leery of the police department—not intentionally—but with everything that had happened at Dennyson Mansion, it would be natural to assume that Irene would be guarded.

The evening that Reagan brought Josh to the mansion was for dinner. Irene wanted Reagan to have someone in her life. She didn't want Reagan to be alone. Irene knew she wouldn't be around forever, and she had hoped Reagan would meet a nice young man one day. And Reagan did.

Josh took Reagan home, and as he pulled into the long gravel drive of Dennyson Mansion, something caught Reagan's eye.

"Oh no, not again!" Reagan gasped.

"What? What is it, Reagan?" Josh asked in alarm.

Off in the distance, to the back of the mansion, was the glowing light again. Reagan could see that it was starting again. No sooner had Josh pulled up than Reagan sprung open the door and darted out as fast as she could. Josh turned off the car, got out, and slammed the door. He took off after Reagan.

Wow, can she run fast! Josh thought, surprised.

He yelled to Reagan. He was fighting to catch up to her. She ran to the back to hopefully make contact with David's spirit.

It was the same scene over and over again—the cottage coming into view, David carrying Melanie, walking through the front door of the cottage, and then David and Melanie vanishing as he slowly walked, glided, through the wooded area. It was a residual haunting, as psychics and mediums would say. It is kind of like a part of a movie being looped, and the scene plays over and over again.

"But why?" Reagan would often say to herself. "Why that specific scene?"

"Reagan, wait up! Where are you going?" Josh yelled to her, out of breath.

"Shhh." Reagan waved and turned with her finger to her lips. "It's starting again."

"What's starting?" Josh asked. He was very confused.

He was confused...until he saw what Reagan saw. "What the hell!"

Now he sees it, Reagan said to herself. *He sees it too.*

Reagan stopped abruptly. Josh almost bumped right into her. He saw what she saw. Just as they got to the back corner of the gardens, and with both of them looking in the same direction, they saw the glowing light coming from the area where the cottage used to be—where the cottage existed before Arthur took it to the ground. Like magic, the cottage appeared—it came to life. Josh couldn't believe what he was seeing. He just stared in total amazement. And all of a sudden, the music started to play. It was faint. It, like always, came from the direction of the ballroom. And like before, every time before, the cottage materialized. And soon after, David appeared—although somewhat transparent. He was cradling his beloved Melanie in his arms. Her lifeless, bloodied body was lying limp in his arms. Her torn bloody wedding dress was dragging on the ground. He turned and went into the woods. He looked like he was searching for something...someone. But this time, before he turned to glide into the woods, he looked at Reagan.

Reagan quietly spoke to Josh, "He's looking at me—at us." Josh had adjusted his footing. It made a rustling sound. "I think we startled him, maybe."

Reagan was ecstatic. *That's the first time David acknowledged me.* She really felt he was looking at her—at Josh.

Reagan slowly walked toward David. She didn't want this moment to be lost. She spoke, "No, please don't go. I want to communicate with you. David, please don't go…"

"Reagan, what are you doing?" Josh asked nervously.

"Josh, shh…just be quiet…please," Reagan replied insistently.

David looked like he was trying to communicate with Reagan. He was trying to say something. In a very faint voice, almost breathy, he said, "Help me…help Melanie…please…"

And then both David and Melanie just disappeared into thin air.

"Dammit!" exclaimed Reagan.

Reagan just collapsed onto the ground. Josh bent down to pull her up. He tried to comfort her.

"Reagan, is this what you see every night?" Josh asked quietly.

"Yes, that's exactly what I see every night. It's the same scene. But tonight it was different. Tonight, David looked at me, acknowledged me, saw me. He tried to tell me something. He did communicate with me! That's big—that's really big!" Reagan was exhausted but excited.

"Well," Josh said out loud, "I may have an idea or two."

Josh and Reagan went back around to the front and came in the front door. Josh wasn't going to leave Reagan after that. They found Irene resting in the leather chair in the library. The soft glow of the floor lamp cast a warm glow. Reagan knew Irene hadn't been sleeping well these past few weeks either, and she felt bad that she was out so late. Reagan knew that Irene had grown quite protective of her. Reagan didn't mind. It was actually comforting to know that someone cared so much.

Reagan gently tapped Irene on her arm. She tried not to startle her. Irene's eyes opened as she focused on Reagan and Josh standing before her.

"Oh my, I must have dozed off." Irene chuckled a little. "You just got home, dear?" Irene asked.

"Hello, Josh," Irene added.

"Yes, Josh just brought me home. I hope I didn't worry you, Irene. I'm sorry. I fell asleep on Josh's couch again," Reagan apologized.

Reagan wasn't sure she wanted to tell Irene about the incident in the back behind the mansion. She didn't want to upset or alarm her. She thought she would sleep on it and maybe tell Irene in the morning. Josh, however, brought the subject up. Reagan was a little perturbed, but she knew Irene should know about it anyway.

"Irene, tonight was different. Tonight I think we communicated with David!" Reagan said with excitement in her voice.

"You did?" Irene replied with much surprise. "Well…that's something…"

"Yes, I know!" Reagan replied.

It was late. Irene had gone up to bed, and Reagan walked Josh back to the foyer. She kissed him tenderly and thanked him for putting up with all her lunacy.

"Well, what else would I have to do!" Josh answered jokingly. "Reagan, I love you—-through thick and thin," Josh said tenderly.

"I love you, too, Josh, very much," Reagan answered back. She was glad they both got their feelings out—finally. It felt good. It felt wonderful.

They held on to each other like they would never let go. They kissed again.

Josh said with a devious smile, "Hmmm… maybe I will move in…"

Reagan smiled.

He kissed the top of Reagan's head and left to go back to his apartment.

It was an event-filled, haunted evening for all three—Irene, Reagan, and Josh. When would these ghostly visions end? When would the questions be answered? The troubled spirits of David and Melanie, like the living, needed answers. Their souls needed to rest in peace. Soon, the anniversary of their murders would come yet again. Would this be the anniversary that the murders would finally be solved? Would there ever be peace at the mansion? They say only time will tell.

Here's hoping.

CHAPTER 31

Hollingsworth Psychiatric Hospital

Brenda came into Bea's (Gina's) room one morning—like every morning since Bea arrived at Hollingsworth. Bea was still in her bed.

"Morning, Bea!" Brenda said quietly. "Rise and shine!" Brenda went over to the window in Bea's room and spread open the draperies.

"Look, Bea—sunshine! It's another beautiful sunshiny morning. It's just waiting for you to wake up and smile!"

Brenda had been assigned to Bea since she arrived at Hollingsworth Psychiatric Hospital. It was obvious that Brenda was the only one that Bea would allow to be around her.

It was pretty much the same routine every day with Bea. Brenda would gently knock and open the door a crack (as to not startle Bea) and say, "Good morning." Brenda would get Bea up, feed her breakfast, and help her get dressed. And, of course, a shower may be needed—at least two to three times a week. This morning, Bea would be visiting with Dr. Goodwin. Brenda would always accompany Bea to

Dr. Goodwin's office for the session and would stay throughout her visit with Dr. Goodwin. Breakfast was finished, and Brenda had just helped Bea with buttoning her cardigan sweater—light yellow. Bea loved the color yellow. Brenda had found some clothing to fit Bea at the hospital's commissary. This was a place within the hospital where clothing would be stored that may be needed for a patient—for any particular reason. Sometimes, the nurses would frequent the resale shops and purchase various casual clothing for women and men. They would keep a stock of these items located in a large storeroom. Along with clothing, there may be toiletries stocked on shelves as well. Any staff member could add items as they wish to the commissary. It was well appreciated and always much needed for the patients. It just worked. The concept certainly came in very handy—such as in Bea's case. She came with no more than the clothing on her back.

"Bea, it's just about time to go for our visit with Dr. Goodwin. You ready, girlfriend?" Brenda smiled at Bea and patted her hand. "Is Teddy coming too?" Brenda asked Bea.

Bea nodded and held tightly on to Teddy. And her other hand was held tightly by Brenda's hand.

"Do you want to walk today? How about walking? We'll hold hands, okay?" Brenda hoped Bea would nod her head in agreement. A little walking—exercise—was good for Bea. It was good to stretch her legs, and it was good for her circulation.

Sometimes, Bea didn't mind walking. She would walk slowly, but at least, she walked. And sometimes she would be tired from the night before. She sometimes had nightmares, and she didn't have as much strength for the next day's activities, so a wheelchair would be the mode of transportation. Dr. Goodwin and Brenda were working on finding out as much as they could about Bea. Since there wasn't much to go on, it was a day-by-day and step-by-step process. They didn't know what triggered these nightmares, and it may not have been anything. There was no stimulus in the Bea's room. There was no television or radio. There wasn't even a clock on her nightstand or on the wall. They tried some soft music once. Brenda thought that maybe some music would comfort Bea—make her happy even. Brenda tried and found a station that played jazz music. When Bea heard a lively, jazzy tune, her mood quickly and dramatically changed. Her temperament became wild and irate. She immediately became uncontrollable.

She held her head, rocked back and forth, and screamed "No, No!" When Brenda and an orderly, Adam, finally calmed Bea back down an hour later, Dr. Goodwin was notified. He was furious with Brenda bringing in an outside source—a stimulus—without consulting with him first.

"Get that radio out of here—now!" Dr. Goodwin exclaimed angrily.

"Brenda, please ask me first before you just take it upon yourself to make decisions where my patients are concerned!" Dr. Goodwin spoke sternly.

"Dr. Goodwin, I'm very sorry. I never imagined a little music could trigger this outburst and episode. I'm very sorry." Brenda was almost in tears.

After catching his second wind and knowing that Bea was again calmed down and returned to her normal state, Will apologized to Brenda.

"I'm sorry, Brenda. But you know and fully understand that in this type of hospital—and especially with this particular patient—we have absolutely *no* idea what stimulates her mind and behavior. And until we can get a better understanding of Bea, I stress again to share with me first any thoughts or ideas you may have. Do you understand?" Dr. Goodwin pleaded.

"Yes, Doctor, I understand," Brenda responded apologetically.

That afternoon was tremendously exhausting—for Bea, of course, and for Brenda and for Adam and Dr. Goodwin as well. After giving Bea a sedative to relax her, another nurse sat with Bea while she rested peacefully. Dr. Goodwin asked for Brenda to come to his office.

"Am I in trouble, Dr. Goodwin?" Brenda asked reluctantly.

"No, no, Brenda. I just want to discuss this new development with you in regard to Bea while it is still fresh in both our minds. Stumbling onto another factor in Bea's behavior—her irate behavior this morning—may not have been a terrible thing. We, of course, are still very much puzzled by this outburst and violent behavior she displayed this morning. But with that being said, it may hopefully bring us closer to where her catatonic nature originated and why." Dr. Goodwin still had that look on his face when he was deep in thought about a patient.

Brenda was sitting across from Dr. Goodwin. She bent her head down and started to cry.

"Dr. Goodwin, I'm so sorry. I never—" Brenda started.

Will came around from his desk, grabbing a tissue for Brenda. He sat on the edge of his desk.

He interrupted her, starting to explain, "Brenda, oh my goodness! Please don't cry." Now he felt bad. "I know we are all very exhausted with this case—with Bea. And actually I want to thank you."

"Thank me?" Brenda replied in great surprise. "Why?"

"Because, Brenda, as terrible as this episode was for Bea, it was a breakthrough! This is the very first time since Bea arrived at Hollingsworth that we have gotten any reaction at all out of her. Something triggered her emotions—the music, that particular style of music. Something made Bea sit up and take notice. Playing that particular style of music must have emoted a response from her. It obviously was very disturbing for Bea to hear that particular music. That is a breakthrough, Nurse Danforth! Neither Dr. Stanbery nor I have been able to reach Bea. But you did! I am tremendously grateful to you, Brenda!"

Brenda wiped away her tears and took a deep breath. "Well then…"

The sessions with Dr. Goodwin after that day were pretty uneventful. One conclusion was certain, however. Will wanted to explore the music issue. They brought in the radio and played several various types of music. The only conclusion that was established? Jazz was not a favorite of Bea's. It was the only type of music that elicited a terrible, negative, active response. An orchestra playing lively jazz music specifically was very awful for Bea—but why?

Bea's clinical file was getting a little thicker. With different tests that were given, these facts were revealed: Bea hated orchestra and specifically jazz music, she hated the color red, she hated seeing blood, and she hates knives and any sharp objects. Some of these were found out by pure accident—hearing and seeing things. Outside, one day, a gardener was trimming bushes. Brenda was with Bea in the dining room, having an early dinner. Bea was watching one of the chefs. He was carving some meat. She was staring at him. And Bea started to get restless and nervous. She was starting to squirm in her chair. Then she noticed the gardener outside. He had a red scarf tied around his neck area. Sometimes, Harry would wipe his brow if it was hot outside.

"Bea, honey, what's wrong?" Brenda was trying to calm her. She tried to have Bea focus on her dinner, but that didn't work.

Brenda quickly told an orderly to bring Bea's untouched dinner to her room. Brenda wanted to get Bea out of the dining area as quickly as possible. She had the orderly get a wheelchair for Bea. Bea was gently guided into the wheelchair—with Teddy of course—and wheeled back to her room. Brenda thought how sad that they had to leave the dining room. It was so cheery in there with the many windows for patients to look out of. It was one of the few times in the day that Bea could possibly interact with the other patients there. Brenda was sad and disappointed that opportunity was lost.

Brenda took the quickest way back to Bea's room. She had to go down the hallway past the nurses' station. A couple bags of blood was being delivered to be stored. Well, needless to say, this was another trigger object that set Bea off. Along with the others, these objects brought out the worst reaction in Bea. But again why?

Dr. Goodwin did have a television in his office. He would turn it on, mostly for background noise. Sometimes he would be working late. He would listen to the national news, etc. The television was on one evening.

He was finishing up some notes on a patient one morning when a knock was heard at his door. He knew it was just about time for another session with Bea.

"Come in," Will answered.

Brenda and Bea walked into the room, hand in hand, and Dr. Goodwin looked up and greeted both with a warm smile.

"Good morning, Bea! Good morning, Ms. Brenda! Please come in and have a seat on my comfy couch! I am just finishing up some notes. I will be right with you both. Okay?" Dr. Goodwin said pleasantly and calmly.

"Good morning, Dr. Goodwin!" Brenda replied warmly. "C'mon, Bea, let's pick our favorite spot on the couch, okay?" Brenda held on to Bea's hand as she guided her over to the couch.

Bea nodded. Bea liked Dr. Goodwin. He was warm and friendly and never spoke harshly or raised his voice.

Brenda and Bea sat side by side on the couch. Bea looked up at the television. The national news was on, and a TV reporter was speaking. The TV sat nicely in a beautiful cherry cabinet. One could view the TV from anywhere in the room. The news was on. The newscaster was reporting on an upcoming anniversary of a horrendous crime—two crimes, two murders, the murders of Melanie Dennyson and David Williams.

All of a sudden, Bea went ballistic! Will shot up out of his chair and rushed over to where Brenda and Bea were sitting. Bea started groaning. The rocking back and forth started. She dropped Teddy and started clutching her head as if in pain. She started repeating over and over again, "No...no...no!"

Brenda rubbed her back and tried to calm her down. Bea just got more and more agitated and more irate.

"I'll go get help. I'll go get Adam—" Brenda started saying.

"No, wait!" Dr. Goodwin replied. "This is something. Let's see where this goes. I assure you,

Bea is in no danger. We have to play this out. Just stay with her Brenda," Will said reassuringly. "I'll call for Adam."

Will quickly called at one of the nurses' stations and requested Adam to come to his office as soon as possible. He went back over to Bea and Brenda.

"Bea, what is it? What's upsetting you?" Will asked firmly.

He looked up at the television screen and the reporter. He saw the subject matter the investigative reporter was talking about.

"Oh boy," Will said reluctantly. "He's reporting about those two murders in Covington—the murders of Melanie Dennyson and her fiancé, David Williams. I do believe, Ms. Brenda, we've opened a can of worms here. We found another trigger object. But it's a doozy!" Will surmised.

Will didn't want to turn off the TV just yet. He wanted to see the rest of the reporter's report—maybe some photos would be pictured. Maybe some photos would yet again trigger more responses from Bea. It was a risk that had to be taken. Adam soon came to Dr. Goodwin's office. He would help calm Bea. Bea liked Adam too. He would be a help.

Somehow Bea was connected to those murders. Will was sure of it. Those puzzle pieces were starting to be added to this puzzle. Things would soon be coming together. A story was beginning to form.

Will didn't want any harm—mental or physical—to come to Bea. But sometimes drastic measures have to be taken to hopefully bring out a breakthrough. Dr. Will Goodwin was hoping this would be one of those times. Maybe Bea would finally come full circle and finally deal with the horrible tragedy she must have been a part of.

Bea had become more and more uncontrollable by the moment.

"Brenda, turn off the TV. We've all seen enough," Dr. Goodwin said. "If you and Adam would please take Bea back to her room. I'm suspecting she will soon calm down. If not, let me know. I'll order another sedative so she can get some rest. When she wakes, please let me know. If she won't sleep, maybe a bite of lunch in her room will soothe her. You and Adam stay with her please. And just let me know of any other developments—if any. Okay?" Will said.

"Absolutely, Dr. Goodwin," Adam and Brenda replied in unison.

"And, Adam," Will interjected. "I will let the nurses' station know you are otherwise occupied with a patient for the rest of the afternoon."

"Thank you, Doctor. Of course, that will be fine," Adam responded.

Brenda found Teddy on the floor. It fell when Bea started her tantrum. Brenda hoped seeing Teddy would calm Bea down a bit.

"Bea, here's Teddy. He fell on the floor. You need to hold him and comfort him. He's hurting, too," Brenda spoke up as she held Teddy out for Bea to grab.

Bea saw Teddy and stopped her rocking. She started to calm down. It worked.

Brenda went and got a tissue. She wiped the tears off Bea's cheeks. An orderly came in with some juice for Bea. Will thought a cup of juice would help Bea as well.

Brenda and Adam sat on either side of Bea as he held onto the paper cup of juice. Bea liked juice—especially apple or grape juice. She was calming back down to her normal state. This was good. It took about an hour and a half this time.

"If you both would take Bea back down to her room now and stay with her. I'm sure she is exhausted with this traumatic experience today. She may need some rest."

"All right. We'll stay with her, Dr. Goodwin," Brenda responded.

Adam noticed that Brenda may have had a question for Dr. Goodwin. He offered to start taking Bea back down to her room while Brenda stayed back in Dr. Goodwin's office for a moment.

"What do you think, Dr. Goodwin?" Brenda asked.

"Oh, with the present developments and the new variables that have just come into view, I, unfortunately, think I need to make a phone call." Will scowled.

CHAPTER 32

Covington Police Department

Josh and Harry were sitting at their desks working. A call came in to Harry.

"Harry Trimble. Uh-huh, okay, will do. Thank you, Jennifer." Harry hung up the phone and looked over to Josh.

"Well, son, seems like our luck may have changed," Harry said calmly and with a grin.

Josh looked up from his desk. "How so, Harry?" Josh asked curiously.

"It seems a doctor from Hollingsworth Psychiatric Hospital just called. Jennifer took the message."

"What did the doctor want?" Josh asked.

"Well, it seems he may have a patient—one of his patients—that he feels somehow is connected to the murders of Melanie Dennyson and David Williams."

Josh dropped his jaw wide open and just stared at Harry in utter amazement.

"Oh my god—no!" was all Josh could mutter.

Harry wanted to put the doctor on speaker phone when he called him back. He, of course, would tell the doctor that he was on speaker and introduce him to his associate, Josh Winters, who would be listening in on the conversation.

Harry and Josh talked before Harry made that call. He wanted Josh to take any notes he could that pertained to the conversation with the doctor. And, of course, Josh would repeat nothing of this conversation and any information to no one. And he was especially not to repeat anything to his girlfriend, Reagan Dennyson.

Harry thought more about the situation as it was. Because of Josh being very close to the situation by dating Reagan Dennyson, he thought that maybe Josh shouldn't be in the initial conversation with the doctor at Hollingsworth. Harry knew Josh would understand his decision. Harry was, of course, the senior officer and detective.

Before Harry made the phone call, he thought he would talk to Josh first.

"Josh, I need to talk with you first before I pick up this phone and make the call to Hollingsworth and this Dr. Will Goodwin," Harry started to explain.

"Okay," Josh replied calmly. "What's up?"

"Because of the delicate nature and because you are dating a Dennyson, I think it would be best that I talk to Dr. Goodwin first. You are too close and very familiar with the only sole living Dennyson relative. And I think I should take this first initial call alone. Understand, son?" Harry was hoping Josh would not take it personally. Harry respected and had full confidence in his professional ability as a fellow police officer and detective.

"Yes, I unfortunately do understand, Harry," Josh replied.

Harry continued, "And, I know you this, but I'm going to stress this once again, you *cannot* and must *not* discuss any of this with Reagan, not just yet. I know and you know that Reagan and that other woman, Irene, will eventually be brought in to this whole thing. It will be inevitable, of course. But for now no speaking of this until we find out what this Dr. Goodwin has to share with us and the caliber and worth—if any—this information will have, okay?" Harry firmly stressed again.

"Okay. Understand," Josh replied. "I'll behave and be patient and not say a word, of course. I guess it's time for any early lunch break. I think I'll go to Rosewood Grille for a change of scenery. Can I bring you something back, Harry?" Josh asked.

"Ya," Harry replied happily. "How about one of those turkey club sandwiches with pickles and some fries! That would be great, Josh. Thank you, son! I love ya!" Harry laughed. "Oh, and some of the really fine coffee would be great too!" A change of mood was good—and needed.

"Okay got it, Chief!" Josh waved.

Sometimes, Josh called Harry "Chief." Harry, of course, was not the chief of police. That honor was given to Chief George Gordon. He was a good man, and hoping to retire soon! As Harry liked to call Josh "son," Josh liked to call Harry "Chief." They were both endearing nicknames. And they were a sign of the closeness and fondness and respected friendship they had developed.

It was just about 11:00 a.m. when Josh came into the Rosewood Grille and Café. It was such a warm and inviting and cozy place. Covington was lucky to have Jayne here in town. He and Reagan would frequent the Rosewood Grille and Café from time to time. It had good food, and they both loved talking with Jayne. Everyone loved Jayne. If someone was having a not-so-good day, it was a sure thing that Jayne could and would cheer them up. She would always be determined to get them to crack a smile sometime before they left her restaurant!

There was an old-fashioned bell fastened to the top of the front door. It hit the door as it was opened. If Jayne was in the back, it was a pleasant signal to alert her that someone was hungry and ready for some good food for the day!

"Morning, Jayne! It's Josh! I'm just coming in for some of your finest coffee and some hot, good food!" Josh bellowed.

Josh was the only one in the cafe at the moment. Soon, around noontime, it would be filled with hungry villagers enjoying great conversation and filling up their bellies with some of Jayne's fabulous dishes. Jayne was a good cook—and she knew it!

"Good morning, Josh!" Jayne smiled as she came up from the back of the restaurant. "Always nice to see you! Harry with you today?" Jayne asked.

"No, he had to stay back to work on some paperwork. But I will be putting in an order for one of your finest turkey club sandwiches to take back to him!" Josh answered happily. "And of course, a big cup of the best coffee in town!" Josh grinned.

"Great! I'll make sure to get that ready for you before you leave," Jayne said.

"Oh…and fries and pickles too!" Josh added. "Can't forget the fries and pickles!" He laughed. "Yep, that would be tragic—for me!"

Jayne laughed and escorted Josh to his favorite corner table near the window. Josh loved to look out onto Covington Square. Covington was such a quaint and lovely town. It was surrounded by trees, and the square was graced by beautiful hanging flower baskets adorning the lighted poles. Color was everywhere this time of year. It really was just beautiful to look at, Josh thought to himself. Simple pleasures…

Jayne brought Josh a glass of ice water and a fresh cup of steamy coffee to start. The aroma of Jaynes coffee was a sheer slice of heaven!

"Jayne," Josh started saying, "I don't know what kind of coffee you brew, but it's the best damn smellin' coffee around!"

"Oh, you're just thirsty…and hungry, I'm hoping!" Jayne laughed. "And thank you, Josh! It's a secret ingredient. It definitely keeps my cafe in business!" Jayne jokingly replied.

"Hmmm…good!" Josh sipped as if it was his first gulp of the day.

"What can I get for you today, Josh?" Jayne asked.

"What's the special?" Josh asked.

"Chicken paprikash is on the board for today!"

"Sold! You make the *best* chicken paprikash I've ever had!" Josh exclaimed.

"I make the *only* chicken paprikash you've ever had!" Jayne chuckled.

Jayne went back into the kitchen and soon returned with a steamy, hot, saucy plate of chicken paprikash grouped with a nice tossed garden salad and a fresh, warm dinner roll to melt in your mouth.

Jayne was the cook and baker of Covington. Covington was indeed very lucky to have Jayne in town.

Jayne had lived in town her whole life. She wasn't alone, however. Jayne had her daughter, Chelsea, there with her, too. Chelsea helped Jayne with the restaurant and also took care of the books and financial aspect of the restaurant. Chelsea went to the local community college after she finished high school. She received an accounting degree and received a minor in business. Jayne knew Chelsea could easily find a better paying job elsewhere—and definitely outside of Covington. But Chelsea was very content to stay here in town and work for her mother.

In conversation, one day, Jayne and Chelsea were sitting in one of the back tables in the restaurant taking a break.

Jaye said, "One day, my darling daughter, this will all be yours!" Jayne raised up her arms and motioned them to encircle the entire restaurant. Chelsea smiled, and Jayne laughed.

"Mom, I love it here. And you're not going anywhere for a very long time!"

Chelsea loved her mother deeply. Chelsea's father—Jayne's husband—had left this earth way to soon. He was never any good about taking care of himself. He would often ignore the red flags. Chelsea would often remember conversations that her mother would have with her father when she was much younger.

"Earl, please, you need to take care of yourself! Let me call Dr. Billingsly. You need to make your appointment for that physical!" Jayne would plead time and time again.

"I'm fine, dear. I just need to sit for a bit—catch my breath," Earl would say all too often.

Well, one evening, Earl met his fate. Chelsea couldn't remember how the commotion exactly started, but she knew how it ended. Her father was having more chest pains than usual. It was a terrible night. Her father had been sitting in the family room/living room in his favorite brown recliner. He stood up to go to the bathroom and collapsed onto the floor. And that was it. Her mother called 911, and the ambulance came. They came right away, but it was too late. Her father was gone. It was an absolutely awful time for her and her mother. Her mother was devastated. What to do? Where to go? Thank goodness Chelsea's mother had a good head on her shoulders. After the funeral service, Jayne had a gathering back at the house. Food was every-where. Friends and family insisted on bringing food over, but Jayne was stubborn and insisted on making everything herself. She was so stubborn.

It was a nice memorial reception after a peaceful service. People were embracing Jayne and Chelsea, of course. So many conversations were all going on at once. You could pick out bits and pieces of many different topics being brought up—sometimes lively, sometimes solemn and somber.

Chelsea was sitting on the living room/family room floor having a sandwich—her favorite, pea-nut butter and jelly—when she overheard her aunt Margaret say to her mother.

"Jayne, you are truly the best cook and baker ever! You should open up a restaurant!"

And well, that's exactly what Jayne did. The Rosewood Grille and Café was being sold. Betsy and Les were retiring and moving down south. Jayne pooled every cent she had, money that Earl had left her, and she bought the restaurant. She did love to cook and bake. It was like mental therapy for her. She couldn't imagine doing anything else—ever!

And, so the Rosewood Grille and Cafe had a new owner. It became very successful. The space next door became available. It was a small shop. Jayne bought it and had the wall between the shops torn down to expand the restaurant. An archway was put in, and the cafe side of the restaurant came to be. It was a coffee and pastry and bakery shop. Jayne became busier than ever. The restaurant and cafe was consistently busy each and every day. She had to hire someone—actually several—to help her. Now Evelyn ran the café side. Jayne shared her baking recipes, and Evelyn brought along a few of her own! They work very well together. Many bakery orders came in, and even Evelyn had to hire a couple more to help. A couple of high school girls help out front, and Evelyn hired an additional person to help the baking in the back. And it worked—it worked well!

Jayne had help in the kitchen of the restaurant as well. Russell was amazing, a self-taught cook. Russell could prepare anything. Like Jayne, he had a gift for putting together flavors and food. Russell was like the brother Jayne always missed having. They, along with Evelyn and Mary, completed the team at Rosewood Grille and Café. They were a team—a family. Russell and Evelyn were like an uncle and aunt to Chelsea. Chelsea would go to the café every day after school. Jayne felt so fortunate to have helpers watching over Chelsea. If Jayne had to be somewhere else other than the restaurant, then Evelyn and Russell were there to help always.

Jayne missed her husband, Earl, each and every day of her life. She knew Chelsea missed her father, too. But Jayne wasn't bitter. She had every right to be. She'd told her husband, Earl, constantly, about not to ignore his health. But she wasn't bitter. She just went on with her life with Chelsea. She went on to raise her daughter to be the best person she could be. Jayne insisted on being a good mother and role model for her daughter—and she was. People often remarked as to just how strong Jayne was. It was her nature and her personality. Whenever anyone remarked to Jayne about her how strong she was, her reply would always be the same: "Well, I have to be. There isn't any alternative. I am who I am. I have a daughter to raise, and that's that!"

CHAPTER 33

Josh finished his delectable lunch in record time, you might say! Jayne stopped over to the table as Josh was consuming his last bite of paprikash.

"Can I interest you in some of my dessert? Just made some fresh cherry pie this morning. You do get dessert with that fabulous lunch I just made you!" Jayne proudly stated.

"Liar!" Josh replied as he swallowed. "Since when do you include dessert with your lunch special?" Josh asked, surprised. "I'll have to investigate this, you know!" Josh laughed out loud.

Jayne loved her patrons, and they loved her. It was always a pleasure coming to Jayne's restaurant. Jayne welcomed everyone like they were all a part of her family. And they truly were!

"Nope, I'm good!" Josh patted his stomach. "If I keep eating at this little diner, I'll put back those ten pounds back on!"

Josh always kidded around with Jayne and referred to her restaurant as a diner. Jayne would laugh.

"Speaking of which," Jayne reminded Josh and herself, "I'll just go and get that turkey club ready for you to take back to Harry!"

"Thanks, Jayne. Thanks for remembering. If I would have forgotten, Harry would fire me! Then I'd have to come here and grovel for a job!" Josh laughed. He could hear Jayne laugh in the background.

Jayne yelled back, "I know! See how I save your butt! I'm always watching out for you, Joshua!"

"Thanks, Jaynie! Love ya like a mom!"

"You should!" Jayne giggled as she headed back to the kitchen. "And by the way, Mother's Day is in May!"

Josh laughed as he went to pay his bill. Jayne would always try to give Josh and Harry and others at the police department food for free.

"Jayne, let me pay. If you did this for everyone, you'd be out of business!" Josh exclaimed.

"Only for my *extra special* customers! Okay, let me change that bill—that'll be $189.95!" Jayne smirked.

Josh paid up and gathered up Harry's lunch. He took an extra cup of coffee to go for himself. He gave Jayne a hug and headed back to the police station.

Josh saw the back room office door ajar and saw Harry sitting at his desk writing. Josh made some noise so Harry knew he was on his way in.

"There you are! I'm hungry! Where's my lunch, errand boy!" Harry laughed.

"Here you go, boss!" Josh acted like he was going to throw Harry the bag—and stopped. "Naw...I don't want to ruin a great sandwich!"

Josh handed Harry his lunch and handed him his large cup of coffee. "Here you go. Enjoy!"

"What do I owe you?" Harry asked.

"Nothin'. My treat, ol' man!" Josh smiled at Harry.

"Thanks, Josh. Kidding aside, I really appreciate you bringing me lunch—and paying for it! And thanks for the best cup of coffee in town! Thank you," Harry said graciously.

"You're welcome, Pops!" Josh grinned. "So," Josh changed the subject, "how'd the phone call go?"

Harry was munching on some fries, and was just about to take a bite out of his turkey club. "Hey, junior, can I eat my lunch in peace first!" Harry wiped his mouth. "Patience, my boy, patience!"

"Sorry, just curious and anxious to hear what the good doctor had to say," Josh said apologetically.

As Harry was swallowing, he told Josh of his conversation with Dr. Will Goodwin. "Well, I think you and I are going to take a little trip. We're going to visit a psychiatric hospital. What are your plans for tomorrow morning?" Harry asked frankly.

"I guess we're packing and heading to a psychiatric hospital," Josh answered.

"We're leaving early. Pack an overnighter—maybe for a couple of nights. We'll see how it goes. Better dig out our expense and travel report documents. You and I are traveling. Oh, and let's stop at

Jayne's and pick up a large thermos of coffee—we're gonna need it! And maybe some of her sandwiches," Harry said. "It's gonna be a long trip."

"Got it!" Josh agreed.

CHAPTER 34

Will was sitting at his desk, swiveling in his over-stuffed leather chair. He knew he had to make that phone call—it couldn't be avoided. He was going to meet with two detectives from Covington Police Department He would have Brenda present in the meeting too. He hoped he wouldn't have to have his patient be present, but he had a feeling that this was going to be a new turning point in Bea's climb to wellness. Will made sure he had his note ready. He thought back to that day when Bea saw that television screen and that reporter talking about the Covington murders. How was she connected to those horrendous crimes? Will couldn't believe that Bea would have committed those crimes. He was usually right about his patients—people. He, unfortunately, came to a conclusion that maybe she may have witnessed the crimes. Bea displayed all the symptoms of that possibility. That poor young lady...

Will was working a little later than usual. It was the night before the two detectives were going to be there. Will had the TV on. He flipped through the channels, seeing if there was any more stations talking about the murders. The anniversary was coming up, and this would be the time where all the stations were

215

replaying interviews, showing photographs of the Dennyson Mansion, where the murders took place. There wasn't anything right now. He glanced at the clock on his wall of his office. Maybe there would be something on the news stations later.

Will made a phone call to one of the nurses' station. He needed to have Brenda come to his office when she had a moment.

"Thanks, Shirley," Dr. Goodwin said. "Yes, when Brenda has a moment. That would be fine. Thank you."

A couple of minutes later, there was a knock on Will's office door. Will wanted to brief Brenda on the impending meeting with the two detectives coming in from Covington Police Department.

"They'll be here tomorrow morning?" Brenda asked.

"Yes," Will said. "I think we should be expecting them around 10:00 a.m. or so. Can you be available?"

"Of course, Dr. Goodwin. I'll maybe have Adam sit with Bea. I will just need to get Bea dressed. Adam can help her with her breakfast," Brenda said as she was figuring Bea's daily schedule out.

Brenda feared for Bea. After the meeting with Dr. Goodwin, she clocked out but decided to come back to Bea's room to spend a little more time with her. Brenda's dedication to Bea was admired by all the nursing staff.

"You're amazing, Brenda," Joan had said one day.

Joan was one of the nurses that Brenda was sharing a break with one day. They were in the break-room. Bea was in the activity room with some other patients. Ms. Linda was wonderful. She was their activities director. Professionally speaking, Linda had her doctorate in physical therapy and a specialization, or additional education, in recreational therapy. She would sometimes be known as a DPT. She was truly perfect for the patients at Hollingsworth. There, the patients had exercise and music and art activities. It was important to emphasize the total wellness of each and every patient at Hollingsworth. It was a special special-needs adult community/facility with round-the-clock medical care. Hence, the accolades for the facility and state-of-the art treatment programs were well known throughout the state and beyond.

After a small break, Brenda slipped into Bea's room and sat down in the chair next to Bea's bed. Bea was taking her afternoon nap. It was almost time for Bea to wake up. Dinner would be soon. When Bea had that outburst this last week, her probable traumatic experience started to unfold. Obviously, Bea either saw or was present to the murders in some way. Things started to make sense. Puzzle pieces were starting to fit together. In several conversations that Brenda and Dr. Goodwin had, they both had one thing on their mind: Who dropped Bea off that one early morning? Could it have been the murderer? If Bea witnessed the murders being committed and person or persons dropped her off that morning, were they involved as well?

There were still mysteries to solve…people to expose…questions to be answered…

CHAPTER 35

It wasn't too bad of a drive to Hollingsworth Psychiatric Hospital. Harry liked driving. It was a time to gather his thoughts. Josh was poring over every bit of information—again—about the two murders, although this is what he and Reagan did almost every night. With a break here and there, they went over each and every fact—again and again.

"Harry, the last of this information on suspects, it was decided that these two women were the most logical candidates—a Nancy Smith and a Gina Brown. That right?" Josh asked.

"Ya, I suppose so," Harry answered. "The FBI was brought in too, at that time. They turned our station upside down to make it a working environment for them. We all just filled in where needed. Then after a while, when they felt everything was gone through, every avenue was searched, they picked up all their stuff and left. There was nothing more to do at that time. The two murder cases were left open. The files were filed away. All the interviews, fact sheets, test and lab findings—everything was neatly put away in boxes. All of the material evidence was locked away in a compartment in the basement of the station."

"Oh, like what evidence?" Josh asked Harry.

"You know, the physical evidence—such as the clothing the two victims were wearing, the murder weapons. They were put away to keep as reference," Harry answered.

"So the blood from the wedding dress—what did the lab results find with that?" Josh asked.

"It's all in the files there—in the reports," Harry responded. "The blood was obviously Melanie Dennyson's. Blood was found coming from David Williams too. They ruled him out, however, in killing her. It didn't make sense that he did it. Then there was also his killing. Someone had to kill him. It was figured that he found Melanie, and the killer was probably still there. Then they killed him too." Harry had recited this same scenario over and over again. He knew it very well.

"You sure he didn't do it? This David Williams kill Melanie? Maybe there was an argument?" Josh was trying to figure out every possible angle.

"No...nope. David had an alibi. He was in the ballroom with his future father-in-law and Irene. The coroner placed Melanie Dennyson's time of death about an hour earlier. Her fiancé was in the ballroom at that time. It had to be someone else," Harry told Josh.

"Do you think it could be this girl at Hollingsworth?" Josh asked.

"Well, my son, that's where we're going to find out just that!" Harry answered.

Harry was hoping. Granted, it would look real good on their records if he and Josh were the detectives that finally cracked these cases wide open and solved them. But sometimes it takes just a little bit of luck, too, to bring everything to a head. And Harry was truly hoping this would be that time.

Josh recited the address again to Harry. It wasn't hard to find Hollingsworth Psychiatric Hospital. Harry turned into the facility. He pulled into the parking lot and pulled into a space. They would check in later at the motel they were staying at. This meeting came first.

They got out of the car, and each stretched out their arms and legs. Josh gathered up a leather notebook and tape recorder.

"Say a prayer, my son, say a prayer," Harry said hopefully.

Harry and Josh were led down a hallway to the administration wing, where the offices were. They passed one door that was closed, and the name on the door was "Dr. George Stanbery." They then came upon "Dr. William Goodwin." The staff assistant who escorted the two detectives to Dr. Goodwin's office knocked on the door.

"Come in," Dr. Goodwin said formally. "Here we go," Will said to Brenda ever so quietly.

Brenda was sitting at the long table alongside the room. Will was sitting at his desk waiting for the two detectives' arrival. Will got up and came around his desk to meet the two detectives at the door. Brenda rose out of her chair to join Will.

"Gentlemen, I'm Dr. Will Goodwin, and this is Nurse Brenda Danforth." Will and Brenda extended their hands out to shake and greet the two detectives.

"Good morning. I'm Detective Harry Trimble, and this is my associate, Detective Josh Winters."

After the initial greetings, Will directed everyone to come and sit at the consultation table alongside the room. Will felt everyone could spread out—paperwork, files could be to displayed more comfortably. There was a thermos of coffee and cups and creamer and sugar as well. A pitcher of cold water and plastic cups were also there. In addition, a nice platter of Danish and cookies finished the ensemble.

"Gentlemen, please have a seat and let's get started," Will said. "And please help yourself to some coffee, water, pastries, and cookies." Will knew the detectives traveled far and more than likely didn't have time for breakfast.

"Thank you, Dr. Goodwin," Harry said. "It is very nice of you to have this for us."

"No problem," Will answered.

"Well, let me start this meeting," Will said matter-of-factly. "I will bring both of you up-to-date on all the information we have about our newest patient, Bea."

Will explained and provided all the information he had on Bea. Brenda interjected with information as well. Will explained the first day that Bea was found at the entranceway of the hospital. Brenda added information where needed. Will also told of the happening that occurred which, in turn, brought him to make the phone call to the Covington Police Department and the detectives.

Harry and Josh listened intently. Before the conversation commenced, Josh asked the doctor politely, "Dr. Goodwin, do you mind if we record this session? It's just policy in any interview process. We do not want to miss any crucial information that is provided. Details are important."

"No, of course not. Please feel free to do so," Will replied.

When will finished divulging all the facts, questions were asked by Harry and Josh.

"Dr. Goodwin," Harry started, "this may be a moot question—and I probably already know your answer—but with being said, can we see and question this Bea?"

Harry already knew what Dr. Goodwin's answer would be, but he had to try.

"No, absolutely not—not at this time. Bea is a very fragile patient—as most are here at Hollingsworth. I do not and will not jeopardize my patient's well-being and fragile state of mind right now."

"Well, Doctor." Harry chuckled. "How do you expect us to move forward with this discovery and hopefully solve these horrendous crimes that have been looming over our town and the remaining Dennyson descendants?"

"We will need to take this step-by-step, Detective Trimble, step-by-step," Will replied.

Josh interjected, "Dr. Goodwin, do you have a photo of Bea? I think if we compare pictures side by side of the two suspects and this Bea, it would help greatly. I know it has been many years since the murders, and what the two suspects may look like now will be different, but at least we could first see if there is any resemblance whatsoever with this Bea and either of the two suspects—women. Would you agree to that, Doctor?"

"Good point and great idea, Josh!" Harry added. "Well, Doctor?"

Will responded, "Yes, I think that would be fine."

"Doctor, do you have a current photo of Bea that we could view and then compare? Your and Nurse Danforth's expertise would certainly be very helpful as well," Harry asked, hoping.

Dr. Goodwin turned to Brenda, who was sitting quietly at the table, taking all the conversation in. Brenda thought for a moment and answered.

"Well, we do have some photos from the dance we had last month for the patients. And we may have the security cameras as a source—like when Bea was in the activities room on any occasion. Would any of those suggestions do? Oh, we also take photos sometimes, if the patient allows, of the nurse that is assigned to them. We take them for our photo board. Sometimes, the patients love to go and look at the photo board and see everyone's pictures. And I think

I have a photo of Bea and myself. Would you just like for me to grab that one? I have it in my locker, Dr. Goodwin," Brenda gave several suggestions.

"That would be great, Brenda. Grab the one from your locker. That would be the easiest one. Thank you," Dr. Goodwin answered.

"Okay, I will be right back," Brenda responded.

While Brenda was gone, it was time for Will to ask a couple of questions of his own.

"So when we compare the photos and say that Bea resembles one of the suspects, what then? What do we do after that?" Will posed the two questions to Harry and Josh.

Harry responded. "Well, if that would be the case, we would have to take this Bea into custody—"

Will interrupted Harry before he was finished, "Even though she is unstable and has the possibility of becoming even more volatile? You can't do that! I have to protect my patient!" Will was getting angry.

"Dr Goodwin, please just calm down!" Harry held up his hand. "We will certainly not exclude you—nor her nurse, Ms. Danforth. We understand how fragile this patient must be, and we would never jeopardize her well-being at any time. We will certainly include you and Nurse Danforth, we assure you, in every step of this process—if it comes to that. You both will be a viable and necessary part of anything that may result from this."

Brenda walked down the main hallway to go to the locker area. She always kept a photo of her and Bea. She had it in a magnetic frame and was attached to the inside door of her locker. She loved that picture of her and Bea. Brenda remembered that day—the day that photo was taken. It was a good day for Bea. She was happy. They had lunch together, and Adam was there too.

Adam was one of the orderlies that usually helped Brenda out when she was with Bea. Adam usually had the same shift as she. On this particular day, Brenda and Bea were going to have a tea party. Brenda was trying to find out what other food Bea might like. They made some hot tea—but not too hot. Brenda let it cool down before she served it to Bea. It was an orange pekoe tea with sugar cubes. Bea loved her sugar cubes. Brenda also had little peanut butter and jelly sandwiches. She had the kitchen staff cut the sandwiches into tiny squares. She told Bea that these were special sandwiches—made especially for their tea party. Bea smiled. She loved peanut butter, and she loved peanut butter and strawberry jam sandwiches. Brenda was ecstatic that she found something else that Bea would eat and love. Bea could be picky. But on that day, she was happy.

Bea liked Adam around too. His voice was calming. Adam was working as an orderly and actually was going to nursing school as well. He wanted to get his RN degree. He wanted to be a psychiatric nurse like Brenda. He would be a good nurse, Brenda felt. The world could use more nurses in the psychiatric field. Brenda was happy that Adam wanted to become a psychiatric nurse, and she was very proud of him.

The tea party was fun for Bea and successful. Brenda, Bea, and Adam had a photo taken to commemorate their fun Tea Party Day. That was the photo that Brenda kept in her locker.

Brenda returned to Dr. Goodwin's office. The door was open.

"Here, Dr. Goodwin." Brenda handed the photo to Will. He smiled.

"That's a lovely photo of you and Bea—and Adam too! I love it. Ah…Tea Party Day!" Will smiled.

Dr. Goodwin handed the photo to Harry.

Brenda spoke to Harry and Josh. "This photo was taken of Bea, Adam—an orderly—and myself. It was a day that we had a tea party for Bea. It was taken this last month. We had the party in Bea's room that day."

Harry took the photo. He looked at it and handed it to Josh. He said nothing. Harry went over to the folder that held a couple of photos of Gina Brown and Nancy Smith. These photos were the photos of them that were taken when they were employed at Dennyson Toys. Harry brought out the photos of each girl. Arthur Dennyson wanted photos taken of each of his employees who worked for him. They were kept in their employee folders when they were created. He thought it was a good idea to have a photo of each of his employees. At times, when he would have meetings, etc., he liked to know each of his employees by face. He had so many employees. He thought the photos would give him that familiarity if he was going to have a meeting with them, etc. or just wander on the floors to visit with his staff. He would do that from time to time. He wanted to talk with his employees and get to know them. He wanted each of them to know just how important they were to him.

Josh handed the photo of Bea back to Harry.

"Just put it on the table, Josh. It's time to compare," Harry said.

Josh placed the photo on the table. Harry placed each of the two photos from the folder on either side of Bea's photo.

"Okay, let's take a look. Let me know what you all think," Harry said.

They all gathered around the photos to compare. Granted, the two photos—the ones of Nancy and Gina—were from a while ago and Bea's photo was recent, but most of the time, resemblances and deductions can still be made. Each one—Will, Brenda, Josh, and Harry—had good vision. Brenda gasped as she reacted and put her hand up to her mouth.

"You see it, too, don't you, Brenda?" Harry asked as he looked over at Brenda.

Harry picked up the photo of Gina Brown and then picked up the photo of Bea. "They are one and the same. Your patient, Bea, is our Gina Brown."

Will breathed a very heavy sigh and replied, "Oh boy..."

They had to think this out very clearly. The next steps would be crucial—very crucial.

CHAPTER 36

Reagan and Irene were sitting at a table near the window at Rosewood Grille and Café. They were sipping their hot tea that Jayne had brought earlier.

Jayne came over. "How are you two? Doing okay?" Jayne asked.

"Good," Reagan replied and smiled.

"Where's that good-lookin' boyfriend of yours?" Jayne asked.

Jayne decided to have a seat with her two friends. There was no one else in the restaurant right now—a lull in the day—and very welcomed, Jayne thought. She patted Irene's arm as she sat down next to her.

"You okay, sister?" Jayne asked Irene.

It felt like Jayne and Irene were sisters. After the first time that Reagan and Irene came into the Rosewood Grille and Café, the newfound friendship quickly developed. It was as if Irene and Jayne always knew each other. It was nice and a welcoming time—just when Irene could use a close friend. Reagan, of course, was close to Irene, but Jayne had similarities to her—losing a husband, being close in age. It was just nice to have a good friend to talk to—someone who really understood. It was equally as nice that Jayne's daughter, Chelsea, and Reagan became close friends as well. It was perfect. On several occasions—mostly on Sundays—when the restaurant was closed, the ladies would take some one-day trips. They would go places, have lunch, visit gift shops and antique shops. They had a good time together. And sometimes, Jayne and Irene would just sit in the restaurant and chitchat for hours over a cup of coffee or tea. Whereas Reagan and Chelsea would take day trips and have adventures, Irene and Jayne would just sit and visit in the library at the mansion or at the restaurant in one of the cozy tables in the back. It was good. Life was comfortable.

The conversation came back around to Jayne's question to Reagan. Reagan looked at Jayne.

"Josh is gone for a couple of days—with Harry, I think. He was very vague. He and I think Harry are working on a case. They were following up on a case, I think. It was kind of strange though. Josh was acting kind of nervous when I asked him why he had to go out of town. I don't know. I know that it is usually privileged information and Josh is not allowed to talk freely about his—or his and Harry's—cases. I understand that. Anyway, Josh is supposed to come home Friday, I think. I sure hope so. I miss him," Reagan said sadly.

Jayne knew this was going to be a touchy subject—and no one was in the restaurant—but she had to ask.

"So tell me about what happened the other night at the mansion. Another sighting of the beloved spirits, I gather?" Jayne asked Irene and Reagan.

"Oh, that," Reagan was the first to reply as she looked over to Irene.

"Well?" Jayne asked again. "What?"

Reagan answered, "It's always the same scene, scenario…"

Irene continued, "But it was different this time." Irene looked troubled.

"How so?" Jayne asked.

"The spirit of David Williams talked to me," Reagan answered. "He said, 'Help me!' It was the first time there was ever any communication between us."

Jayne turned to look at Irene and her reaction. "Irene, say something."

"I'm tired, Jayne…just tired. I'm tired of all of this…the anniversary coming up and dealing with all those interviews again. I'm tired of the ghostly apparitions, the music being heard in the ballroom. I'm tired of taking care of the mansion. I'm *just* tired…"

Irene was exhausted, to say the least. Reagan and Jayne and even James noticed the toll that all these burdens had on Irene. Sometimes, Reagan was afraid that Irene would have a heart attack. She was slowing down and getting older. The mansion was slowly sucking the life out of Irene. Reagan knew Irene needed a change—a big change—in her life. Dennyson Mansion and all its baggage was just too much for Irene to bear any longer. A change was needed for Irene and soon. Reagan knew it.

It was another Sunday afternoon, and Jayne and Irene were sitting in the library at the mansion. They were having a cup of English breakfast tea and talking.

"Irene." Jayne was having an epiphany. "Let's run away! I'll sell the restaurant and you leave the mansion to the two lovebirds—Reagan and Josh. Let's leave and go down south. We'll buy or rent a nice condo—near a beach. What do you say? We'll hook up with a couple of sugar daddies and live the rest of our lives in pure bliss! What do ya say?"

"Wow!" Irene responded in a bit of a shock. She laughed a little and answered, "Actually, that sounds like heaven to me! And no ghosts, no drama, no interviews, and no mansions!"

"Great!" Jayne exclaimed. "I'll get the ball rollin'!"

They both laughed and clapped their hands in a high-five—well, "high ten!"

CHAPTER 37

Josh and Harry were sitting in their motel room. The motel was the closest to the hospital. It was just down the road. It was a small motel room but clean. It was a well-known motel chain, and Josh and Harry didn't require anything fancier. "No use spending needless money," Harry would often say. "It's on the police department's dime. We don't want to abuse it. Hell, they're even paying for our meals, too."

Harry was honest—always had been. Josh and Harry—even though there were years between them—made a good, solid team. They worked well together.

Harry was sitting at the round table in the corner of the room. You could tell he was figuring things out. Josh just came out of the shower, dried off, and put some comfortable lounge pants on and a T-shirt. He was drying his hair with a towel as he came out into the room.

"Bathroom and shower is all yours, boss," Josh told Harry.

"Okay, thanks," Harry replied as he was jotting some notes down. "No running for you tonight?"

"No, I'm taking it easy tonight. Just a little tired, I guess," Josh replied.

"Understand. Me too, kiddo, me too," Harry responded.

Harry was in deep thought. He had to think things through. He didn't want to botch this case up—not that he ever did botch a case up. They were on to something. These murders could finally be solved. The case could finally be closed once and for all! He knew it—he felt it. They were so close...

Josh came over and sat down with Harry. Harry looked at Josh.

"You figuring more things out, Harry?" Josh asked.

"No, just asking more questions, son."

"Like what?" Josh asked.

Harry slammed his hands down on the table and raised his voice. "Where the hell is Nancy Brown! She is the answer to this whole damn mess! I just know it. It's her. It's gotta be her. Where the hell is she? You can't just fall off the face of the earth without a trace, without someone knowing! We gotta find her, Josh. We gotta find this Nancy Brown, then we'll solve these damn murders! It's her...I can feel it in my bones!"

CHAPTER 38

Jake's garage

"Hey, Butch, hand me that wrench over there," Jake yelled over to Butch.

"I'm comin'!" Butch replied.

Butch was finishing up his lunch at Jake's Garage. He'd been working there for years. It was easy. Jake had a sign on the front door one day. Butch saw it and applied—pure and simple, just the way Butch liked it!

It wasn't a bad life. It wasn't a rich one either. But it was a comfortable life for Butch. It was definitely a time for a change for Butch...well, for Nancy Brown anyway.

Nancy Brown was no longer. Nancy Brown became Butch. It took time for the change. After dumping Gina off at Hollingsworth Hospital, Nancy went back to the apartment, gathered up a few of what belongings she had, and just left. It was time to move on. It was time for a change—a drastic change. Gina would be all right. Nancy had confidence that Gina would never come out of her catatonic state. Nancy felt she was safe. Her appearance was totally changed...and her identity. When she and Gina left that night of the murders, Nancy went to work and changed her and Gina's appearance. Gina looked okay. Unfortunately, Nancy couldn't do a whole lot with her appearance. She wouldn't sit still. There was too much damn rocking back and forth. Well, that was her fault—Nancy's fault. Nancy didn't mean for Gina to witness her murdering that damn bitch and then her wimp of a fiancé. She didn't figure on that either. It was just too much for Gina's fragile mind. She just went crazy—nuts! Nancy knew she had to change her appearance and identity—and quickly. So the transformation began. And the end result? Nancy became Butch, with very short dark hair. She dyed it black. One of the few people that Nancy (Butch) loved in her family was her Uncle Butch. His real name was "Henry," but for some reason, he had the nickname "Butch" since he was a young boy. As a small child, Nancy watched, in horror, as the life of her uncle slowly drained out of his body. She watched her dad cradle her Uncle Butch, his brother, in his arms when he had that fatal heart attack. As she was playing outside, she watched her father and her Uncle Butch laughing and talking. Then suddenly Uncle Butch clutched his chest and gasped for his last breath of air. As he fell to the ground, her father caught him and cradled him in his arms. He was gone. She watched the tears roll down her father's cheeks. Her Uncle Butch was a wonderful man, and Nancy felt it would be in his honor and memory to take his name as hers. She smiled. He would have liked that.

Butch's new clothes would be jeans, overalls, T-shirts, denim shirts, ball caps, and unfortunately, a new pair of boots—damn, she'd loved those boots!

Nancy had to bury the evidence, and it was a good thing, too. The feds were looking for a match to the boot prints made in the cottage that night. And they were looking for the murder weapon—the pitchfork. Before they left that night, Nancy had dug a deep hole in the back behind the apartment building. There were overgrown weeds and garbage thrown back there. She dug a big hole and dropped the boots and pitchfork into the hole. She covered them over lots of dirt and extra weeds and garbage. She was quite proud of herself—as usual.

"No one's gonna find them here!" Nancy said to herself. "Safe again!"

Well, maybe not *that* safe…

CHAPTER 39

The small apartment building on the other side of town was falling in such disrepair. The owner had died, and it was left to his only son. He didn't want the apartment building. He was living elsewhere—out of state. He quickly sold it to a developer. It was decided to become a strip mall with a few new stores and shops. It seemed like the answer to many locations that had old, dilapidated buildings. The land was great, but the old buildings had to come down. They needed to make way for new buildings, new stores. The location was slated for business development anyway. It would be an easy transition. It would certainly be a much more profitable moneymaker as well. So the tearing down of the apartment building and the clearing of the land began.

CJ Construction Company was the best construction company around. It was run by Charles "Chuck" Jacobs and his two sons, Sammy and Kenny. They made a good team. Their company had the reputation for being thorough, reasonable in price, and they got the job done right and in a timely fashion. Well…unless, of course, there were glitches to hold them up from completing their project. Mostly, things went as smoothly as planned. Occasionally, there would be issues that would occur. It happened, and Chuck Jacobs understood. Chuck was usually calm, flexible, and reasonable. He was never hotheaded. He could usually handle any problem that came his way. "It happens sometimes. You just have to roll with it and get through it. Getting upset and hotheaded will never solve anything."

And with this construction project, it did happen, and of course, it just so happened to be a Monday morning as well. Why do *all* the issues happen on a Monday morning?

The Jacobs were at the site bright and early Monday morning. Chuck and his two twin sons, Sammy and Kenny, worked with him side by side. Sammy and Kenny were identical twins and knew the construction business as well as their pops—as they called their dad, Chuck.

There was a commotion in the back at the site. The property was leveled, and the apartment building itself was gone. Rubble was being removed. It was just about finished. The excavator and bulldozer were in the back. The land in the back was being cleared. The dirt was being removed. The next steps would commence—leveling and digging.

Stan Bruber was directing Bill Noble in the excavator. Bill was about to claw down to remove some more dirt.

Stan started waving his hands and screaming, "Hey! Hey! Bill, stop! Stop!"

Bill stopped and killed the motor.

"What the hell, Stan! What gives?" Bill stuck his head out and yelled.

"Don't you see 'em?" Stan yelled at him and pointed to the ground.

"See what, man?" Bill yelled back in frustration.

"Boots! A pair of boots and something else… something wooden."

Chuck heard the yelling and ran over, his two sons following him.

"What's wrong? Why are we stopping, guys? What's up? What's holding you up, Stan? Bill? What's the problem?" Chuck just kept shooting out questions. He knew they were all on a tight schedule, and he wanted to get this part done today.

"Boss, I'm sorry, but Bill just uncovered a pair of boots and something wooden."

"Just a pair of boots? So what!" Chuck exclaimed.

"Well, boss, the excavator hit something wooden too. Part of it is sticking out of the ground. Come take a look."

Bill climbed down out of the excavator, and the three men and Chuck's sons went over to where the boots and a wooden/metal object was unearthed.

"Well, boss, what do you think?" Stan said.

"What the hell! There's a pair of old boots and… it looks like a farm tool. A pitchfork maybe?"

Chuck was rubbing his forehead and scowled. "Okay, you guys take a fifteen-minute coffee break and no longer!" Chuck bellowed. "And don't mention this to anyone just yet. We need to get a handle on this."

Both men headed over to the trailer to grab some coffee.

Chuck and Sammy and Kenny went over to the area where the boots and pitchfork were exposed in the dirt. They stood there staring at the objects. Chuck was figuring out what to do.

"What do you think, Dad?" Sammy asked. "Should we pull out the boots and pitchfork?"

Kenny added, "Hey, Dad, I don't mean to be morbid or anything, but I think that pitchfork has dried blood on it, and it looks like a lot."

"Ya," Chuck answered his son, "it kinda looks like it, doesn't it? Well, we're actually ahead of schedule. I think we gotta call the police department and tell them what we found—just to be sure. Dammit! Not what I wanted to come across today!"

Chuck started walking away as he pulled out his phone to make the call to the Covington Police Department. He needed to talk to the chief.

"Hey, boys, will one of you go and get a tarp from one of the trucks and cover up those items? The other one, just stay put and keep a watch on it. Thanks!" Chuck smiled at his two sons.

"Covington Police Department. Sergeant Abrams."

"Sergeant, this is Chuck Jacobs from CJ Construction Company. I need to talk to Chief Gordon immediately please."

"Okay, Mr. Jacobs," Sergeant Abrams said. "Everything okay?"

"No, not really," Chuck answered. "We're here at that apartment site on the other side of town. We've been clearing the ground. We're getting the ground prepped so the new strip mall can be put in. One of my men was using the excavator, and I think he uncovered something that Chief Gordon and the rest of you will be interested in seeing. We came across a couple of items that were obviously buried for a reason. You guys need to take a look at them. My sons covered them with a tarp. Nothing has been touched."

"Okay, Mr. Jacobs, I'll put you through to the chief. And I know you said it, but please don't have anyone touch or remove those items. Send your crew out on an early lunch, if you can. I'm sure the chief himself will want to come out with a couple of officers and investigate. I'll put you through. Hold on," Sergeant Abrams said.

"Will do—-and we won't, promise!" Chuck replied back. "And you know, Sergeant Abrams, you don't have to put me through to the chief. I explained everything to you already. Just send some guys out to the site, please—as quickly as possible. Unfortunately, I can't afford to give all these guys a real long lunch. I'm sure you understand, Sergeant Abrams."

"No problem, Mr. Jacobs. I'm sure the chief and a few officers will be there shortly. And thanks for letting us know. We appreciate it," the sergeant said.

"No problem, Sergeant," Chuck responded. As he hung up the phone, he said under his breath, "Dammit, this is really going to be a long day!

Sergeant Abrams hung up the phone and went back to Chief Gordon's office. He knocked on his door.

"Enter," Chief Gordon replied.

"Chief, I think we may have a break in those Dennyson murders!" Sergeant Abrams said.

Chief Gordon put down his pencil and looked up at Sergeant Abrams. "Oh really, Sergeant? Do explain."

Two squad cars pulled up to the site. Chief Gordon, along with Sergeant Abrams and a new patrolman—Mike Edgars came. Chuck's sons, Sammy and Kenny, stay back at the site where the two items were found.

"Chief," Chuck greeted the chief of police with a handshake. "Officers. This way."

Chuck led them back to where the items were uncovered.

"Nothing's been disturbed, right?" Chief Gordon asked Chuck.

"No, George, nothing's been touched," Chuck replied.

Chuck and George Gordon went way back. Unfortunately, Chuck's twin boys weren't always the most well-mannered boys in town. Both Sammy and Kenny had their growing pains and "boys will be boys" behavior. And the behavior lasted a little longer than Chuck and his wife, Jenny, would have liked. Punishments and lectures were given—more frequently than either parent wanted. And then there was the straw that broke the camel's back that brought all their raucous, out-of-control behavior to a screeching halt. Needless to say, Chuck and George talked, and Chuck asked George for a special request.

"George, I think it's time," Chuck said one evening. "I'm requesting that little favor."

"You sure, Chuck?" George just wanted to make sure he was hearing and understanding Chuck correctly.

"Ya, I'm positive," Chuck replied disappointedly.

"Okay." George knew it was probably time for a little tough love.

After that night, both boys were locked up in jail—separately. After that night, there were never any more problems or issues or shenanigans of any kind again. Both boys became model citizens. The fear and the scare of being put in jail and in separate cells was enough. Thanks to Chuck, their father, and George, things were quiet and calm—thank the Lord!

The police officers removed the items with rubber gloves—and very carefully. Both items, a pair of boots and a bloodied pitchfork, were carefully bagged and taken back to Covington Police Station.

Chief Gordon sent the officers on their way. He said he would see them back at the station to go over the new evidence, etc.

"Be careful with those two items, boys. I do *not* want anything to happen to them. Understand?" Chief Gordon reminded the officers.

"Right, Chief. Understood," Sergeant Abrams replied.

Chief Gordon would follow in the other cruiser. He just wanted to speak—to thank Chuck.

"Chuck, you have been a lifesaver today! With the anniversary of those two murders coming up, you may have just found the holy grail! I thank you and your eagle-eye crew!" George was extremely grateful for Chuck's amazing find. "You probably found the needle in the haystack that we've been hoping for—for a very long time! I thank you. And I owe you *big* time! I owe you a beer! Hell, I owe you a whole case of beer!" George exclaimed.

"No problem, Chief! My men found the items. I just called you guys. And a case of beer sounds *really* good right now!" Chuck laughed.

"Kidding aside, Chuck, please call us if you or your men find anything else, okay?" Chief Gordon pleaded.

"You bet, George. You know I will! I certainly will do that. I do hope those two items are everything you hope them to be," Chuck said with a hopeful grin.

"Oh, I think they are," George replied. "Thanks, Chuck."

And as Chuck was walking away from George, he yelled, "And I or my men *don't* find anything else! This is killing me!"

Chief Gordon waved his hand back at Chuck. "God, I sure do hope this town is done with killings! I'm gettin' too old for all of this!"

CHAPTER 40

In one of the rooms at Covington Police Station, two items were displayed on a long metal table. Chief Gordon and a couple of police officers were there. There was usually a DNA lab they usually outsourced to. Chief Gordon was waiting for someone to arrive. Olson Labs was the company that Covington Police Department usually used as a source—along with other surrounding police departments if needed. Olson Labs were reliable, thorough, and quick to get the materials analyzed, and the results were provided in a timely fashion. Usually Margaret Redding would be the representative coming. Margaret was a no-nonsense type of person, and there was never any question as to the reputation, confidentiality, and quality of the findings. She was good.

Margaret pulled into the Covington Police Station. As with every case, it was always confidential. And with this particular case, there was no exception.

Margaret entered into the front of the police station and was greeted by one of the officers.

"Ms. Redding, welcome. Right this way." The officer held out his hand to shake Margaret's and led her down a hallway and down the stairs.

Officer Brody led Margaret down the stairs to the room that Chief George Gordon was—and where the two items were laid out.

"Right this way, Ms. Redding. Chief Gordon is waiting for you," Officer Brody said.

"Thank you, Officer Brody," Margaret replied dryly.

Margaret knocked on the door and waited for a reply from Chief Gordon.

"Enter," Chief Gordon answered.

"Chief," Margaret greeted Chief Gordon with an extended hand.

"Margaret! Thank you for coming so quickly!" Chief Gordon replied.

"No problem! What do we have here, Chief?" Margaret looked at the objects in question.

"Well, I think we have found two objects that are linked to the Dennyson murders. I think these are the boots that made those footprints that were found in the cottage on the Dennyson Mansion property that night. And I'm going to make a prediction that this is the murder weapon that killed Melanie Dennyson, and these are the boots that were worn by the killer," Chief Gordon said.

"Okay. Well, we'll see," Margaret replied.

"So what now, Margaret?" Chief Gordon asked.

"Well, I'll wrap up—very carefully—these pieces and take them back to the lab. And actually, very exciting news for us—and for you today. Remember that grant I said I was working on? Well, I was awarded two grants. And upon receiving those grant monies, I was able to purchase a 'magic box.' This is so exciting for me—and the lab!" Margaret said so proudly.

"A magic box, Margaret? Really? One of those rapid DNA machines? That is exciting news!" Chief Gordon replied. "Congratulations, Margaret!" Chief Gordon held out his hand. "I've been reading up on those—fascinating! And expensive!" Chief Gordon chuckled. "I read about it recently. It can be hooked up to the National DNA Database and can provide DNA results in possibly ninety minutes! Is that true?" Chief Gordon asked Margaret.

"Yes, that is true, Chief! You have been read-ing!" Margaret answered with a laugh. "And we now have one!"

"That *is* good news! It couldn't have come at a more perfect time I'd say!" the chief said. "I'd like to sit down with you and talk for a bit. I want to run by a couple of other things with you—if that's all right?"

"Certainly," Margaret answered the chief. "Where do you want to go and talk?"

"Here's fine," Chief Gordon replied. "Please take a seat." Chief Gordon motioned Margaret.

There was another round table located on the side of the room, with four chairs placed around it.

"We can sit here," Chief Gordon said. "Hey, can I get you a cup of coffee, tea, water—anything?"

"A cup of coffee sounds great!" Margaret replied happily. "I could use a cup of strong coffee now!"

"We can definitely get you one of those! I think strong coffee is the *only* kind of coffee we have around here!" Chief Gordon laughed.

George left the room and went to get Margaret—and himself—a couple cups of coffee. Margaret took off her coat and went to sit down at the table, but she hesitated. She decided to go over to view the items that lay on the long metal table. It was always a puzzle to Margaret. She loved to piece puzzles together. Solving mysteries was Margaret's passion, her life, her job. She loved to make her predictions and see just how close she would be to the answers. Mostly she was usually spot-on and correct, which is why she was very well known and praised and respected in her field. She was just *that* good!

Margaret reached into her shoulder duffel bag and pulled out a pair of latex gloves. It was time to take a look.

Hmmm, Margaret was thinking. Definitely blood on the pitchfork. She was surprised it wasn't wiped off—not that it would have made a difference. Blood can still be detected, even if not seen by the human, naked eye. But murderers are sloppy. They still think just wiping off the blood is enough. Criminals/murderers do stupid things. They *don't* think, and that's why they are usually caught—just not always right away. Margaret continued thinking, *Those boots look fairly not worn too bad—that's good.* A manufacturer's label would be found on the boots somewhere. That could be traced—definitely possible.

George came back with two cups of coffee in large Styrofoam cups. He saw that Margaret was bending over the metal table looking at the two pieces of evidence. She was turning over the boots, obviously looking for a manufacturer.

"I couldn't remember how you take your coffee, so I brought you both cream and sugar," Chief Gordon said apologetically.

Margaret was in deep thought. "Black is fine, Chief. Thanks."

"Well, what do you think, Margaret?" George asked as he handed Margaret her cup of coffee.

"I think these boots belonged to a female. They're fairly new—maybe a couple of months old. They hadn't been worn much—the heels are not worn down too much. The shoelaces are not terribly worn—not frayed yet. I'm thinking if you have a photo of the footprint—or footprints—found in the cottage, these boots will match right up. Also, this pitchfork—when we get some blood samples off of it, it will be a match to Melanie Dennyson's DNA," Margaret said very matter-of-factly.

"Well, that's a lot of information to surmise in just a couple of minutes. Just think of the information you'd have for me if I was gone longer!" George laughed.

"So what *do* you think, Chief?" Margaret asked curiously.

"I think, Ms. Margaret, you are spot-on! I am in full agreement." Chief Gordon nodded.

"Okay, well, I'll get these back to the lab and call you later," Margaret said. "What are you going to do next, Chief?"

"Well, we know that Nancy Smith and Gina Brown lived in that apartment complex. With that size 10 in the boots, I'm gonna say those were Ms. Brown's boots. Now we gotta find Ms. Brown!" George concluded.

George and Margaret finished up their conversation. With the help of a police officer, the items were carefully preserved and wrapped up to make their safe trip back to Olson Labs.

"Now take good care of those items, Margaret." George pleaded. "They're our *only* hope and solution to all this. God, I wish you could just transport and bring that DNA machine here—hook it up—and not have to move this precious cargo."

"Well, it does fit on a tabletop—the DNA machine. It's the size of a desktop computer," Margaret replied matter-of-factly.

"It does?" George answered hopefully and with a smile. "Can you bring it here?"

"I don't know…maybe. I think I can. It would take a little time to hook it up. I will need to bring the vials, cartridges, too, to collect the samples. I'll check to see how long it will take to hook up to the National DNA Database from here. Hopefully, that wouldn't be too much of a problem. Let me make a couple of phone calls. I might be able to make your wish come true," Margaret answered.

"Thank you, fairy godmother!" Chief Gordon laughed as he clapped his hands together.

There was hope.

CHAPTER 41

Harry was ready to make that phone call to Chief Gordon at the station. Josh was sitting with him in their motel room. The last two days were incredible—surreal. Luck was on their side with this visit.

"Hey, Jennifer, it's Harry. Could you please put me back to the chief? I need to talk with him right away." Harry felt numb and tired. "Ya, I'll wait," Harry replied.

Chief Gordon was back in his office when the call came in.

"Chief, Harry on line 4 for you," Jennifer said calmly.

"Okay, thanks, Jennifer."

The chief picked up line 4. "Harry!" Chief Gordon spoke enthusiastically. "How are you and Josh doing up there? Are you still at Hollingsworth? What do you two boys have for me? Good news, I hope! I haven't heard from you. I was starting to worry about you two!"

"Sorry, Chief! A lot has been happening up here at Hollingsworth. And I think I have some breaking news that you'll be very happy to hear about!" Harry replied proudly.

"Well, that *is* great news! I think I have some new breaking news for you and Josh, too!" George replied, equally proud to say.

And as Sherlock Holmes used to say, "The game is afoot!"

Chief George Gordon was sitting at his desk. He was working on his late lunch. *Thank God for Jayne and Rosewood Grille and Café*, he thought to himself.

Things were going to happen very quickly within the next few days. And hopefully, on the day of the anniversary of the Dennyson murders, he'd have some final news to share! Here's hoping.

CHAPTER 42

Harry traded the rental sedan and upgraded to a roomier van. He and Josh had a few more passengers going back with them this time. Dr. Will Goodwin, Bea, Nurse Brenda, and the orderly Adam. Dr. Goodwin packed everything he thought he would need—medicinewise—for Bea.

And he brought Adam along for good measure. Surprisingly, Bea wasn't too hard to handle. She didn't put up much of a fuss. Although she never took day trips or traveled, she was unbelievably calm. Maybe down deep inside her psyche, Bea wanted this to be all over too. The main factor for Bea's calmness, of course, was Brenda—and Adam as well. They both, especially Brenda, was Bea's solid rock, her solitude, maybe her version of her sanity. Bea's calmness *was* Brenda.

Everyone was heading back to Covington. Harry, and probably Josh too, wished for a "crystal ball" moment. To be able to know that everything would finally be over—the murders would finally be solved. It would be indeed a dream come true. God, Harry hoped everything would run smoothly…

Brenda sat right next to Bea, holding her hand like always. Bea held tight to Teddy, and Adam sat on the other side of Bea. Dr. Goodwin chose to sit in the far back of the van. That way, he would be invisible and be able to write some notes, read more information, catch a quick nap, and collect his thoughts about the upcoming days ahead. His thoughts—first and foremost—would be to protect his patient, Bea. She was very special to him, although only very few, if any, knew just why.

Will's thoughts took him back to the happiest days of his life—with his wife, Joyce, and their beautiful baby daughter, Laurel. Tears began to well up in his eyes as he thought back about those beautiful days long ago and just how blissfully happy he and Joyce were. It took such a long time—years—before Joyce and Will could conceive. Several miscarriages gave them both very little hope of ever having a child of their own. They gave up trying—especially with the close call Joyce had that last time. They then talked and decided that maybe it was time to consider adoption—and they did.

Little Laurel was a beautiful little angel that came into their life. It was a miracle, too, just how—with relative ease—the process from start to finish was. Joyce and Will heard about so many horror stories of how couples had to wait—years even—for adopting. Of course, the cost was very expensive. There was a lot of paperwork to fill out, matching up possible couples to infants/children. If the mother was giving her child up for adoption, she could very easily change her mind—right up to the delivery and maybe even after. Will heard of that happening—occasionally, but it did happen. Will and Joyce both wanted an infant—a little girl if at all possible. And they got their wish. Laurel was a beautiful little bundle of joy. She was pink, her cheeks were rosy, her hair was actually the color of Joyce's—a sandy blonde. And if that wasn't perfect enough, little Laurel had the most beautiful big brown eyes to match Joyce's as well. Will and Joyce's life was perfect. Their family was complete. They were so happy.

One day, while Joyce had Laurel on the floor on a fuzzy, cozy blanket, she noticed something different—something odd about Laurel. Something just wasn't right.

Joyce yelled for Will. "Will, come here quickly please!" There was panic in Joyce's voice.

Will was in the kitchen studying for an upcoming exam.

"Honey, what's wrong?" Will came rushing into the living room. "Honey?" Will asked in a raised voice.

"Something's wrong with Laurel." Joyce started to cry. "Will, there's something wrong. I know it!"

Will thought that Joyce was probably just over-tired—exhausted with being a new mother. She was putting all her efforts and time into little Laurel. There was never any time left for herself, for anything or anyone else. "Honey, you're just imagining it. I'm sure Laurel's fine."

Will patted her shoulder and tried to comfort her. She was tired. Will was tired.

"No! Will, something's not right. I can't put my finger on it, but something *is* wrong with Laurel!" Joyce raised her voice. She was insistent.

Will knew there was no reasoning with her. So he just comforted her and said they could make an appointment right away with Laurel's pediatrician. It was too late to call that day, so Will would make the call right away in the morning.

Laurel was just three months old. It was hard to tell if her development had been anything other than normal. She was growing and gaining weight. Her hearing seemed to be normal, but Joyce was right. Something was off.

Little Laurel was diagnosed with having autism. Most children are diagnosed with autism between two and six months old. Studies have found that boys tend to be impacted with autism more so than girls. And sometimes, the characteristics and potential signs of autism go undiagnosed. They may hide in plain sight.

Joyce was right. Tests were done on Laurel, and she displayed several signs of autism spectrum disorder. They, along with the pediatrician, hoped it wouldn't get more severe as Laurel grew. There was promise, Dr. Graham explained to Will and Joyce. Catching it early, with applied behavior analysis or ABA therapy and other intervention methods, and implementing these procedures would be critical in Laurel's development.

Laurel was starting to walk. Joyce had to watch her constantly. Sometimes, Laurel would bolt. It was hard enough to keep up with a "normal" developed toddler, but with a toddler that had autism, it was tremendously more difficult. And the reasoning factor just wasn't present.

Joyce would take Laurel to a nearby playground. Joyce was with Laurel one day. They were near one of the toddlers' swings. She took Laurel out of the swing. Laurel wanted down. Joyce was just catching up with Cassie. They weren't deep in conversation—just casual "how are yous, what have you been up tos." Laurel squirmed out of Joyce's grasp, and she flew—bolted. There was a duck pond nearby. "Why did they put that pond there near the children's playground—so close!" Joyce repeated over and over again.

Laurel got too close and tumbled into the pond. Ducks were squawking. Joyce ran and screamed "Laurel!" Joyce ran, practically tumbling herself. She ran in and scooped up Laurel as quickly as she could grab her. The water was ice cold—even though the spring weather was mild and breezy. Laurel had somehow hit her head.

It was too late. Joyce had someone call 911, and EMS came quickly. She tried to resuscitate Laurel. Joyce kept trying—crying in between attempts. The EMS came and took over, but it was too late. Little Laurel was gone.

From that day on, it was like living a nightmare—day in and day out. Joyce could never get a decent full night's rest. She had nightmares every time she dozed off. The doctor gave her sedatives. Will couldn't sleep either. Both understood all too well the results of sleep deprivation. Plus, Joyce kept hearing a child's cry at night. She would jump out of bed at night and run somewhere…anywhere…to where she heard the cry. And then the crying stopped. It was silent. Will couldn't deal with the disturbances any. He needed his sleep. He needed to be fully awake for his exams. He and Joyce didn't sleep in the same bedroom any longer. He said it would be just temporary—just until he completed his exams. That promise never happened. Then the fighting started. Will and Joyce were fighting all the time now. It was terrible. Neither one ever got over the death of their little angel, Laurel.

Joyce ended up divorcing Will. She just couldn't take it anymore—living in that house with the constant memories of Laurel. She knew she had seen the ghostly apparition of her little girl too. She even tried to communicate with Laurel but was unsuccessful. Joyce felt she would go crazy. At times, she felt she was already there. Will was hurting too. He was suffering—Joyce knew. But men, they handle grief differently. They keep it all inside. In the end, divorce was imminent.

Joyce ended up moving down South with her sister, Meg. It was probably for the best. Will wished her well and made sure that Joyce agreed to keep up with her grief therapy sessions with Dr. Marcus. He was a college roommate of Will's and actually a friend as well. When Will heard that Joyce wanted to move down South and live with her sister, Will made the phone call to Jared. They kept in contact over the years, and Will was very grateful they did. He never thought in a million years that Jared's services would ever be needed, not ever—until now.

Back to reality.

CHAPTER 43

Will bounced back to reality.

"Dr. Goodwin, you okay?" Brenda turned around and was trying to get Will's attention. "Harry's stopping to get some food. Do you want anything, Dr. Goodwin?" Brenda asked again and was looking concernedly at Will. She patted his arm.

"Oh, I'm sorry. I guess I probably dozed off for a while. I know I was in deep thought. I'm sorry. What was your question, Brenda?" Will asked apologetically.

Brenda repeated herself, "We're going to stop for food. Would you like a burger, a sandwich, anything, a drink?" Brenda asked patiently.

"Yes! That sounds great! Thank you! Anything sounds good!" Will answered appreciatively.

Harry pulled into a fast-food restaurant and into a parking space. He thought it would be easier to get everyone's requests, then go in and order.

"I'll go, Harry," Josh offered.

"I can help," Adam added in. "I need to stretch my legs a little."

"That would be great! Thanks, Adam!" Josh answered.

It didn't take long to get food orders. Harry just decided they could just as easily eat, peacefully, in the parking lot and enjoy their lunch. Bathroom breaks could be taken, and legs could be stretched.

Bea was fine, too. She loved her hamburger, fries, and strawberry milkshake. She was content. Brenda was surprised just how content she was. Brenda brought along all Bea's favorites—her favorite books, some drawing pads and colored pencils, a coloring book, and a new box of crayons. It was a surprise Brenda had for Bea: two new coloring books, always about animals, woodland animals, farm animals—it didn't matter. She bought Bea a new box of sixty-four-count crayons too. Bea clapped her hands together and smiled the broadest smile Brenda had ever remembered seeing. Brenda loved Bea like she was her very own.

Chief Gordon was impatiently waiting in his office for the impending arrival of Harry and Josh and their precious cargo.

Harry made one more stop before arriving in Covington. Brenda took Bea to the restroom while the gentlemen waited patiently in the van.

"Okay, boys," Harry said. "This is the final stop before reaching Covington. Now would be your chance to go to the little boys' room." Harry chuckled.

"Right, boss!" Josh answered with a smirk. "Got it!"

Adam contemplated and replied, "Okay, maybe better go then." And out the car door he went.

Dr. Goodwin took the break time to ask Harry a question. "Detective Trimble," Dr. Goodwin asked, "may I ask—just to confirm—what the plans will be when we reach Covington?" Will had a worried look on his face and a tremble in his tone of voice.

Harry replied matter-of-factly, "Josh and I will drop you, Bea, Nurse Brenda, and Adam off at your hotel so you can freshen up. Within an hour or so, we'll come back and pick you three up and back to the station for our meeting with Chief Gordon. Dr. Goodwin, please know that we are all in unison in keeping Bea's—or Gina's, rather—well-being our utmost concern and priority. We know that she is in an extremely delicate state of mind. And to add, Doctor, you have to understand that our first and foremost priority is utilizing Gina to help us solve these horrendous murders once and for all! Gina Smith, I know in my gut, is the very key to all of this. And it is Gina that will be able to pin Nancy Brown to these murders. Then we will finally be able to put all this to bed. The Dennyson family and descendants, alive and deceased, will be able to rest in peace."

Dr. Goodwin caught that last thought and replied, "The Dennyson family...'alive *and* deceased,' Detective?"

"You heard me, Doctor, alive *and* deceased! The last living descendent—a Ms. Reagan Dennyson—and the woman who along with her inherited Dennyson Mansion, Irene Buckley, have had quite a bit of ghostly ruckus going on at the mansion. It escalates more so around the anniversary of these

murders. Throughout other times, supernatural phenomena occur as well. Now don't get me wrong, Doc,
I'm not some sort of a ghost-chasing, spirit-medium
nut! And with that being said, many people—including various staff members at the Covington Police
Station and Dennyson Mansion have seen and heard
some very strange and unexplainable things at that
site. So I'm just sayin'," Harry replied.

Brenda, Bea, and Adam had just returned to the
van, so the conversations stopped abruptly. After the
three got settled back into their seats, Harry started
the van back up, and off they drove on the last leg of
their trip.

It would have taken a much shorter time if it
was just Harry and Josh traveling, but with the extra
people, it did take longer. Harry, along with Josh,
just wanted to get back to home base. They were anxious to get things rolling.

Harry dropped Will, Adam, Brenda, and Bea
off at the Covington Inn. It was the nicest—and
only—hotel in town. The Covington Inn used to be
the old Covington Bank and Trust until it was sold
in the early 1900s. It was purchased by the Malleys—
John and Marie. They transformed the bank and
trust into a beautiful inn. And it had been in existence ever since. The owners had both passed away,
and it was now being run by John and Marie's daughter, Sarah, and her husband, Mark. They were both
as gracious of hosts as Sarah's parents both had been.
They greeted everyone with much warmth.

Sarah and Mark made a few minor improvements and added a quaint patio and small English garden. It really added to the Covington Inn charm. The only other adjustment that was done years ago was to the basement and cellar area. There had always been peculiar noises being heard randomly, voices would be heard, and sometimes things would go missing. Staff would always get a creepy feeling going into the basement and cellar area. Closing up late at night, staff would experience lights going on and off. And then one night, Jessie and Dan were straightening up in the dining area. The kitchen was all cleaned up, the chef went home, and a random gunshot was heard coming from the cellar. When the inn was Covington Bank and Trust, that was the area where the vault was located. There were always stories, urban legends, that an argument had ensued between the owner, Henry Shaw, and his partner, Samuel Thomas. Then a gunshot was heard. The partner, Mr. Thomas, was found guilty of killing the bank owner, Henry Shaw. Samuel Thomas was put to death, but up to his dying moment, he swore he didn't kill his partner, Henry Shaw. He claimed there was another individual down there with them. This other individual was never found. The police only found the owner's dead body and the partner kneeling down next to him. The other individual, a Mr. Theodore Albright, was never found. Mr. Thomas said he just vanished—as if through a wall or secret passageway. Police searched and never found a secret passageway. After that, the vault and room leading into it were sealed up. But to this day, at a specific time of night, voices may be heard—like people arguing and then a single gunshot.

The food was always the charm that brought everyone to the inn. Of course, anyone could dine in the inn's dining room or eat out on the beautiful patio area. Chef William was well known to the area and created an amazing, wonderful menu, along with the addition of delectable wines from various local wineries. He added a five-course chef's choice tasting menu. Chef's choice was added to the menu this year. He also has wine tastings and specific food features quarterly/seasonally during the year. Holiday gatherings, Sunday brunch, and weekend specials all added to the inn's special appeal. Covington Inn was a wonderful addition to the enchanted charm of the town. It added to the quaintness and charisma. But along with that charm and all those wonderful old, seasoned buildings of Covington came the additional baggage of spirits who liked to dwell there.

It had been said, on occasion, a guest or a staff member might see John or Marie walking about. The gardens were expanded, and the patio and surrounding area were added. One might witness Marie walking about on one of her early evening strolls. She loved her little garden and all the beautiful flowers. Her daughter, Sarah, and husband, Mark, and the staff felt that Marie was very pleased with the beautiful changes. The sitting area, where guests could relax and enjoy piano music provided by Mr. David Markham, was John's favorite place to haunt.

At nighttime, notes on the piano would be heard playing. Of course, no one was in there. John always loved the piano and music. Although he never played the piano, one could sometimes hear notes playing. It was felt that it was John playing the notes and feeling regretful that he never took up piano lessons. "John, you should take up the piano. Martha could teach you," Marie had often said to her endearing husband.

"I know, Marie. But there is so much else needed to be done here at the inn. My enjoyment for the piano—learning how to play—should have been done so much earlier in my life—not now," John would always reply. "I do love that beautiful mahogany grand piano. I will never part with it—ever!" John would always add.

CHAPTER 44

Harry dropped off Dr. Goodwin, Brenda and Gina (Bea) and Adam at the inn. He'd called several days ago and talked with Sarah. He explained that he needed a couple of rooms, adjoining if possible, for three guests. Without going into too much detail, Harry asked Sarah to take extra special care of these guests. He told Sarah to get them whatever they wanted or needed and send the tab to him and charge the Covington Police Department He also added that these guests and their names were to be kept confidential. Sarah and Mark were always understanding if there were any specific requests or requirements concerning their guests at the inn. In this particular situation, as in the past (with the Covington Police Department and Harry), Sarah and Mark never asked too many questions, and requests were always honored. Harry appreciated that. Through several conversations with Sarah and Mark, Harry always thanked them profusely for being understanding and compliant. Sarah always had this uncanny way of just knowing when to ask and when not to ask and when to just keep everything between the inn and the Covington Police Department. It was all good.

Like always, Sarah met her guests upon their arrival, and today was no exception.

Dr. Goodwin and Adam shared a room, and Brenda and Gina/Bea shared a room. Sarah was able to provide an adjoining room as well. One of the improvements that Sarah and Mark made in the inn was to have one adjoining set of rooms on each floor. Sometimes, guests requested these rooms, and it was a good call on Mark's part to install them a couple of years ago. Mark had very good insight and business sense when it came to running a hotel. Sarah was grateful for Mark's insight and knowledge. They balanced each other out very well, which many would say why the Covington Inn was such a lovely place to stay and so successful. Mark also created the website for the inn. It was a site that was easy to navigate through. It was pleasing to the eye and quite functional. Restaurant events would be advertised, room and restaurant bookings could be placed, and even a space for Chef William's corner for upcoming feasts, cooking tips, cookware and kitchenware endorsements, and usually a recipe, or two, of the month feature. People had displayed wonderful feedback and comments of the Covington Inn, and there was talk of the inn being featured on one of the national morning shows in the near future. Needless to say, Sarah and Mark and Chef William were very excited. It would be wonderful for the city of Covington, and something other than the murders for Covington to be noted for. Finally, if and when these murders of Covington were solved, the dark umbrella that hung over this city would disappear. Sarah and Mark and Chef William might become Covington's heroes. Here's hoping.

Mark led Dr. Goodwin, Adam, Brenda, and Bea up to their rooms. Bea smiled when Mark opened the door to her and Brenda's room. Bea smiled joyfully at the beautiful soft and lovely shade of golden butter yellow-painted walls and an accent wall with wallpaper of a small, dainty floral pattern. It was a room that was very inviting and welcoming. The gentlemen had a rich navy-blue-and-beige room. And their accent wall was a pleasant striped pattern with a touch of dark red.

Brenda had Bea lie down to nap for a bit while Brenda relaxed in a small cozy easy chair to read for a while. The door to the adjoining room where Adam and Will were staying was open a crack.

Adam was conversing with Will. Will thought this would be a good opportunity to get to know Adam a little better. Sometimes, in grave situations, one had to look for the silver lining. Will often enjoyed talking with his staff, although this wasn't the most ideal of situations to have that occur.

"So, Dr. Goodwin," Adam started the conversation, "what do you make of all of this?"

Adam was sitting in one of the easy chairs in the room, and Will was sitting at the small round table nestled in the corner. He had some papers spread out and was obviously working on something. Will looked up from what he was doing. Adam, at that moment, thought that maybe that was the wrong time to start a conversation.

Adam immediately apologized, "I'm sorry, Dr. Goodwin. I didn't mean to interrupt you while you're working."

Will looked and responded, "No, no, it's quite all right, Adam. I'm just jotting some notes down pertaining to the developments in Bea's—or rather Gina's case." Dr. Goodwin chuckled. "I have to remember… it's Gina, not Bea. So much to remember, so much to ingest," Will said as he shook his head.

Adam responded back, "I know what you mean. There has been so much happening so fast. I wonder how this will all end."

"I can't say for certain, Adam, how this will all end. And you are correct to say that it is a lot to take in, isn't it? As you know, Adam, we have patients that sometimes have very complicated histories. And we deal with each and every one as best as we can. And with that being said, this case with Gina/Bea and her horrendous past and the very touchy incidences surrounding her…well, let's just say, this tops the chart for an unusual and bizarre situation, to say the least!" Will replied in bewilderment.

"It does, Doctor, this certainly does," Will agreed, shaking his head.

Will looked over to the adjoining door that was ajar and thought to himself that this particular discussion should probably stop. He didn't want Gina/Bea to possibly overhear any of their sensitive conversation about her. That would be inappropriate. Will opted to change their conversation and ask Will how his schooling was coming along.

CHAPTER 45

Harry and Josh got back to the station. They were both exhausted, and both probably would have opted for a nap, a long nap, to rejuvenate. But not now. Chief Gordon was impatiently waiting to talk to Harry and Josh. The other day, Chief Gordon talked to Harry on the phone, and both debriefed each other with their most incredible information. It would be hard saying which piece of information was more incredible—both were just as much an intricate part of this puzzle. Each acclimation was equally part of the holy grail of findings. And soon, with the additional intricate pieces of this puzzle, the Dennyson murders could be solved. The Dennyson files could be labeled "solved" and put to bed.

Harry and Josh joined Chief Gordon in his office. Harry knocked on the door.

"Come in, gentlemen," Chief Gordon replied. "Welcome back home. I've been patiently waiting for the two of you. Glad to see you back. If you would, Josh, please close the door. Wow, you boys look like hell! I'm sorry, I know you both have worked very hard on this case. But every step we take in the right direction brings us all that much closer to solving these crimes. And it looks like we are very close to doing just that. I am very pleased with the both of you and the detective work you both so diligently put forth." Chief Gordon smiled at both Harry and Josh.

"Thank you, sir," Harry and Josh replied together in unison.

Chief Gordon motioned to Harry and Josh to sit down at the two chairs facing his desk. "Please have a seat, gentlemen. It's time to plan out the rest of this operation. Before I begin, I must direct a few questions to you, Josh." Chief Gordon looked at Josh.

"Okay, Chief," Josh replied reluctantly. "Have I done something wrong?"

"Oh my goodness, no, Josh. You have not," replied the chief. The chief continued, "Josh, this case, as you know, is of the utmost important to us. We need to handle this as with all of our serious cases—with kid gloves," Chief Gordon said candidly.

"I understand, Chief. I really do," Josh replied. Josh was thinking he knew exactly where this portion of the conversation was going.

Chief Gordon continued, "With the additional fact that you are intimately linked to Ms. Dennyson, I need to ask you, Josh, if you will be able to continue to separate this case from your relationship with Reagan. I need you to be honest with me, Josh. If you have any hesitation at all with any of this, Josh, I need to know right now." Chief Gordon pointed his finger on his desk.

"Chief, if I may interject?" Harry proceeded, "Josh has continuously, since the very beginning of this case and with all the new developments, kept his relationship with Ms. Dennyson and this case separate. Everything has been kept confidential and will continue to be kept confidential. I have never questioned Josh's loyalty and professionalism in regards to this case." Harry stumbled over his words a little. "I just wanted you to know that, Chief," Harry finished.

Josh looked over at Harry with a warm sense of companionship and comradery. He always felt a closeness with his partner, but at that moment, Josh knew Harry's "declaration of faith" in him was real and sincere. Josh was touched. He smiled at Harry, and Harry nodded his head and smiled back as he put his hand on Josh's shoulder.

"And I understand that, Harry, I really do— and I agree with you totally. But again from this day forward, things will escalate and move very quickly. More information will be coming out. It may become more difficult for Reagan. I just need to hear this from Josh. Well, Josh?" The chief looked over to Josh for a response.

"Chief, I am fine—really," Josh said firmly and reassuringly. "You will have no problems with me." Josh tried to sound as convincing as possible. "I know and understand fully just how critical this case is. My relationship with Reagan—Ms. Dennyson—will not cloud my professional judgment. And, please believe me when I say this most sincerely—Reagan wants this case solved just as much as we do. I think, Chief, after you talk with Reagan—whenever that time will be—you will be convinced and reassured as well."

"Well, okay then," Chief Gordon replied. "I thank you, Josh, for your candidness and reassurance. Then I guess we can now move forward on this case," Chief Gordon answered with a smile.

Chief Gordon explained how the DNA process would be happening, which brought him to the next topic of discussion.

"I sent out, again—just like we do with every anniversary of these murders—the photos of Nancy Brown and before, an additional photo of Gina Smith. After finding Gina Smith, obviously, I sent out just Nancy Brown's photo. And along with Ms. Brown's photo, I sent out a composite photo of what Nancy Brown could or may look like today. With that being said, through a very good suggestion, it could even be a possibility that Ms. Brown could look like a male. On every anniversary of these murders, photos of these two broads will be surfacing everywhere. And Ms. Brown, more than likely, becomes very nervous. It is a good and likely possibility that she may have changed her physical appearance drastically. All this girl wants to do is blend in. I've sent off these photo composites to all the police and sheriff departments—city, county, and neighboring states. Somebody has to have seen her—or him—somewhere."

Somewhere…

CHAPTER 46

It was Thursday morning. Jake was working on a vehicle when Sheriff Middaugh drove up.

Butch was off that day. The garage wasn't full—just one vehicle needed some repairs.

Jake heard footsteps on the gravel leading up to the garage. He slid out from under the car and wiped his hands off with a rag.

"Mornin', Sheriff. What can I do for you today? Cars all working okay?" Jake asked Sheriff Middaugh.

Sheriff Middaugh chuckled. "Mornin', Jake. Ya, they're all working great, thanks to you and Butch. You both keep our vehicles and many others in this town purring just like kittens!"

Sheriff Ray Middaugh was going to approach this subject very carefully. "You alone today, Jake? Is Butch here?" Sheriff Middaugh asked.

"Just me, Sheriff. Butch has the day off today. What can I help you with? I'm sure you just didn't want to stop for a visit—although you know you are always welcome!" Jake exclaimed with a smile.

Jake and the sheriff went way back. Sheriff Middaugh and Jake's father were always very good friends. Jake's father, Bernie, passed away several

275

years ago, and Jake took over the garage. Jake always was there with his dad, helping him on weekends and after school. The sheriff and Jake's father, Bernie, liked to go fishing. They were very excited one very early morning. They couldn't wait to get out into the lake for some good fishing. The weather was perfect. Bernie had a decent fishing boat. He took such pride in that boat, Ray remembered. It was an older boat that someone in town was selling—it needed some repairs. But Bernie looked forward to doing the repairs himself. The engine needed help—as Bernie said. No challenge was too big for Bernie! Finally, the repairs were completed, and it was time to take her out for a run. Bernie was so excited. And one morning, along with his best friend, Ray, he took her out. Ray remembered it was a glorious morning—a perfect morning. The lake was a sheet of glass. It was early morning. The quietness of the day was just starting. He and Bernie watched the sun come up as they were sipping their coffee sitting in that boat. It was a perfect morning. The stillness of the early morning, the cool, brisk air, the birds, some animals stirring in the brush. There just wasn't anything better than that! And then Bernie's heart attack. Ray had suggested many times to Bernie to go see Doc to get a look at that ticker. Bernie said he would—right after he got the boat repaired. After finishing their cups of coffee, Bernie had stood up to reach for his fishing rod. He felt pain in his chest and then his left arm— Ray remembered.

Bernie stumbled and collapsed onto the floor of the boat. Thank God that Ray always took his radio with him—even on his days off. Ray quickly radioed. He quickly rowed to shore. The squad was there. But it was too late. Bernie had passed. It took a long time for Ray to get over Bernie's passing. They were going to retire together, go down South and fish all day every day.

They were both so looking forward to those wonderful days ahead. No more car and truck repairs for Bernie and no more sheriff headaches for Ray—just peace and quiet, some good bourbon and whiskey, and fishing.

"Dammit," was all Ray could say to himself for many days, weeks, and months following. "Not good timin', not good timin', ol' friend," Ray would say to himself.

After that day, Jake couldn't even look at that boat. "I'm gonna burn that ol' son-of-a-bitchin' boat!"

Sheriff Middaugh took Jake home after the funeral. The boat was sitting in the back behind the garage.

"Now, Jake, you don't mean that. It wasn't the boat's fault that your father died. You know your father loved that boat. It was his pride and joy. If you want, I'll haul it out of here. You can decide what you want to do with it later—when you have some time to think more clearly," Ray said to Jake as he put his arm around him.

With tears in his eyes, Jake said to Ray, "No, you're right, Sheriff. I guess I don't mean that. I don't want to burn it. Sheriff, I want you to have the boat. Dad would want you to have it. Please take it, Sheriff." Jake started to cry. "Sheriff, please. She's yours. I know Dad would want you to have her."

Ray hugged Jake. He always watched over Jake from that day on as if Jake was his very own. He promised Bernie, that very night—in his prayers—that he would. And Ray never went back on his promises.

It was so hard for Jake to remove his dad's name from the garage. Instead, he put up "IN MEMORY." It helped.

"Jake, can you take a few moments away from that car? I need to discuss something with you. It's pretty important," Sheriff Middaugh asked solemnly.

"Sure, Sheriff, no problem."

Jake motioned Sheriff Middaugh to his office in the back of the garage. It was his dad's office—and now it was Jake's.

"Sheriff, can I get you something? Coffee, a soda?"

"No, I'm good, Jake. Just some conversation for a bit will do."

"Okay, well, have a seat. What do you want to talk about—discuss?" Jake said curiously.

"Butch," Sheriff Middaugh said very frankly.

"Butch? What about Butch?" Jake replied with much surprise. "He's a good worker. I never had any trouble with him since he came to work here. What's the problem, Sheriff?"

"Well…to start, I and detectives and police in another town called Covington think Butch is an alias…and in a whole lot of very serious trouble," Sheriff Middaugh said to start.

"Really, I would have never thought that, Sheriff," Jake replied. "Really, Sheriff?"

"Ya, I'm afraid so, Jakey," as Sheriff Middaugh and Jake's father used to call him. "Take a look at these photos sent over to us from Central."

Sheriff Middaugh handed Jake three photos, all of Nancy Brown—one as Nancy Brown as she was, a composite of what she might look like now, and then as a male. The third photo shocked Jake almost right out of his chair.

"Jesus! I think that's Butch, Sheriff!" Jake exclaimed. "I wasn't prepared for that, Sheriff—not in a million years!" Jake was truly in shock.

"Yep, me too!" Sheriff Middaugh agreed.

The sheriff and Jake talked at length.

"Jake, I need you to do something for me. This is crucial and very important," Sheriff Middaugh asked as he looked at Jake very seriously.

"What do you need for me to do, Sheriff?" Jake asked.

"I need for you to get a blood sample from Butch. I don't care how you get it, but I need it by morning. Can you do that, son, without any issue? You can't—and I can't stress this enough—ever lead on that you know anything about this, his identity…anything! Your life may be in serious danger. From what I understand, under pressure, this Nancy

Brown—Butch—can and will become dangerous if for any reason she/he feels threatened. Do you understand, Jake?"

"Ya…I guess, Sheriff. But really? Butch? Butch and I are pretty close, and…wow, I guess I just can't wrap my head around this, Sheriff. It's pretty hard to believe and all…" Jake was really finding this impossible to believe.

"Can you do it, son? If for any reason that you think you can't, then we'll have to find another way. But this would be the easiest." Sheriff Middaugh looked at Jake with hope.

The sheriff pulled out a glass vial and handed it to Jake. "Here, when you get the sample, you'll need to collect it in this vial. And then give me a call, and I'll come collect it. Okay?"

Jake took the glass vial from the sheriff. He held it gently and looked at it. *This little glass vial,* Jake thought, *would be Butch's demise.* He really didn't want to do this to Butch. He liked Butch. They were buddies. Butch was a great guy and really the only good friend that he's had in a long while. He couldn't be a girl—lady. That photo was wrong. It could be a twin, a doppelganger, someone else! Butch was a good guy. Jake could never believe that Butch would hurt a fly—ever! He didn't even have a temper. Jake remembered that guy that had come in with a car issue. It was right around when Butch started working for Jake. He was new, but he was a quick learner. Jake felt he could fix the issue with this guy's car. Butch needed to finish something up—not too serious. They guy came back in and was madder than ever. I watched from the office to see how Butch would handle the guy. It was important to be able to handle whatever issue came into the garage. Butch handled it great. He was calm and fixed the problem right away. He offered his hand in a handshake and apologized to the customer. They ended up laughing, and the guy even apologized back to Butch for being an ass about the whole thing.

"Okay, Sheriff. I'll try—it won't be easy, but I'll try," Jake answered reluctantly.

"That's my boy, and don't lead on about me comin' here today or anything about our conversation or anything. Understand?" Sheriff Middaugh pleaded.

"Understood, Sheriff," Jake said sadly. Jake felt like he was losing a best friend...his best friend.

CHAPTER 47

"Dammit!" Jake said to himself. He'd stayed longer than he had planned that night at the garage. Jake was hoping to get out of there by four and head to the Rusty Bucket. It was ten-cent wing night, and a bucket of beers was $6 tonight. The waitress—and sometimes bartender—Lindsay was there. He liked Lindsay—she was fun. He kind of thought that she liked him too. Jake didn't think he was bad looking. Pretty decent for a guy, he thought. He was okay, he thought. Lindsay was a fox, and Jake wanted to get to know her better—not just at the bar but maybe on a date sometime. One day, Jake thought many times, *I need to leave this town, go to someplace new, and maybe find a new career and settle down, have some kids.* Maybe that time was coming sooner than he expected.

"Damn," Jake said himself again. Jake felt really awful about having to deceive Butch and all. Jake liked him—a lot. But shit, he's a girl! Jake never would have figured that ever—in a million years!

Jake held the vial and turned it round and round. He tried to figure just how he would get that sample of blood. He knew what to do—he and the sheriff had worked it all out—but Jake knew that sometimes not everything works out as planned. It may not go as planned.

He went out into the garage. The sheriff had given Jake two vials. He said if he could get several samples—if possible—that would be great. Jake went over to clean up the area around the car he was working on. He swept up the area with a broom. He had his glass of beer in one hand and set it on the edge of the car's hood. He wasn't thinking. Because of the wetness of the glass, it slid right off the hood of the car and crashed to the floor in a million pieces—big and small.

"Shit! Goddammit!" Jake yelled out loud. "Now I'll be here for another damn hour!" he exclaimed in a frustrating voice. He started to sweep up the shattered glass and stopped abruptly. "Shit, what am I doing?" Jake spoke out loud to himself. "Karma, fate—I'll just leave it. I'll be here in the morning, and so will Butch. Maybe this will work out after all."

Jake went back to his office to clean up, put the photos away in his desk—the vials too. He was ready to turn off the light when he heard something—someone out in the garage.

Jake yelled out, "Anyone there?" His office was all glass windows facing the work area of the garage. He looked out into the garage space and saw Butch!

"Shit!" Jake said under his breath. He wasn't ready for this—definitely not right now! But he had no choice, and his mannerisms had to be the same—nothing different. He couldn't let Butch know—or even suspect—that anything would be different between them. "Ahhh…man." Jake drew a deep, heavy sigh.

Jake came out of his office. "Hey, Butch!" Jake exclaimed. "What're you doin' here, man? You just in the neighborhood, really? I thought you'd be at the Rusty Bucket belting down a few ales! It's $6 beer night, bro!"

"Ya, I was just headin' back to the apartment, and I saw a light on and was just checkin' to see if everything was all right," Butch replied calmly.

Jake thought to himself. *Ahh, shit!* Butch was being considerate and thoughtful and concerned about Jake's Garage. *Damn, this is gonna be so damn tough.* Jake hated this. It would be the hardest thing he ever had to do! *Shit!*

"I was just closing up," Jake told Butch. "I wanted to finish up on Baker's car and all. I stupidly had a beer and was walking over to the car. I set it down on the hood, and the damn glass slid right off and fell to the floor. I'm too lazy. I'll just clean it up tomorrow—in the morning," Jake said to Butch.

"I'm here, man. I'll get it. You go. I'm sure you're beat. I'll clean it up," Butch replied back to Jake. "You just go, dude. I can get this. You go relax and have a few at the Rusty Bucket. I know you've been itchin' to see that gal Lindsay again. Dude, really, go! I got this!" Butch looked at Jake and smiled.

Jake just looked back at Butch. There were so many thoughts going through his mind all at one once. He hoped his expression wasn't one of confusion. Although his dad always told him that he wasn't very good at hiding his feelings. Jake thought to himself that this wouldn't be one of those times. He thought about the stuff that the sheriff had said about Butch. None of those things—the things the sheriff said that Butch did—could ever be possible. Butch just wasn't like that—he couldn't be like that! Nope, the sheriff was wrong. It must be somebody else!

"Nahh, I can't let you do that, Butch! It's my damn mess. I should be the one cleaning it up!" Jake replied.

"Bro, I'll get this!" Butch insisted. "Go home—or to the Rusty Bucket! You know, man, it's the least I can do for you. If it wasn't for you, Jake, I don't know where I'd be today. You gave me a chance, a chance…at a new life. I mean…a new beginning." Butch started to stumble over his words. "I mean… well, you know what I mean, bro."

"Ahhh…no problem, dude, really. You've worked hard each and every day since you've been here with me. You're a quick learner and a hard worker. I appreciate it, man. And you're a good friend, dude. You came into my life when I really needed a friend—a buddy." Jake looked directly at Butch. He was hoping to get his message across sincerely. "I will always remember that, dude."

As fate has a way of stepping in and taking control, Butch had bent down to pick up the shards of glass, and he cut himself on a large piece that was protruding out.

"Damn it! Ouch!" Butch yelled. "Shit!" Before Butch could wipe his blood on his pants or shirt, Jake yelled, "Hey, man, hang on! Let me get something to wipe you up." Jake ran into the office.

Think, think. What can I get to collect—wipe up—the blood? Damn it! Jake thought to himself.

"Hey, man, hurry up! I'm really bleeding here," Butch screamed. "I think I might have to go to an urgent care—emergency—if this bleeding doesn't stop!"

"I'm comin', man!" Jake yelled out from his office. "I'm just getting clean rags. You don't want dirty rags, do you?"

For emergency/urgent care, there was Doc Baker in town. Jake thought he should maybe call Sheriff Middaugh back. He gave him a direct number to call—if anything came up—and it did.

"Hey, Butch, let me wrap your hand up in this clean rag." Jake had just rushed out of his office with a clean rag. Jake wrapped Butch's hand tightly. "You know, I could drive you to Doc Baker's. I have to tell him about his car anyway. Maybe you should get your hand checked out." Jake was hoping Butch would go along with it. "Hey, Butch, stay here. Keep the rag around our hand. I'll go call Doc Baker, okay?" Jake said to Butch.

"Ya, sure. Thanks, man," Butch replied in pain.

As Jake started for his office to make the call to Doc Baker, he turned around to face Butch. "Hey, Butch...I'm sorry, man." Jake meant that comment very sincerely, more than Butch knew.

Butch nodded his head. "I know, man. It's all right. I'm the one that was insistent on staying—it was my decision to stay and help you. How would you have ever predicted that I would cut myself? I was the careless one—not you, bro," Butch replied, smiling. "It was my own fault—not yours."

Jake quickly went back to his office and closed his door slightly, hoping that Butch would not hear one of his conversations. He made two phone calls—one to Doc Baker and one to Sheriff Middaugh. His conversations were brief.

"C'mon, Butch, let's go. Doc Baker just said to come right over. He'll take a look at your hand. Just leave your car here. It'll be fine. I can just pick you up in the morning. Of course, only if you'll be up to coming in. Of course, you can stay home. I know you won't be working on any cars anytime soon. And the only reason for you to come in is to answer the phone and keep me company." Jake smiled and hoped Butch would be okay.

"Okay, thanks, man," Butch responded.

Jake knew Butch was hurting. He could tell how much pain he must have been in. He never felt so bad in his entire life. Jake had this overwhelming sense of guilt and betrayal. He wanted to die.

Jake drove Butch over to Doc Baker's office. Doc Baker had his office attached to his home. He loved having his office right there. It was convenient and not as costly as having to go to a separate office building. Doc Baker was a good doctor. He had been a doctor for close to fifty years. He was considered by many a country doctor. Being in a very rural area, the nearest hospital was around twenty miles away. Dr. James Baker was everything anyone could want in a doctor. He was knowledgeable, resourceful, kind, always calm, a quiet man. He could—and would—calm any person down if need be. His voice was soothing. His office was always open, even if office hours were over. Day or night, Doc Baker was there and available to tend to the sick, injured, or patients that just needed a calm voice, medical information, a consult, or just someone they could take their problems to. He was invaluable.

After Jake spoke to Sheriff Middaugh, Sheriff Middaugh called Doc Baker.

"Jim, it's Ray Middaugh. We have a very strange situation here. There's something I need to discuss with you. And I believe you just received a call from Jake over at the garage. There's something I need for you to do for me. It is imperative that you keep this in the strictest of confidence." Sheriff Middaugh told everything to Doc Baker. As always, as in every normal and bizarre case, Dr. Jim Baker took it in stride—calmly, with little obvious reaction. No matter what the situation was, Jim Baker was calm. He listened intently to Sheriff Middaugh as he explained all the incredible details surrounding Butch. Sheriff Middaugh knew without a doubt that Jim Baker would keep everything in confidence. He would do whatever was needed to be done without hesitation or reservation. Although he liked Butch, Doc Baker followed the sheriff's instructions to the letter. The sheriff knew that Doc Baker would make sure that when Jake would slip him the two vials, he would collect the blood samples and call him when Butch and Jake left. Making sure he wouldn't be seen by Butch, the sheriff would give ample time and then come over to Doc Baker's and collect the samples. And then ultimately, the final proof would then be known.

CHAPTER 48

There was a little lull in the conversations in Chief Gordon's office. Harry was ready to go back to the inn and pick up Dr. Goodwin, Brenda, Bea, and Adam.

"Chief, do you mind if I at least give a call to Reagan?" Josh asked. "I don't want her to become suspicious. She's expecting me back today and all…"

"No, go ahead, Josh. But remember what I said," Chief Gordon reminded Josh.

"Yep, I understand, Chief," Josh replied.

"Josh, where have you been? I've been so worried about you! And I missed you!" Reagan exclaimed.

"I know, I know. I'm so sorry, Reagan. We're working on a case, and we had to get some stuff completed," Josh explained.

Josh hated to lie or rather, mislead Reagan, but she would know soon enough—and why.

Harry called Dr. Goodwin to let him know that he would be on his way back to the Covington Inn to pick them up.

Dr. Goodwin hung up the room phone and told Adam, who was just stretching out on his bed to rest for a while, that Harry would soon be there to pick them all up and take them to the police station.

Adam sat up, stretched, and rubbed his eyes.

"Okay, Doc. I'm awake," Adam yawned and responded.

Dr. Goodwin knocked gently on the adjoining door that led into Brenda and Bea's room.

"Brenda, it's Dr. Goodwin. It's time to go. Detective Trimble will be here in a couple of minutes, okay?" Dr Goodwin hoped they weren't both asleep.

Brenda opened the adjoining door a crack.

"Okay, Dr. Goodwin. I'll get Bea ready to go," Brenda responded.

Brenda closed the door gently. A thought came to her mind—something she should have mentioned to Dr. Goodwin.

A few moments later, Brenda knocked on the door and waited for a reply from Dr. Goodwin or Adam.

"Yes, come in, Brenda. What do you need?" Dr. Goodwin asked curtly.

Dr. Goodwin was feeling the pressure and anxiety of everything that has happened these past several weeks. A dear patient of his would soon have her world turned upside down, and he was so uncertain of the results and impact this would have on her very soul and mind. For all the great strides he has made with Bea, this impact could put her back to the catatonic state they found her in.

Brenda stepped into the room. "Dr. Goodwin. I have a thought, and I wanted to mention it to you before Detective Trimble arrives, which I know will be in just a few moments."

"Go on, Brenda. What's on your mind?" Dr. Goodwin asked as Adam looked on.

"Well…if Bea is associated with these crimes in any way, wouldn't she be afraid to be anywhere near a police station? And with that, wouldn't she be afraid to see any police officers in uniform?" Brenda spoke quietly so Bea wouldn't hear her.

"Good point. Well taken," Dr. Goodwin answered with a scowl. "Maybe I'll head on downstairs and talk to Detective Trimble. I'm sure he's waiting outside for us now. Just wait with Bea. Adam, you too. I'll be back up to get you three."

As Dr. Goodwin headed toward the door, he turned to Brenda. "You're a very good psychiatric nurse." He lifted up his hand and pointed his finger at Brenda. "And you would make a fine doctor." Dr. Goodwin smiled as Brenda smiled back.

Harry was waiting downstairs—outside in an unmarked police vehicle. He was expecting his precious cargo any minute. Dr. Goodwin came out, but it was only Dr. Goodwin. "Dammit, now what!" Harry said out loud in frustration. Where were the others?

"Ahh, shit!" Harry said to himself. "I knew this couldn't go smoothly as planned. What now?"

Harry put down his window, waiting for impending doom—or at least, some bad news.

"Doctor, what's the problem?" Harry asked hesitantly. "Where are the others?"

"Well, there is no problem, Detective, really. Brenda brought up an observation, per se, and I feel it warrants our consideration," Dr. Goodwin responded.

"Okay…" Harry looked puzzled. "Shoot!"

Will explained to Harry Brenda's thoughts about Bea seeing police officers in uniform and a police station. "With what happened, Bea would therefore, be frightened and very reluctant—maybe scared—to go anywhere near a police station, let alone see police officers in uniforms."

Harry thought about it for a moment as he rubbed his hand across his mouth.

"Well, Dr. Goodwin, I guess that's just a chance we'll have to take. Hell, maybe going to the police station and seeing police officers in uniform will snap her right out of it and she'll come to life again!" Harry waved both his arms into the air and replied sarcastically.

"Or maybe Bea will just submerge even further into a catatonic state and then we'll never be able to reach her again!" Dr. Goodwin answered Harry very abruptly.

"That is a gamble—a chance—that law enforcement officers have to take each and every day. Today, might not be a life-or-death situation, but a gamble all just the same."

Which way would fate decide to turn? Would karma be on the side of the Covington Police

Department and Harry and Josh? Would karma be on the side of Reagan and Irene, and would peace finally be with all the spirits of the Dennyson clan? Or would fate and karma finally catch up with Gina and Nancy?

Time would soon tell their fates…

CHAPTER 49

Dr. Goodwin went back up to the rooms to collect Adam, Brenda, and Bea. He gathered his medical bag up as well. He, of course, had Bea's medical records—what little he had—and plenty of medication that may be needed if Bea got out of control and required it. He hoped not, but that hope was slim today, Will felt. He was glad and very grateful that Adam agreed to come along on this trip.

Brenda had freshened up and got Bea ready to go.

"Bea, are you ready to go for another short ride?" Brenda asked in a soft-spoken voice—always soft-spoken.

Bea was sitting on the edge of her bed. Adam was sitting beside her. Bea responded much better to a soft tone of voice—not harsh. Today, calmness would be much needed. Both Brenda and Adam feared for Bea's well-being today. They were both sure that Dr. Goodwin felt the same way.

"Bea, don't forget Teddy!" Adam reached for Bea's teddy bear, which was lying behind her on the bed, and gave it to Bea with a smile.

Bea reached out her hands to take her teddy bear from Adam. She really liked Adam. Whenever Adam came around her, Bea always greeted him with a big, warm smile. She felt safe when Adam and Brenda were around her.

"She's gonna need that bear today," Adam remarked with a discouraging huff.

"Adam, please!" Brenda scolded him. "Positive thoughts. We have to think positively. We have to think positively..." Brenda's thoughts trailed off as she thought what would this afternoon bring.

They all went downstairs and climbed into the unmarked police vehicle. Harry was waiting impatiently. Dr. Goodwin sat in front with Harry. Brenda and Adam sat on either side of Bea in the back seat. Harry looked back at Brenda. He wanted her to remember to pay close attention to any reaction from Bea—any facial expressions that Bea might exhibit. Even the slightest reaction—a stare, a vocal response, anything that would denote a response that would indicate something to help piece this story together. He wanted to know anything at all that might set Bea off. Harry was hoping these surroundings would spark a familiarity with her—a store, a shop, the library, a school, a park, just any location that might be familiar to Bea. Adam and Brenda were to watch her carefully.

"Do you want Adam and I to point locations out to her, Detective?" Brenda asked Harry earlier.

"No, no, I don't," Harry replied. "I want to see if she looks up, pays attention, and becomes aware of her surroundings solely on her own—of her own accord," Harry answered.

Harry slowly pulled away from the Covington Inn after everyone was buckled up. He wanted Bea to hopefully soak up everything around her. He was hoping to see a glimmer, a wake up, something that might bring her back to reality.

Here's hoping.

CHAPTER 50

Brenda and Adam noticed nothing in Bea's expressions, reactions, etc. She was just sitting still, holding on to her Teddy—her comfort. Harry glanced occasionally into the rearview mirror so he could watch Bea. He drove a little slower than usual, as well, thinking that maybe Bea would react to something—anything. But nothing...

Harry, in a low-toned voice, spoke to Brenda. "Ms. Danforth, start suggesting," Harry said in a monotoned voice.

Brenda knew what Harry was implying. Adam looked over at Brenda as Dr. Goodwin closed his eyes as if to say a prayer or two.

"Bea, look at those beautiful flowers over there in the park. They're yellow—your favorite color!" Brenda said in an uplifting, pleasant voice.

Bea looked up. Brenda and Adam searched Bea's face for any expression—a reaction of maybe a familiarity of the surroundings. Bea smiled her usual smile—not anything different than her typical smile. No reaction.

"Bea, maybe we'll get ice cream later! Do you see that ice cream stand over there?" Brenda tried again to get a reaction out of Bea.

Bea looked at the ice cream stand with several people standing in line for ice cream.

"I like ice cream," Bea responded. "Strawberry is my favorite." Bea smiled.

Bea didn't verbalize a lot. Once in a great while, maybe one sentence, one or two words, but that was all. This was a breakthrough—a little one, but still a breakthrough. Brenda knew Harry was looking back at her, at Bea. Brenda just shook her head to let Harry know that nothing was clicking with Bea, except for her comment about the ice cream.

And then the Covington Police Station came into view. Harry was slowly turning into the police station parking lot, but he continued to pull around to the back so they could all enter through the back entranceway.

Bea was looking outside the car. She was slowly becoming fidgety in her seat. She started to yank at her seat belt. Then she saw a few police officers in uniform—she became irate. Her reaction escalated very quickly. She continued to squirm in her seat, trying to get out of her seat belt. She became agitated and started shaking her head and repeating, "No… no…no!"

Adam and Brenda had Bea between them. They continued to try and calm her down, but it was no use.

Dr. Goodwin started to reach into his medical bag. Harry patted the doctor on his arm.

"No, Doctor, not just yet. I need Bea to be awake—coherent. Please, let's just get her inside. There is a room that's all set up for us. I have this, Doctor, please," Harry insisted.

"Bea will not leave this car, Detective! There is no way we're going to get her to leave this car! You don't understand. You're going to make this situation even worse! I must protect my patient!" Dr. Goodwin pleaded.

"We just have to get her into the station. Dr. Goodwin, trust me. We've handled all sorts of irate, uncontrollable people. We can handle this. Let's go!" Harry demanded.

Adam got out of the back seat first. His concern was that Bea would bolt and run away.

Then all would be lost.

Adam said to Brenda, "Hang on to her. I'll get her from this side."

Adam made a suggestion to the detective. "Detective Trimble, it might be a little easier if you could please lose the police officers in uniform. That is what's upsetting Bea. If they're gone, she might calm down a little."

"Good point. Will do," Harry responded.

Harry got out of the car and yelled over to the officers. "Boys, would you please go inside? We have an irate person here who needs *not* to see anyone in uniform. Thank you."

Adam and Brenda told Bea that the "uniform people" were gone. Brenda looked at Bea. She made sure to make eye contact and repeated it again.

"Bea, calm down. It's okay—they're gone now. Please don't worry. You are safe now. You are safe with me and Adam and Dr. Goodwin—and Harry." Brenda purposely left out using the word *detective*.

"We will not let anyone harm you. You are safe. We will keep you safe!" Brenda kept repeating it over and over again to Bea.

Bea calmed down somewhat when the police officers were not in view any longer.

"Okay then, can we go in *now*?" Harry asked impatiently.

"Detective, I know you understand, but please, a little patience with my patient." Dr. Goodwin brought a little levity into a very tense situation.

Harry chuckled a little.

"I get it, Doc." Harry smirked as he glared over at Will.

Adam tried again. "C'mon, Bea, we're just going to get out of the car and walk a little ways. Maybe Brenda and you could use the bathroom, okay?" Adam tried anything to get Bea out of the car—any simple distraction.

Bea clutched tightly to Teddy as she moaned a little, rocking just a little.

"Okay, Beatrice," Adam said lightly. He knew he would then distract Bea. She hated being called Beatrice. She would always say that it wasn't her name. She would always get mad at Adam. But there was a reason why Adam would do that. It would distract Bea and take her away from the current issue. She would say her name was Bea, not Beatrice.

"My name is Bea, *not* Beatrice! I'm mad now." Bea scowled.

"I'm sorry, Bea. I won't call you that again. We friends?" Adam usually knew that when he smiled at Bea, she would smile back and all would be okay. He was hoping that would work today.

"Okay, Bea, let's you and I go to the bathroom." Brenda pointed over to the building. "It's just over there. Okay?"

Brenda said to Harry, "We will go to the bathroom. I am not going to lie to her, and I'm not starting now, you understand?" Brenda said quietly but firmly.

Somehow, by the grace of God, they got Bea into the police station. Harry told Brenda where the nearest women's restroom was, and Brenda quickly took Bea there. She smiled and acknowledged Josh by the back entranceway, but she knew he understood her not staying to chat. Adam followed behind Brenda and Bea. He saw Josh and quickly smiled and shook his hand. He wanted to follow Brenda and Bea just to make sure there weren't any problems. If there was, Adam would need to be there to help Brenda. He waited for them outside the door.

Josh greeted everyone at the back entranceway as they all came in from the back parking lot.

"Harry, Dr. Goodwin." Josh shook Dr. Goodwin's hand. "Nice to see you again. Everything okay?" Josh asked Harry and Dr. Goodwin.

"Brenda, Ms. Danforth, took Bea to the restroom. Adam is waiting for them. I'm going to take the good doctor here to interview/interrogation room 1. Could you please wait for them and then bring them down? Also, there are to be *no* visible officers in uniform that can be seen—just until we get Bea settled into the room. Okay?" Harry asked Josh.

"Got it, boss. Also, the chief wanted to meet Dr. Goodwin briefly. Then he will be in the observation room," Josh said to Harry.

"Great. Thanks, Josh," Harry replied.

"You bet," Josh answered dutifully.

"And, Josh," Harry added, "it was never my intention to keep you out of the loop."

"I know, Harry," Josh answered with a smile.

"Are we good?" Harry asked Josh.

"Of course—all good!" Josh said reassuringly.

Harry walked Dr. Goodwin down the hall while Josh found Adam waiting for Brenda and Bea outside the women's restroom.

"Hey, Adam!" Josh extended his hand.

"Josh, hi!" Adam reciprocated the gesture.

"All good here?" Josh asked.

"Yep, all good," Adam replied.

"They didn't bolt, did they?" Josh asked with a laugh.

"Nope, they didn't." Adam laughed. "I can hear Brenda talking to Bea. I think they're good—for now at least," Adam replied, hoping.

Brenda and Bea came out of the bathroom.

"No uniforms, I hope?" Brenda asked Adam quietly. "Hi, Josh, it's nice to see you again. I'm sorry that Bea and I didn't stop to greet you before. I know you understand," Brenda said apologetically.

"Hey, Brenda, no problem. I'm going to take you all down to a room. You both can stay with Bea of course," Josh explained.

"Hi, Bea," Josh said pleasantly. "It's so nice to see you again!"

Bea smiled back at Josh. She liked Josh too.

Josh led them to interrogation room 1. Harry wanted to make the room as comfortable and inviting as possible for Bea. Harry had gotten some water bottles, coffee, juice for Bea and found some cookies in the break room. He didn't want the room to look cold and uncomfortable—for anyone.

And now we wait...

CHAPTER 51

Chief Gordon had introduced himself to Dr. Goodwin. He assured him the session would be as painless as they could possibly make it. But rest assured, Chief Gordon also wanted Dr. Goodwin to understand that this was still a murder investigation—a double murder investigation. The Covington Police Department—Harry and Josh—had their jobs to do. Chief Gordon and the Covington Police Department had an obligation to fulfill to the Dennyson family and to the community of Covington. They would do their very best to keep Bea safe and as calm as they could. But Bea is the key to this murder investigation, and they would do everything and anything in their power to solve these crimes once and for all. Chief Gordon, along with Harry and Josh, all knew they were close to finally solving these horrendous crimes—very close.

Everyone was settled in the interrogation room—Harry, Dr. Goodwin, Brenda, Adam, and Bea. Josh decided to join Chief Gordon in the observation room directly next door.

Bea was a little uneasy sitting in her chair. Brenda had poured Bea a glass of juice and gave her a sugar cookie.

"Two hands, Bea," Brenda reminded her. Bea smiled back as she sipped her fruit juice and took a bite out of her cookie.

"Mmmm, good, Bea?" Adam asked her.

Bea smiled back at Adam. All good so far.

Harry started, "Okay, Dr. Goodwin, let's get started. Also, we will be filming and recording this interview session."

Harry recorded, out loud, the date and time. He also asked for verbal agreement from everyone to allow the recording and filming of the session. He had to receive permission from Bea also. This could be very tricky and extremely crucial, and Harry had to make sure there would be no question whatsoever as to Bea's approval. Harry had discussed this situation with Dr. Goodwin earlier. They were ready to begin.

Dr. Goodwin gave a nod to Brenda to ask Bea for the approval. Bea was the most comfortable with Brenda. She felt relaxed.

"Bea, is that okay if they take a picture of you and Teddy? And if there is anything you want to say, that is okay too. Can you say that is okay, Bea? Just answer me," Brenda asked very calmly.

Bea looked at Brenda and smiled. "Okay."

Harry breathed a sigh of relief and thought to himself, *Good, now we can proceed—baby steps.*

Bea sat across from Harry. Dr. Goodwin sat at the end of the table, and Adam and Brenda sat on either side of Bea. They were facing the observation mirror so Chief Gordon and Josh could view them clearly.

The observation room was just about intact. There was just one more person missing. Chief Gordon was waiting for Dr. Sheila Chamberlain. She was a behavioral psychiatrist that the police department had utilized several times in their investigations. She also had a degree in forensic psychiatry. This form of psychiatry specifically dealt with the interfacing of mental health issues and the law. This included matters of civil, criminal, and administrative law as well as evaluation and specialized treatment of individuals involved with the legal system at a variety of levels—including those incarcerated in jails, prisons, and forensic psychiatric hospitals.

Chief Gordon did not disclose to Harry that Dr. Chamberlain would be present, but he trusted Sheila. Another set of eyes and professional psychiatric ability was always needed for special cases. And this case was extra special. Chief Gordon didn't want to miss anything, and he certainly wanted to cover all his bases. He wanted these murders solved, put to bed, and case files closed for good. Then he would retire South! And then Harry could have his position. But not just yet.

The video and recording equipment was set, and people were all in place. A quiet knock was heard on the observation room door. Dr. Chamberlain was

307

here. Chief Gordon quietly opened the door as he shook Sheila's hand. She sat down next to him. Josh smiled and greeted her.

Interrogation room 1 was ready. Harry gave Chief Gordon a small signal to let him know that they were ready to begin. Harry waited a few moments, and the session began.

"Ready, Doctor?" Harry directed the question to Dr. Goodwin. Will nodded.

"This is Detective Harry Trimble at the Covington Police Department on Friday," Harry started. "Dr. Goodwin, for the record, please state your full name and occupation and where your practice is located and which hospital you are associated with."

In turn, Brenda and then Adam followed with telling who they were, their occupations, and where they were employed.

Harry explained that he would be showing Bea a few photos, which were of Butch/Nancy Brown. He also had to tell Bea they knew her real identity was Gina Smith. Here came the gamble, but it *had* to be done.

"Bea," Harry started, "I'm going to show you a couple of pictures. Could you please look at them and let me and Dr. Goodwin and Brenda and Adam know if you know who this person is in these pictures?"

Harry waited for a response from Bea—a nod of her head, a smile, anything. Bea continued to look down as she tightly clutched Teddy. She wasn't really focusing on anything other than her stuffed bear.

Brenda made a motion to Harry. Harry nodded in agreement.

Brenda tried a different approach. "Bea, could we look at some pictures together? Remember how we would walk down the hallway and go to the photo board and look at everyone's pictures? You would point to the people you know and laugh at their silly faces. Do you remember?"

Bea looked up and nodded to Brenda. Good. Baby steps.

Adam braced himself, along with Brenda and Dr. Goodwin. Harry placed two photos of Nancy Brown—of how she used to look. He gently placed them on the table in front of Bea. Harry then nodded to Brenda.

"Bea, do you know this girl?" Brenda asked gently. "Bea, look at the pictures," Brenda asked again as she pointed to the two photos of Nancy Brown.

Bea brought her eyes down to the photos. Her eyes widened, and the rocking started. She dropped Teddy to the floor, grabbed her head, covered her ears, and shouted, "Nooo! Nooo! Nooo!"

Well, there was the reaction Harry was finally hoping for. Now it was crucial to get to Bea before a full-blown episode became too uncontrollable.

Harry jumped right in and proceeded but not with caution but in full force and head-on. He was determined to crack her wide open.

"We know your name is Gina Smith. *Bea* is *not* your real name!" Harry raised his voice sternly.

"Detective, please!" Brenda yelled.

"Detective Trimble, that's enough!" Dr. Goodwin screamed. "You will *not* handle my patient like this! I will *not* have this!"

Among the chaos, Adam tried, without success, to calm Bea down. It was a circus.

Harry wasn't going to listen to any reasoning. He knew he had to continue on with full power and direction.

Harry kept drilling Bea. "Your name is Gina Smith. We know that! Who is this? Do you know who this is?" He pointed with force at the photo of Nancy Brown. "Gina, is this Nancy Brown?" Harry was shouting now.

On that last note, Bea—or Gina—was gone. She was in full-blown, uncontrollable, rocking, moaning, semicatatonic state of mind.

Chief Gordon, Josh and Dr. Chamberlain all were witnessing all this through the observation window. Josh just stared. Chief Gordon turned to Dr. Chamberlain for some kind of remark or comment. She just watched with a sick-looking smile on her face—like she was enjoying Bea's agony, the commotion, and tumultuous reactions going on. Chief Gordon, at that moment, had a different opinion of the doctor. It was a side of the doctor he didn't like seeing.

Dr. Chamberlain spoke up and smiled, "Well, we could try hypnosis." She smiled again.

There was a speaker button that when pushed, anyone in the observation room could speak to anyone in the interrogation room. Chief Gordon thought this would be that time.

"Harry, we may have another alternative. Could you please step out so we can discuss this? Dr. Goodwin, I am sorry for this reaction. Please calm Bea down as best as you can. We will be right back with you," Chief Gordon said apologetically.

"I'll be right back—not that any of you would want that. Dr. Goodwin, I am sorry, but it had to be done. We have to solve this case, and we are so very close," Harry said solemnly.

"And now we have to clean up your mess, Detective Trimble!" Will turned back to tend to Bea. Although Brenda and Adam were very upset, they could not display their emotions. They had to keep in control—for Bea's sake. They all felt betrayed by Harry. They felt, especially for Bea, that they were led into a lion's den with no protection and no defense.

Harry knocked on the door of the observation room and waited for a response. Chief Gordon opened the door and stepped aside for Harry to step in and close the door.

"Harry, you remember Dr. Sheila Chamberlain," Chief Gordon said.

"Dr. Chamberlain." Harry did not hold out his hand to greet her. He looked quite puzzled. Dr. Chamberlain was never a favorite of his.

Harry quickly shot a glance back to Chief Gordon and then to Josh. Josh shook his head very slightly to let Harry know that he knew nothing of Dr. Chamberlain being present for this session.

"Harry, I called Dr. Chamberlain in, as sometimes I do. I think having another behavioral psychiatrist here will give us additional insight. Of course, you also know Dr. Chamberlain is a specialist in forensic psychiatry," Chief Gordon said matter-of-factly.

"Yes, I'm aware," Harry answered dutifully.

Harry hated Dr. Sheila Chamberlain. Her methods were borderline barbaric. She would go to the extreme degree to get whatever response she could get from a patient. She had quite the reputation—and not in a good way. She had unorthodox ways of getting the responses she desired. Harry felt that all she wanted to do was make a name for herself—however she could. She had little or no regard for her patients. She had been reprimanded and called on the carpet many times for her savage ways of getting information out of patients. Harry was *not* happy, and Josh just stood there in bewilderment. Harry didn't remember if he ever told Josh about Dr. Chamberlain—or her brutal methods. She was merciless. She had a devilish smile and piercing eyes— the devil's spawn!

"Chief Gordon, would you mind if we stepped out and talked for a moment?" Harry asked calmly, but underneath it all, he was screaming.

Chief Gordon replied, "Sure, Harry, of course." Chief Gordon excused himself.

Harry opened the door, and they stepped out into the hallway. Harry motioned to an unoccupied room so no one could overhear their heated conversation that was about to happen. Harry wasn't looking forward to the discussion he was about to have with his superior—the chief of police. If anyone did overhear, and of course, the chief of police would know, Harry could be cited for insubordination. They both went into the unoccupied room. Harry closed the door behind him.

"Jesus, George, what the hell were you thinking! You're sending that poor, helpless, girl right into the lion's den. Christ, the gas chamber!" Harry was outraged.

"Really? Really, Harry?" George yelled right back at Harry. "How is your opinion of Dr. Chamberlain *any* different than how you drilled that poor girl today like a military master sergeant? For God's sake, Detective, you put that poor girl into a catatonic state! Now, how is that *any* different than what you believe Dr. Chamberlain does!" Chief Gordon yelled back sarcastically.

Harry found a chair and slumped down into the seat. The chief was right. How he treated Bea today was exactly the way he felt about Sheila Chamberlain. Harry rubbed his hand across his face. He was tired. No, he was exhausted.

"Ahh, Chief, I'm sorry. This case…I should retire!" Harry was disgusted with himself.

"Oh no, you don't—not before me!" Chief Gordon shook his finger at Harry and chuckled. "I'm the first to go—not you! When I retire, this whole mess will be yours to run—however you like, I might add! Now reality is, we both have to get back to that interrogation room and check the status of that fragile girl, and that doctor, nurse, and orderly that probably want to take a couple of contracts out on both of our lives!" George just wanted to bring a little levity to this conversation that needed to be over.

Chief Gordon knew Harry hated Dr. Chamberlain and her unorthodox methods in dealing with psychiatric patients. George knew this would be an extremely uncomfortable situation, but he wanted this case closed. And if bringing in Dr. Sheila Chamberlain would do that, then so be it! This discussion needed to end between Harry and George. Neither Harry nor Chief Gordon wanted to leave those people unattended—in either the observation room or in interrogation room 1.

CHAPTER 52

Brenda and Adam tried to console and calm Bea down as quickly as possible. When Harry left the room, Dr. Goodwin stood up and came and sat right in front of Bea—across from her. He needed to make eye contact with his patient.

"Bea, look at me," Dr. Goodwin said sternly. "It's all right now. No one will harm you. You are safe," Dr. Goodwin tried to reassure Bea.

"Bea." Brenda took Bea's face in her hands and turned Bea to face her close as she looked into her eyes. "Bea, it's okay. Do you trust me? Bea, do you trust me?" Brenda pleaded.

Brenda was looking for a nod to bring Bea back around. Adam was right next to Bea, too.

"Bea, look at me please," Brenda said again.

Brenda tried one more thing. "Bea, I love you. I won't let anyone hurt you. Please believe that. I won't let anyone hurt you—ever."

Brenda dropped her hands from Bea's cheeks. She gently grabbed her and held her like a mother would console her child. She held on tight as to hopefully stop Bea's rocking.

Bea started sobbing, but it was a different sounding sob—like a normal human being crying uncontrollably. Brenda looked at Adam and smiled. Maybe the act of Brenda holding her brought her out of her catatonic state? Who knew, but the important part is that it helped.

Dr. Goodwin noticed it, too.

"Brenda, I do believe you are a miracle worker!" Dr. Goodwin exclaimed solemnly. "A simple gesture of a warm hug can do miracles—I've seen it happen before," he added in surprise.

Dr. Goodwin had witnessed this in the past time and time again. Sometimes when a patient is uncontrollable, such as moaning, rocking back and forth, etc., an act of just embracing them in a warm hug helps the patient. It is a very comforting act. And on the other hand, Dr. Goodwin had seen it backfire, and the patient became more belligerent and possibly more violent. But sometimes, you just have to try.

Bea wouldn't let go of Brenda. She held on tight.

"Ah, honey," Brenda said in a soft, comforting way, "it's going to be okay. You're going to be okay."

Brenda didn't pull away from Bea's grasp until she felt she could.

There would be much talking that needed to take place, but again baby steps.

Brenda loosened her embrace and placed her arms on Bea's shoulders. She pulled back just a little so she could look at Bea.

"Honey, are you all right?" Brenda asked Bea.

Bea/Gina tried to form words and talk, but nothing was coming out of her mouth.

Bea slumped back in her chair. She looked like she was going to say something—like someone who was trying to gather their thoughts. She was trying to find the words to say. It was so very difficult for Bea to speak. Dr. Goodwin had seen this phenomena before. An occurrence happened to snap a patient out of their state of limbo. It was as if they were coming to as if they were waking up from a coma. It didn't happen that often, but he had seen it occur in a few of his associates' patients. He often thought it would be an interesting topic for a dissertation. Maybe since he actually was having one of his own patients experiencing it, he may write an article on the topic for a medical journal.

Bea opened her mouth to speak. "I'm fine…not fine…"

It may have only been one or two words, but it was a breakthrough and miracle all the same. It was as if Bea/Gina came out of a coma. Either the photos of Nancy Brown or Brenda's grabbing to hold on to Bea/Gina in a hug triggered or tripped a circuit in Bea's/Gina's mind. Adam gave Bea a tissue as he looked over to Brenda and smiled.

"Here, Bea, here is a tissue for you," Adam said warmly.

"Adam," Bea said, smiling at Adam. Bea gave Adam a warm hug.

Dr. Goodwin watched as this amazing miracle happened.

"Well…well…" Dr. Goodwin smiled at Bea. "Welcome back, Bea. We are so glad you are here with us."

Brenda thought it was time to ask Bea a question since she seemed in a controlled state and calm.

"Bea, you know this girl in the picture, don't you?" Brenda asked.

There was no more rocking or moaning or irate behavior as a result. There was just Bea's answer.

"Yes, I know her…"

Well it was a shame, to say the least, that Harry and Josh missed the most pivotal, amazing moment. It was truly a breakthrough. And if anything could make Dr. Will Goodwin any happier, it was a breakthrough in one of his patient's recovery. It was truly a defining moment in Bea's/Gina's healing process. She was going to be okay. She was going to be a survivor. Will needed to document the session today. He had a lot of writing to do. It was an unexpected good day. It was a day that Dr. Goodwin wouldn't have been able to foretell. But it was a damn good day!

The silence was broken.

"Adam, would you do me a big favor and go find Harry and Josh and have them come back in here, please?" Dr. Goodwin asked.

"Certainly, Dr. Goodwin. I would be glad to," Adam replied.

Adam got up from his chair and left interrogation room 1. He hoped to find Harry and Josh very quickly. The police station was big enough, but he was hoping for immediate direction to find them. He didn't figure they were still in the observation room, or they would have been right over witnessing this miracle today with Bea/Gina. Adam thought he'd better check next door anyway.

Adam knocked on the observation room door. Josh opened it.

"Adam," Josh greeted him. "I saw you coming. We—Dr. Chamberlain and myself—witnessed everything. This is great news and at the best possible time," Josh said with relief. "Adam," Josh continued. "This is Dr. Sheila Chamberlain, a behavioral and forensic psychologist. She has joined us today as an extra pair of eyes and ears and of course, professional opinion."

Adam shook Dr. Chamberlain's hand. "It is a pleasure to meet you, Doctor."

"It's nice to meet you, Adam," Dr. Chamberlain responded.

"Well, I guess you and Josh have obviously witnessed our breakthrough with Bea or rather Gina. This will be so confusing as to what to call her now. And I'm sorry that Detective Trimble and Chief Gordon didn't get to see this. Dr. Goodwin will certainly be very occupied documenting this new development," Adam responded.

"I am very familiar with Dr. Goodwin's reputation, Adam. He has published several articles in several medical journals, and it is widely known about his successes with his hospital and patients. His hospital has a stellar reputation as being one of the best in the US. I will very much look forward to officially meeting him," Dr. Chamberlain commented with a smile.

Harry's heated discussion ceased with Chief Gordon. Apologies were exchanged. These murders brought out the worst in everyone. Covington, Covington Police Department, the chief, the detectives, Reagan, and Irene—all were tired. So many people just wanted these murders solved and put to rest.

And it looked like they could be put to rest soon. But the final piece of the puzzle had to be found—Nancy Brown.

CHAPTER 53

Irene and Reagan were sitting in the breakfast nook at the table. The anniversary of the murders was fast approaching. The ghostly apparitions of David and Melanie, the visibility of the cottage, the music in the ballroom—everything was escalating and being heard and being seen more often. It always occurred around the anniversary, but for some reason, it had been magnified like this the past several months as well.

"Irene, have you seen any other entities around? Any spirits?" Reagan asked as she sipped her coffee. Reagan was curious.

"If you mean Arthur and Anne, sometimes, but I just see them. There is no communication, however," Irene sadly replied.

"Have you heard from Josh lately, Reagan?" Irene asked.

"One phone call, then one phone message the other day. Irene, something is happening…I can feel it! I can sense it!" Reagan answered ominously.

"Yes, I sense something too," Irene agreed. "There *is* something in the air, so to speak."

"I miss talking to Josh. He seems to be very preoccupied with a case, but he won't tell me. I know everything must be confidential…I get that," Reagan said. "But there's something about the case he, and probably Harry too, are working on now is so strange…It's just strange, that's all. Irene, do you think it's about the murders?" Reagan asked.

"Well, my dear, I guess you and I will just have to wait to find out. Be patient and wait for Josh to tell you when he's ready," Irene said to Reagan in a nurturing way.

"I guess," Reagan responded with a frown.

It definitely wasn't business as usual at the Covington Police Station. The chief had sent a couple of officers out to get a take-out lunch order from Rosewood Grille. Chief Gordon released Dr. Sheila Chamberlain for the day, although he did mention to her that, more than likely, he would need her assistance when they found Nancy Brown and brought her in. Dr. Chamberlain agreed with enthusiasm.

"Now, Doctor, when I do call you in, everything must stay on the up and up—no edgy shenanigans or unorthodox methods. This next interview/interrogation will have to be run right by the book. I do *not* want any hang-ups or issues where we would have to let this suspect go. Do you understand that, Doctor?" Chief Gordon stated firmly.

"Yes, yes, Chief Gordon," Sheila responded with a little laugh. "I understand. I'll be a good doctor. No deviousness! I promise!" Dr. Chamberlain said with a chuckle.

"Good! As long as we have a firm understanding with each other. I want these murders solved once and for all with absolutely *no* problems whatsoever!" Chief Gordon continued. "I'll just need you in the observation room and then maybe with us for further questioning of this Nancy Brown—if needed. I'll need your professional opinion and guidance."

"Of course, Chief Gordon. You will have my professional expertise, and I promise to go right by the book." Dr. Chamberlain raised her hand in a salute and smiled.

Dr. Chamberlain left. Chief Gordon wanted everyone—Dr. Goodwin, Brenda, Adam, Bea/Gina to stay put in the interrogation room 1. Harry and Josh had just joined them.

Harry knocked and opened the door to the interrogation room and entered with Josh. The natives were getting a bit restless. It had been a long, exhausting morning. Bathroom breaks had to be given, and a bite of lunch was definitely in order.

"Hello, everyone," Harry said. "I want to apologize that I abandoned you all. It certainly was not my intention. I had to talk with Chief Gordon and go over a couple more details before we can move to the next step in this process." Harry looked at the three individuals sitting at the table and made a hypothesis that something had happened here. "Am I to understand that we made a breakthrough, Dr. Goodwin?"

"That would be correct, Detective Trimble," Dr. Goodwin said bluntly.

"Well, this *is* good news!" Harry smiled. "On that note, how about a little lunch to celebrate, huh? Let's leave this cramped room and go across the hall to a somewhat more comfortable room and area. I have purchased some boxed lunches from our finest restaurant—the Rosewood Grille. My treat! How does that sound to everyone? Harry asked.

"Detective," Dr. Goodwin interjected, "I think I—we—need to ask: what's next?"

"Well, this may not be what you want to hear right now, Doctor, but how about we eat some lunch first? Then we'll conquer your question. Does that sound okay, Doctor?" Harry asked with a smile. "With filled stomachs, we can then talk about what's next."

Adam answered right away, "Well, I don't know about everyone else, but that sounds great to me!"

"Well then, if that's all right with the rest of you, 'cause it seems like Adam here is going to take off without us, let's change our scenery, shall we, and head to a more casual place. We have our conference room down the hallway. It's a little more comfortable and roomy, and I have lunch waiting for us. Does that sound okay?" Harry asked joyfully.

"Bea, does that sound okay to you? Do you feel comfortable and able to walk a little down the hall to have lunch?" Dr. Goodwin asked Bea/Gina.

Dr. Goodwin had taken Bea's/Gina's vitals—her blood pressure, listened to her heart. Everything, so far, seemed to be fine.

"You can call me Gina, Dr. Goodwin," Bea/Gina replied.

Bea/Gina was still talking slowly and in a measured tone. Dr. Goodwin thought a thorough physical would definitely be needed and, of course, a full psychiatric analysis—due to the new breakthrough.

They all left the interrogation room and walked down the hall. Harry opened the door to one of the conference rooms. Everything was already set up, buffet style, at the far end of the long center table. Paper plates, cups, plasticware, beverages, and a nice selection of salads, sandwiches, fruit, and cookies were displayed. Everyone dug in and enjoyed all that Rosewood Grille provided. It was well needed and well deserved for all! Everything was delicious.

They all took a seat around the large conference table. Harry waited a little before he started talking about the next portion of business. He wasn't quite sure just how he was going to approach the subject matter. But they had to move to the next step...and the sooner, the better.

Harry observed Bea's/Gina's behavior. She was still, of course, being guarded by Brenda and Adam. They were sitting on either side of her—their usual spots. There was very little conversation going on as well.

Brenda broke the silence and spoke up, "Detective, would you mind if I took Bea...I mean,

Gina, over there to the couch and have her rest for a while before you continue your questioning? I'm sure you can understand how Bea/Gina must be feeling. I can see she is a bit tired from this morning and, of course, the wonderful lunch you provided for us today." Brenda wanted to keep the conversation as light as possible.

Dr. Goodwin and Adam chimed in as soon as Brenda finished her sentence, "Yes, thank you Detective, for that wonderful lunch. It was wonderful!"

"You are all very welcome. It was our pleasure! I know this day has been very trying for you. I know we need to continue. Brenda, yes, of course, let Gina rest a little while. It's no problem. There will be more questioning for Gina. And, I promise, it will be in a very calm fashion. I promise," Harry assured the three.

Harry turned to Dr. Goodwin. "Doctor, will Gina be able to answer some more questions?" Harry asked kindly.

Dr. Goodwin wiped his mouth with his napkin and replied, "Well, why don't you ask her yourself, Detective? She's still here with us." Dr. Goodwin raised his hand toward Gina.

Everyone turned to look at Gina sitting calmly at the table, finishing her sandwich and staring at her cookie. She was still very quiet, but something had changed—a couple of variables were added. She no longer grasped tightly at her teddy bear, and she did recognize that her name was Gina Smith—not Bea.

These were very big steps. Now the night surrounding the murders had to be discussed. And, hopefully, much more information and puzzle pieces had to be fitted into place.

Brenda still had her arm around Gina. Adam had wiped a cookie crumb from Gina's mouth.

Brenda asked again, "That nap we were discussing earlier, Detective, would that be okay when Gina finishes her lunch? Just a short one. Please. She'll be a little more rested and may be able to answer your questions. Would that be okay?"

"Of course. We'll have this discussion in maybe a half an hour. Would that be okay?" Harry was trying to be patient and understanding, although he had been waiting for this moment for a very long time.

Brenda directed her next question to Gina. "Gina, honey, maybe after a short nap, would you mind answering a few more questions for Detective Trimble and Detective Winters—Josh?"

Gina reluctantly nodded her head as she finished her cookie.

"Gina, are you all done? Did you have enough food for lunch?" Brenda asked Gina.

Gina replied, "All done. Thank you."

Brenda had finished as well. She got up from her chair and reached her hand out to Gina. Gina grabbed her hand. Adam helped Gina up.

"There you go, Gina. Are you ready for a nap?" Adam asked.

Brenda and Adam and, of course, Dr. Goodwin knew Gina was tired. Her eyes were very tired from the long morning she had. Brenda led Gina over to the couch at the end of the room. The sun was shining in through the big windows, and that always made a room much more inviting. There were two swivel chairs, both adjacent to the couch. There were two end tables and a coffee table in the center. It had a living room effect. It helped to make the conference room less formal and stuffy looking.

It didn't take long for Gina to doze off. There was also a soft throw blanket laying on the corner of the couch. Chief Gordon's wife had to take the credit for that section of the room. She said it made the conference room have a variety of places where people could sit—more versatile. Chief Gordon never thought that area would ever be used, but he was wrong today. It was actually utilized more than he thought. If it was a small meeting with just a handful of people, then it was a perfect area for conversation. He never thought it was necessary to soften an area or try to make it comfortable. It just wasn't needed he thought. But today, as for a few other times, it was needed. The chief hated when his wife was right!

While Gina was napping, Brenda sat in one of the swivel chairs and read. Adam sat in the other swivel chair and had decided to grab a few winks as well.

Chief Gordon, Harry, Josh, and Dr. Goodwin sat at the conference table. Chief Gordon had just joined them in the conference room. It was a good time to go over what was to be happening within the next few days and weeks.

The conversation was low in volume, and the chief led the conversation.

"Well, first off, I want to thank you boys for doing a great job. And, Dr. Goodwin, I certainly want to thank you and Brenda and Adam over there for all your cooperation, patience, and expertise in this extremely delicate situation. I'm going to tell you that these next few weeks—and however longer it will take—will be crucial. It is important that we all stay together—in unison—and on the same page. I am waiting for some results from a blood sample that was sent to me a couple of days ago. If this pans out and the identity of this person is who we think it is, then we may have closed this case once and for all." Chief Gordon was so hoping.

Harry and Josh looked at the chief, and both smiled as well as Dr. Goodwin. It was true, these next couple of weeks were going to be very crucial.

While Chief Gordon was addressing the detectives and Dr. Goodwin, there was a small knock at the door. Josh rose up from his chair since he was nearest to the door and opened it a crack. It was one of the officers.

Josh turned around. "Chief, Harry, you're both wanted. Chief, Sheriff Middaugh is on the phone waiting to speak with you in regard to the photos and composite. And, Harry, Margaret is here waiting to speak with you about the blood samples."

"Oh, okay. Thank you, Josh," Chief Gordon answered. "If you will excuse me, gentlemen, duty calls. Harry, why don't you take Josh with you and go talk to Margaret about those samples? Doctor, will you, Brenda, Adam, and Gina be okay for a little while longer while we take care of these matters?" Chief Gordon asked politely.

"Sure, we'll be fine," Dr. Goodwin replied. "I will start working on my notes from today. And I see the lounge area looks secure for the moment." Dr. Goodwin laughed.

Brenda looked up from the book she was reading. "We're fine over here."

"You sure all is okay?" Dr. Goodwin asked Brenda.

"Yes, I think so—so far," Brenda responded.

So far, so good…but not for long.

CHAPTER 54

Things were finally coming to a head. Chief Gordon talked with Sheriff Middaugh in regard to the individual named Butch who worked at the nearby garage. He hoped the blood sample retained by the town doctor was a sufficient amount and enough to make the connection and positive identity.

"Chief Gordon, it's the darndest thing. I would never have suspected this here Butch. He was never a troublemaker. He never got into a lick of trouble of any kind. He's been working with a good friend of mine—his boy, Jake. Jake owns a garage up here on Highway 41. I can't believe he's been here under our noses for all that time. I understand how you want to solve these horrendous crimes, but I sure hope Butch is not your man. He's very likeable up here in these parts. It would hard pressed for anyone, including myself, to ever imagine that Butch would ever be capable of such awful crimes of passion," Sheriff Middaugh explained.

"I understand, Sheriff. Sheriff, do you have any reason whatsoever to think that this Butch would skip town?" Chief Gordon asked.

"No, no, not really, Chief—not unless we give him reason to, I guess," Sheriff Middaugh responded.

"Sheriff, I can't tell you how important it is to keep an eye on this Butch/Nancy Brown. I, along with two of my detectives, will be leaving within the hour to come and pick him/her up. Do you think you could put him up until we get there?" Chief Gordon asked.

"What's the premise of arresting or holding Butch for? Chief, I gotta have a reason for bringing him in—you know that," Sheriff Middaugh added.

"How about suspicion of a double murder? Read him his rights and lock him up. Do you have enough manpower to do that, Sheriff?" Chief Gordon was hoping for a yes.

"I do, Chief, but again, I can't just lock Butch up for no reason at all," Sheriff Middaugh again stressed.

"I *don't* care, Sheriff! Make one up! Get him on a traffic violation—anything! I just want you to contain him in a cell—just until me and my detectives can get there. Do you understand?" Chief Gordon was getting a little frustrated and running out of patience. "Don't miss a step or a single trick with this, Sheriff. If for any reason you—as well as your men—screw this up, we'll *all* be in a heap of trouble. Got that? We can't let this suspect slip through the cracks again!"

"Okay, Chief, I got it." Sheriff Middaugh breathed a heavy sigh.

Chief Gordon continued, "Don't let him slip away—please. We have two very well-known murders at stake here. There is *no* room for error anywhere!"

Sheriff Middaugh understood, but he still couldn't believe Butch was even capable of one murder—let alone two, and brutal murders at that! But evidently it was true, providing there was a match with the blood samples and the miracle of DNA. The sheriff did *not* want to make this next phone call to Jake.

"Jake, it's Sheriff Middaugh here. Is Butch in your office with you now, or is he in the garage working?" the sheriff had to ask.

"Hi, Sheriff. Butch is working out in the garage on a brake system. How did everything go? Do you have answers yet, Sheriff?" Jake asked.

"Well, that's why I'm calling you, son. I need to come get Butch and bring him in. I have to lock him up till the chief and two detectives come from Covington to collect him. They'll be here within the next forty-eight hours. We have to keep Butch locked up until then. Jake, does he suspect anything—anything at all?" Sheriff Middaugh asked and hoped for a no.

"No, I don't think so. Everything's been fine. I also have to tell you"—Jake was watching the garage so as to make sure Butch wasn't overhearing his conversation—"I found a stash of money that I usually keep in my desk drawer missing the other day."

"How much was in there, Jake?" Sheriff Middaugh asked.

"Around $2,500 or so, Sheriff," Jake answered.

"What the hell, Jake! Why are you keeping that sizable amount of money in your desk drawer? Did you have it locked up? And why isn't it in the bank, son?" Sheriff Middaugh raised his voice in exasperation.

"I know, I know. It was stupid. Ol' man Sterling paid me in cash for work on his car, and I forgot I put it in my desk drawer. I was planning on making the deposit the next day, but I guess I forgot about it. Sterling brought it to me late one night while I was closing up, and I guess I just forgot," Jake replied.

"Son, don't you have a key for night deposits at the bank?" the sheriff asked.

"No, I'll get one—promise. It's on my list for the things I need to do." Jake was tired.

"Oh well, make sure you do, son—make sure you do. That's a lot of money to lose. Jake, did you happen to give ol' man Sterling a cash receipt?" Sheriff Middaugh asked.

"Yep, I did," Jake responded.

"Jake, did Butch know that money was in the drawer?" The sheriff was fishing and thinking this was his way out of finding a reason to arrest Butch. This could be his lucky day—but not for Butch.

"Well, ya, he was here. Butch was the one that repaired Sterling's truck. He saw ol' man Sterling pay in cash for the work, and he saw me put the money in the drawer in my office. Do you think he took it, Sheriff? I can't believe he would do that. He was so proud of fixing that old truck for Sterling. I can't believe he would do that, Sheriff." Jake sounded so disappointed.

"And next question, Jake. Did ol' man Sterling see you and Butch there?" Sheriff Middaugh knew this was important for Jake to confirm with a yes.

"Yep, 'cause, ol' man Sterling made it a point to thank Butch for fixing his truck and making it work again. He was very grateful, Sheriff," Jake answered.

"And again, just to confirm, you know that Butch saw you put that money in your desk drawer, right?" Sheriff Middaugh just wanted to make sure there were no unturned questions.

"Yep again, because he asked me why I wasn't going to take it to the bank and put it in the night deposit," Jake responded again.

"And you know you didn't remove it—put it somewhere else?" the sheriff asked.

"Sheriff, no, I left it right here in the drawer—in an envelope." Jake was getting a little perturbed with the sheriff's line of questioning.

"Okay then. Well, I'll be over shortly to question Butch. *Do not*, I repeat, *do not* say anything to Butch, you hear?" Sheriff Middaugh stressed.

"This is going to be very awkward, Sheriff. Butch has been nothing but a good, solid worker—and a good friend, I might add. I don't want you to arrest him on my property—at my place and in my presence. Please, Sheriff, please don't make this awkward for me and for Butch," Jake pleaded. "Arrest him somewhere else if you have to. I should have been paying him more anyway. I'm considering this back pay to him. Why can't you just leave this alone, Sheriff? Just pretend you didn't hear about this? Can't we just wipe this whole conversation away and forget about it?" Jake asked again.

"Jakey, I have to do this. But I'll tell you this much, I will come in and question Butch first, okay? I still have to bring him in. I have a chief of police and two detectives comin' for him. I don't have a choice, son. I don't!" Sheriff Middaugh tried to explain.

"Then arrest him at his apartment—without me knowing, Sheriff. That's the least you can do for me, okay?" Jake was insistent.

"Okay. Tell me when he's leaving. Just give me a heads-up. Can you do that, at least?" Now the sheriff was losing patience.

"Ya, I can do that, but that's all I'll do!" Jake replied. He knew he was leading Butch right in a lion's den. It just didn't feel right to him.

CHAPTER 55

Chief Gordon, Harry and Josh regrouped after their prospective meetings and phone call. Chief Gordon motioned Harry and Josh into his office before heading back to the conference room where Dr. Goodwin, Brenda, Adam, and Gina were resting.

"Boys, I talked to Sheriff Middaugh. I do believe we've found our Ms. Nancy Brown. Sheriff Middaugh will be bringing her—or rather, the identity and name she has been going by for all these years, Butch—in. She has been playing the role as a man, and from what I gather, a foolproof identity. Sheriff Middaugh said that they had absolutely no idea that this Butch was Nancy Brown. He—or rather she—has been a model citizen and worked as an auto mechanic at their nearby garage, Jake's Garage, up on Highway 41. No one ever knew. No one ever suspected a thing. How about that?" Chief Gordon remarked in full surprise. "I had a very hard time trying to convince Sheriff Middaugh that this Butch was indeed a murderer and linked to one of the most widely known double murders. Well, to say the least, the sheriff was shocked—as well as the owner of the garage that this Butch worked at," Chief Gordon exclaimed.

Josh and Harry just stared in utter amazement. The notion that Josh had about Nancy Brown changing her identity was true.

Harry gently slapped Josh on the arm. "Way to go, Winters! You nailed it! Your suspicion about Brown was spot-on accurate! Chief, that was Josh's suggestion that we send a composite around to the neighboring police and sheriff departments and circulate a composite of what Nancy Brown might look like as a male," Harry told Chief Gordon like a proud father.

"Very good, Josh! You're a damn good detective, and I feel a promotion will be pending for you because of this, son! Well done!" Chief Gordon said in enthusiastic gratitude.

"Thanks, Chief, Harry. I don't know what to say. I just kept thinking to myself why this character hasn't surfaced, etc. This is what I learned at the academy—never assume and consider every possible angle. Think out of the box," Josh humbly replied. He added, "And if I needed to lay low for the rest of my life, what would I do?"

"Well, the academy taught you well, and that's why you graduated at the top of your class, Josh! The town of Covington and the Covington Police Department thank you! Hell, and let's add the media, all the Dennyson spirits—living and non-living—thank you! And last, but certainly not least, I thank you, Josh!" Chief Gordon leaned over and extended his hand to Josh to give him a well-deserved handshake.

It was time.

After the briefing in Chief Gordon's office, all three headed back to the conference room to speak with Dr. Goodwin, Brenda, Adam, and of course, their star witness, Gina.

Chief Gordon opened the door of the conference room. He glanced at the conference table and saw Dr. Goodwin working diligently at his laptop, probably entering data in regard to Gina's breakthrough. Gina was sitting up with the blanket that his wife had crocheted across her lap. Brenda and Adam were talking with her.

"Okay, folks, we need to keep moving on this. Brenda, Adam, and Gina, if you would please join us back at the table. Doctor, if you don't mind, could you finish up your thoughts and let's talk for a couple of moments. Unfortunately, the detectives and I have to leave very soon. We need to leave town for a short while," Chief Gordon briefed everyone.

Brenda and Adam helped Gina up from the couch and came back over to the conference table to reoccupy their seats. Dr. Goodwin looked up and smiled with confirmation. He finished up his last thought and closed his laptop. They were all sitting and waiting for Chief Gordon to continue—including Harry and Josh.

"At this time, I will turn this conversation over to Harry and Josh," the chief said.

Harry started off and directed his thoughts to Dr. Goodwin. "Dr. Goodwin, these next set of questions are critical. I am—or rather, Josh and I—are going to ask Gina some questions that may be very uncomfortable for her to answer. I will need yours and Brenda's and Adam's input as we continue." Harry waited for confirmations from the doctor, Brenda, and Adam. Gina just looked forward without emotion. Harry, Josh, and Chief Gordon were wondering what could be going through her mind. What could she be thinking about? Was she remembering that night of those awful murders? Did she take part in any of the murders? Could she have killed Melanie or David or both, or was she just a witness to the crimes? In reality, everyone was dying to know. Harry and Josh started.

Harry first let everyone know that this session would again be recorded. He received verbal agreements and permission from everyone. He exclusively asked Gina for a verbal agreement. Everyone complied.

"Gina, if you would please speak up a little louder and reply, that would be very helpful. Is that okay?" Harry asked.

Brenda looked at Gina. She and Adam were sitting on either side of her again.

Dr. Goodwin asked Gina, "Gina, do you understand Detective Trimble's question?"

Before any specific questions surrounding the murders were asked, Dr. Goodwin asked Gina some basic questions. It was to receive a few responses and reactions. He wanted to test the waters, so to speak. He needed to get a feel for Gina's reactions, answers, her behavior. Normally, after a breakthrough with a patient, Dr. Goodwin would be in his office—his own surroundings in a much more controlled environment. It would be with him and his patient and no one else present. But, unfortunately, this couldn't happen today. He prayed that Gina would not have a relapse and to go back into her previous state of mind. That truly would be tragic—and the possibility of her recovering would be very slim.

Gina knew everyone's name in the room. She knew she was at a police station. She understood what snapped her out of her very lengthy catatonic state of mind. She was a little slow in her speech response, but more importantly, she was fully aware of people around her and the surroundings and why she was where she was.

The questioning and the process was long. Patience was very much needed in this session.

Everything had to be asked correctly. The details had to be delivered and asked perfectly.

Gina divulged all the facts as she remembered them. Dr. Goodwin was very surprised that she had recovered so quickly. Her speech was still much labored, and it took her a little longer to get her thoughts out, but her recall was vivid and clear.

Gina told everyone that she'd known Nancy since they were little—that Nancy was her best friend and that they did everything together. She told them about going off to college together and meeting

Melanie Dennyson. She told everyone of just how much Nancy hated Melanie. She also said of a couple of other killings that Nancy had done. Gina described just how frightened she was sometimes of Gina's rage. She talked of the plan that Nancy had for her and Gina to come and work at Dennyson Toys and hope-fully work for Melanie. Gina explained how Nancy worked out each and every detail right up to the eve-ning before Melanie's wedding to David Williams. That night, Nancy went berserk and became out of control—more than ever before. It was fuzzy, but Gina remembered that night. She followed Nancy into the cottage and saw what Nancy did to Melanie. She said she crouched down in a dark corner, and all she remembered was the sound of the pitchfork going into Melanie, the screaming, the blood, Melanie fall-ing, Nancy screaming and being so enraged and out of control. Gina remembered like it was a dream, a very bad dream, waking up or coming to in a dark small space like a shed and her head hurting so bad. It hurt so bad that she felt nauseous. Gina said it was the worst headache she had ever had. She faintly remembered Nancy telling her to stay put—that she would be right back. She needed to find her car keys. And that's when Nancy returned to the dark cottage and found David bent over Melanie. Nancy finished another job of brutally killing one last victim. Gina remembered how Nancy boasted about killing David. He was obviously another hated victim of Nancy's.

"Gina, we have to leave now. We want you to understand that we have to go get Nancy and bring her back for questioning. We will be arresting her for the crimes of murdering Melanie Dennyson and David Williams. I want to stress to you that we are *not* holding you responsible in *any* way for these two murders. I want to make sure you know that. I need you to respond that you understand that, okay?" Harry explained patiently and slowly so that Gina understood completely. He also wanted Dr. Goodwin, Brenda, and Adam to understand that as well. It was pertinent and very important—especially to Dr. Goodwin, that the Covington Police Department was *not* going to hold Gina responsible for the crimes and anything leading up to them. Harry wanted them to know, and Chief Gordon spoke in agreement, that Gina would be free of any of the crimes that were committed. She was also an extremely valuable source in finally solving these horrendous crimes.

Harry asked Gina again if she understood everything he had just said. She responded with a yes.

"I know," Gina replied quietly. "She should pay for what she did to Melanie and to David…and to me!" Gina started to cry uncontrollably.

Brenda had her arms around Gina. "Honey, it's going to be all right now."

"Gina," Chief Gordon interjected, "please know you did *nothing* wrong. You are only a witness—our witness to these brutal happenings. We are extremely grateful that you are helping us to solve these murders."

Gina asked timidly, "Will I have to see Nancy?"

"Not if you don't want to," Chief Gordon replied. "But if you do not, I would like for you to sit—along with Dr. Goodwin and Brenda and Adam—in the observation room next door. While we are questioning Nancy, we need to get confirmation from you that that is her. She will not be able to see or hear you in any way or even know that you are here in this building. Do you understand, Gina?" Chief Gordon explained and stressed to Gina.

Dr. Goodwin directed a question to Gina, "Do you understand everything Chief Gordon is explaining to you, Gina?"

"Yes," Gina replied calmly. "Will Nancy go to prison?" Gina asked.

"Yes," Chief Gordon responded. "Probably for the rest of her life. But please know she will never be able to hurt anyone ever again. She will get help. She'll be taken care of," the chief replied.

"Will she die?" Gina asked.

"That will be determined by the court and the judge assigned to the murder cases," Harry answered.

Gina was thinking about that—Nancy having to die for the crimes she committed. Gina wasn't sure how she felt about that. She wanted her to just stay in prison and get help.

Chief Gordon turned to Josh. "Josh, I need for you to make that phone call now to Ms. Dennyson—to Reagan. I would like for you to brief her and bring her up-to-date on the current information. When we get back and have Nancy Brown secured in jail, we will all go over to the Dennyson Mansion and have an official meeting with her and that Irene and whatever staff is still present at the mansion. Dr. Goodwin, I know this has been very rough for you and your staff to be away from your hospital and work for this trying time, but if you and, of course, Gina could stay just a little while longer, it would be tremendously appreciated," Chief Gordon said earnestly.

Brenda added, right after Chief Gordon was finished with his statement, "I'd like to stay, too, Dr. Goodwin, if that's all right. I want to stay with Gina."

"Of course, it's okay," Dr. Goodwin replied. "I have been in communication with the doctor back at Hollingsworth. Everything is good there. I can stay for a while longer, Chief Gordon," Will replied. "And, Brenda, you certainly can stay as well. Adam, Dr. Goodwin asked, how about you? Do you wish to stay?"

"Unfortunately, I really need to get back to Hollingsworth—work, of course, but school as well. I'm sorry," Adam replied apologetically.

"No problem. I can certainly understand that. If you need any assistance with your professors and you need any written explanations of your being away, please don't hesitate to ask and let me know, Adam," Dr. Goodwin answered.

"Thank you, Dr. Goodwin. I will certainly let you know. I appreciate that," Adam said in response.

Chief Gordon summed up the entire morning with several thank-yous to Dr. Goodwin, Brenda, Adam, and Gina, of course. He wanted to emphasize how grateful he and Harry and Josh and the rest of the Covington Police Department were in their valuable help in solving these unsolved murders. He wanted to thank Dr. Goodwin and Brenda and Gina for staying, and he appreciated their patience. Their patience was well noted and much appreciated. If they would just return to Covington Inn and sit tight for just a couple of days longer, he would be grateful. Chief Gordon promised this would be routine, and they would be back in just a couple of days. And then they could wrap this case up for once and for all.

Things were falling into place—finally. Chief Gordon, although accompanying detectives to gather up a suspect was not a common practice, went along with Detectives Trimble and Winters. This case was touchy, to say the least, and had to be treated with absolutely *no* room for error.

Josh made that call to Reagan—finally. He was apologetic yet again because their conversation had to be brief. He explained everything and brought Reagan up-to-date on what had transpired these past few days. He explained everything that had been happening, and he wanted to let her know that he, Harry, and Chief Gordon were leaving town shortly to go and pick up Nancy Brown. He explained about the construction company finding the long-lost boots, the pitchfork, which was the murder weapon that killed Melanie, and of course, finding Gina Smith. He apologized to Reagan about how this was so much information to take in all at once and how he couldn't divulge the information until now. He was finally granted permission from the chief to do so.

Reagan understood. After she ended her conversation with Josh, she sat in disbelief. She couldn't believe that this all could be finally over and come to an end. She understood how the chief, Harry, and Josh had things to do, to finish up and finally bring everything to fruition, but Reagan had something to do as well.

Reagan went to find Irene. Irene was upstairs resting in her room. Reagan knocked gently on her door.

"Irene, it's Reagan. You awake?" Reagan quietly asked.

Irene was just sitting in her chair as she had dozed off for a couple of moments.

"Come in, dear," Irene replied. "I'm awake."

Reagan slowly opened Irene's bedroom door. "I'm sorry to bother you, Irene, but I wanted to let you know that Josh called me. I need to bring you up-to-date on the new information about the murders of Melanie and David," Reagan said matter-of-factly.

"I knew it!" Irene exclaimed. "Come and sit here with me, dear," as Irene got up from her chair and went over to the small settee in the sitting area of her bedroom.

Irene motioned Reagan to come and sit beside her.

Reagan explained how Gina and Nancy were both found. Nancy had done the murders. The murder weapon was found along with a pair of boots at a construction site. It was the apartment building where Nancy Brown and Gina Smith lived. The construction company found the items when they were digging and leveling the land so a strip mall could be built. Gina Smith was here with a doctor and her nurse from Hollingsworth Sanitorium. Nancy Brown was soon going to be brought in. She was found living elsewhere.

"Irene, Josh instructed us that we are to say nothing—tell no one—of this information, not just yet. It will all be known in a press release. It will be on the exact day of the anniversary of the murders," Reagan explained in utmost disbelief.

"Oh my, how dramatic…and how ironic," Irene said. "To think all those questions about the murders will finally be answered publicly. Arthur and Anne and Melanie and David will finally find some peace. They will finally be able to rest in peace," Irene said solemnly as she closed her eyes.

"Irene," Reagan said, "there's something else we have to do—you and I. It's important, and we have to do it on the day—or night rather—of the anniversary of the murders."

The other night, Reagan had gone out into the gardens and watched quietly again the recurring playback visions that had been happening in the back near Melanie's forgotten cottage. When Reagan would run and try to make contact with David.

"Irene, I know now why David won't talk to me. He doesn't know me. He doesn't know who I am. But David knows you, Irene. He knows you, and so does your Melanie." Reagan came to this epiphany the other night. *Why would David acknowledge me— talk to me. He doesn't even know me.*

"Irene, you have to go out there with me and try and communicate with David. For some reason, watching David carry Melanie out of that cottage and then saying, 'Help me!'—he doesn't know or think that he died. And maybe he thinks he can still save his beloved Melanie. Irene, we have to tell him that they both have died so they can be reunited and pass over together. Irene, are you listening to me?" Reagan put both of her hands on Irene's shoulders and looked into her eyes that were tearing up.

Irene was listening to Reagan, but her thoughts took her back to that horrid, awful night. She replayed the moments that led up to when her and Arthur walked back to Melanie's cottage, finding Melanie's lifeless body and David's crumpled body over Melanie's. Blood was everywhere! It was the most horrific, terrifying moment that two people could ever see and experience! Life would never, ever be the same again at the Dennyson Mansion.

"Irene?" Reagan gently gave Irene's shoulders a rub. "Irene?"

"I'm sorry, dear. I was just remembering that terrible, terrible night that all happened." Irene was almost in tears.

"I know. I understand, Irene. I'm so very sorry," Reagan apologized. "But, Irene, we *have* to—you and I—have to bring Melanie and David to rest. You have to be a part of this. They know you!" Reagan pleaded again. "And there's also one more thing," Reagan began to say.

"What's that, dear?" Irene asked, looking puzzled.

"I think it would help if we could somehow, in a modest way, recreate that night. And I think it would be good to have a doctor here, so David could bring Melanie to him. That's what David wanted to do that night—to find someone who could help Melanie, like a doctor. He wanted to find someone to help him with Melanie. We need to give that to David. He needs to be rid of the guilt that he must have been feeling that night of not taking care of his Melanie. Don't you see that, Irene? Do you understand?" Reagan tried to make her point. She so wanted Irene to agree so Melanie and David would finally be at peace.

The best-laid plans.

CHAPTER 56

Sheriff Middaugh and his two deputies saw a dim light and heard the TV when they approached Butch at his apartment. He informed his two deputies, Mike and Jason, that this could get rough. Butch had no clue that he was going to get a visit from the sheriff's department He also informed his two deputies that there was not to be anything mentioned about the murders or his real identity.

"Just call him Butch and keep the story straight about bringing him in for questioning about the missing money from Jake's desk drawer. Got that, boys?" Sheriff Middaugh reviewed.

Butch's apartment was actually a side-by-side double house. Butch lived on one side, and an older single guy lived next door. Both were quiet and were never a problem, the owner told Sheriff Middaugh one day.

The sheriff knew this wasn't going to be pleasant. He had to admit, he really liked Butch. He never had any squabble or one ounce of problems with the boy. And now finding out that Butch had been impersonating a man...well, that was something, he thought. And doing what the chief said he did, well, that was certainly a lot to take in and ingest.

"Got it, Sheriff," Mike and Jason replied in unison.

Sheriff Middaugh knocked on Butch's door.

"Butch, it's Sheriff Middaugh. Can I have a word with you?" the sheriff treaded slowly.

Sheriff Middaugh wasn't sure if Butch was going to come open the door or somehow slip out the back, so for that reason, he motioned Mike to go around back and watch and wait. He didn't think Butch had a gun. He had asked Jake the other day if he knew if Butch had one.

"You know," Sheriff Middaugh said to Jake, "I know you guys talk, and maybe through your many conversations, Butch might have mentioned that he had a gun."

Jake didn't think so.

Sheriff Middaugh was glad that Butch came to the door to answer. He was grateful there wouldn't be any running or tasering involved that night. He was getting too old for that, which made him think about retirement soon—maybe go South...

Butch looked scared when he opened up the front door. For the first time in his/her life, there was a frightened look in his eyes. Maybe these past years of living a comfortable, quiet existence made Nancy realize what she had been missing all these years—peace in her life. There had been no agitation, conflict, rage in her life as Butch. She liked living life as Butch, as a man. It was less complicated. There was no drama. Butch actually made a friend, a true friend, a comrade in Jake. Maybe there was something to this "I just don't feel right" as a woman thing.

Morphing into Butch, becoming Butch, Nancy could become whoever she wanted to become. She could leave her previous life in the past. It could—and would—stay there in the past where it belonged. She could start all over again with a clean slate. She wouldn't make the same mistakes ever again. No more killings. Hell, she didn't even want to own a gun! There would never be a reason to have one. Everyone was really nice around here. It was a place with clean, simple, no-fuss living. It was a place to start over, a new place to call home.

Butch opened up the front door. He looked disheveled, barefoot, like he'd fallen asleep on a couch or in a chair while watching TV.

"Sheriff Middaugh?" Butch looked absolutely puzzled and confused. "How can I help you?" Butch asked as he smoothed out his hair.

"Butch, there's a problem about Jake missing some money from his desk drawer. He alerted us the other day. I need you to come down to the station to make a statement. You know anything about that, Butch?" Sheriff Middaugh asked nonchalantly.

By then, Mike had joined the sheriff and Jason at the front door. He had heard him talking and fig-ured staying in the back was needless now.

"Sheriff, you think I took money from Jake?" Butch asked, surprised.

"I'm just asking, Butch. It's missing, and it's a lot of money—that's all. You're the only one who works there with Jake. I'm just asking you if you know anything about it. Please don't get upset. I just need you to come with me to the station, Butch. We need to get a statement from you—that's all."

"Umm…Sheriff, I made that deposit for Jake," Butch answered frankly.

"You made that deposit for him?" Sheriff asked with a surprised look. Mike and Jason just looked on.

"Ahh, shit!" Butch exclaimed as he slapped his hand against his head. "I totally forgot to give Jake the damn deposit slip! Shit! I wanted to surprise him. He's been real busy lately, and I know he has a lot on his mind. I saw him put the money in his desk drawer. I know where he keeps the books and deposit slips. I thought I'd surprise him by telling him I made the deposit for him. Here it is…" Butch reached into his back pocket. Mike and Jason, automatically had their hands on their guns. But it was hard to do so. They, too, were friends of Butch's.

"Guys, guys, look. I'm just going for my wallet. You can grab it if you want." Butch put his hands above his head. "I'm telling you the truth."

Butch was telling the truth. The deposit slip was in his wallet. He had forgotten to give it to Jake. He apologized and said he was sorry. He even understood and held no grudges against Jake for not knowing or wondering if he took it. Butch didn't feel any grudge against Mike or Jason, especially since they knew one another. He understood. He also held no grudge against Sheriff Middaugh. Butch knew they were all just doing their job. Butch was going to surprise Jake. It was one less thing that Jake had to worry about.

The sheriff had to think quickly now. What was he going to do? It was legit—Butch didn't steal any money. He said he would never do something like that. Butch was grateful that Jake even hired him with very little—none, actually—mechanic's experience or knowledge. And Jake spent days—and sometimes nights—teaching Butch everything he knew about auto repairs, just like his father taught him. Butch was genuinely so very grateful.

Sheriff Middaugh hated when things didn't come together and go as planned. But it was bittersweet as well. He was very glad to confirm his thoughts that Butch wouldn't do anything like that. And of course, Jake was so relieved and feeling guilty.

"Butch, could you still come down to the station now—with Mike and Jason and me? It would be just to clear everything up?" Sheriff Middaugh was grasping here.

"I guess, Sheriff," Butch answered. "Just let me get some shoes on." Butch left the door opened and yelled over his shoulder, "You guys can come in if you want. I promise not to bolt!" Butch chuckled.

The sheriff and his deputies came in and thought to themselves that Butch had no clue just how true they thought that could have been.

"I'll wait for Butch, Sheriff," Jason offered. "If you and Mike want to just sit and wait in the cruiser. We'll be out in a minute—Butch and I."

"Okay, Jason." Sheriff Middaugh motioned Mike to join him in the cruiser while they wait for Jason and Butch to come out. The sheriff didn't feel there were any worries here.

Sheriff Middaugh said under his breath and in a very low voice, "Well, boys, here we go. Just go with the flow. I'm winging it here."

Mike and Jason nodded nonchalantly.

Sheriff Middaugh and the deputies took Butch down to the station. Butch rode in the back seat with Jason, while Mike rode in front with Sheriff Middaugh. The sheriff was driving a little slower than usual. He was thinking, *Now what?* He was listening to the small talk that was being exchanged between his deputy, Jason, and Butch. *Damn*, Sheriff Middaugh thought to himself, *sometimes I really hate this job!*

Sometimes people changed. The people in the rural town knew nothing of Nancy Brown—her personalities, her traits, her behaviors. That girl was gone, existing *only* in the past, a past life you might say is dead. She was nowhere to be seen or found again! Butch was the new Nancy Brown. How can this be? In life, a miracle, if you must say, can and once in a while does happen. Butch was truly a new entity, a new person, with characteristics such as kindness, thoughtfulness, a drive to succeed, to honestly be good at something. The evil, deceitful, diabolical, lying, cheating, killing, and pure evil traits/tendencies and trademarks of Nancy Brown did not exist any longer. They did not exist in Butch. The new characteristics—one may label attributes, those that are genuine—are characterized in a positive way. Those features were those that surfaced and existed now in Butch.

So what happens to those individuals with these dilemmas and situations, these turnabout mannerisms? The oddities and peculiarities of the human mind is a vast black hole. Mental experts study for years and years the workings of the human psyche. They make many comparisons, assumptions, hypotheses, educated guesses. It only takes one individual, one animal, one entity to change the variables. It only takes one to skew the results, to change course in one's thinking.

This may be the case in Nancy Brown, who was now Butch. Just how does one do that in the most sincerest of ways? And also, of course, the opposite can happen as well…the phenomena of not only going from the baddest of the bad to the "goodest" of the good, but the reverse—going from good to evil. The variables in one's life changes. It creates who we are, but *we* have the power to create *who* we *want* to become…

CHAPTER 57

Butch was sitting behind bars now. The sheriff was sitting at his desk, wishing he had retired last year. Jason offered to stay while Mike went home— one deputy was all that Sheriff Middaugh felt was needed. Before Mike headed home, he went to pick up some food to bring back to Sheriff Middaugh, his fellow deputy, and to Butch. Not any one of them would ever imagine Butch doing those awful murders up at Covington. All three felt terrible about locking Butch up. His reaction was truly a "deer in the headlights" reaction. He never saw it coming. And yet he willingly walked right into the jail cell. He waved off the handcuffs that Sheriff Middaugh hoped he wouldn't have to use. There was a calmness about Butch that night.

Butch had known that someday, the past and the previous existence of Nancy Brown might catch up with him. He knew that what he did—or rather, what Nancy Brown did—could surface again someday.

Sheriff Middaugh said to Jason, "I want to talk with you and Mike when he returns with the food, okay, Jason?"

"Sure, Sheriff," Jason responded. "You okay?"

"Fine," Sheriff Middaugh said very solemnly.

Mike returned with sandwiches and drinks and several bags of chips. "I didn't know what everyone would like, boss, so I bought a little of everything." Mike chuckled.

"Fine…that's fine, Mikey. Please take food to Butch and then join me and Jason back here, okay? There's something I want to discuss with the both of you boys," Sheriff Middaugh replied.

"Okay, boss," Mike responded in a curious, questioning tone. "Be right back."

Mike returned from delivering the food to Butch. Mike felt he was giving Butch his last meal. And like Jason and maybe the sheriff, he was not real happy about it.

"Okay, boss, I'm here." Mike came into the office and sat down next to Jason.

The door of the sheriff's office was open a crack, but soon closed. The sheriff didn't want anyone, including Butch, to hear of this next conversation that was about to happen.

"Boys, I've been a sheriff here for thirty-some years. I've seen, heard, and done many things that I had to do as a sheriff—as you two can attest to. Sometimes, the decisions, duties were difficult, and some, on the other hand, very easy to perform. But this case, this situation has stumped me…stopped me in my tracks, so to speak," the sheriff explained.

"How so, Sheriff?" Jason asked.

"We know Chief Gordon and his two detectives are on their way right now to pick up Butch. And we know what they are picking him up for. Of course, we don't know those behaviors that were present in that individual who committed those crimes. We just know Butch and the type of person he is. He is not that person any longer—anymore. That person that committed those brutal, awful, evil murders in all likelihood is dead—gone. Those characteristics of *that* murderer, that person, do *not* exist anymore."

"So what are sayin', boss?" Mike asked.

"I am going to go back and talk to Butch. You boys are to stay here. I am going to let Butch go if he agrees to do exactly what I am proposing. If he accepts what I am proposing, I will turn him loose. It will be up to him to choose his life. We will corroborate our stories to a tee, no variances. We will all be in unison. We—all three of us—must agree that Butch is a decent *guy*. He is *not* that person who committed those crimes. He's different now. I want all three of us to give Butch that second chance for life. He'll therefore need to evaporate for a time, and when those men from Covington leave, he can come back, if he chooses, and live his life out here—with us. If either or both of you disagree, I'll deny I ever had this conversation with you. If you both agree with my decision, then we die with it. After this…soon, I'm retiring and heading down South. There will be a new sheriff—most likely you, Michael—to take my place. If we decide on this and explain to Butch, the conversation dies here. We are to *never* speak of this again—ever," Sheriff said very firmly.

"What about Jake, Sheriff?" Jason asked.

"I'll take care of Jake—that'll be easy. Jake likes Butch. They're best buddies. Jake will be in full agreement. I am sure of that. So we all in agreement, or do either or both of you want to take this conversation further?" Sheriff Middaugh was hoping for solidarity and agreement.

The sheriff left his two deputies with one last thought: "Sometimes, we don't always go by the book. Sometimes, our judgment leans toward playing God. Sometimes, it's not always leading with your head. Sometimes you just have to lead with your heart. Now maybe Butch won't do what I think he'll do, but I don't think so."

Mike looked at Jason, and Jason looked at Mike. Both nodded in agreement with Sheriff Middaugh, but both wanted to be in the room here when Sheriff Middaugh talked with Butch.

"We both want to be here, Sheriff. We want to be here when you talk with Butch," Mike said.

Jason nodded in agreement.

"Okay, then," Sheriff Middaugh answered. "Go get Butch, Jason, please."

Jason went down the hall to unlock the jail cell that was holding Butch. Butch was resting quietly on his bunk.

"Butch, Sheriff and Mike and I want to talk to you, okay? I'm unlocking this cell, but I need to know that you're not going to try and escape, okay?" Jason was hoping, and thinking Butch would comply.

"No, Jason, I'm not going to try and escape," Butch answered.

"I have your word on that?" Jason asked.

"Yes," Butch answered frankly.

"Okay." Jason was so praying that that the alter personality wasn't going to suddenly show up and emerge now.

Jason led Butch, in handcuffs (just to be on safe side), down the hallway to Sheriff Middaugh's office. The door was open. Jason had Butch go in first.

"Jason, take the handcuffs off of Butch, please," Sheriff Middaugh instructed him.

"Butch, do you believe in second chances?" Sheriff Middaugh asked as he motioned Butch to sit in an adjacent chair.

Butch was rubbing his wrists. "I suppose so, Sheriff. Are you guys going to shoot me?" Butch asked.

"No, Butch, we are not going to shoot you." The sheriff chuckled a little. "But…I'm going to give you your second chance, Butch. It will be a chance to continue living the life you have been living for the past years here. We, unfortunately, know now who you really are—who you, in our eyes, were. We all feel that you are not *that* individual—that person—any longer," the sheriff said.

Butch interjected, "You all know who I am—well, who I was?"

Jason and Mike nodded, along with the sheriff.

"Ya, man," Jason answered. "You're Butch!"

Butch, for the first time in a long time, had panic in his voice. "Sheriff, guys…I'm *not* that person anymore. Please believe me! I'm not!"

"Now let me finish," the sheriff replied, raising his voice. "We three—Jason, Mikey, and myself—have made a pact. And here's how it's going to go—if you agree. I will need your word, of course, Butch. And I'm going to say this before I continue, we'll *never* have this discussion, this conversation, *ever* again. What is talked about, decided, and agreed upon will 'die' in this room tonight. I will button everything up. Only I will be the one talking to the chief and his two detectives. This situation will never be discussed again. From this point on, you will be Butch Lawson. I'll take care of it. I must ask you, Butch, will you stay with us here in the county?"

"Yes, oh my god, yes!" Butch answered with surprise. "I want that more than anything! I promise I won't escape—bolt. I just want to stay and live here in peace," Butch said with relief.

"Okay," Sheriff Middaugh continued. "Well, here's what we're going to do then…"

Life is about second chances, new beginnings, a new start. There are angels put here on this earth to guide us, to teach us, to lead us maybe in different directions, better directions than the pathways we would have normally taken.

There are sometimes miracles that happen to mold us into different human beings. There are variables that will surface to change our direction, to make us think differently, to act differently, to be different, pure and simple. It can be totally unexplainable, with no logic whatsoever. A wise person once said, "Make a decision. In three days, it may not have been the best decision to make. But at *that* moment, at *that* specific time, it *was* the *right* decision to make. Don't look back. For it's better to make a decision than to do nothing at all."

So decisions were made that night in the sheriff's office. Secret pacts were made and kept. Confidences, lies, were created, created for the greater good.

For the greater good...

CHAPTER 58

Jason took Butch home with him. Jason was going on vacation for two weeks. He had a place where Butch could lay low for a while. They stopped real quick at Butch's place to grab clothes and then left for Jason's apartment to grab what he needed. And then the two were gone.

Sheriff Middaugh went to pay a visit to Jake. He explained what was going on. He told him about the mistake of thinking Butch took the cash. He gave Jake the deposit slip.

"I don't know what to say, Sheriff. I really just don't know what to say!" Jake responded in pure amazement.

"Are you in agreement, Jakey? Are we all on the same page?" the sheriff asked.

"Hell, ha!" Jake answered. "Sheriff, I like Butch. I was always on that page! I will always be on his side—always!"

"Okay then. Here's how this story is going to go down. There are to be absolutely *no* variances, Jake—got it? We have to *all* have the *exact* same story. The chief and the detectives will be here in the morning.

We *can't* have any screwups!" Sheriff Middaugh said loudly.

"I got it, Sheriff. I know nothing!" Jake replied dutifully.

"Hey, also, do you have any photos of you and Butch or just of Butch around here?" the sheriff asked.

"Uhh, I think maybe a couple," Jake answered. "But why?"

"Burn 'em now!" Sheriff Middaugh ordered. "I do not want any photos of Butch around so they can see what he looks like. You understand?"

"Yep, got it!" Jake responded. "I got it. Burn 'em. Right! Sheriff, it's going to be okay. Your heart is in the right place. We will protect Butch," Jake reassured the sheriff.

Sheriff Middaugh explained to Jake how Jason was taking Butch to higher ground and was keeping him in a secluded cabin located in the dense, wooded area. "No one will find them there. Then in several weeks, hopefully when things die down, Butch and Jason can come back home. Then Butch can settle back in to the life and lifestyle he had been happily living."

Sheriff Middaugh went back to the station, where Mike was waiting for him. The sheriff had a few other things to set up before the chief and his two detectives came.

"Mikey, hit me!" Sheriff Middaugh said it very matter-of-factly.

"What?" Mike asked in utter amazement.

"You heard me! Hit me!" the sheriff repeated.

Sheriff Middaugh had to make it look like Butch had fled. The story would be as follows: Sheriff Middaugh was alone with Butch at the station one evening. He let Butch out of his cell so he could use the bathroom. The urinal was backed up and couldn't be used. Butch had to use the restroom closest to the sheriff's office. Butch hit him over the head and knocked him out with a heavy flashlight that the sheriff was holding.

Everything was in place. Sheriff Middaugh bandaged up his forehead. Deputy Mike was with him at the station, and a black sedan just pulled into the station lot.

"It's showtime!" Sheriff Middaugh declared. "And here we go!"

CHAPTER 59

"What the hell is going on down here!" Chief Gordon yelled at the top of his voice.

Detectives Harry Trimble and Josh Winters sat in total disbelief. Chief Gordon was ranting and raving and pacing the floor.

"Did you not call in anybody for extra help? Did you not chase after Nancy Brown? Didn't you send a posse out—comb the area? What the hell have you both been doing around here? Playing tiddlywinks?"

Harry and Josh had never seen the chief so irate or so upset.

Hell, they were in complete shock. How did you lose a suspect? This was a simple task that had now become the bumble of the century!

"Chief, we've been searching these areas. Have you looked behind us? Those are some pretty dense forests up there! We'll find him—her! For right now we, unfortunately, have turned up nothing. Don't start accusing my department for slacking off and not doing our jobs!" Sheriff Middaugh barked right back at the chief.

"Well, you didn't...you didn't do your jobs or Nancy Brown would be here and we would be leaving to take her back to Covington!" Chief Gordon yelled.

Chief Gordon was steaming and throwing things and swearing. They had been *that* close to closing this whole case once and for all. Now Nancy Brown was on the loose again, and no one had seen her—and maybe never would again.

It took a lot for the chief to even come anywhere near to a calm state of mind.

"We need a composite of this Butch," Harry said to the sheriff and his deputy. "We need a photo—a sketch of what this Butch looks like now. You have a photo, Sheriff, of this Butch? We have to have something to go off of—anything," Harry asked, growing impatient.

"We have no photos. We didn't book him for anything, so therefore, we have no official photo. You told me to just hold him and you'd be down to pick him, or rather her, up. I did that," Sheriff Middaugh told Harry firmly.

Josh asked, "Sheriff, the place where Nancy Brown/Butch worked, would they have any photos?"

"That's Jake at Jake's Garage. No, I asked thinking you boys would want something to use as a reference. But Jake said he never had any photos of Butch. I'm sorry," the sheriff replied calmly. "I know he's—she's gone. And we royally screwed up. I have the bump and headache to prove it. But rest assured, we will keep looking for this Nancy Brown. You can be sure about that!" Sheriff Middaugh made sure he sounded sincere.

Sheriff Middaugh went to make a pot of coffee. He needed an excuse to leave the area. He felt drained. His epic performance would possibly be his last!

"So what now, Chief?" Josh asked Chief Gordon. "We came down here, and we now go back empty handed?"

Harry was looking out the window with his hands on his hips. He was dumbfounded. Never had he thought they would come this close to solving such high-profile murders—one of the most well-known murders—and have the sole murderer just slip through their fingers again!

"Harry, make some calls around to the neighboring sheriff departments and alert them of Nancy Brown possibly being in their area. Tell them that she has changed her identity and goes by the name of Butch now. Tell them to comb their areas thoroughly—no stone left unturned! Tell them to look for a male—short, dark hair, around 5'8". Give a generality on the weight—maybe around 180 lb. or so. Maybe, just maybe, by the grace of God, someone will report seeing someone like that in their area. Here's hoping," Chief Gordon said.

"Okay, Chief. I'll get right on it," Harry replied dutifully.

"Oh, and, Harry?" Chief Gordon added. "Tell whoever you talk to this identity of Nancy Brown/Butch could now be altered. More than likely, she could be changing her look again."

"Got it, Chief," Harry responded.

"Damn it!" Chief Gordon yelled out loud again.

Nothing! That would be the adjective to describe the results of anything Chief Gordon and Detectives Trimble and Winters turned up. Nothing!

The chief didn't want to leave the area. He thought, like Harry and Josh did, that this Butch might come back to the area. Maybe this Butch forgot something. It was a stretch, but somehow it gave the sheriff and the two detectives some hope.

"What would bring her back here, Chief? Don't you think that would be a stupid move?" Sheriff Middaugh replied. "It would be a pretty stupid move to come back to the same area that he/she lived. This Nancy Brown, I think, would know we would be always watching, waiting to see if she would return. That wouldn't be too bright." The sheriff hoped it was believable. Although he thought if he kept this conversation going, the chief was going to have him shot.

"Absolutely true. But I'm grasping here, Sheriff Middaugh." Chief Gordon tried so hard to keep his temper intact.

Chief Gordon was thinking. He looked at Harry and at Josh. They, too, were thinking. Were they all thinking the same thing? Was something here just not right? Were they missing something?

Sheriff Middaugh interrupted the silence, "Chief, what can we do? What do you want us to do?"

"Find Nancy Brown!" the chief bellowed. "You lost her...go find her!" The chief was so frustrated and tired and hungry.

"Is there a place around here to get a bite to eat?" Chief Gordon asked Sheriff Middaugh.

"Just down the road, about two miles, there's a restaurant/diner in town," Mike answered.

"C'mon, boys," Chief Gordon said to Harry and Josh. "Let's go get something to eat and discuss our next move." The chief was exhausted.

"Sheriff, we will be back. Please do whatever you can. Call in favors to whoever you know. We need to locate Nancy Brown. She couldn't have gotten too far. Oh, and, Sheriff, did she own a vehicle? Did she have a mode of transportation?" Chief Gordon asked.

Sheriff Middaugh responded, "Butch had a pickup truck, but it's still at his apartment. It hasn't moved. Remember, I picked him up to bring him in. The truck's still there."

"Hmmm…that's still strange though," the chief said. "Why wouldn't Nancy go back to her apartment and pick up her truck? She could have dumped it somewhere and hitched a ride to wherever she thought to go. Interesting…"

While at the diner in town, Chief Gordon called back to the Covington Police Station and explained the mess to Lieutenant Markham.

"Oh god, what a mess, Jim! Send out the pictures and composite again, like before, and we'll hope for another miracle. Unfortunately, we'll be coming home with nothing. Pray for a miracle." Chief Gordon did pray.

CHAPTER 60

The anniversary of the murders of Melanie Dennyson and David Williams was just two days away. Josh called Reagan to touch base with her on the updates concerning the case. He explained how the sheriff's department literally lost Nancy Brown. She gave them the slip and left town. They—the chief, Harry, and himself—were all at a loss. Nancy Brown slipped through their grasp once again.

There wasn't anything else to do at the sheriff's department They couldn't just sit around and wait for Nancy Brown to return. Like that was going to happen!

Chief Gordon, Harry, and Josh headed back to Covington empty handed. It was certainly not what they expected to happen. It was definitely not the outcome they were hoping for. They all thought this case would finally be wrapped up, sealed, and closed up for good. But that's not the way it happened. It was a very solemn and quiet ride back home to Covington.

Chief Gordon broke the silence. "Boys, what should I have done differently?" Chief Gordon asked.

He was riding in the front seat while Harry was driving and Josh was in the back.

"I don't know, Chief." Harry was the first to speak up and respond. "But, Chief, something just isn't right with all this. There's something missing in all of this," Harry said in a very puzzled way.

Josh chimed right in, "Ya, Chief, there are a couple of puzzle pieces missing. I know that something isn't right with what went down."

The chief responded, "Yes, I agree with the both of you. There is something that just isn't right with what happened. And we three may agree to an answer, but we can't prove anything. Sheriff is a pretty seasoned officer and well respected in those parts. He isn't one to usually mess up a case, get sloppy, or make any mistakes. Something just doesn't add up, for sure."

There were several more moments of silence. These three men were all thinking of possibilities. They were trying to figure things out and trying to fit the puzzle pieces together.

Josh broke the silence, "Chief, Harry, what if Nancy or this Butch had some help escaping?"

Harry answered, "What kind of help are you suggesting, Josh?"

"And why, Josh, would anyone help this Butch get away?" Chief Gordon interrupted.

"Simple," said Josh, "because they like him. Maybe as Butch, he made friends there—loyal friends, maybe friends in high places. Obviously, he not only changed his physical identity but changed his personality totally as well. He did a 180. He certainly wasn't going to keep being the same person that he/she was. No one would ever want to bring attention to themselves like that. We've heard about this time and time again with these killers. They do an about-face. They lead normal lives until they grow old and die. We know many high profilers that have done that, and only by a fluke do police, federal agents, etc. stumble upon them years later—for a simple violation. What do you both think about that?"

"The only thing is," the chief answered, "I can't believe he and his two deputies would stick their necks out and jeopardize everything—their jobs, their careers, their reputations—for a killer." Harry nodded in agreement with the chief.

"Well," Josh answered, "as I learned in the academy, and of course, both of you know this, sometimes things just don't make sense. It doesn't have to make sense. People make all sorts of irrational decisions when emotions are a factor."

Chief Gordon replied, "Well, that's true."

It was a very long ride back to Covington. Harry, the chief, and Josh were all very tired, to say the least. They headed right over to where Dr. Goodwin and Brenda and Gina were staying—at the Covington Inn. They were beat, but they knew they had to talk with them to bring them up-to-date on the latest information. It was to be a conversation that neither of the three wanted to have. They were avoiding it like the plague.

All three were in the lobby when just the doctor entered the lounge area.

"Gentlemen, nice to see you return safely, and I hope you found what you were looking for." Dr. Goodwin greeted them with a smile.

"Hello, Doctor," Chief Gordon replied in a very tired voice.

"Oh…that doesn't sound promising." Dr. Goodwin reacted with a surprised look.

"Let's just say that our journey did not lead us to the package we had hoped to bring home," Chief Gordon replied sadly.

"No package?" the doctor asked.

"Nope…no package," Harry replied.

There were a few other people in the lobby and lounge area. They were all within ear's distance, so of course, the men could not speak freely.

"Doctor, would you like to join us for a drink in the bar and lounge area?" Chief Gordon asked.

"I'd love one!" Dr. Goodwin replied enthusiastically.

The four gentlemen found a secluded booth in the corner of the bar and lounge. They would know if anyone was or could be listening in on their impending, extremely delicate conversation.

Brenda was with Gina upstairs in their room. Brenda was working hard on Gina's ability at communication. It was going to be a long process of acclimating Gina and helping to strengthen her mental stability.

The chief and Harry described their trip to collect Nancy Brown. The doctor listened intently. They were all sipping on their favorite beverages as they hoped their drinks could cushion some of the disappointment they were feeling. It was true—alcohol could sometimes numb the pain.

"Frankly, I don't know what to say," Dr. Goodwin responded after everything was divulged.

"There's nothing to say, Doctor," Chief Gordon replied.

"Dr. Goodwin," Josh asked, "is there a possibility, in your professional opinion, that these people who knew Nancy Brown as Butch would have become good friends with him/her?"

"Well, of course!" Will answered. "There's always a possibility that this Nancy Brown/Butch struck up friendships, lasting and close friendships with all or any one or several of those people. That is true for anyone. It's human nature, for God's sake! Anything's possible. And of course, remember this, you *do* have Gina Smith. She remembers."

"I know, Dr. Goodwin, but it's not enough. We can't solve a case without the murderer who committed the crimes," Chief Gordon answered disappointedly.

The future was in the hands of fate.

PART 4

The Final Journey

CHAPTER 61

Jason and Butch were eating. Jason fixed some pork and beans. They were sitting in the cabin that belonged to Jason's uncle. They had been there for a couple of days. It was a cabin tucked just far enough away from civilization. It was a cabin that belonged to Jason's uncle Ned. His uncle had passed away a couple of years ago, and he'd left his cabin to Jason. Jason had many fond memories of spending many a summer up there with his uncle Ned. They were very close and shared many wonderful times up in the cabin. They were so much alike in their mannerisms. One would swear they were father and son—not uncle and nephew. Jason was more like his uncle Ned than his own father. Jason and his father were very different. They were still very close but different. Ned knew Jason's job as a law enforcement officer could become very stressful, so he wanted Jason to have his cabin as a getaway space—somewhere he could go to collect his thoughts and rest and rejuvenate. So the cabin was now Jason's.

"You know who I am, what I am—or what I was—and you're a deputy, and still you chose to help me? Stay with me?" Butch asked. "You sure you want to do this, Jason?"

"I know it doesn't make much sense," Jason replied back to Butch.

"Man, you could lose your job if you're ever found out," Butch said.

"And so could Mike and Sheriff Middaugh, don't forget," Jason replied.

"Why? Why would you guys *ever* put your jobs, your reputations on the line for a slug like me?" Butch asked in bewilderment.

"Simple, Butch. We think you've changed. You're not *that* person that committed those murders those years back," Jason said with compassion.

"But…I still committed them. They were awful, brutal crimes. I was such an evil person back then. I should pay for what I did," Butch said in a judgmental way.

"You'll fry if you're caught—you know that. They'll give you the death penalty…or life!" Jason said abruptly and firmly. "You could turn yourself in, you know."

"I could, but I don't want to die, even though I deserve to," Butch replied in a scared tone of voice.

Jason wanted to turn this conversation around and get off the subject completely. He didn't want to upset Butch any further. It wouldn't do any good.

"Hey, Butch, I need to go into town to pick up more supplies. I shouldn't be gone too long. Will you be okay for a while?" Jason asked Butch.

Butch wasn't really paying attention. His mind was elsewhere. He was thinking about the past and all what he did, all that was done, all the words he said.

"Butch, you hear me?" Jason asked again.

"Oh, ya, man. Sorry, just thinking about things," Butch answered, trying to cover up his solemn behavior.

"I just have to go to this little store. It's like a general store. I'll be back. Any special requests? Any special foods I can pick up for you?" Jason wanted Butch to know he cared and was concerned.

"No, I'm good, but thanks, man!" Butch responded warmly. "I really appreciate everything you and the sheriff and Mikey are doing for me. I really don't deserve it. I will be forever grateful to all three of you. Thank you so much. I have never had anyone in my entire life treat me with such compassion and caring."

"You sure you're okay then?" Jason asked yet again.

"Ya, I'm good. It's all good," Butch replied, trying to assure Jason.

"Okay then. I'll see ya in a bit, bro. I'll try not to be long." Jason, at that moment, really didn't want to leave Butch. An inner voice inside of him said, "Stay."

"I'll see ya," Butch said.

CHAPTER 62

Jason left. Butch heard the door slam and then again on the truck door. He was alone now. Butch got up from the couch and walked over to an old wooden table. The cabin was small. He knew what he had to do. He found some paper in one of the drawers. The cabin wasn't equipped with a lot of supplies, but all the basics were there. He found some notebook paper and some pens and pencils. He needed to write. He needed to write a letter. He sat down on the old, worn-out couch and started to collect his thoughts.

My name is Nancy Brown. I go by Butch now. I have been living my life as a man for several years. I have changed. I am not the person I once was. I am not Nancy Brown. I know that I have killed. I killed Melanie Dennyson and David Williams and two others before them. They were two college-aged girls. My best friend and confidant at the time was Gina Smith. She had absolutely nothing to do with any of those crimes—those murders. She was a witness only. Please do not hold Gina responsible in any way. It was of my own doing. And because of her witnessing those brutal, horrific crimes, she went into a catatonic state. I was the one to drop her off at Hollingsworth Asylum/ Sanitorium. I knew I could no longer take care of her in her state of being. I knew the doctors and staff at Hollingsworth would take good care of her. I also escaped out of the jail where I was held until Covington Police could come and get me. I hit the sheriff over the head and fled. I do know, in my heart, that I was wrong. I know what my fate will be if I am caught. I will either get life in prison or the death penalty. Please believe me when I tell you that I am a changed person. I do not feel the hatred, the rage, the anger, the spite, the revenge, the evil that I used to feel every single day. I had found a new life for myself as Butch. I found a reason to live a good life. I found the goodness and kindness in people. I learned a trade and was given a job that I truly didn't deserve. I was shown kindness and friendship, loyalty and joy. These are all things that I have never experienced my entire life. But I must tell you, I am miserable now. I know that I have ruined several lives over what I have done. My actions have changed other human beings' lives—and not for the good. Please know that I am suffering…and suffering greatly. It isn't fair that my life is spared out of sheer luck and others have suffered and died because of the actions I have done. I'm not sure if Gina will ever come out of her state of mind, and for that, I am truly sorry. I am so sorry, Gina, for what I did to you. Please forgive me. I am so very sorry that you have seen the horror that I have done and still stayed around me to live with the horrible person that I was and became. You didn't deserve that. You showed me loyalty when I didn't deserve it. You showed me a kind of dedicated, devout friendship. You deserved a better friend. I take full responsibility for all the lives—living and deceased—that I have maimed and destroyed. I take ownership and blame for all of it. And, if there is a heaven, I know I won't be going up there. I do not belong there. If there is a hell, I am sure I will be there... or maybe I'll be in between, in limbo or purgatory, serving my penance. I will finish what is needed to be done. I will solve this crime. I know I will not meet you both in heaven, so please know, Melanie and David, that I am so truly sorry for the terrible pain and suffering that I have caused you both. I know you are both together, but you never got to be man and wife. And you never got the beautiful wedding you both deserved. Melanie, you were an angel and always treated me so kindly. You didn't deserve the tragic, brutal ending you received. And, David, you were always kind to me, and all you did was love your Melanie with all your heart and soul. Any

woman would be eternally grateful to have such a loving partner.

I am closing this letter with
such tremendous remorse and
guilt and sorrow and pain. It is
with great sadness that I know, in
my heart, that I have to say goodbye to this world and await my
penance in the next. And for that,
I am truly sorry for myself…that
I have made such bad, terrible
decisions in my life to bring me
to this.

May God bless all who I
have hurt. May the deceased find
peace, and may the living feel
some sort of closure and solitude
now that I am gone.

With sorrow,
Butch/Nancy Brown

CHAPTER 63

Jason took a little longer than he expected. He knew Butch would be okay. He kept saying that to himself. He shook off the nagging thought that Butch just didn't right. He seemed preoccupied. He probably didn't want to share his thoughts with him at the time. But he thought there would be plenty of time and opportunity for them to talk. Jason would have time to somehow feel better about everything that was going on. He knew Butch had some things that were troubling him. Shit, Jason couldn't imagine just how much shit he was probably thinking about. Butch had to be carrying around so much damn guilt. It had to be such a heavy burden for anyone to carry around. Butch had enough in the cabin to keep him occupied until he returned. There were some playing cards, puzzles, books to read.

Jason pulled up to the gravel area located next to the cabin. The cabin was pretty much hidden by evergreens and other foliage. Jason stepped out of his Ford Ranger with a couple of bags of food and supplies to keep him and Butch okay for a while.

Jason opened the door. The scene that Jason saw ahead of him wasn't anything he ever, in a million years, would have expected to see. It was horrific. Jason dropped the bags to the floor. The first thing he saw was Butch slumped over on the couch.

Butch sat lifeless on the couch with a large kitchen knife protruding from his chest. He'd stabbed himself. There was blood oozing out from the point where the knife entered his poor, lifeless body. He was gone. Butch was dead.

Jason knew not to touch anything, but he was so distraught. He dropped to his knees and started crying. He tried to find a pulse…nothing.

"Ahhh…man…Butch…why?" Jason said now out loud. "Man, why did you do this? We had *all* this worked out. You could have come back. We would have gone back in a couple of weeks. It would have blown over. You would have been home free, buddy!"

Jason talked out loud like he thought Butch would have heard him. But Butch didn't hear him, not that Jason would have known. Unfortunately, Jason couldn't or didn't have the gift of seeing or hearing spirits.

Jason saw the letter that Butch left sitting on the coffee table in front of the couch. He picked it up. He read the powerful, remorseful words that Butch composed. He must have written it when he left to go get food and supplies. Jason thought to himself, *I shouldn't have left Butch alone…*

Jason knew what he had to do now. He said a prayer out loud to Butch, as if he might have been listening. He said that he needed to leave his body there for a short time. He had to go get Sheriff Middaugh and Mike.

"Buddy, may you finally rest in peace and feel no more pain and grief and remorse. I love ya, man."

Jason wanted to place a blanket or sheet over Butch's body, but he knew he couldn't do that. He straightened everything up, and he placed the letter Butch had written back on the coffee table where he found it. He took one last look and closed the front door and locked it. He gently pulled the door closed. There was nothing else he could do. He drove back to the station to get Sheriff Middaugh and Mike. They would then head back up here. Jason vowed to come back up here again and find a peaceful, serene resting place for Butch. He wanted to find a headstone that would complement everything that Butch was. He, at least, deserved that much.

CHAPTER 64

It seemed like a very long drive back down the gravel road from the cabin.

It was nearing closing time at the sheriff's department. Jason hoped the sheriff and Mike were still at the station. He was nearing the area, and Jason stopped across the street behind a building so his Ford pickup wouldn't be seen. He wanted to make sure he didn't see the black sedan from Covington still there. It was gone.

"Good," Jason said to himself. The coast was clear—or so he hoped.

Jason quickly pulled in around the back to be on the safe side. He entered the back of the building. He saw Mike's pickup truck and the sheriff's car in the front, but he still pulled around to the back. He knocked on the back door since it was always locked. He had a key, of course, but the sheriff and Mike wouldn't have expected him, so he just announced himself loudly so hopefully the sheriff and Mike could hear him as he turned the key into the latch. He just thought to himself that he hoped he didn't make a bad judgment call and think that the chief from Covington and his two detectives were gone.

One could have taken the sedan and left one or two with the sheriff and Mike. But actually, with what just happened several hours ago, it just wouldn't matter. Not now…

Mike met him at the back entranceway. "Jason, what the hell are you doing here? And where's Butch?" Mike yelled.

Sheriff Middaugh was right behind Mike when Jason came through the doorway. "Uh-oh…what happened, Jason?" The sheriff had a feeling that Butch might not have kept his word and bailed.

Jason replied, "Butch is dead…"

Jason explained everything to the sheriff and Mike. There really wasn't that much to tell. The sheriff, Mike, and Jason were sitting in Sheriff Middaugh's office.

"Okay, so are we all in agreement?" the sheriff asked his two deputies. "No questions?"

Sheriff Middaugh wanted to make damn sure they all had their stories straight. It was a simple story, not complicated.

"So, Jason, again, does anyone other than yourself know about the cabin?" the sheriff asked.

"No, Sheriff, just me," Jason responded.

"Good," Sheriff Middaugh replied. "I'm gonna make the call into the chief. And know from this point on, there's no turning back. We got this, boys?"

"We understand," Mike responded. "Make that call, Sheriff."

Jason interrupted, "Wait, Sheriff, before you make that call, I have a question."

"What's your question, Jason?" the sheriff asked. "You okay? I know this has been a lot for you these past couple of days."

"I just want to know when this is all wrapped up, do I have your permission to bury Butch's body up at the cabin? He really liked it up there—even if it was for a very short time. I think he deserves at least that," Jason asked.

"Sure, Jason, I think that can be arranged. Covington isn't going to want the body. And it would be very nice if he's here around us—around the people he called his friends," Sheriff Middaugh said solemnly.

The sheriff was thinking to himself if there was anything he might have missed being said. Because once that phone call was made, it would surely be out of their hands for good.

Sheriff had one more thought. "Jason, are you positive that you didn't touch anything?"

"Well, there are my fingerprints on the door-knob to the front door and probably around the cabin. But if you're asking if I touched the knife, then no. I did check for a pulse, but I didn't move his body. I read the letter he left but placed it back onto the coffee table in front of the couch. That's it, Sheriff," Jason replied.

CHAPTER 65

Chief Gordon hung up from the call that he just received. "Well, this is something I didn't expect to happen," he said to himself.

He opened his door and went in search of his two detectives. He found both Harry and Josh in their office. He knocked on the door that was opened just a crack.

"Boys, got a minute? I do believe we have a break in the case," Chief Gordon said in much surprise.

"Really?" Harry said in a surprised voice. "Did they finally find Nancy Brown?"

"Well, in a manner of speaking, yes...yes, they did," Chief Gordon said matter-of-factly.

"What's up, Chief?" Josh asked curiously.

"Well, quite a bit, actually. The good news is, to start off, Nancy Brown has been found. But the bad news is, she's dead," the chief responded with somewhat of a sad tone in his voice.

"Are you kidding, boss?" Harry spoke out loudly.

"I really wish I was. No, I am not kidding," Chief Gordon said in a discouraged voice. "Boys, we need to gather a team together and head back down Highway 41. Then we're going to go find us a cabin in the woods..."

CHAPTER 66

The scene around the cabin was anything but desolate. There were two unmarked vans there (for good reason). The medical examiner or ME was on hand. It would be determined when the time of death occurred back at the coroner's office. The weapon that was used was still present in the body. The suicide note was present. And there were no other fingerprints found at the scene aside from Jason's. A couple of cans of pork and beans were found in the trash. Not much else was found. Simple and bare necessities were in the kitchen area—supplies used. A few kitchen utensils were found in drawers, and a few plates, bowls, cups, and glasses were neatly stacked in the cupboard.

The cabin looked like any other seldom-used vacation cabin would look like. It housed just the basics—not a lot of furniture but just enough to make it comfortable, Chief Gordon, Harry, and Josh thought. The chief had his team sweep thoroughly for fingerprints and for anything out of the ordinary.

Sheriff Middaugh and his two deputies were there, too. Jason thought that maybe he needed to tell the chief that it belonged to his uncle Ned. If they asked the park rangers in the area, they would know that. He didn't want the chief and his staff to think the sheriff's department was hiding anything. He and the sheriff and Mike had talked about it on the way to the cabin. They needed to have some truth in their story.

"Chief, can I talk with you for a second?" Jason asked as they were all congregating in the front living room.

"Sure, uh...Jason, is it? Sure, of course. What's on your mind, son?" Chief Gordon quickly glanced at Harry, then Josh, and then to Jason. He certainly didn't want to make those quick glances too obvious.

"Chief, this is my cabin. Well, it was my uncle Ned's, and then he willed it to me when he passed away. I didn't think that Butch would even know about this cabin. The only ones that knew about it were Sheriff Middaugh and Mike and myself. And actually, Jake from Jake's Garage knew about it, too. I was trying to think how Butch may have known about it. Maybe he heard Jake talk about it at some time." Jason hoped to God he sounded honest and sincere.

"Well, okay, Jason," the chief said. "And let's talk about the details. So tell me, Sheriff, who found this cabin, and how did you fellas find that Nancy Brown was here?"

Jason spoke up again. "Actually, Chief Gordon, it was me. Sometimes, I come up here to get away for a bit. We, of course, knew that Butch—or rather, Nancy Brown got away from him when the sheriff contacted me and Mike. I mentioned to Mike and Sheriff Middaugh that maybe he or rather she might have gone up this way. I thought we should check it out. We are all pretty familiar with these parts. There are plenty of places to hide out up here. I told the sheriff I'd check out the area. Mike came with me, and then we found Butch dead."

"Well, okay then," Chief Gordon said soberly. "I guess we have our story."

Jason shot a quick glance at the sheriff and then over to Mike. He was a little puzzled that the chief didn't even ask him one question or even ask to clarify any details.

The medical examiner and team put Butch's body on the stretcher and covered him/her with a blanket. The evidence was bagged. The team dusted for any possible fingerprints. Nothing was found, aside from Nancy Brown's fingerprints on the knife.

"Well, looks like we're just about finished here," Chief Gordon said to everyone. Chief Gordon walked over to where Harry and Josh were talking in low tones. "Boys," Chief Gordon said quietly, "you got anything else to add?"

"Nope, I guess not. We have our murderer—although not alive. We have a suicide note and the weapon. So I guess that wraps it up—neat and tidy," Harry said.

"Something bothering you, Harry?" Chief Gordon asked. "Josh, you got anything to add? You usually do by now."

"No, I guess not either, Chief," Josh responded.

"Hmmm…you both look like you have something else on your minds. Well, I guess I'm reading you both wrong," the chief said, somewhat confused.

Harry and Josh looked at each other and smiled at the chief.

What else was there to say? What else was there for anyone to say? The case was just about wrapped up. Nancy Brown was found, dead, but she was found. With the final paperwork—reports, the coroner's report—the evidence collected and bagged, the crime scene searched, the dusting for fingerprints all completed, they could all say that these murders were now solved once and for all.

Now for the breaking news and the release of the information to the public and to the world—the press release.

It couldn't have come at a more perfect time that the brutal murders of Melanie Dennyson and David Williams were finally solved.

CHAPTER 67

The Covington Police Department was bustling and very active that day, the day of the anniversary. The chief was getting ready to be televised and break the announcement. News reporters and television stations were there, impatiently waiting for the news to be revealed. All that was known was that there was new information being released to the news media in regard to the high-profile murders of Melanie Dennyson and David Williams. Chief Gordon made sure everyone was in place. Detective Harry Trimble and Detective Josh Winters were standing right behind the chief as he approached and stepped up to the podium. He was soon ready to make the breaking news announcement. There would be *no* question and answer period after the announcement.

Chief Gordon made sure there were several police officers stationed at Dennyson Mansion as well. He also had two officers inside with Irene and Reagan. They needed protection, too. He knew with this breaking news, there would be a swarm of news media—news reporters, etc.—descending on the grounds of Dennyson Mansion. Wrought iron gates were installed to keep the news media and reporters out and away from the entrance to the estate. That was a smart observation and decision that Josh gave to Reagan and Irene—to install wrought iron fencing and gate around the entire estate for protection and to hopefully keep unwanted people at bay and away from the premises.

Reagan and Irene and James were comfortably sitting in chairs, watching the TV as the stations broke away from their regular programming for the breaking news report. A police officer was also in the room as well as several other officers that were added. They were spaced around the mansion and grounds for security purposes.

"We interrupt your regular programming to bring you this special report…"

Chief Gordon stepped up to the podium. Reagan and Irene were holding each other's hands as they watched the television screen and Chief Gordon. They could see Harry and Josh standing still directly behind him, hands folded before them, with no expressions on their face. The chief reported finding the murderer of both Melanie Dennyson and her fiancé, David Williams. They showed photographs of both Melanie and David as Irene had tears rolling down her face. They then showed a photograph of Nancy Brown. It was the photo that came from her personal file while she was employed at Dennyson Toys. They also showed a current composite drawing of her as alias Butch Lawson.

Irene gasped as she held her hand up to her mouth. Seeing that before photo of Nancy Brown made her remember—faintly—the girl that she remembered with her Melanie. Irene never liked her. Occasionally, when Melanie and Irene would talk, Melanie would talk of Nancy and a Gina that worked with her. Melanie was having some issues with them concerning their work. Irene always felt a funny feeling about that Nancy. Irene would sometimes warn Melanie about those two girls—especially that Nancy Brown. Irene kept warning Melanie to just be careful around them. "Something just isn't right about those two, Melanie!" Irene would say.

"Oh, Irene," Melanie would laugh and respond, "why do you do that? You have to look for the good in people!" Well, it didn't matter anymore, did it?

After the breaking newscast, Reagan stood up and turned off the television. She turned to Irene and James, who was sitting there as well. "Okay… well, there's one more thing we have to do," Reagan addressed Irene and James.

CHAPTER 68

Evening would soon fall upon Dennyson Mansion. It was the eve of Melanie's and David's wedding—the anniversary. It should have taken place years ago, but it was brutally stopped by a horrible, terrifying occurrence—two murders.

Reagan knew it would be silly to have a full orchestra or orchestra ensemble playing in the ballroom, so she actually got four CD players with the exact jazz CD playing simultaneously in various locations of the ballroom. She wanted to have a big sound—a sound that could also be heard in the gardens and could be heard in the area where Melanie's beloved cottage one stood.

James would impersonate a doctor. Reagan got a doctor's bag. She actually borrowed it from a doctor at the nearby hospital. She wasn't sure Josh was going to be able to make it, but she knew they were wrapping up everything at the police station. Chief Gordon and Harry wanted to be here, too.

It was time to begin.

Reagan and Irene were dressed up like they were going to a party—an engagement party. Irene actually wore the exact same gown she wore that night so many years ago. Reagan had a beautiful, stunning midnight-blue gown on. They wanted to look their best for the party. James joined them. He had a navy suit on, and he was carrying "his" doctor's bag. He was waiting for his cue.

All three were standing at the back of the ballroom. They were holding each other's hand and looking intently into the gardens—specifically to the back wooded area. They were waiting for things to appear.

Reagan broke the silence. "It's time."

"Reagan, wait!" Josh had just run into the ballroom with shortness of breath. He was accompanied by Harry and Chief Gordon. And to Reagan's surprise, others descended into the ballroom as well—Jayne and Chelsea, Dr. Goodwin, Brenda, Adam, and Gina. Jennifer from the police station came, too. She brought her sister, Jackie, with her. Evelyn was there from the cafe. Everyone was dressed in elegant evening attire. They would join Reagan and Irene and James. They were all now waiting…

Reagan turned around to see all her friends with her and Irene and James. They were there for support. They were there to show just how much they cared not only for Reagan and Irene and James but for the Dennyson family—Arthur and Anne and, most importantly, Melanie and David. Reagan and Irene were almost in tears.

It was time, long overdue.

CHAPTER 69

Reagan opened the glass doors out into the gardens. She propped the doors open so the lively jazzy music could be heard throughout. She hoped the music could be heard in the gardens and all the way back to where Melanie's cottage once existed. The music spilled out into the gardens and to the back of the beautiful lit gardens that led, or would have led, to Melanie's cottage—that quaint, beautiful, charming cottage where Melanie and David found their doom that horrifying, gruesome night.

The beautifully lit pathway was being walked upon once again, but this time by Reagan, Irene, and James. The others stepped out, too, but stayed back to watch, to see.

Reagan, Irene, and James suddenly stopped. The cottage was slowly coming into view.

"We have to hurry," Reagan said softly.

They came to where they would be within talking range and be able to view David coming through the front door of Melanie's cottage cradling his beloved Melanie in his arms.

"James, be ready," Reagan said calmly to James.

"I'm ready, Ms. Reagan," James replied, holding tight to his doctor's bag.

And there he was, David's spirit coming through the cottage front entranceway carrying Melanie's lifeless spirit in his arms.

"Irene, ready?" Reagan asked.

"I'm ready, dear," Irene replied with a deep breath.

"David," Irene spoke loudly, "I've brought you a doctor to look at Melanie."

David looked over to Irene. James slowly approached the apparition.

And under his breath, James replied, "I'm going to need a stiff drink—or a couple—after this!"

"David," James spoke up. "I'm Dr. James. I can help you. Put Melanie down. I can help her. I brought my medical bag." James held up his doctor's bag so David could see it. James was hoping he would understand.

For the first time, David complied and gently placed his beautiful fiancée lightly down on the ground. He still was bent over her and didn't get up, but he raised his hands to invite the doctor to look at his cherished Melanie.

Irene walked slowly a little closer and saw her sweet Melanie for the first time since that horrible, terrifying night. Tears were now rolling down faster down her cheeks as she saw her Melanie still looking so beautiful and angelic in her wedding gown. She looked just the same as she did that night she died.

James, acting as Dr. James, bent down and leaned over as if to check for a pulse and a heartbeat. He thought to himself that this was the hardest thing that he ever had to do, and it was something that he thought he *never* could do, and with that being said, something he *never* thought he would be asked to do.

"David, I am so very sorry. Your beautiful Melanie is gone. There is nothing I can do to save her. I am truly sorry, son," James said solemnly and sincerely.

Irene spoke up now. "David, you are dead, and Melanie is dead. We know who killed you both. Please, you and Melanie must go into the light—together. You both can be at peace now. Your souls will be joined together now…forever."

David looked at Irene puzzled. He still didn't understand.

Josh was standing right behind Reagan. Josh spoke in a whisper to Reagan as he tapped her on her wrist, "Reagan, I have an idea. I know what has to be done. Please trust me. Give me your white ribbon belt now, please."

Reagan quickly slipped her white ribbon belt off and gave it to Josh. Josh, in turn, quickly removed his tie and placed the white ribbon around his neck to temporarily look like a minister/priest might look. It certainly wasn't great, but it would do for the purpose of acting like a minister/priest, someone that could conduct a ceremony—a wedding ceremony. He could marry David and Melanie in a mock ceremony.

Josh stepped through to stand with Irene.

Josh spoke up now, "David, I can marry you and Melanie right here, now. Melanie, you need to get up now. You need to stand next to your husband-to-be, David. I will marry you both tonight."

Melanie fluttered her eyes to open them. Her spirit floated up, and there she was, in her torn and bloodied but still beautiful wedding dress and beautiful veil that was given to her from her beloved mother, Anne. She was smiling as if she had woken up from a coma. She smiled at Irene, and she then turned to smile at her beloved David, her betrothed.

Melanie and David looked at Josh as if to say, "We're ready...we're finally ready to become man and wife."

Josh did the best that he could to remember the vows. He recited them to Melanie and then to David. He then pronounced them man and wife. He added these words:

"You both have finally been united in love and are now surrounded by all those that love you. You are now Mr. and Mrs. David Williams. You both now can go in peace and love. You are now joined in the sacred union of marriage. David, you may now kiss your beautiful bride."

Melanie and David embraced and had their final kiss. It would be their last kiss.

It was now Irene's turn to say her final thoughts. It would be her final thoughts for her beloved Melanie and her now husband, David.

"Melanie, my dearest Melanie, I love you with all my heart and soul. I was there for you when you were young and watched you grow into a beautiful, confident, and caring woman. David, you are a wonderful man, and we all know that all you wanted to do was to love and protect your dearest love, Melanie. You two must go now. Go into the light. Your spirits are joined and can be together forever for eternity. Your souls are now one. It's time for you both to find eternal rest and peace. Your family are all waiting for you both to join them in eternity. It's time…"

As Irene finished her speech, more spirits floated and joined Melanie and David at their sides: Arthur and Anne, Vincent and Carole, and Rachel, Richard and Irene's Gordon. Melanie mouthed the words "thank you," and David did as well. They were now complete. Each took one last look at Irene with much love and joy.

Irene and Reagan were crying now. All their loved ones were all there and looking at them, smiling. It was a glorious miracle and a glorious moment. There wasn't a sound to be heard, with the exception of the distant music coming from the ballroom…a light, jazzy tune.

Melanie turned to look at her beautiful little cottage slowly fading away. It would be seen no longer.

Melanie and David turned and glided to the walkway of the wooded area and joined all their loved ones who they cherished all so dearly. One last time, Melanie and then David turned and smiled at Irene and Reagan and James and Josh. One by one, the visions of each spirit faded, and then the last two— Melanie and David—vanished too.

Melanie and David were gone.

They were at peace now. They joined their family who had gone before them and joined the beloved family members that passed away after them. They were *all* at peace now...forever.

EPILOGUE

Things have settled down at the Dennyson Mansion now. Things have settled down in Covington. Things have settled down at Hollingsworth Sanitorium, too.

Gina had returned to Hollingsworth Sanitorium, and Dr. Goodwin and Dr. Stanbery had given Gina a series of tests. Everything was registering normal with Gina Smith. Her speech was getting better. Brenda adopted Gina, and because Brenda was a nurse and could take care of her, Gina was released from Hollingsworth. She went to live with Brenda. On occasion, Gina would accompany Brenda back to Hollingsworth for visits and activities. She was happy, and she was going to be all right.

Adam finished his studies and became a registered nurse. He now works as a nurse at Hollingsworth.

Dr. Will Goodwin is doing well and stops to visit Brenda and Gina. He and Brenda have become close. Laughter is often heard as a new family may soon form.

Dennyson Mansion is quiet now. James has retired and moved away. Reagan will always be eternally grateful for what James did for her that night. He showed much courage and loyalty. He finished that fine aged Scotch he was saving for that special occasion. He finished it off that very night and was quite content.

Irene retired, too. Jayne gave the Rosewood Grille to her daughter, Chelsea. Reagan and Chelsea are still best friends and spend many days together. Evelyn stayed in to help run the restaurant and bakery. Irene and Jayne have decided that traveling is what they want to do. They both want to see the world and all it has to offer. New adventures await them…to wherever life takes them.

Josh is now living at Dennyson Mansion with Reagan. They are engaged to be married. The wedding will *not* be on the anniversary of the murders, but in the spring out in the gardens of Dennyson Mansion. It will be a time for new growth and fresh blooms and romance. Reagan will not be returning to nursing. With much work ahead of her, she will be opening Dennyson Mansion as a museum. The name will be changed back to its original name: Covington Manor and now Museum.

Chief Gordon has retired from Covington Police Department. Harry Trimble is now chief of police and is in contact with Chief Gordon from time to time. Chief Gordon is enjoying a much-needed peaceful existence down South—fishing and enjoying a peaceful life with no murders or ghosts in his sight. Josh is now chief of detectives and is now in the process of training a new recruit. Harry knows this new recruit will be in good, solid, and smart hands. He has no worries about that.

FINAL THOUGHTS

Life is funny.

As we grow up and become adults, we imagine what our lives are to be like, what our futures will hold.

We make plans, and those plans change. We find careers, and careers change. We think we know exactly what we want, and we change. Change *can* be good.

Our lives are part of the "grand design," a wise man told me once. Are our lives already mapped out for us? Do we have choices to go down one pathway or another? Do we take the short path where we think it's simpler, or do we take the longer, more complicated pathway that we think may be more difficult to follow?

We make choices—not always the right ones. We are not psychic—only "chosen" ones have that gift. We do not have that crystal ball and turban to guide us and help us make the right and correct decisions.

We stumble and fall, for if we all made *no* mistakes, how would we learn? What would we learn? Straight As don't make the perfect student.

What's important in our lives? What makes us rise every day with the sun and lets us slumber peacefully at night?

It's the people we surround ourselves with each and every day. They help us to stay strong, to teach us when we need to know, to pick us up when we fall.

We move forward. We don't look back. We make mistakes. We learn. We learn to love. We learn to trust. We reach out for friendships and love, and we reach out *in* friendship.

The spirits of our loved ones are always with us and surrounding us, protecting us. Sometimes, we feel them near. Sometimes, we can see and know they are there. They send us messages for us to hear.

It is *faith, hope, one day at a time, the faith to continue*, the *hope to continue and inspire and dream*, and *the promise of the future*, and the promise of a new day. It is splendid for life is *whatever* you make it to be, the effort you put into it. We will have joys—and we will have sorrows. Your faith, your hope, and the promise of one day at a time will guide you through to each day of your journey. It will guide you down the pathway you must follow each and every day.

Blessing and love to you.

The end…for now.

ABOUT THE AUTHOR

 C. L. Stevens resides in the quaint lakeside community of Bay Village, located on Lake Erie, west of Cleveland, Ohio. She has happily resided there all her life. Her husband, Keith, and two grown, married children—Clark "C. J." (and Steph) and Erin (and Nick)—and her tricolored collie, Jovie, round out her loving, fun-loving family. Ms. Stevens has been a writer for many years and finds her passion in bringing her stories to life! This first murder/mystery novel holds a very special place in her heart as she dreamt the whole book—with music!

Printed in the USA
CPSIA information can be obtained
at www.ICGtesting.com
JSHW080926201023
50312JS00001B/1

9 798889 600923